Never Coming Home

Evonne Wareham

D1333768

First published 2012 by Choc Lit Limited
Penrose House, Crawley Drive, Camberley, Surrey GU15 2AB, UK
www.choclitpublishing.com

A CIP catalogue record for this book is available
from the British Library

ISBN-978-1-906931-70-4

Printed and bound by CPI Group (UK) Ltd, Croydon, CR0 4YY

*To my mother, for always believing in me,
and to the Cheerleading Team – Mary, Evelyn and Tracy,
and the newest recruit, Bernice.*

Acknowledgements

A lot of people have helped with this book. First and foremost – my Choc-Lit Tasting Panel Readers. Did you know you've changed my life? Thank you. The whole team at Choc-Lit, who get the show on the road, and keep it there, and still find time to eat chocolate, and my fellow Choc-Lit authors, who have made me so welcome. The Romantic Novelists' Association, particularly the organisers and readers of the New Writers' Scheme, who have critiqued, encouraged and knocked the corners off manuscripts, and got me where I am today. The *RT Book Reviews Magazine* and Dorchester Publishing – their American Title contest brought *Never Coming Home* into being. On the technical side, Nigel Hodge shared his expertise on forensics. I hope I've done his help justice, within the confines of telling a story. Any errors are down to me. Family and friends and colleagues have supported me, and the book, on the way to publication.
Thank you all.

Prologue

October 4th
He wasn't meant to be there.

Not on that road, at that time, on that day – but the job in Atlanta had fallen apart, the client was screaming and someone had to sort out the mess.

Sometimes owning the company sucked.

Once he'd cleaned the brown stuff off the fan – and the walls and the floor – any sensible man would have taken the next plane out.

Except Devlin hated to fly.

Driving – well – that was something else. He'd take the plane in the end, but he could afford an hour or two on the road first. And right now –

Right now the sun was going down, with a lot of bright, hot colour. Dusk and the empty highway ahead, and the Boss on the radio, keening about bad desire.

He could take the time, if he wanted.

Sometimes owning the company wasn't so bad.

He almost drove past it.

There wasn't much to see. Some rubber on the road, a few broken bushes. Something – that weird sixth sense, that had saved his ass more times than he ever wanted to think about – made him pull over. Just to take a look.

Then he was scrambling through the bushes and down the gritty slope, feet sliding on loose shale, towards the car.

It was a beat-up black Chevy. On its back, wheels in the air. Like an upturned bug.

The briefest look at the woman behind the wheel, dangling grotesquely from the still-fastened seatbelt, told him she was beyond anything but prayer.

All Devlin's attention was on the other side of the car.

In the scrubby dust beside a rock, lit by the dying rays of the sun, was another victim.

This one was still moving.

5th October

Kaz Elmore had the corkscrew in her hand when the doorbell rang. She let out a low-pitched groan. It had been a long day. With no pressing need to get home, she'd lingered on-site, then found herself driving across London at the height of the rush hour. Her back was aching and her skin prickling from the unexpected afternoon sun.

There was a full bath upstairs, with her name on it. The fragrance of lavender bath oil drifted through the house. Only the sudden impulse for a glass of wine, to drink while she soaked, had brought her back down. She could already taste it – cool and slightly tart, condensation beading the rim of the glass ... *Grrr!* Opportunities for self-indulgence didn't come by that often. She was trying to make the most of this one. If she was allowed to!

Her mouth twisted in a rueful grin. Five minutes more and she could have ignored whoever was standing on the step, finger pressed to the bell. Now, silhouetted by the kitchen light, she was clearly visible through the glass.

'If you're selling double glazing, mate, I know *exactly* where I'm going to bury the body.'

Kaz padded along the hall. A pile of mail was stacked, unopened, on the side table. Her eyes skittered towards it. She'd leafed through it already. There was nothing there. It was much too soon to expect a postcard, even if Jeff ... The doorbell pealed again.

'Hold on!' Flipping the catch, she eased the door open a crack, peering through the gap. 'Uncle Phil!' Annoyance forgotten, she unhooked the chain and threw open the door.

'Hi! This *is* a surprise. I was opening a bottle of wine, or are you still on duty? Come in.'

Kaz was half-way down the hall before she realised her uncle wasn't following.

'What?' She turned towards him, a sudden tightness in her chest. His face was bleak. His official face, eyes flat. Her stomach lurched. 'What is it?'

'There's no easy way to tell you this, love. It's bad news. The worst.'

Chapter One

'You know, Dev, you don't have to do this.' Bobby Hoag leaned on the doorjamb of his partner's office. Devlin was tossing files into drawers and packing his laptop into its travel case. 'Have you thought about it?' Bobby persisted. Behind him the reception area was deserted, the lights dim. An open window wafted the smoke from Bobby's cigarette into the rainy Chicago night. 'It's been more than six months. By now these people will have settled, put it behind them. And you're going to rake it all up again?'

That got Devlin's attention. He looked up, scowling.

'Would you ever put something like that behind you?'

'Well – no,' Bobby admitted. 'But even so – if no one has got in touch, in all this time –'

'I've thought about this, Bobby.' Devlin zipped the slim travel case and propped himself against the desk, folding his arms. 'Christ, it's not something I want to do. Maybe I won't, when it comes down to it. This trip is about work, first and foremost. It just happens to be London, and the woman is in London.'

'Cheyne Walk, Chelsea – you're not the only one round here who can use the Internet.' Bobby answered the raised eyebrows. 'Classy address?'

'One of the best – which makes the whole thing ...' Devlin shrugged.

'Curiosity.' Bobby's face opened up in relief. 'Now *that* I can understand.'

'Don't worry, mate, I'm not going soft on you.' Devlin picked up the case. 'Maybe I'll still decide not to bother the lady.' He shrugged. 'In six months, she hasn't bothered me.' He looked at his watch. 'I have to go.' He pointed a finger.

'Hold the fort. Stay away from fast women and slow horses. Don't let anyone pay us in nine-dollar bills.'

'Hah!' Bobby snickered. 'I wasn't the one who got scammed into taking those shares in a diamond mine.'

'You can laugh buddy – if that mine ever comes good, I'm gonna be up to my ass in pretty wimen. Pretty wimen *love* diamonds.'

Devlin settled grudgingly into his seat. He'd been prowling the aisle of the plane until one of the exasperated stewardesses, perky blonde, with dimples, had suggested he might like to stretch out and relax. He'd given in, but only because of the dimples.

It wasn't the flying that got him. It was the whole business of putting himself in someone else's hands. The airport thing, trapped in ever-lengthening limbo between check-in and actually boarding the damn aeroplane, and then the plane itself. Someone else had to drive it, and that bugged him. For all he knew, there was a bunch of assholes up there in the cockpit, playing strip poker, while this high-tech piece of scrap metal flew itself into the handiest mountain.

He scrubbed his eyes with the heels of his hands and accepted a mineral water from the flight attendant. She was watching him warily. Probably wouldn't have served him whisky, even if he'd wanted it. So – yeah – he was a control freak. With attitude. The hell with it. It had kept him alive for thirty-six years. With concentration he relaxed his limbs, focusing on the end of the journey. The job he had come to finish was no problem. It was the other thing. Was he going to find this Katarina Elmore or not?

Now that was the question.

He was no nearer an answer when the taxi pulled in to a quiet street, off Park Lane, and set him down. The hotel was discreet and comfortable, his two major requirements these days. It was also expensive. Money hadn't been an issue for a year or so, but in this case the client was paying. Probably a trade-off against tax, or something. Devlin didn't know and didn't care. He didn't do money on a corporate scale. Left all that to Bobby, who was sharp, reasonably honest and keen to stay attached to his balls. They went back a long way, him and Bobby.

Devlin sighed. These days Bobby also dealt with corporate relations. He set up the deals. Devlin got wheeled out to add gravitas, once the contract was ready to sign – and handled the bulk of the hands-on stuff. To each his strengths. It hadn't always been that way. They'd watched each other's backs, out in the field. But that was a different life. Another place, another time. His name hadn't been Devlin then. And Bobby hadn't been Bobby. When you dropped out of that world, everything changed.

He checked in, emptied his bag, rang the client and arranged to meet the next day. It was nearly six. Lunch time in Chicago. He'd slept on the plane – nothing much else to do. He wasn't going to want his bed for a while. So – he could have an early dinner and reacquaint himself with English TV on the set in his room. He could do a show, or find a club with cold beer and hot women. He still remembered a few of those. He could just go for a walk. He rang down to reception. 'Can somebody call me a cab? Yeah – Cheyne Walk.'

The house was in a kind of mews, not directly on the river. Compact, made of old brick. It was a world away from the backstreets of Hackney where he'd grown up. That was an even longer time ago. Yet another name, and another life. He frowned. He didn't need stuff like that surfacing. He was American, nowadays – it said so on his passport.

He'd asked the cab to drop him on the opposite side of

the road. Reconnaissance. Even now he didn't have to knock on that neat, blank front door. Bobby's words echoed. He would be stirring up something that maybe was better left. She'd made no attempt to contact him.

The paint on the house was shiny; the windows were clean, with boxes on the sills overflowing with spring stuff. He could recognise daffodils but the other things, blue and white, kind of like bells? No idea what they were. Pretty though. Like someone cared. There was a slim tree in a pot beside the door, with more daffodils. Someone had made an effort. Life was going on here.

If the woman has got herself together? Are you just going to fuck it all up?

Leaving now would be the easy way.

Since when did you choose the easy way? If it was you – God help you – you'd want to know. Maybe she'd been afraid to ask?

He crossed the street and rang the bell.

He thought for a moment that there wasn't going to be an answer. He couldn't deny the flicker of relief. Then the door opened.

'That was quick. I didn't expect – oh!'

The woman was a looker. Still youthful, with a pale cashmere sweater and jeans, clinging to an admirable figure – but the expression lines around the eyes and mouth told him she was too mature to be the one he was looking for.

'Can I help you?' She'd taken a pace back, frowning, as if she was trying to place him.

'My name is Devlin.' He had a card ready. Not that it said a lot. He handed it over. She was frowning now at the slip of pasteboard in her hand.

'Security consultant?'

'I was hoping to see Mrs Elmore?'

'Ah.' She looked as if she was about to hand the card

back. Instead she slipped it into a pocket. No reaction to his name, Devlin noted, puzzled. 'My daughter isn't here at the moment. Perhaps you can call again.' She was closing the door.

Devlin tamped down the gut reflex to stick his boot in the narrowing gap. The palm of his hand was the civilised way. 'Can you just tell me when she will be home?' He'd started this thing, now he had to finish it. Besides, there was something going on here that he didn't understand.

'I ...' The woman hesitated.

'It's important that I speak with her.'

Something in the woman's expression changed. Her focus on him sharpened.

'Important to whom, Mr Devlin?'

'I think to both of us. You, too.' He took a breath. 'I was there ... I was with your granddaughter when she died.'

Chapter Two

'With Jamie? Oh God!'

The woman's hand went to her mouth and her eyes widened. Devlin had a sudden panic flash that she might faint.

Keep talking Devlin. Keep her attention.

'Look – I'm sorry. I know it's been a while. I didn't know whether I should get in touch or not. I thought that if Mrs Elmore wanted to speak to me then she'd have contacted me. But as I was in London ...'

She wasn't reacting, just staring. She was made of sterner stuff than he'd thought, though. There was a little more colour in her face.

'Look –' He was floundering. 'Maybe this wasn't such a good idea, after all. I'll just go.' He raked his hand into his hair, starting to turn away.

'No! Please.' She did react then, putting out a hand to him. 'It's just ... No one told us ... We didn't know anything about you.' She let the door swing wide. 'I think you'd better come in, Mr Devlin.' She gestured for him to enter. 'This has been a shock. I think we should start again. I'm Suzanne Saint.' She held out her hand. Devlin took it. The familiar ritual of a handshake seemed to steady her. 'My daughter should be home at any minute. When she gets here you can tell us both. Go through, please.'

Devlin went through the door she indicated. The room stretched from the front to the back of the house, cool, airy, lots of white paint, luxuriant plants, pictures on the walls. One in particular.

It was hanging alongside rather than over the fireplace. The oil paint was thickly applied. The smudgy, mixed-white background made the central tracery of lines, in multiple shades of red, stand away from the canvas. The pattern seemed abstract until you looked closer. Then you saw it – the clear profile of a woman.

Devlin's eyes went automatically to the right-hand corner. The signature he'd expected was there – a slashing letter K incised, like the mark of Zorro, in red paint. 'An Olivier Kessel.' His voice sharpened. 'This is you, isn't it?' Realisation hit him as she nodded. 'Hell – you're the other Suzanne!'

She grimaced before she smiled. 'A long time ago. I'm flattered that you saw it. Not so many people remember that story now – which can be a blessing.' The smile grew rueful. 'It got a little stale, hauling around that *other* label.'

Devlin raised his eyebrows, intrigued, betting that if he kept quiet, she'd say more.

She hooked a strand of pale gold hair behind her ear. 'It was one of those bright ideas that got stuck and kept being replayed.'

Devlin suppressed a smile. Let a silence lengthen for long enough and the impulse to fill it became almost unbearable. First rule of interrogation. Her eyes had narrowed, assessing him, aware of what he was up to. Smart lady. He nodded encouragingly and got a soft laugh in response.

'You want me to rake over my old glories for you, Mr Devlin? All right then. It came from a young journalist who interviewed Oliver, oh – sometime in the early seventies – Oliver was still Oliver then, that important extra 'i' came a little later.' The expressive eyes sparkled with knowing mockery. 'The reporter needed an original angle to sell a story about a more-or-less unknown artist. He came up with this idea of linking two *brilliant* –' she made quotation marks in the air with her fingers, grinning '– artistic talents, who'd both used a woman named Suzanne for inspiration.

Of course, at the time, Oliver was delighted to be linked to Leonard Cohen. People were only just beginning to suggest that *his* talent was in any way remarkable and not many of them – ' The grin was decidedly wicked now. 'It was a totally daft comparison – there was absolutely nothing else to link Oliver with Cohen, but you know how these things go. Then the article got syndicated in the States. Oliver's career began to take off and he declared, very dramatically, that I was his Muse.' The grin widened. 'Being a muse is a very ambiguous activity, you know. No job description. In retrospect it seems principally to have consisted of cleaning a great many paintbrushes and standing around in draughty studios, half-naked. But I was young, and in love to the point of imbecility.' She gave the painting a considering look. 'I sat for hours for that thing. It seemed only fair that I should end up owning it. And a few others.' She was still smiling, but her eyes had narrowed again. 'Oliver's early work isn't that well publicised these days. You know your art, Mr Devlin.'

'Just Devlin, please.' She'd given him information. Interesting information. He'd enjoyed hearing it, so he owed her. 'I once babysat a private art collection from L.A. to New York, for an exhibition, and back again. There were a number of Kessels. The guy was a fan. The whole art thing interested me, so I did some research, browsed a few galleries.'

'Babysat? Oh yes – Security consultant.'

Abruptly her face folded in on itself. She'd remembered why he was here.

That's how it must be, this far down the line. For a few minutes you forget – have a conversation, get lost in a memory, something from before ... Then the unthinkable comes crashing in again.

'Would you like some tea?' she asked jerkily. 'I'll put the kettle on.'

He let her go ahead, taking time to survey the rest of the room. There were photographs, family groups, in happier times. Katarina Elmore – another looker, if these informal shots were anything to go by – but in a totally different style. The husband was there too – ex-husband – tan, good chin, good teeth. And a child. Another girl, dark like her mom, aged about four or five. Devlin picked up the slim silver frame to get a closer look. He hadn't realised there was a younger daughter. No pictures of *his* girl. Too painful to have the memories around? Might be a comfort to the mother and grandmother, but for the other kid? How hard was it going to be, growing up in the shadow of an older sister? A dead older sister.

He followed the sound of clinking china into the kitchen. A big room, with the evening sun coming in through the window, mismatched wooden units, warm terracotta tiles. Suzanne was fiddling with cups and saucers. A large spanner sat on the work surface.

Suzanne saw him looking at it. 'The man who serviced the boiler forgot it. I thought you were him …' Her face clouded. 'If he hadn't rung, to say he was coming back for it, I'd have already gone home. There would have been no one here.'

'I would have called again.' *Would you?*

Ignoring the prickle at the nape of his neck, Devlin wandered over to the refrigerator. Amongst the saver coupons and postcards there were children's drawings, attached with magnets. Devlin examined them, something to occupy his attention while Suzanne completed the performance of tea-making. Not exactly the million dollar art occupying the main room. Except … Devlin's spine stiffened in surprise. The pictures bearing the legends Mummy, Daddy and Gran were recognisably people, not the usual scrawling matchstick figures with green hair. 'Hey, these are good.' He indicated the drawings.

'Aren't they?' Suzanne turned towards him, a flash of animation in her face. 'Quite remarkable for her age. Oliver was so excited –' The animation faded. 'All that's gone, too. Her father – they were supposed to be going to Florida, to Disneyworld ...' Suzanne pulled the teapot towards her.

Devlin looked back, away from her swimming eyes. He could see it now. There was a tiny J in the corner of each picture. Jamie. *His* girl had painted these. His throat tightened. *Maybe it* was *a mistake to come here? What can you really tell them?*

He could still feel it, raw in his throat. He'd scrambled down that damn slope, but when he got there ... This child, with so much promise, had blinked up at him, and tried to smile. That smile – the relief in it had damn near hauled his scabby heart straight out of his chest. She'd trusted him to rescue her. Trusted him to make everything right. He'd known in an instant that there was nothing he could do, except be there for her, put his arm around her. Let her *feel* that she wasn't alone. The next second she'd coughed up a little blood – and died. The look of surprise on her face would be with him forever. These drawings were hers.

Devlin swallowed hard. 'Look – this is disturbing for you, my being here. I don't have that much to tell you ... It was very quick ...'

'No!' Suzanne put out her hand to cut him off. She was shaking her head, emphatically. 'We'll wait for Kaz – I think she has the right to be the first to hear how her daughter died.'

She finished loading the tray. Devlin took it from her and carried it back into the other room. They both turned at the sound of a key in the lock.

'Mum? Are you still here? Don't tell me he didn't turn up!'

Suzanne closed her eyes, opened them. 'In here, darling.'

13

Devlin found he was bracing himself. He didn't know what for. Yet.

She was as striking as her mother, but with a wilder edge. The dark curls were barely kept in check by a flamingo pink scarf. Flawless skin. Wide, dark eyes. Wide, full mouth. There were smudges under those eyes, and tension in the set of her head that shouldn't be there. Even so, it was a face to make a man acutely aware of his loins.

For Christ's sake, you're here to give her your sympathy, not to come on to her!

Devlin dropped his eyes before they could betray him, and found that she was wearing – a dark brown boiler suit. His heart all but stopped when he realised that she'd halted in the doorway to stare at him, with it half-unbuttoned. The T-shirt beneath clung to the kind of figure that turned heads. Or made a man's mouth go dry. Devlin swallowed. The shirt gave him a clue. *Gardeners do it in the bushes.* Katarina Elmore was a gardener? Why hadn't he known that? *Because you didn't want to get in that deep, did you?*

Kaz stepped into the living room. There was a man in the house. And definitely not from the gas company. Not unless they were kitting them out in expensive Italian tailoring these days. Blinking, she took in the tea things on the table. Her mother was entertaining? Suzanne was fluttering – there was no other word for it – around a complete stranger. Kaz's bewilderment escalated. Suzanne didn't *do* fluttering. Mind, he was *some* stranger. The sharp lines of the expensive suit gave one message, the hint of five o'clock shadow another. There was a lot of him, six foot two at least, with the shoulders to match. And muscle in all the right places. Too rugged to be handsome, a touch of Steve McQueen about the eyes. Fabulous mouth. A face for dreams. Or maybe nightmares.

What the hell is something this hot doing in your living room?

'Mum?' Her heart had picked up a little speed. She felt it bump gently against her ribs. Something was stirring. She remembered it vaguely. Lust. This guy had danger written all over him. Sexy danger. *Oh boy!*

With difficulty Kaz hauled her eyes away from Danger, and his fabulous mouth, and towards her mother. Suzanne's face was strained. There were lines creasing her forehead.

'Darling, this is Mr Devlin ... er ... Devlin. He ...' Her mother's voice faltered. 'He's from America – to see you.'

'America?' A sudden blast of inexplicable cold lurched through Kaz, thoroughly dissipating lust. She could see now that Suzanne's eyes were half-closed and hazy with tears.

'He was there, darling. He was there ... when Jamie died.'

'What?' Kaz blinked, swallowed. Cold, lust, everything was gone. Something squeezed her chest, and kept on squeezing. White, hot rage.

'What the hell kind of freak are you? And what do you think you can get from us?'

Devlin took an involuntary step back. He'd imagined tears, shock, confusion. He hadn't expected blazing anger. 'Mrs Elmore –'

'Get out! Get out of my house – now!' Her voice was like a blade, thrown directly at his unprotected rib cage. He knew his hands had gone up to defend himself. He put them to better use waving her off. She was advancing towards him, blood in her eyes.

'Kaz!' Suzanne's voice was a strangled gasp.

'Stay out of this, Mum.' Kaz barely spared her a glance. 'I don't know what sick game you're playing, Mister, or what you expect to get out of it. I don't want to know. How dare you soil my daughter's memory!' Her voice was shaking.

'My uncle is a policeman.' She hauled a mobile phone out of her pocket, brandishing it like a weapon. 'I'll give you twenty seconds to leave, then I'm calling him.'

'OK.' Devlin opened his palms. 'I hear you, and I'm going.' He didn't know what was going on here, but the way out was that way. He took a step, then paused. Bugger it, he wasn't running out, tail between his legs. *Try for a little dignity here.* 'I'm sorry for your loss. I didn't intend to add to your distress.' Deliberately he turned to Suzanne. Her face was white. 'It was a pleasure to meet you, Ms Saint. Goodbye.'

He was going to have to pass Mrs Elmore to get to the front door. Her body was almost vibrating with fury. He side-stepped quickly. Even brushing against her arm might shoot sparks. And probably be construed as assault. He skirted carefully around her. She swung in a circle to watch him.

'No!' Suzanne's shout stopped him at the door. 'Don't leave, Mr Devlin.' He turned cautiously. Tears were coursing silently down the older woman's face. 'She was your daughter, Kaz, but she was my granddaughter. I loved her, too. I believe him. I want to hear what he has to say. I wouldn't let him tell me until you were here. Darling, *please.*'

She crossed the room to her daughter, putting an arm around her. Devlin saw Kaz quiver, but she didn't shake her mother off. Suzanne's voice was low and intense. 'When it happened ... we were devastated. Jeff did everything he could to spare us, I know, but ... but maybe it wasn't the right thing after all. I wake up nights and I wonder ... whether ... whether ...' She half-choked, then tried again. Devlin found there was a lump in his throat. 'We know so little. You didn't even see her ... If Mr Devlin can tell us something, I want to hear it. Then we can judge. Please, darling,' she begged again. Her voice was brittle, and almost too soft to hear.

Devlin stood, poised, for a very long three seconds. He almost felt Kaz Elmore's breath shudder out.

'All right.' Her shoulders sagged a little as she rounded on him, then jerked back. The sparks were still there, but she'd damped them. He could feel the effort zinging off her. 'I'll listen, because my mother wants it. Sit there.' She glared at him, pointing towards the sofa in front of the fireplace.

Devlin scrunched down a grin that had come up from nowhere. It would undoubtedly be seriously misconstrued. 'Yes, ma'am.'

He folded himself onto the lime-green sofa, as instructed, and waited. Kaz disappeared briefly into the hall and came back without the boiler suit. The jeans fitted as well as the T-shirt. The women sat down, facing him. Suzanne poured tea and handed him a cup. Kaz's knuckles were tight on hers. She had both hands wrapped around it, as if she needed the warmth. When she looked up, her eyes were still combative. Devlin leaned forward, opening up, letting her come to him.

'If you were there when my daughter died, why is this the first we've heard of you?' she demanded at last.

'I don't know, Mrs Elmore.' He'd been wondering that himself. 'The cops certainly knew all about me.' One detective in particular had shown a disturbingly high interest in what he'd been doing on that road. The guy's enthusiasm had only waned when the lab results confirmed the cocktail of drink and drugs in the driver's bloodstream. 'Maybe they didn't pass the information on to your ex-husband?'

'Or he didn't tell us,' Suzanne suggested. 'You remember how it was.' She looked at her daughter. 'And Jeff had to cope with the guilt he felt, as well.'

Kaz shrugged and fixed dark eyes on Devlin.

'Your daughter was in the States, with your former husband, on an access visit, right? She was in the car with your husband's PA when the accident happened?'

17

'PA!' Kaz snorted. She dumped her cup down on the table, fiddling with the ends of her scarf, as it brushed her shoulder. Devlin breathed in, wondering if she was going to let that wild hair loose. There was a pang of disappointment when she dropped her hands to her lap. 'I didn't want to let her go, not all that way, but he'd promised her Disney. They could have gone to Paris. And then he leaves her with his girlfriend while he's off on some deal or other. They weren't anywhere *near* Disneyworld.'

'No,' Devlin agreed. Not by the direct route.

Suzanne put her hand over her daughter's, stilling the working fingers. 'Jamie would have been happy, darling. She was seeing new things, and having some attention from her father. And she liked Gemma.'

'I know.' The fingers convulsed, then her eyes were back on Devlin. He waited, but she didn't speak.

'I didn't know whether I should get in touch with you,' he said softly. 'A phone call didn't seem – if I did it, I wanted it to be in person … I figured you might contact me – but if you didn't know, then that explains that one.'

'If I'd known about you, I would have got in touch.'

He didn't doubt. Something subtle unknotted in his chest. It had been hard not to wonder … if it was simply that no one had cared enough.

Her gaze was impossible to look away from, it simply nailed him to the lime-green sofa and kept him there. He sensed the shift in her. The anger was receding. Now she wanted to know. He took a breath. 'It was almost dusk, but still quite light. Something on the road – I don't know – made me stop. As soon as I was out of the car I could see the smash. It was quite a way down the slope.' Abruptly he was back on the edge of the highway, feeling the shale under his feet, hearing it slide. 'Once I got down there –

there was nothing to be done for the driver. Then I spotted your daughter. She'd been thrown clear.'

He swallowed, reaching for his cup. He took a swig of cold tea, felt rather than saw Suzanne's half-hearted move to re-fill his cup and Kaz's answering move to stop her. The eyes didn't let him go. *Finish this.*

'She was still alive when I got to her, but the injuries were bad. I was there with her for … maybe less than two minutes. She knew I was there, though. She smiled … I think she was trying to speak. She didn't seem to be in any pain. Then she died.' He'd sat there, for a while, then he'd called 911 and the whole circus started. 'That's it.' He shrugged. 'I'm sorry. I know it's not much, but maybe it helps … to know she wasn't alone.' He cleared his throat. 'If there's anything more you want to ask …'

Suzanne's hands were over her eyes. Kaz sat straight. Those dark eyes were full too, but he understood that she wouldn't cry in front of him. 'I guess I'll leave now.' He stood. 'You had a beautiful daughter, Mrs Elmore. I'm sorry that I never knew her.' He held out his hand. After a second Kaz rose and took it.

'Thank you.' Her voice choked. 'For coming, and for telling us. I apologise for my anger. I thought – I don't know what I thought. When it first happened, there were a few reporters … I wasn't in any state to give interviews, but one of them talked his way in. I gave him a couple of quotes and I thought he'd left. I found him in the kitchen. He had Jamie's drawings –'

'It doesn't matter,' Devlin broke in. 'I wish you well, Mrs Elmore, you and your other little girl. I'll see myself out. I think your mother needs you.' Suzanne's face was buried in her arm, shoulders shaking. 'Tell her goodbye for me.'

'I will.' Kaz turned towards her mother.

All he wanted now was to get out. Leave them alone with

their grief. Grief he'd stirred up. *Shit.* The next thing after that he wanted was a stiff drink. Something was making his eyes heavy. Maybe it was jet lag?

He'd reached the door, in three quick strides, before she spoke again. 'Mr Devlin? What made you think I had another daughter?'

'What?' He swung back towards her. 'It was the pictures.' He nodded to the photo frames on the shelves behind her. 'The little girl. I assumed she was Jamie's younger sister.'

His breath jarred. In a second her face had gone from soft to sharp again, the eyes hostile.

'Those photographs are all of Jamie.'

Devlin felt as if a pit had suddenly opened at his feet. He scraped his hand over his face. 'I don't understand.' Cold sweat was settling between his shoulder blades. He crossed the room quickly, to pick up the nearest of the frames. He had to be sure. He held it out to her. 'You're telling me *this* is Jamie.'

'Of course it is. I only had one daughter, Mr Devlin.' She was moving towards him, tense with suspicion. He didn't blame her. 'Look – I don't know what's going on here ... If this is some sort of game –'

'No! It's not a game.' He held up his hand, mind reeling. *What the fuck is this?* 'I don't know what's going on either ... but I have to tell you that this is *not* the child who died in that car wreck.'

Chapter Three

All Kaz could do was stare at him.

Her eyes seemed to be locked on his face. He didn't look deranged. *Dangerous, but not insane.*

Behind her Suzanne had risen to her feet. This was grotesque. She could feel her mouth working, trying to find words.

'Are you trying to tell me that my daughter wasn't in the crash?'

Amazingly she'd formed a sentence. Her brain had begun to splutter past the shock, to compute information. Information that didn't make sense.

She took a long look at Devlin, feeling confusion crowding her again. What she was seeing in his face – it didn't look like anything she might have expected. His expression was as stunned and bewildered as hers must be. And there was something else in there too. Something that looked like – pain? *Pain?*

'I'm not trying – ' His voice sounded rusty. 'I *am* telling you. Jamie – she's what four, five years old?'

'She would have been five. On Christmas Eve.' The memory had nausea rising. Kaz gritted her teeth. 'What has that got to do with it?' She couldn't understand why her voice sounded so steady, when inside she was dissolving. Now there was something new in his face – excitement?

'The girl who died in that car had to be ten, maybe eleven years old. And she was blonde, with braces on her teeth.'

'Could there ...' Suzanne had moved silently to stand behind her. Instinctively Kaz put out her hand and felt her mother's fingers grasping hers. 'Could there have been two girls – did Gemma have a child of her own?'

Kaz felt a rush of emotion, too complex to classify. Devlin and her mother were both looking to her for an answer. She tried to focus. 'She could have, I don't know.' She stopped. 'She was only twenty-four.'

Devlin was frowning now, turning the thing over. As if he really believed –

'It's possible then that she had a child, but not likely.' He shook his head. 'There was never any suggestion of more than one child –'

Kaz put her hand to her head. The whole thing was surreal. What was she doing, even thinking about this?

There were dark wings beating on the edges of her eyes. She felt strange. As if she was going to faint. She'd never fainted in her life. *No time to start now.* She really couldn't –

She heard Devlin curse. Felt the room move as he leaped forward. *His reflexes are very fast.* For some reason that seemed funny, not sinister at all. She wanted to giggle but it didn't make it to her mouth.

He had her off her feet and onto the sofa while she was still too fuzzy to resist. 'Do you have any brandy?'

Points to Devlin. Not fazed by swooning females. Store that away for future ... for future ...

'It's in the kitchen.' Suzanne hurried off to get it.

The doorbell rang. Voices in the hall. The gas man, reclaiming his spanner.

Kaz lay still for a moment, getting her bearings. 'I didn't faint. I never faint.' It was important to get that clear.

'No,' he agreed. Smooth. His face, as she peered at it, looked totally blank. Put her in mind of a brick wall.

'You're not pouring brandy down my throat.' She was clear on that too, even if the room was still showing an alarming tendency to come and go around the edges.

'Hell no – the brandy's for me.'

For a long moment they gazed at each other. His hand

was still on her shoulder. Kaz could feel the warm strength of it through the swirl in her head. Hope, fear, anger. No wonder she'd … uh … got a little fuzzy at the corners.

'If you're making all this up –'

'I swear. I'll swear on my mother's grave if you like. She'll kill me if she finds out – but what the hell?'

'I think maybe you're crazy.' She leaned back and shut her eyes. Shut him out for a bit. Let herself re-group. His hand was still there, though. Warm. She had an irrational desire to cling to it. Totally irrational, as he was the cause of the problem. She opened her eyes again. 'Have you escaped from somewhere?'

'Nope, and I'm not delusional, and I don't see little green men and I don't talk to my refrigerator.'

'Talking *to* the fridge is okay. It's when it talks back that you're in trouble.'

Kaz sat up and swung away from him. He stepped back, letting her go. She needed to be away from him, to think, but she missed the feel of him. The room stayed where it should be. Mostly. Suzanne came back with a bottle of cognac and three glasses. Kaz could see from her eyes that she'd caught the end of the conversation. Mercifully, she didn't ask.

'Don't worry about it,' Devlin advised her as he accepted a glass. Instead of going back to his seat, he settled on the floor next to Kaz's feet, looking up at her. Within reach. She sipped brandy, studying him. The appearance was all macho alpha male, yet he didn't feel the need to dominate. Jeff would have been pacing the room, waving his arms. Probably yelling. 'I think we need to consider what we have here,' he suggested softly. 'The implications.'

'There was another child. There's been some sort of mix up, although I can't think what. Or …' Her voice faltered. Her chest was too tight to breathe. 'Or you're telling me that my daughter may still be alive.'

'Don't go there yet.' He leaned forward. 'When you got the news, what happened?' He was watching her face intently.

'My uncle – he's a detective inspector with Scotland Yard. He came to tell me. Jeff contacted him, thought it would be better if Phil broke it to me.' *Or was too much of a coward to do it himself.* 'I flew out. Jeff had done all the formalities, identified the body.' Her eyes widened. 'I didn't see her. I wanted to. He said that her face … that she was too badly mutilated.' She'd thrown up all night, until the hotel doctor had given her an injection to stop the retching. 'We had the funeral – cremation. I brought the ashes home. We scattered them off the Albert Bridge. Jamie liked to go there, to see the boats on the river.' Her voice husked as her throat closed over.

Suzanne leaned in and patted her hand.

'After it happened – I was completely numb,' Kaz went on after a moment. 'It wasn't until weeks later that I began to ask questions. That was when I found out that Gemma was drunk.' She stared down at Devlin. 'My ex-husband told me my daughter was dead. If she isn't …'

'Then he must have her.' Devlin nodded. 'Was the divorce acrimonious – arguments about custody?'

'At first, a little, but in the last year we'd been getting on much better. And Jamie still loved her dad. That was why I agreed to the American trip. I didn't want to come between them, just because Jeff and I …' Her hand went to her mouth. 'Oh God – was he planning to take her for over a year?'

'Could be.' Devlin hauled himself off the floor and onto the arm of the sofa. A weird, disconnected part of Kaz's brain admired the way his muscles dealt with the movement. He was long and lean and looming alongside her. She glanced away, aware of heat in her face.

It wasn't the look of him, it was the fact that she'd nearly fainted. That must be what was making her cheeks pink. Something about disrupted blood flow. She was still disoriented, from almost passing out. Devlin had caught her. How embarrassing was *that*? Enough to make anyone – well –

Is blush the word you're looking for?

She wriggled her shoulders. Women of twenty-nine didn't blush. It had to be something else. What would the man think? That she made a habit of swooning into a stranger's arms? Even though she'd told him she didn't?

She had to pull herself back to hear his next question. She wasn't sure that he hadn't repeated it

'Do you know where Jeff is now?'

'No. We didn't keep in touch – after Jamie ...' She shut down on the sudden stab, the memory of pain. 'He said he wanted a clean break. I didn't argue. He still gets post here sometimes. Last time I forwarded something it came back "Gone Away". I don't know where he is.'

'Then you can't take the easy route and ask him.' Crooked grin, very Steve McQueen. 'I guess you should think about this. Get some advice – maybe your uncle?' He was standing up. Leaving?

Kaz stifled what felt like a thread of panic. There was no reason for it. She could handle this. She *wanted* him gone. She needed ... space ... To get her thoughts in order. That was it. No space with him sitting on the end of the sofa, watching her. So strange to feel that he understood.

'I've kind of dropped a bombshell into your life,' he said quietly.

'You could say that.' She shook her head. It didn't make it any clearer. 'Like you said. I need to think.'

'I'll go now.'

Suzanne uncurled from her position in a chair under her portrait. 'I'll see you out.'

'Goodbye, Mrs Elmore.' He raised one shoulder in a half-shrug. 'I'm sorry.'

'Don't be, Mr Devlin.' She looked up at him. It was important to say this. 'If everything you've told me is true, you've just given me back my daughter.'

If, if, if. Kaz reached for the brandy and poured herself another shot, shuddering as it hit the back of her throat. She heard the front door open and the murmur of voices, then the sound of the door shutting. Mr Devlin had left the building.

'Darling, I don't think you should get your hopes up.' Suzanne came back, to put her hand on Kaz's shoulder. 'It seems – incredible.'

'That's why I believe it.' Kaz breathed in sharply. 'It's just *too* incredible. What's the alternative? A mix up? Two car crashes involving one woman and one child on the same stretch of road, *at the same time*? Or is Devlin a liar?' She shook her head as her mother sank into the seat next to her. 'Why would the man make up something like that? It was all so casual. If he hadn't said that – about my other daughter.' She shivered. *He'd been about to leave. He could have walked out of here, without you ever knowing.*

'He could be a very good actor?'

'I don't doubt that he is – but why come here? What's in it for him?'

She'd been trying to work that one out, and for the life of her she couldn't see – which meant ... 'Mum, his story makes sense.'

She shut her eyes. Everything slotted into place, with a horrible symmetry – which meant that Jeff ... She swallowed down lurching nausea. She had to go slowly. She was taking the word of a stranger against the man she'd been married to for six years. *And is that why you're willing to accept the word of a man you don't know, because you do know Jeff?*

She had to take this slowly, one step at a time. No hopes. Not yet.

Her mother was watching her, her face screwed into lines of tension. 'I don't want you to – Be careful, darling.'

'I intend to.' Kaz conjured up a weak grin. 'You were the one who told me to listen to the man!'

'I didn't know then what he was going to say.' Suzanne reached for the brandy.

Kaz got to her feet. 'I'm going to ring Uncle Phil.'

'A bit of a mystery man, your Mr Devlin.' Phil sniffed appreciatively at the plateful of his sister's signature dish, beef bourguignon, on the table before him. 'I haven't been able to get much on him, and what I have got I don't like.' He stuck in his fork. 'I've got a couple more leads I'd like to follow up.'

'But what about Jeff, and the crash?' Kaz had contained her impatience for two restless days and sleepless nights, while her uncle did what he did. This afternoon she'd been ready to *spit* the nails into the rustic pergola her team were constructing for a woman in Islington.

'First things first.' Phil chewed appreciatively. 'Can't beat a nice piece of beef.' He grinned at Suzanne.

Kaz set her teeth. It had been her mother's idea to have this conversation over dinner in her flat in Notting Hill. 'You know your uncle functions better on a full belly.'

'First thing you do –' Phil took a sip of wine – 'when you get a story like this – you look at the source. Ask yourself, is it reliable? Quite frankly, love, this bloke Devlin doesn't bear close scrutiny. He started the security outfit three years ago. Doing well, mind, from what I can gather. Takes on the more exotic jobs. Walks close to the line on occasion. Before that – nothing.'

Kaz raised her head with a jerk. 'What do you mean?'

'What I said – nothing. ' Phil pulled a face. 'Well, not nothing exactly. All the right stuff is there, but it's too clean. Too perfect.' Phil shook his head. 'I called in a couple of favours. Didn't bring me much. The man's past ticks all the right boxes, but there's no proper history. He simply didn't exist. Not as Devlin, anyhow. Which makes me think that there is something very nasty indeed in Mr Devlin's past.'

'Criminal?' Suzanne's brows rose, as she offered him more potatoes.

'Not necessarily.' Phil helped himself generously. Kaz breathed heavily, then bit her tongue as her mother shot her a cautioning glance.

'What then?' Kaz leaned forward, when it was clear that Phil wasn't going to say any more without prompting. 'He was some sort of spook? A spy?' She splayed her hand on the table. 'Look – Devlin has a murky past. Seeing the man, that does not surprise me.' *You don't get that poised, dangerous edge from a lifetime working in an office.* 'But what about what he *said*?'

'Can't separate the two.' Phil finished his meal with relish and pushed away his plate. 'Very nice, Suze, as always.'

Kaz wondered if it was physically possible for a human to steam from the ears. She might be about to find out. When had her Jack-the-lad Uncle Phil turned into such an – old woman!

'You going to finish that?' Her uncle pointed at her barely touched plate. Kaz pushed it towards him. 'Don't want good food going to waste.' Phil began to shovel. Kaz sipped her wine, waiting. Phil could hardly miss the impatience in the silence. He looked up, shaking his head 'I don't like saying it, Kaz love, but you're on a hiding to nothing if you set your hopes on anything that man told you.'

'Why would Devlin make up a story like that?'

'Some sort of confidence trick?' Suzanne suggested softly.

'But what? And why?' Kaz turned to her mother.

'Maybe he just gets off on manipulating people – hope, grief.'

'You could be onto something there.' Phil waved his glass. 'I'm sorry, Kaz.' His voice softened. 'I know that you want to believe, but here we have a man with a dubious past, telling you a story that is, quite frankly, too incredible to be true. That your ex-husband staged some sort of conspiracy, to steal your daughter?'

'Jeff saw his chance and took it. He identified this other child as Jamie.' Kaz had been thinking about it. She'd thought of nothing else for forty-eight hours. Every angle, every possibility. She had no doubt that Jeff was capable of it. He'd take any kind of chance, when he wanted the outcome enough. *Even marrying a woman he didn't love. Surely there was* something, *at the beginning? Huh! You don't want to think you were that much of a fool.* If he'd already been planning to disappear with Jamie, this had been a gift. *It really comes down to one thing – do you believe Devlin? Do you want so desperately to believe that you're falling into whatever trap he's set?*

'Have you asked the American authorities at the crash site? The Sheriff or whoever?'

'I'm checking whether there was more than one accident,' Phil agreed cautiously. 'And I'm looking into Jeff's whereabouts. That would be the best thing. Get in touch with him, and you could clear the whole thing up.'

'Yes,' Kaz agreed reluctantly. *Or you could just go for the jugular and chop off the bastard's balls. With blunt scissors.*

'Patience, love.' Phil grinned at her. *Not so daft that he doesn't realise what you're thinking. Didn't get that high in the police force just on a smile. Plus he's known you all your life.*

'I'll do what I can,' Phil continued. 'But I think you need to accept that you had an encounter with a particularly nasty con man. If he gets in touch again, you call me immediately.' He looked at his watch. 'I ought to be going. You want a lift, Kaz?'

'No, thanks, I'll catch a cab later.'

Kaz stared moodily into her wine as her mother escorted her brother to the door. She hadn't forgotten her initial reaction to Devlin. It hadn't been that far away from Phil's. Even now, her uncle *might* be right. *But now you want to believe Devlin.*

'He suggested you should see someone.' When Suzanne came back she topped up their glasses.

'A shrink?' Kaz grimaced. 'I've done all that, Mum, bereavement counselling, therapy. I'm still seeing Deborah regularly. This isn't in my mind and I didn't go looking for it.' She dug her hands into her hair and tugged. 'I'm bloody glad you were in the house when Devlin turned up, or *everyone* would think I was barking. *I* might think I was barking. We *didn't* invent him, did we?'

'No – but I suppose we might have allowed ourselves to be preyed upon.'

'But why?' It always came back to that. She'd looked at it from every direction. She simply couldn't see the angle. If there was one, it was too deep for her. 'If Devlin had tried to get us to employ him, offered to introduce us to a medium, asked for money for his story?' she demanded, exasperation roughening her voice. 'He didn't do any of that. He came to tell us how Jamie died. The rest was an accident. He was as shocked as we were.'

'I believe that too,' Suzanne confirmed quietly.

'Oh, Mum.' With the tightness in her chest threatening to choke her, Kaz reached out and gathered her mother into her arms. 'Thanks.'

'You never have to thank me. *Never.*' Suzanne was vehement as she sat back. 'But what are we going to do?'

'I don't know,' Kaz admitted. 'Phil isn't going to do anything more, is he? Despite what he said about following leads?'

Suzanne sighed, mouth working as she made up her mind. 'Possibly not,' she said at last. 'He has got a lot on with this latest case and he's done his best, as he sees it, by warning you off. I have to say it. Mr Devlin does sound a bit ... scary.'

'A *lot* scary,' Kaz agreed. 'But it doesn't matter. I've got to *know*, Mum.' Kaz banged her hand restlessly against the arm of the chair. 'The only way that I'm going to find out is to take Devlin's bait, if it is bait. I have to talk to him again. First thing in the morning I'll ring his hotel. I hope he hasn't checked out already –' She tipped her head back as realisation hit, like a punch in the gut. 'He didn't tell us where he was staying.'

'Which sort of proves that he didn't intend to maintain contact.'

'He knows where we are, though. If he wants us.' Kaz wrinkled her nose. 'What do we do now? Ring all the hotels in London, on the off chance?'

'I suppose – hold on a minute.' Kaz leaned forward eagerly as her mother gave a start. 'He gave me a card. What was I wearing that day?'

Kaz stood beside her mother's wardrobe with the card in her hand.

'I hoped he'd have written his hotel on the back,' Suzanne sighed.

Kaz wasn't going to be beaten now. 'There must be someone in his office when he's not there. What time is it in Chicago?'

Devlin saw her before she saw him.

He'd paid off the cab a short distance from the hotel. She was sitting in the window, scanning the street, but in the opposite direction.

They'd have told her at reception that he was out. He wondered how long she'd been waiting. She was more formally dressed today, in a dark business suit, the vibrant hair ruthlessly secured in a chignon. There were several small tendrils escaping to curl around her face. The jolt of lust – he couldn't call it anything else – was disconcerting. He'd been telling himself over the last two days that the physical reaction he'd had to Kaz Elmore was nothing special. That he really *didn't* want to see her again. And now here she was.

When Bobby had telephoned, to warn him that the woman was looking for him, he should have told his partner to stall her. He didn't do damsels in distress, not even damsels that were as sexy as all get out. *Especially* not damsels who were as sexy as all get out. It was the thing about the child that had hooked him. Bobby had laughed. Devlin had called him an asshole and rang off.

His business in London was done. He should be getting on a plane home this afternoon. A feeling in his gut told him that wasn't going to happen. It had nothing to do with the tendrils of hair that were curling around Kaz Elmore's face. That was just sex.

Kaz Elmore wanted something from him. He had a pretty good idea what. If he wasn't damn careful, he was going to give it to her. Unwittingly he'd lobbed a grenade into her world. That didn't mean it was down to him to sort out the pieces. *Just keep reminding yourself of that, buddy.*

There was a tight feeling at the back of his neck. He couldn't imagine what it might be like to lose a child. Shit – he'd never cared enough, about *anyone*, for it to hurt. That was the kind of guy he was. It was a personality defect, plain and simple.

His career had picked him, when he was too wet behind the ears to know any better. He'd been recruited and trained and turned loose and then he did what he did, because he was good at it. He'd been good at it for nearly ten years. When he got tired of waking up in some Godforsaken place, with sealed orders for God-knew-what, he'd bailed out. He'd had enough clout and enough data on them by then to make deals. His mouth twisted. They'd sent him to therapy and tried to kick him upstairs, make him the guy who did the picking, rounding up the next crop of kids, but he wasn't buying it. He had told them his terms.

They still called him, occasionally. If they had a loose end to tie up ... Sometimes he told them, sometimes he didn't. Sometimes he really didn't fucking remember. That had bothered him, when the jobs and the places ran into each other. Whoever they were, whatever they'd done, they needed to be remembered. That was when he finally *knew* he had to quit. When the faces began to blur.

Now there was a beautiful woman waiting for him and something inside him, that he really didn't need, was shifting. Conscience, responsibility, a need for ... justice. Dammed if he knew. Sensible thing would be to get the hell out of Dodge. *Jesus.* He squared his shoulders and headed towards Kaz Elmore.

Kaz sat on the edge of the chair, peering out of the window, wondering how long this was going to take. The receptionist had been polite, but noncommittal.

No, Mr Devlin was not in the hotel at present. Yes, Madam might wait here in the foyer if she wished, but as Mr Devlin had left no message as to when he might return, would Madam perhaps prefer to call back later?

No. Madam would stay. She had nowhere better to go.

She moved restlessly. She'd dressed carefully. She'd wanted to look cool and professional. Would that impress Devlin?

Come on – you dressed this way because you were afraid of looking too sexy.

She breathed in heavily. All right! Yes! She could admit it. She found Devlin attractive.

Isn't that really why you're here?

This is about hiring Devlin for his *professional* skills.

Oh yeah. And you're not hoping this good-looking guy is going to be some sort of white knight?

Kaz planted her hands firmly down on the chair, on either side of her, bracing herself. This was not being needy. She was *not* expecting Devlin to take care of her. She was done with all that. Just because he'd caught her, when she'd nearly fainted, and she'd liked the feel of it, of him, didn't make him her saviour. All that Phil said about him was probably true – and some. Which suited her just fine. She was here to make a business arrangement.

She shut her eyes, channelling strong, independent woman for all she was worth. She was here to *negotiate*. Devlin had skills, she needed them.

Knowing your limitations is a sign of strength; it does not mean that you're still some happy-ever-after, needy heap. Devlin is a gun for hire. You're hiring. You can do this. You can work with the Devil if it means that you see your daughter again.

She opened her eyes, took a deep breath. She should be putting her speech together for when he arrived, not cluttering her brain with a lot of other stuff. If Devlin –

'Mrs Elmore?'

Kaz gulped. Damn! He was here, before she was ready! Hell, he was even bigger than she remembered. She struggled up, off the chair. He was looking at her with a totally unreadable expression.

'I'd appreciate a few moments of your time,' she said formally. She wasn't getting anything from his face – welcome, curiosity, impatience, nothing. *He must really clean up at the poker table.*

He nodded abruptly. 'Shall we go someplace more private?' Kaz's heart spiked. Did he mean his room? She set her teeth. Whatever.

He ushered her to a private room at the back of the hotel, decorated to look like a library. Deep leather sofas and walls of old books. Coffee arrived as they were sitting down. He'd seen her, waiting in the foyer. Of course. She pulled in the deepest breath. She had to get a hold of herself and the situation.

Then he smiled at her. He was lifting the coffee pot and grinning. He looked about as lethal as the plate of shortbread biscuits nestling on the tray. Had her uncle really warned her off this man? *Of course he did – the man is a chameleon. That's what you'll be paying for.*

'I've been told that I should stay away from you.'

Devlin handed her a cup, with a considering look. 'Your uncle? The cop.'

'Yes.'

'But you're here anyway.'

Kaz hesitated. She'd wasted the time when she could have been preparing her speech. All she had now was the truth. Devlin would probably prefer it that way. *So go for it.*

'My uncle says you're dangerous, that you're trying to con me.'

'And what do you think?'

Her heart lurched. 'That you may be the only chance I have of ever seeing my daughter again. I need to trace my husband. Phil said he'd try, but I think he's humouring me. Have you ever killed anyone?'

Devlin's hand jerked, almost upsetting his coffee. *What the hell?*

There was a long beat of silence. He couldn't meet Kaz Elmore's eyes.

'I'll take that as a yes.' She was leaning forward, intent. On him. He *had* to look at her. *Those dark eyes. Jesus.*

'Good.' she said briskly, as if he'd answered. 'After I've found my daughter, and made sure she's safe, I may need help to wring my ex-husband's neck.' As if they were discussing the weather. *And her a mother!*

He needed to concentrate. His mouth wasn't working. He had to get his mind back in control.

'I want to hire you, Mr Devlin. It's not just for Jamie.' Christ, she wasn't even giving him a chance to react, just ploughing straight on. 'If my little girl wasn't in that crash, then it was someone else's daughter who died in your arms. She *did* die in your arms, didn't she?'

This time the sudden silence in the room seemed to breathe.

Vaguely Devlin could hear the noises of the hotel, a long way in the background. In the front of his mind he was back on the highway, with a little girl ... but now Kaz Elmore stood at his shoulder.

He'd never even told that part to Bobby ...

With her dark eyes skewering him to the leather sofa, Devlin could only blink. *So much for the hard man image.*

She sat back, apparently satisfied. 'I want my daughter returned to me. I want justice for a mother I don't even know. I think you're the one to help me get them.'

Devlin swallowed. Hauled his wits back from wherever it was they'd danced off to. *Get your butt in gear, salvage something here. Get out of this!*

'My firm provides security, protection, expensive baby-sitting,' he pointed out hoarsely. 'I'm not a private detective.'

'But you've done other things. Before. You can do this.' Her eyes didn't let up.

'That was a long time ago.' Now she'd got him admitting – what? *Much more of this and she's gonna have the number of the Swiss account and all the shares in the mine.*

'I bet you don't forget. Besides which – ' The little breath she took told him she had her clincher. 'I think you want to know, just as much as I do. That dying child pulled you in. Now that she no longer has a name, or a family ... You're the only one who can stand for her. You're involved, as much as I am. So – will you take my money? Give me – what – a week of your time, at whatever the going rate is?'

She blinked when he told her. But clearly it wasn't going to dissuade her.

'Do we have a deal, Mr Devlin?'

Devlin exhaled. This woman was Trouble. Definitely capital T. Trouble with his name on. *Since when did that stop you? You've been stuck in a nice warm rut for quite a while now. What if you're losing your edge? One way to find out. Sucker.*

'Okay. One week.'

'Oh!' She gave a little jump of surprise, he noted, with a glimmer of mean satisfaction. 'That's great.' Her voice wavered. Now she had him, she seemed at a loss what to do with him. 'Where do we start?'

Time to take the game back.

'We need to talk about that, but first I have something to show you. Upstairs.'

'Oh, yes. I ...' She got up. He stood too. There was a strand of hair curling across her face. She pursed her mouth, blowing upwards to dislodge it, but it fell back. Devlin reached out and brushed it aside for her. He saw the flash of emotion in her eyes. It wasn't just him –

The air in the room went abruptly to treacle.

'You feel it too, don't you?' Her eyes were like saucers, jet black, and the words came out on a gasp.

'Uh huh.' No point in denial.

'What ... what do we do about it?' There was a tremor in her voice. Then her chin came up. He knew that look. She'd sleep with him, if that's what it took. To get her child back. Brave, desirable, ruthless, vulnerable, a mother. And attracted to him. Definitely Trouble.

He sighed. 'Nothing. We do nothing. We both just have to get over it.' He gestured that she should precede him out of the room. 'Golden rule of security work – don't make out with the client, it's bad for business.'

Chapter Four

They stood at opposite corners of the lift, as it rose silently to the ninth floor.

Kaz's shoulders sagged as she tried to sort out her emotions. Relief, confusion, shame, a weird thrill of ... power? What was happening to her? For a moment there she'd lost herself. Known that if it took more than money to convince Devlin to help her, then she would offer it. Had offered it? And been refused. She exhaled. She'd hired Devlin. That was key. Forget the other stuff. *Need to get this back on a business footing. Let him know where you stand.*

'I want you to know Mr Devlin, that although I'm ... attracted to you, I appreciate that we have a business arrangement and I'll keep my side of the bargain.'

'Good to know.' His eyes were on the lift indicator. 'And it's just Devlin. Or some clients call me Dev.' She must have made some involuntary movement of disapproval, narrowed her eyes or something – though how could he know, when he wasn't looking at her? 'Protection gets up close and personal. You're lying on top of a guy, stopping someone from putting a bullet in him – gets kind of friendly,' he explained smoothly as the lift stopped.

Kaz followed him out, not sure what to make of the remark. Had he ... The image he'd put in her head ... of them lying on the floor together ...

She caught his eye, and saw the amusement. He *had* known what he was doing. Of course. *Teasing you.* She straightened her shoulders, gave him a cool stare, and swept through the door he was holding open for her.

He had a suite, so she wasn't confronted by a bed the minute she walked in. Devlin crossed to a side table, opened a laptop and punched a few keys, gesturing for her to join him. She looked curiously at the screen.

'After I left you, I got my partner – you spoke with him last night – to check out a few things.' Devlin had called up a list of e-mails. Kaz watched him loading a file. 'If the girl wasn't Jamie, then she had to be someone else.' He gave a lopsided shrug when Kaz threw him a *duh* look. 'Bobby checked out disappearances of nine-year-old girls and upwards, in the Atlanta area. This is what he found.' Devlin swung the laptop towards her. The image cleared, then resolved. Displayed on the screen was a picture of a young girl. Blonde, pretty, carefree, her smile showing up the braces on her teeth. 'Sally Ann Cheska. Eleven years old. Been missing from home for six months, three weeks, two days. Last seen October 1st, last year.'

'Three days before the accident.'

'You said it. And *that's* the girl who died.'

'Oh God!' Kaz sat down on the nearest chair, with a thump.

'Makes it kind of real, doesn't it?' Devlin looked broodingly at the screen. 'My partner is doing some digging. If he finds anything more, he'll call.' He looked at his watch. 'You want to order lunch from room service while we talk?'

Kaz speared a piece of lettuce, then let it drop back onto the dish. The Caesar salad was delicious, but she had no appetite. She put down her fork. 'That little girl, Sally Ann, what could she have been doing with Gemma?'

Devlin dipped his head. Not quite a shrug. 'Seems like she was a runaway. The woman probably picked her up on the road.'

'A good turn that went horribly wrong?'

'Looks that way.' He was eating grilled swordfish, impassive. 'One interesting thing, she wasn't reported missing until 8th October – over a week later. Bobby's looking into that too.'

'So –' Kaz picked up her glass. The wine Devlin had chosen was easy on the palate and a shade too welcome to her overstretched nerves. She sipped cautiously. 'At the time of the crash, no one was looking for her? That would have made it easier for Jeff to do … what he did.'

'Yes.' Devlin picked up his own wine. 'Tell me about him – Jeff,' he demanded abruptly.

'What do you want to know?' Kaz gave up the pretence of eating and wrapped her hands around her glass. 'Jeff is – oh – everything from a fairy tale. Prince Charming, the Pied Piper, Peter Pan, Robin Hood – except he doesn't believe in sharing the loot with the poor.'

'A reckless, charismatic hustler, willing to take a chance to make a buck,' Devlin translated, after a moment. 'Capable of sizing up a situation fast and making it work for him?' he suggested quietly.

'Even when it's the death of his girlfriend and an unknown child.' Kaz put her glass down with a bang. 'Yes. My ex-husband is slick enough' She looked away, her eyes burning. *Damn.* She thought she'd cried herself out over Jeff, years ago. But these tears were hot. *Anger.*

'If he had everything in place to snatch his daughter, then this was a gift for him.' Devlin's voice was very soft, reflective.

Kaz pinched the bridge of her nose. 'When I think … All the arrangements … flights, hotels … the funeral. He was *comforting* me, for Christ's sake!'

'Did you sleep with him?'

'No!' Kaz's body jerked. 'No,' she repeated more quietly, meeting Devlin's eyes. He'd shocked her but, curiously, she wasn't offended. Taking prisoners clearly wasn't Devlin's style. He was blunt. And intuitive. She hadn't slept with Jeff, but she *might* have. She shivered. Once the horror had got a grip on her she'd been too numb, too sick – but that first night, when Jeff had held her as she wept …

They'd cried together …

Devlin was watching her, eyes hooded. 'It wouldn't have been impossible, in the circumstances,' he suggested.

'I know.' She let out a pent up breath. 'All that time he was with me.' *Those awful, endless hours.* 'He had Jamie hidden somewhere. Who did he leave her with?'

'Friend, another girlfriend, a business associate, a paid sitter?' Devlin topped up their glasses. 'It's a possible lead. If we can find out, they might know something. If anyone comes to mind, feel free to share.'

'Nothing at the moment. Do you think that they might still be in the States? Will I need to come back with you?'

Devlin's face went blank. 'You don't need to go anyplace. Wherever they are, I'll handle it.'

'No.' Kaz shook her head for emphasis. 'I'm coming with you. If …' She swallowed. '*When* we find my daughter, she'll need me.' She slanted her chin up, ready to fight dirty. 'How much do you know about five-year-old girls?'

'Squat,' he admitted, after a short, interesting pause. There might have been a hint of amusement at the corner of the mouth. Or maybe it was just a nervous tic, at the thought of being alone with a five-year-old. He held up a hand. 'Okay. You don't need to draw me a picture. If I get a concrete lead, I'll call you.'

'Not good enough.' Kaz leaned over the table. 'I want to be part of it. All of it.'

'No way! This guy snatched your daughter and told you she was dead. This is not some fucking treasure hunt.'

'You don't need to protect me.' Kaz felt herself bristling, made herself relax. Emotion wouldn't cut it with Devlin. 'I was married to the man – I know him – he's a chancer. He's

42

never been violent. Of course, if there is another reason for not wanting me along, then tell me now, and we'll deal with it.'

She saw the irritation flash across his eyes, before he battened it down. She had intuition, too. He didn't want her because he didn't want a civilian involved. No inconvenient baggage, and no camp followers. Well, too bad. Even so –

'Look – I don't think this is a game, I'm not playing detective. I won't get in the way, or interfere. But I can't sit at home and wait. She's my *daughter*.' Despite her efforts, her voice hitched.

'Yeah, well.' Devlin shifted in his seat, deep unhappiness in every line of his body. She saw him shake it off. Resignation? Or was he planning something? She needed to keep her wits sharp here. 'You come along – ' he continued at last. 'You do as you're told. When I tell you. *Before* I tell you!'

'Absolutely,' she agreed, concealing relief. For whatever reason Devlin had decided not to fight her, she could be grateful. 'Thank you.'

'Hrr.' It was a low pitched growl. 'Seems to me, as husband's go, your ex was pretty much a waste of space. So – why d'you marry him?'

Kaz shrugged. 'Because he asked me?'

Devlin's spiked glance told her *exactly* how that wasn't good enough. She took a reckless slug of her wine. *You may as well tell him the truth.* 'Jeff … swept me off my feet,' she said, after a second's pause. 'He was all those storybook things I told you. Every girl's fantasy. And … I wanted to believe him. I wanted the whole thing, with him. Husband, home, family. Roses round the porch. My mum and dad … They never married. You knew that?' She skimmed over Devlin's swift nod. She'd got used to it now. The admission didn't wound any longer. 'Oliver and Suzanne – it never seemed to matter to them – it was all part of the bohemian lifestyle.' Kaz wrinkled her nose. 'When they split up, it was just Mum and me. She was great, and I still saw Oliver occasionally, when he was in London, but I always wanted to be part of a family. Childhood dream, and all that. We – I thought Jeff and I were starting something of our own. Jamie was meant to be the eldest of six kids. I wanted that solidarity. I wanted to belong. It was all about what *I* wanted. I didn't see … ' She studied the pattern made by a speck of salad dressing, spilled on the tablecloth. 'I really *did* think Jeff wanted all those things, too.' She looked up. Devlin's face wasn't telling her anything. 'I was blinkered and self-absorbed and pathetically needy.' She kept right on looking at Devlin. Now there was an expression in his eyes she couldn't read. 'And Jeff had his own agenda.'

'And that would be?'

'My father.' She heard the flatness in her voice. 'If I'd been able to deliver, then it would have been fine. But I wasn't.'

'Jeff wanted what from your father? Money?'

'Not that simple.' Kaz shook her head. 'Jeff is a frustrated artist. He wanted my father's patronage, to be his protégé. To be fair – and that hurts – Jeff isn't without talent, but he likes life easy. He wasn't prepared to apply himself. Not in the way Oliver demanded. Jeff thought he was going to cut a swathe straight to the top of the art world. My father was the route he chose. Through me, though I didn't realise it for a long time.'

She stifled a wince at the memory. The screaming, door-slamming row when Jeff had finally thrown the truth in her face. Even after six years, and a baby together, she hadn't seen it coming. She'd shut her eyes to so much.

Devlin's silence somehow made it easier to talk. 'Oliver welcomed Jeff at first. Despite all his efforts, he'd never managed to find a glimmer of promise in me. No artistic ability at all. When I brought him a son-in-law, ready to kneel at the foot of the master – Oliver was thrilled. Unfortunately

Jeff didn't take very well to kneeling, and his ambition was bigger than his talent.' She paused, sipping wine. 'I wanted so much to make the marriage work. When I found that I was pregnant we bumped along for a while. Jeff does love Jamie – but … There were other women. In the end even I had to admit it was over. Sad, sordid, banal story.'

'Bad luck.'

'Bad choices. Too many assumptions. Won't make that mistake again,' she said firmly. She sat back, closing the subject. The conversation ball was in Devlin's court now.

Devlin frowned. He got the message. No-go area. Her chin was up, with a tilt he'd already begun to recognise. Courage. It was setting a slow simmer in his gut – something suspiciously like anger. Jeff Elmore was a grade-A asshole, as well as a kidnapper – but there was something else here, too. 'Your father thinks you have no artistic talent, when you have two gold medals from the Chelsea Flower Show?' He sat back a little when she stared at him. 'I just checked out your website,' he defended himself. He'd wanted to know about the gardening thing, so he'd done a little fishing. And come away intrigued. 'Designing and building a garden – that takes skill.'

There was surprise in her eyes. 'Arranging plants and flowers – it isn't like working in oils and canvas.'

'Well it impresses the hell out of me – seeing as I don't know a daisy from the hole you'd plant it in. It might not be painting, but in my book it's art. It's just different, that's all.' He saw a flicker in her eyes. Pleasure. The simmering in his gut damped down. Warm. They sat for moment, just looking at each other. Then he dragged his mind back to the matter in hand.

'Would your father know where Jeff might be? Have they kept in contact?'

'I wouldn't think so. Jeff was a disappointment and Oliver doesn't *do* disappointment.' Her mouth twisted. 'My father is a great man. A genius. I respect that. But there's a certain single-mindedness. High expectations.'

Devlin eased back in his chair. 'I guess geniuses don't necessarily make hands-on parents either – not much time for bedtime stories and trips to the zoo?'

She looked startled. 'I can't begin to *imagine* Oliver at a zoo. A sculpture park maybe.' She gave a lop-sided grin. 'When I was seven years old I remember wishing for a dad who'd push me on the swings and tuck me up at night, but that's not what Oliver is about. Even then, I understood that my father was different.'

Devlin digested the information, put it with a certain look in the eyes. *Understanding* didn't stop something hurting. He was beginning to get some interesting insights into Katarina Elmore. More, probably, that she realised. She was opening up to him. At a guess, she didn't do it often.

That was one of his particular skills, getting people to open up. Usually the setting was more – hostile.

The thought dumped him back into reality, cold turkey. He had no business sitting here, thinking warm fuzzy thoughts. He really had no business sitting here, period.

Kaz Elmore had a knack of getting to some soft underbelly that he hadn't acknowledged any time in the last century. The length of the eyelashes flirting against her cheek might have something to do with it, but not all. There was just – something about the woman …

She'd sighed. How the hell did a mere exhalation of air send something hot and sharp up under a man's ribs? *His ribs? Who are you kidding?*

'When Jamie was born I thought for a while that Oliver was going to turn into a hands-on *granddad*.' He saw the shame in her eyes. The memory of a fleeting envy – for her own kid. Honest, to a fault, this Mrs Elmore. His fingers twitched, wanting to reach out to her. He held them still. 'I thought he'd be outraged, that I'd been thoughtless enough to make him a grandfather, but he really took an interest. He always kept up with Jamie's progress although he had a new partner and another daughter of his own. A new family.'

The wistfulness, that she surely wasn't aware of, goaded him.

'You're certain of that? That they are a family?'

She looked up, startled. 'Well, I haven't seen him for quite a while ... the divorce ... and Jamie ... ' She stopped, shaking her head. 'It isn't like when my mother was with him. Valentina is very quiet, a home-maker. It must be different. And he's older.'

Devlin shrugged. Dysfunctional didn't necessarily mend, just because it got old. If Olivier Kessel was a crap father then, he was likely still a crap father now. But Kaz Elmore had not just survived she had succeeded, without him. He took a moment to consider that. She was a determined lady, and now she was his client. C.L.I.E.N.T.

He had all he needed. He pushed back his chair, to signal that the meeting was over. Time to get the show on the road and the disturbing Mrs Elmore off the premises. Give a man room to do what he had to do. *Like figure out what the fuck he's got himself into? Oh, yeah – that.*

Kaz felt a small flutter of disappointment when Devlin got to his feet. Reluctantly she followed. Confidences were over. Devlin was back to business again. She'd told him a lot, more than she should, and he'd undoubtedly guessed a whole lot more. Yet she didn't feel exposed. She was comfortable with him. Surprise made her frown. *Take care around this man.*

'What?' He was watching her.

47

'Uh – you didn't answer my question, a while back,' she improvised. 'Is Jeff still in the States?'

He flipped a hand. 'It's a big place. Plenty of room to hide. D'you think that he'd stay? Would he want to?'

'I don't know. I would say not, but ... How would he get Jamie out of the country?'

'There are ways – but a small girl isn't like an adult. We can't rule out that he just slipped under the radar. And got away with it. I guess cancelling her passport wasn't the first thing on your mind.'

Kaz caught her breath. Her stomach swooped, giving her a queasy spasm. She still hadn't grasped all the implications of this. 'He could have just got on a plane?'

'No one was looking for her.'

'Because she was meant to be dead.' Kaz shut her eyes, taking it in. 'You'll check on that?'

'Of course. And I need you to give me a list of friends, family, acquaintances, anyone you think might help him, any place you think he might go.'

'I have some old address books. I could ask – No!' She pulled up short, realising the crater yawning in front of her. She could have jumped into it, headlong. The thought made her palms damp. 'I can't tell anyone about this, can I? At best they'll think I'm unstable.' Bitter recollection of her uncle's scepticism piled into the sinking feeling in her stomach. 'And if anyone does know anything, they could warn Jeff.'

'You need to tread carefully.' Devlin didn't sound concerned. 'But a little healthy curiosity about the whereabouts of your ex-husband wouldn't look too odd. Just don't go calling half of London.'

'I won't.' She took a moment to gather herself, looking around for her bag. 'Thank you for lunch. For everything.'

'You're welcome. I'll be in touch when I have something from Hoag.'

'Oh. Yes.' For a second a swirl of blackness made her hesitate. 'We will find her, won't we?' The qualm of doubt was hollow around her heart.

'Maybe not in a week. Don't worry.' Both his hands covered hers. Then he let go. 'We'll work something out.' He slid another business card across the table. 'E-mail address, and my mobile number. You can send me the list. Let me know who you're going to speak to – just your closest friends. I'll take care of the rest. And I'll follow up any leads you get.' A hint of warning in the pitch of the voice.

'Yes.' She shivered as she picked up the card. 'Thank you.' She wrenched herself together and headed for the door.

Devlin stood back while the waiter cleared the table. The glass with her lipstick on the rim was already loaded onto the serving trolley. She'd been wearing some light, clear fragrance. He wondered how long *that* was going to hang around to bother him. It had been an interesting two hours. Stimulating. Kaz Elmore had issues. She was strong, feisty, all those I-will-survive words, but she still had issues. Some, he guessed, that she didn't even know about. With her ex-husband for sure. And with her father, too.

Devlin snagged a cup of lukewarm coffee, before the untouched pot got hauled away, and retired to the window to brood. Seemed like Kaz Elmore had got herself tangled up with a couple of men who were major-league assholes. And was still beating herself up about it.

And now she had him.

Kaz watched the door of the tube train open and close, without really seeing it. Her mind was too full. Of Devlin, of Jeff, of her father. Her shoulders twitched impatiently. Why the hell had she dredged up that old stuff from her childhood? This was about finding Jamie, not about her past.

She'd schooled herself not to think too much about Oliver. She'd tried to be what he wanted, not to mind when his impatience showed, not to care when he barely acknowledged her existence. He was a great man, and why should great men make time for bastard daughters, who didn't even have talent to recommend them? The tiny part of her that had longed for her father to look at her with approval, love, *something*, was part of another fairy tale. It was a neediness that shamed her, one that Oliver would have found completely incomprehensible. She was past that now. The search for a hero was well and truly over. 'No more knights in shining armour.'

A startled grunt from the man sitting opposite her jerked her back to reality. She put a hand to her mouth to stifle a giggle.

She'd talked too much to Devlin about things that didn't matter, but it was no use worrying about it now. The man had skills. A small shiver trickled along her spine. Skills, and a fabulous mouth. And she'd insisted she was going to work with him. Which she was, so too bad for both of them.

Next time she'd hold her guard higher.

Kaz tracked her mother down at the select dress agency she ran with two friends. Luckily the tiny shop on the King's Road was empty. Suzanne had her arms full with the billowing skirts of a lace-and-taffeta ball gown.

Kaz closed the shop door and leaned against it.

'I hired Devlin. He'll help us find Jamie.'

'Darling, I'm so glad.' Suzanne dumped the dress and crossed the shop to give her daughter a quick, hard hug.

Kaz searched her face. 'It is the right thing, isn't it? Going after this?' she asked, suddenly uncertain.

'What else can you do? If Devlin's story is true, and I think that it is, despite what Phil says, then he has some kind of stake in this, too. If it's a scam, you still need to know. It's a case of giving him enough rope, to see if he'll hang himself.'

After a moment Kaz nodded. 'He'd already found out who the other little girl was. She went missing a couple of days before the accident.'

'Oh no!'

'Yes.' Kaz exhaled shakily. 'His partner is investigating that end. Devlin knows what he's doing, Mum. He's focused and professional and I … We have a deal. One week.' Her hands clenched and she moaned softly. 'What can we do in one week?'

'It sounds as if Devlin has done quite a bit already,' Suzanne said briskly. 'If we must, we'll find the money to employ him, for however long it takes. I'll sell another of your father's precious sketches. There's a dealer in Singapore who's always pestering me for more. And it will annoy your father, which is a bonus.' She paused. 'There are other things than money, though.' She shot her daughter an ambiguous look as she bent to pick up the abandoned gown. 'I wasn't always faithful to your father, you know.'

'Mum?'

Suzanne shook out the dress and reached for a hangar, the light of reminiscence in her eye. 'The way we lived – you know how it was. There were always beautiful, creative people around. I remember … there was one boy in particular, Jed. He was part of the group at the palazzo, in Venice, another artist.' Her smile softened. 'Your father disliked him intensely. Jed was very talented. He'd already had a couple of shows, in Paris and London. I think Oliver realised that I was more than fond of him, even as self-absorbed as he was.'

'What happened?' Kaz questioned, totally diverted.

'There was a terrible accident. Jed had a crazy habit of decanting his painting chemicals into old wine bottles. There was a mix up. He drank something – it was horrible.

But that's history.' Suzanne shuddered. 'What I'm trying to say is that Devlin is an attractive man. I may be wrong, but I sensed some chemistry between you.' She grinned, looking wicked and youthful. 'So, if you feel that you want to offer him an additional – inducement – then I would perfectly understand.' She laughed. 'Have I shocked you?'

'Yes. No.' Kaz pushed her hand into her hair, dislodging a handful of pins that scattered onto the floor with a machine-gun clatter. Picking them up helped cover her flush. When she straightened she had herself in hand. 'A few centuries ago you would have been burnt as a witch,' she accused.

'For being a mother?' Suzanne tipped her nose in the air. 'Mothers know these things.'

'Yeah, well.' Kaz shifted her feet. 'All right, yes, there is ... attraction. And I have already thought about what you suggested,' she admitted. 'And it's not one-sided.' She had the satisfaction of seeing her mother's eyes widen. 'I didn't offer, but it ... sort of came up in conversation.'

'And?'

'Devlin doesn't mix business with pleasure.'

'Oh. Pity.' They looked at each other, then dissolved into howls of laughter. It had more than a touch of hysteria in it. Kaz sobered first.

'Mum, I'll do anything I have to do, to find Jamie, but getting involved with Devlin – he may be on our side, because we're paying him, but I'm sure that he's every bit as dangerous as Uncle Phil says. I have to get my daughter back, but if I start seeing Devlin as some sort of life line ...' She tailed off. 'He's a means to an end, that's all.'

Kaz had only remembered the invitation to the dinner party at half-past five.

Now, at nine, they were just finishing the main course. Kaz had no idea what she'd just eaten. It might have been emu, for all she knew. Her eyes flickered around the room, like the eyes of a stranger, the dark red walls, the gleaming tableware, the faces flushed with wine and warmth and conversation. What was she *doing* here?

Her skin itched. She wanted to stand, to shout it out. My daughter is *alive*. Her father has her. I've just hired a man who probably kills people for money, to help me find her. *Oh God.*

She took a deep, ragged breath and hauled herself back to now. These people were her friends, couples who still welcomed her, despite the divorce, and she knew how rare that was. She tuned back, with difficulty, to her hostess, in raptures over a recent trip to Italy.

'I almost forgot, talk about coincidence. Who do you think we walked into, right in the middle of the San Lorenzo market?'

'I think we're about ready for the pudding, darling.'

Kaz turned, just in time to intercept the warning glance between husband and wife, the quick jerk of the head towards *her* and the embarrassed flush on Gwen's face as she rose from the table. 'Of course. Has everyone finished?' she asked brightly. 'If you'll just pass along those dirty plates.'

Thirty seconds later Kaz was on her feet, gathering dishes. She carried them through to the kitchen.

'You saw all that, didn't you?' Gwen dumped plates into the sink. 'Subtle as a brick, my husband. And I'm no better. I'm sorry, Kaz, I didn't think. I don't want to upset you. I have *such* a big mouth –'

'Gwen.' Kaz held up her hand to stop the flow of apologies. 'It doesn't matter. Please – just tell me – who did you see in Italy?'

Devlin scowled at the laptop, re-reading his partner's e-mail.

53

So far Hoag hadn't found any answers, only more questions. Loose ends. Loose ends that Devlin didn't like. He shoved his hand into his hair. Nothing was quite –

The mobile phone next to the computer began to vibrate, threatening to hop off the end of the table. He grabbed it and pressed the switch.

'Devlin?' Her voice was high, excited. Drunk? There was a sound in the background like traffic.

'Where the hell are you?'

'I had to come outside, in the street, so no one would hear. I'm at dinner, old friends. They've just come back from Italy. Devlin –' Her voice shook, then steadied. 'They saw Jeff, in Florence. Three days ago!'

Chapter Five

Bobby Hoag stepped sideways to avoid the hunk of rusting metal that might once have been part of an SUV. Maybe. Just beyond it a dog was going crazy, barking and snapping. Bobby sent up a silent prayer for the links on the choke chain that was stopping it from ripping out his throat. He gave the fangs a wide berth and kept going.

As trailer parks went, he'd seen worse, but not often. He'd travelled quite a way along the highway from Atlanta to Nashville, and down a few side roads, to find this one. Not a place he'd want to raise a kid.

Luanne Cheska was sitting on the steps of a run-down trailer, a cigarette in one hand and a beer in the other. *A good healthy breakfast. Couldn't be beat. Guaranteed to set you up for the day.*

Bobby assessed her swiftly, looking for any resemblance to a dead child. It was there, if you looked. The blonde hair was natural, the mouth full-lipped and lush, the hands wrapped around the neck of the bottle delicate. Under the smudged layer of last night's make-up, the bone structure was good. The claim to beauty and the match to her daughter ended there. The bloodshot eyes and overblown figure, in spray-on T-shirt and jeans, didn't exactly bring up the word maternal.

'Hi, handsome, you lookin' for me?' She raised the bottle in salute as she gave him a slow once over. Bobby felt sweat breaking out on the back of his neck. He planted his feet solidly on the ground and returned the stare. He had a nasty gut feeling –

'Mrs Cheska? It's about your daughter –'

Luanne's feet slapped down on the dirt as she rocked back. Her face had flipped from lazy welcome to beyond ice.

Bobby sighed. On a scale of friendliness and co-operation, it looked like the dog was going to score higher.

'What d'you want to know about Sally Ann? You sure as hell ain't the police.'

'Your daughter is missing –'

'That bitch from Lynchburg, she sent you here, didn't she?' Luanne stabbed the bottle at him, waving it like a weapon. 'You try and raise a kid on your own, no one wants to know. Soon as the little slut runs off someplace, the whole world comes sniffing around. I'll tell *you* same as I told the cops, when she sent them here. I don't know where that girl is. She wants to run off, nothing I can do to stop her. Now get the hell out of my face.'

Twenty minutes later Bobby slid behind the wheel of his car. His head was ringing. Luanne Cheska's mouth would shame a trucker, but she'd liked his money. He had the name and number of the bitch from Lynchburg.

Mrs Laura Kettle, denizen of Lynchburg, Tennessee, had faded blonde hair, good jewellery and a dress splattered with tiny pink flowers. Bobby found himself looking into a pair of shrewd grey eyes. She served him tea, in a bone-china cup.

'Tell me, Mr Hoag, just what is your interest in my granddaughter?'

'Overlapping investigation, ma'am,' Bobby responded promptly. 'I'm looking into the disappearance of another young girl. Been employed by the family. Need to see if there's maybe a pattern.' He shrugged. 'Probably not, but I have to check it out. You were the one who reported Sally Ann missing. Not your daughter.'

'If you've met Luanne, then I guess you'll know why that was.' Bobby waited. Slim fingers twisted themselves into a knot in the woman's lap. 'Is this going to help find what happened to my granddaughter?'

'I can't say, ma'am, but if I find anything, I'll be sure to let you know.'

Mrs Kettle sat still for a moment. 'I suppose – if I've told the police, I may as well tell you. I should never have agreed to what Luanne wanted – ' She closed her eyes, let out a breath, opened them. 'This is hard to say, but it's the truth. My daughter is an unfit mother. When Jake was around, my son-in-law, Sally Ann's father, things weren't so bad. But when he left ... Luanne said she wanted her freedom. Needed to find herself.' The words were bitter. 'Didn't want to be bothered with a growing girl. Sally Ann lived here with me for four years. Then, early last spring, Luanne came for her. Said she'd met someone, wanted to be a family again. He was supposed to make a home for them. Luanne said he was a good man, able to provide for them, wanted to meet his Luanne's little girl.'

Pain flashed across the woman's face. 'Grandparents don't have much say, Mr Hoag, not when a mother wants to take her child, but Luanne – she had to have her chance to be a real mother, and I had to give it to her. I still think that.'

She paused, swallowed, began again. 'Sally Ann was excited. She wanted to go with her mom. I told her though, if she ever needed me, she was to call and I'd come get her. Gave her the change, for the phone. End of September last year, we had a big storm and a power outage. Phone lines went down, too.'

Mrs Kettle looked away. The fingers spasmed again. 'I had no reason to think that my granddaughter would have tried to get in touch with me when the line was out. I'd spoken to her just the day before. She said everything was okay, but she sounded –' The woman hesitated. 'There was just something, you know? So I rang Luanne. Turns out the number she'd given me for their new home was some bar in Atlanta. She wasn't living in the city, as I thought.

When I finally tracked her down, in that trailer park, she was drunk – and alone. My granddaughter had been missing for a week.'

'You think Sally Ann tried to reach you and when she couldn't get through she set out on her own, to come here?'

'I'm sure of it.' The grey eyes were awash now, with an anguish Bobby couldn't begin to measure. 'She was coming to me, and someone took her. To do ...' Her voice jarred. She stared at Bobby. 'Sometimes I find myself praying, Mr Hoag. Praying that my granddaughter isn't alive any more.'

'So, looks like the child was on her way to Lynchburg when she ran into Elmore's girlfriend.' Devlin rammed the mobile phone closer to his ear, to cut out the noise of the airport announcements. 'You backtracking on that? See where they hooked up? Good. There was something else too, about the accident report. We really need to get a look at it. Can you – ' He tipped his head away from the phone, to listen, cursing softly. 'They just called our flight. Yeah *our*. Yeah *flight*. Uh! You too buddy. I'll e-mail you once we land. Keep digging.'

The phone was at the top of the house. It rang for a long time, the sound echoing in the empty room.

When it was finally answered: 'Kaz Elmore has arrived in Florence.'

Silence, then a breath. 'Is she going to find anything there?'

'It's possible.'

'Do what you have to do.' The command was curt. 'I have something else for you also. Her uncle, Philip, the policeman. Is he becoming a problem?'

'He might.'

'Then deal with it.'

'You know I'm not in London?'

'If you can't do it yourself, get someone. Reliable. I don't want any fuck ups.'

'I will do it. Personally. But there will be a delay with the other.' A soft warning.

'Just get it done.'

'Payment?'

'You can put it on my account. You know I'm good for it.' A harsh bark of laughter. 'Don't call again until it's completed. Call soon.'

Chapter Six

Kaz pushed open the shutters and stepped onto the tiny balcony. The square below her was coming to life in the early morning sun. The proprietor of the café opposite was putting out tables and chairs on the piazza. Pigeons sidled hopefully around a few early coffee drinkers at the counter, before being shooed back out onto the square through the wide open doors. Kaz blinked as a waiter flourished white linen and gleaming cutlery, bouncing light into her face. The hotel Devlin had organised was small and quiet, despite being in the heart of the city.

She stretched, welcoming the sun on her bare arms, mind idle for a moment, imagining what it would be like to be here in Florence on holiday. Just wandering the streets with –

Abruptly she turned back into the room. She didn't have time for daydreams.

'*Grazie, signor.*' Kaz slipped the picture of Jeff back into the side pocket of her bag, as the man shook his head. On the other side of the road she could see Devlin getting a similar reaction from the girl behind the counter of a small sandwich bar. She sighed and crossed over to him. Together they completed the remaining shops in the narrow street. Nothing.

Kaz swore softly, under her breath. 'We've been here three days already. In that time, someone might have thought, even vaguely, that they recognised him!'

'Not necessarily.' Devlin might have been frowning, but it was hard to tell with the wraparound shades. 'We knew it was a long shot.' He lifted his shoulders. 'What do we have? A brief sighting at a stall in the San Lorenzo market? He could have been staying on the other side of the city, even outside it.' Devlin was scanning the street. 'Or he could have moved on by now.'

'Thanks. *That* I really needed to hear.' Kaz glowered at him. 'Look, we have to keep doing this. This is all we have – ' She could hear the edge of desperation in her voice. The week Devlin had promised was oozing away. The high she'd felt when they boarded the plane was long gone. They'd begun at the market, at the stall that most closely resembled the one where Gwen said she had met and spoken to Jeff, and worked outwards. In the evenings they toured hotels and restaurants. The snapshot of Jeff that she'd had enlarged was dog-eared and curling at the edges. Her feet were sore and her temper short. If Devlin –

'I didn't say we should stop.' He swung round to look at her. 'I just think we should chill for a while. Have lunch, make like tourists for a few hours.' He gestured down the cramped street at the tranquil, ever-looming presence of the Duomo, the huge, red-domed Cathedral, glimpsed at the end of it. 'This is a beautiful city. Maybe it wouldn't hurt to take a look at it.'

'I ...' Kaz opened her mouth to argue, then shut it again. The tight ball of frustration in her stomach was winding tighter with every shrugged shoulder and shaken head she received. Some people didn't even glance at the damn picture before they were brushing her off. She wanted to grab them, shove it in their faces, scream at them to *look*. She let out a shaky breath. 'It would be wasted time.'

Devlin was still scanning the street, this time in the other direction. 'You know, what we've been doing might have more effect than you think.'

Kaz squinted up at him. 'How so?'

'Ripples in a pool.' He turned towards her. 'Think about it. We've been showing the picture all over the city. People talk. A guy in a bar says something to another guy, who has this friend –'

' – who knows something.' Kaz examined the idea. 'And then they come to us?'

Devlin nodded. 'Sometimes it works that way.'

Kaz chewed her lip. 'What if … what if all this simply does the opposite, drives Jeff deeper underground?'

'Chance we have to take. We talked about this before.' Devlin looked bored. 'Subtle wasn't an option here. Sometimes you have to shake the tree.'

'Pools, trees. You turning into an environmentalist on me, Devlin?' She gave a shaky laugh.

'Nope, a poet.' He grinned suddenly. Kaz felt the knot in her stomach unclench and regroup in a different way. 'Must be something in the air.' He gestured towards the restaurant behind them. 'Let's eat.'

They took the last vacant table outside. Kaz gave her order, barely looking at the menu, and sat back in the shade of the umbrella. Devlin was watching her.

'What?' Irritated, she leaned forward and pushed the wraparound shades up onto the top of his head, so that she could see his eyes. The dusty blond hair was springy under her fingers. She withdrew her hand, fast. 'I can't see what you're thinking when you have those things on.'

'Maybe you don't want to know what I'm thinking.' The predatory smile rolled over her skin like a touch. Kaz swallowed. He was tormenting her, for invading his space. When he glanced away though, at the waiter who'd just placed a bottle of mineral water on the table, the relief was tinged with something else, something that shivered along her skin. Downtime, in a city like Florence, with a man like Devlin …

He was attracted to her, but he had his professional code. She had to respect that. She'd thrown herself at a man once before, and got burned. She mustn't do it again.

He was pouring the water, pushing a glass in her direction. He leaned back, lazily, nursing his own glass. Kaz inhaled shakily, sensing the threat withdrawn.

Devlin buried a smile in his glass. The move with the shades had surprised both of them. Then she'd reacted as if she'd been burned, setting irritation and awareness buzzing in his gut. He'd flicked out that barbed response on a reflex, then regretted it when he saw her face. It was like shooting fish in a barrel. He didn't need her vulnerability to make him feel like an asshole. She was too tightly wound and too tightly wrapped a package for him to unpick. However much he wanted to.

The shock of that one rocked him. Kaz Elmore didn't just make his groin ache. She had layers, and he wanted to explore them. *Shit*.

Now she was looking at *him* as if she was peeling skin. With deliberation he let his limbs relax, easing back in the chair. He saw her ease back too, both of them stepping down from code red. *She's a Client. Out of bounds. Remember that, buddy. This is lunch, not combat.*

Conversation; that was the thing. She was looking expectantly at him. What the hell had he been about to say? Oh, yeah.

'The way you speak Italian. You didn't learn that in an evening class.'

'No.' She swirled the water in her glass, then thanked the waiter as he put a plate of antipasti on the table. Devlin helped himself to salami and olives and waited. Looked like she was sorting through memories. For him, or for herself? 'I lived here, and in France, until I was twelve,' she said finally. 'Oliver rented a palazzo in Venice, before he bought the château in Provence. I grew up in both places.' He could see one kind of wariness being replaced by another.

'Not exactly your average childhood,' he offered casually.

63

'Not at all. Oliver was the centre of – what? A commune? An entourage?' She picked out a black olive. 'You know the rock stars in the '60s and '70s – Elvis, the Beatles, the Rolling Stones – the way they had this whole group of people around them, agents and managers, gofers, backing groups, stunningly beautiful girlfriends – even wives? That's how it was with Oliver. Wherever we lived, the house was always full. Twenty, thirty people, sometimes. Mum was his favourite model for over twenty years.' Devlin heard the defensiveness and the pride.

'So – what happened when you were twelve?' he prompted.

'When I came home from school, Mum was in the hall, with our bags packed. She wouldn't tell me why, just that we were leaving. I heard later that Oliver had brought another woman home, to the château. As his fiancée. She was supposed to be the daughter of an exiled Russian count, but I never found out whether that was true. He married her shortly after, in New York. They were going to found this incredibly talented artistic dynasty. We left that night.'

'I can see how your mother might want to do that.' Devlin nodded. 'But Oliver didn't get what he wanted. No dynasty,' he elaborated, as he met her eyes.

'No Russian countess either. She left him after six months, for a racing driver. The divorce was messy and expensive. He's steered clear of marriage ever since.' Kaz smiled in acknowledgement as the waiter put a plate of risotto in front of her.

'But you're not his only child.' Devlin picked up his fork.

'Not now.' Kaz shook her head. 'My half-sister, Chiara, was born a couple of weeks before I discovered I was carrying Jamie. So Oliver has another chance at his artistic dynasty.' Devlin watched, interested, as the smile got a little crooked. She skewered a shrimp and held it up. 'This is delicious. How is your tagliatelle?'

Chapter Seven

Philip Saint ambled down the corridor, sipping coffee from a takeaway mug. Nothing in the nondescript passageway gave any clue as to what the building was. It could be any office block, in any city.

At this time of day Scotland Yard was as quiet as it ever got. Behind a closed door someone was yelling into a phone. In the room next to Phil's three officers were crowded around a screen, intent on some grainy CCTV footage. Phil raised a hand as one of them looked up, but kept on walking.

In his own office he slumped down heavily behind his desk. There was no one else about. He'd been out for – what? An hour? The pile in the in-tray was stacked and toppling. Again. Sometimes he was sure that all that paper bred, right there in the tray, while he wasn't watching it. Was that the answer? Sit and watch it?

It couldn't be more useless than spending half the day interviewing witnesses who'd suddenly been taken blind or deaf. Those that weren't suffering from total amnesia, that is. He swilled down the last of the coffee. The current case had reached a brick wall. Frustration was mounting, shortening tempers within the team. Sodding CPS. In the old days –

Phil crushed the carton, pitching it into the bin. He needed a break in the case, and he really needed to make time to see Kaz, to find out how she was doing. That bloody Yank, stirring up trouble, just when she'd begun to come to terms –

He shifted restlessly, slumping further into his chair.

The row of post-it notes, next to the phone, had to be more interesting than the admin crap in his in-tray. He peeled off the top one, frowning at the number scrawled on it. Underneath, the message-taker had scribbled *Lyon*.

Abruptly something clicked in the back of Philip's mind. He hauled the phone towards him and began stabbing in numbers.

Fifteen minutes later he replaced the receiver with a low whistle. He hadn't known what to make of Devlin – except that he was disturbing things that were best left alone, but he'd never imagined Jeff – what the hell did he do now? Kaz –

His hand was still on the receiver when the phone rang again.

'Hello?'

'I want a meet.'

'Who is this?'

'You don't know me. I know you. I was in the pub, lunchtime. You weren't asking the right questions, or the right people. You're looking for the shotgun, right? I know where you can find it.'

Phil sat up, heart accelerating. 'If you have information –' he began carefully.

'Not over the phone. I know other stuff. You want it, you come and talk. In the Park, bench in Birdcage Walk, Queen Anne's Gate entrance. Twenty minutes.'

The line went dead.

Phil looked around, checking that he had the right spot. There were any number of benches in St James's Park, but this one, set a little apart, in front of a stand of bushes, had to be the one. He sat down, wiping away the film of sweat from his forehead with the palm of his hand. He'd jogged over to get here on time, but it wasn't just that which had made him sweat – if he could get one piece of hard evidence, it would be enough to lever this bloody case open.

His heart was pounding. He forced himself to breathe slowly. The whole thing might still be a windup.

He patted his pocket, where kept his cigarettes. Always a good opener – gave the snout the chance to ask for a light.

Head down, fumbling with the wrapper, the first inkling he had that he was no longer alone was the cold touch of metal on the back of his neck.

Chapter Eight

'C'mon.' Devlin urged Kaz towards the entrance of the Academia Gallery. 'We can't visit Florence and not look at Michelangelo's *David*. Think of it as part of my artistic education.'

Kaz narrowed her eyes. She suspected that Devlin knew more about art than she did.

'We can spare a couple of hours,' he persisted. 'And when did you last see a museum in Florence without a mile-long queue outside? It's fate.'

He was right. There were only a handful of people standing in line before the ticket office. Kaz gave in.

They ambled around the bright, air-conditioned space, discussing what they saw. Kaz found the half-realised statues of the slaves, or prisoners, that had never made it to Julius II's tomb, more exciting than the massive *David*, and said so. Devlin naturally disagreed.

Kaz stood in front of a Botticelli Madonna, letting the beauty of the picture wash over her. Devlin was behind her, on the other side of the room, talking to one of the attendants. He'd been right about taking time out. She could feel the tension slipping out of her, except for the ever-present buzz of sexual attraction, and she was learning to cope with that.

Devlin was easy to be with, she found, with surprise. And she couldn't help that little lift of her heart when she turned and saw him walking towards her. What woman could? The way he moved, the way he looked, the way the jeans clung to narrow hips. The way his eyes sought hers.

She turned quickly back to the painting.

She really hadn't meant it to happen. She was almost certain of that, because she wasn't quite sure how it *did* happen.

They were half a block away from the hotel, walking single file around a car slewed, Florentine style, with two wheels on the pavement. Abruptly the bell in the church tower above began to toll. Startled, Kaz hesitated. Devlin stopped within a hair's breadth of her back. She could feel his warmth.

She turned, confused, and his face was so close.

And then she just reached up.

His mouth was firm and hot and, when he took control, searching. Her head was ringing and it wasn't just the bells. *No prisoners.* She leaned her hands against his chest and simply melted into him.

Devlin lay on the bed, staring at the ceiling, remembering the feel of Katarina Elmore's mouth, and wondering if he was ever going to get a taste of all that sweet, soft heat again. Probably not. He sat up, cursing quietly.

She'd stunned him, stunned herself, when she reached for him. He'd seen that when they finally broke apart. Her eyes had been so wide and dark. At that moment, God alone knew what she was thinking.

She'd caught him unawares, for a second time, when she swung on her heel and dived across the square. He'd followed. He might have yelled at her to stop. He wasn't sure.

Once at the hotel she bolted to her room, without a word or a backward glance.

Devlin looked over at the clock. That would be half-an-hour ago.

She would be packing her bags now, he was pretty sure of that, and all bets were off over whether she would want to keep working with him. He shoved the heels of his hands into his eyes and rubbed. *This was not meant to happen.*

His control was shot to hell. One bloody kiss, and his belly was getting tight and his groin hard and heavy, just thinking about her.

He gritted his teeth and rolled off the bed. He'd have to speak to her, and soon. To say what? God knew. Apologise? Demand she apologise to him? Now there was a thought. Despite himself, his mouth twisted into a grin.

She'd got them into this bloody mess. Which didn't mean that it wasn't down to him to get them out again. If the worst happened, there were a couple of guys in Florence, good ones, he could hook her up with. Freelancers. He'd worked with them … before. They'd keep an eye on her while she hunted for Jeff.

He really hoped that it wouldn't come to that. He wasn't ready to say why, except that it wasn't only to do with the ache in his belly. Kaz Elmore was tapping into something in him that was shifting. Something that had started at the side of a deserted road six months ago?

That thought was enough to prod his libido back into its cage.

Stripping off his shirt, he headed for the bathroom, to see whether a cold shower could finish the job.

Kaz padded along the landing, a bottle of the hotel's best Barolo clutched in a sweating palm. The sight of the door to Devlin's room almost had her running back to her own.

She stopped, gathering her resources. She had to do this. She *wanted* to do this. She was scared witless and her knees were knocking, but she was right where she wanted to be. She half-smiled. She'd finally got it. Life was too damn short to let something as good as Devlin pass her by.

The man could kiss.

The thought of all the other things he might be able to do had her stomach juddering with heat and nerves. She wasn't looking for happy-ever-after any more. She couldn't think of a better way of proving it than going to bed with Devlin. If he would. If he wouldn't, she was just going to have to seduce him. She swallowed. Well first, they'd have a drink.

She squared up and rapped on the door.

'Devlin, it's me. Can I come in? I just wanted –'

Whatever else she was going to say died on her lips as she stepped into the room. He'd released the door and moved away from it. He was standing in the middle of the floor. A pair of dark jeans clung to lean hips and that was it. Bare feet, bare everything else.

Her mouth went dry as she took in the definition of muscles under the smooth, lightly tanned skin. She hadn't realised just how spectacular his body was. She simply hadn't looked, hadn't let herself. There was a faint fuzz of hair showing above the zipper of the jeans. She wanted to put her hands just there. He was reaching for a shirt. She had to stop herself snatching it out of his grasp.

'Kaz?' He was looking from her face to the bottle of wine. She put it down carefully, on the nearest piece of furniture. She had to get her mouth moving, as he didn't seem able to get further than her name.

He hadn't got the shirt on yet. He was just standing there, holding it. She wrenched her eyes away from his chest and up to his face. Frowned.

'Uh ... your hair is wet.'

'Just out of the shower. Cold shower,' he elaborated.

'I see.' She nodded, beginning to smile. 'Did it work?'

'No.'

'Thank God for that.'

She stepped forward, took the shirt out of his hands and dumped it on a chair.

'I brought a bottle. If you really want, we can drink it. Or you can kiss me again, and we'll move on from there.'

For an evil second she thought he was going to opt for the bottle, or even scoop her up and shove her back onto the landing. Then he hauled her in, and went for her mouth. Firm, fast, hard. Everything went misty. Bliss.

The groan Devlin gave when he finally let her go sent a hot thrill of pleasure through her.

'You sure know how to stage an ambush.' His forehead rested against her hair. 'Here I am, half-naked, trying to resist a beautiful woman offering me great sex –'

The thrill this time was panic. She leaned away. 'I don't –'

'S'ok.' His hand was warm against the back of her neck. 'My resistance was shot to hell quite a while ago.' He lifted his head to look at her, holding her eyes. Seeing everything. 'You and me – it will be great. *That* I can promise.' His voice was very soft, very sure. The ache inside her quivered and bloomed.

'I don't expect you to promise anything else.' When her voice wavered, she let out a breath. With Devlin, everything was going to be different. This was what she was doing here.

She eased forward, letting her pelvis rest against his hips, feeling his hardness even through the stiff fabric of the jeans. She had one more speech and then she was done. 'I have to say –' Her fingers clenched against his chest. 'If I didn't want this, I wouldn't be here. But I remember what you said, about not mixing business with pleasure. So whatever state your resistance is in, I can still leave. If you want.'

'Woman, you have to be dangerously crazy if you think I'm letting you out of here.' He was grinning. 'What do you want? Down on my knees and beg? I can do that.'

'No!' Her hand curled at the denim waistband, holding him. 'I just –'

He put one finger to her lips, to quiet her. 'I know what you were doing, and I appreciate it, but right now neither of us is going anywhere.'

This time the kiss was a slow, sweet simmer that set little fires of need spurting over her skin. It was like a long hello, she thought, dreamily, as his mouth explored hers. A prelude and a declaration.

When he lifted her and deposited her on the bed, without letting go of her lips, she was breathless. Her palms were on his chest. His heart was tripping steadily under her fingers. Her own was all over the place. Just like Devlin's hands and his mouth. *God, his mouth.* On her eyelids now, and her jaw, leaving hot yearning trails wherever it touched. She made an impatient sound in the back of her throat, scrabbling for the buttons on her shirt.

'Not yet.' He scooped her hands away, pinning them above her head with one of his as he ran the other slowly over her breasts. She squirmed. 'Devlin.'

'Hold on, baby, it's gonna get a lot hotter than this.' She could hear him laughing, feel it in his mouth as he dealt with the buttons. One at a time. With kisses in between, and long nibbling trails.

He stripped her slowly, revelling in each layer of skin as he uncovered it. His tongue and his teeth on her tight, hard nipples sent fire spiralling deep inside her. To where the need was.

Dazed with pleasure, she gazed up at him. She'd thought it might be crazy, wild. She'd never expected it to be so *focused*. Every move he made, every touch, every caress of his mouth on her heated body, was flawless. And he pulled something out of her. Response, or instinct. Something that knew when to touch and when to hold, when to yield and when to demand.

She felt tears pricking the back of her eyelids and blinked them away.

For a second they hung suspended, motionless, Devlin

poised above her, watching her face. Kaz put up a hand to touch his cheek. He turned his head, to nuzzle a kiss into the palm.

'I want you.' Her voice was so thready she wasn't sure he'd heard. Fathoms deeper than she'd ever wanted before, she shifted her hips to take his weight, opening to cradle him, as his body pinned hers. His eyes hadn't left hers. Darker than she'd ever seen them. Intent. On her.

She put up her arms and dragged him back to her lips as he slid inside her and began to move. The gasp she gave was lost in his mouth, but she knew he felt it. He shifted slightly and stroked deep, taking all she was offering and giving it back to her.

As their lips parted she couldn't take her eyes off his face. Desire, power, strength, giving.

Chapter Nine

'It's incredible.' The Commissioner of the Metropolitan Police dropped the late edition of the *Evening Standard* on his deputy's desk. Banner headlines flared across the page – *Hit Man in the Park*. 'A police officer gunned down – executed – in a public place, in daylight. I don't have to tell you that I want all the stops pulled out on this one.' He threw himself into a chair. 'What do we have so far?'

'Doesn't seem any doubt that Phil was responding to a call from a supposed informant. He logged it before he left. We're tracing it, but it will almost certainly be from a stolen mobile phone.'

'Which is now at the bottom of the river,' the Commissioner finished for him. He saw the light in his deputy's eyes. 'What else?'

'This is interesting. Just before the last incoming call Phil *made* a call. To France.'

Chapter Ten

Devlin raised his hand in front of his face, inspecting it. It was still trembling slightly. With an effort, he dug an elbow into the bed and heaved himself up. Kaz was stretched out beside him, eyes closed. Her chest was rising and falling, so she was still alive.

He propped himself up on a pillow and watched her chest. It made good viewing. When he had his strength back he was planning on kissing those two gorgeous peaks a whole lot more. Gonna do a little teasing too, and fondling. Breasts, throat, thighs. He had a programme.

Christ, he was getting hard all over again.

His body was still quaking in aftershock. He reached up to brush back a strand of hair that was falling over her face. The feel of that hair, rippling against his body.

He breathed out, a long shudder of remembered pleasure, dropping a kiss on the bare shoulder that was closest to his mouth. If there was a part of this woman that didn't turn him on, he hadn't found it yet. He was going to need a lot more time. A whole lot more. Like an intensive study. When he got the proper use of his limbs back.

He could feel a stupid watermelon grin turning up his mouth when her eyes flicked open. He'd put that dazed expression there. He was damn near immobile, she was punchy. *Looks like this thing is just full of possibilities.*

'Hi.' He rolled over carefully, kissed her on the mouth, very gently. Boy, she tasted good. He dipped a little deeper.

'Devlin.' She was kissing him back, but he could feel her laughter under his lips. 'You can't want to go again already.'

'Babe, you have no idea.' He eased back, leaning on an

arm so that he could look at her. 'Katarina Elmore, you are one hell of a woman.'

'Thank you.' The smile was pure, feminine, cat-got-the-cream satisfaction. Didn't you just love it when your woman looked like that?

He outlined her lips with an exploring finger. 'So, now that you've had me, are you gonna fire me?'

'Now that I've had you, are you going to quit?' she countered, rolling so that her face was level with his.

'Nope.' He slanted his head. 'But I am going to stop taking your money.'

'Devlin!' She sat up in a rush. 'I didn't do this to –'

'Hey.' He pulled her into his arms, her head against his chest. Which felt really good, even though her muscles were tense against him. 'I never thought you did.'

He raised himself slightly, to kiss the back of her neck, waiting for her to relax. Her hair was in his face. He brushed it away. It smelled of green grass and vanilla. Bugger. Sensory memory. Scent was the strongest trigger there was. New-mown fields and baking now and he was always going to think of her. He rocked her gently, teasing out the last resistance from her shoulders. And found they were shaking. With laughter. Bemused, he put a finger under her chin, to tilt her head up. 'What did I say?'

'Not you.' She was blushing a little, through the giggling. His chest constricted, unexpectedly. 'My mother. I just remembered. I probably shouldn't tell you this, but she told me that if I had to sleep with you, to get you onside, that she had no problem with that.'

Devlin let out a bark of laughter. 'An interesting woman, your mother.'

Kaz braced her hands on his chest, looking into his face. 'I'm not here in your bed for any other reason than that I want to be.' She put her hand over his mouth to keep him quiet while she talked. 'What we just did. Well for me, it was damn near perfect. I just wanted to say that. I'll take your help, to find my daughter, as a friend, as a lover. But if you need to go, because of your business or anything, you tell me, and that's okay.' She blinked. Why was being in his arms like this giving her the power to tell him he could leave? She could feel strength running into her as if it were coming out of him. It was the craziest thing. 'Deal?'

'Deal.' He took one of her hands and pressed a kiss into her palm. 'Now, about this damn near-perfect thing. You want to try for perfect?' His mouth was wandering up her wrist. Licking. Involuntarily, her hips flexed. 'It'll take a bit of time,' he cautioned.

Kaz caught her breath as his hand strayed across sensitised flesh. 'Take all the time you need.' She wriggled against him, saw his eyes darken. 'I'm entirely in your hands.'

Chapter Eleven

It felt strange, yet right, to be wandering along the Ponte Vecchio with Devlin, part of the crowd flowing across the bridge to or from a late dinner. His arm rested loosely on her shoulders. She tucked her fingers into the waistband of his jeans.

The sky was the soft blue-black, not-quite-dark, of night in any city. Pools of deep golden light spilled out from the shops, some no more than kiosks, that lined the bridge. The wares of the goldsmiths glittered behind plate glass. Couples were huddled close to the windows whispering and stealing kisses. Leaning sideways Devlin drew Kaz easily out of the path of two small boys who screamed as they chased each other. Elderly ladies with bored dogs on tooled leather leashes stopped to gossip, blocking the pavement. Families ate ice cream. Kaz gave a sigh. This was good. Normal. Something she'd all but forgotten.

They walked on, through the dusk, and the cluttered maze of streets.

'You want to go in?' Devlin paused at the entrance to the square that led to their hotel. Kaz looked around. The evening was soft and warm, enticing her to linger.

'We could have coffee?'

The bar opposite the hotel was small, but now even more tables overflowed into the piazza. The pigeons were still pecking around, hoping for crumbs. Kaz looked up. She could see the window of her room, with its tiny balcony. They'd shown Jeff's picture to people here, on the very first evening. Got the first round of polite smiles and headshakes. But tonight she wasn't going to think about that. *Only tonight.*

She chose a table on the square, watching Devlin ordering their drinks, admiring the view as he leaned on the counter. The guy had a spectacular rear. She'd never taken time to admire it before. Glancing away, she caught the eyes of the Italian girl sitting at an adjoining table, who'd been looking the exact same way she had. The young woman smiled and made an approving gesture and they both dissolved into giggles. Devlin, coming back to the table with tiny cups of bitter espresso, looked them over suspiciously.

'It's a girl thing,' Kaz didn't explain as he put the coffee down in front of her. 'Thank you.'

'Huh!' Devlin hooked out a chair with his foot and planted the spectacular rear on it. 'Guy at the bar says they have another place, in the Oltrarno district. One of the waitresses, she works both bars and another restaurant at lunchtime. Might be worth trying her with the photo.'

'She's not here now?'

Devlin shook his head, looking out across the square. Kaz studied his profile. She'd known this man for less than two weeks. She was alone in a foreign city with him. He'd just given her the best time in bed that she'd ever had. In her life. 'Who are you, Devlin?' she asked softly. 'Why should I trust you?'

The word sent a tremor through her, but it was out now.

He looked back at her. 'Goes with the territory,' he said unexpectedly. 'You protect people and their possessions for a living, they have to be able to trust you. That works with me. I don't know why.' There was a shadow in his eyes. Then he grinned. 'Plus, in this case, I have what every nice girl needs.'

Kaz frowned, not entirely sure she wanted to be described as a nice girl. It sounded boring. 'And that is?'

The grin got wider. 'Your mom's approval.'

'I should never have told you that.'

Devlin shrugged. 'Done is done. She's a cool lady, your mom. Very cool. She and your dad, how did that happen?'

'She was a model. Fashion.' Kaz dropped a sugar lump into her cup. 'People don't remember it much now, but she was on the cover of *Vogue*, twice, before she was eighteen. She had one of those Svengali type managers. José.' Kaz found herself smiling. 'She still has press cuttings and photographs. There's one – she's got these huge panda eyes and legs like a racehorse and José's in floor-length fur and ringlets. He was very good with money. Put it into property for her. The house in Chelsea, her flat in Notting Hill and her shop. She owns them all. Plus a lot of paintings and sketches from my father.'

Devlin leaned back in his chair. 'Is José still around?'

Kaz shook her head. 'Aids – 1989. But my father lured her away from him long before that. He'd seen her photos and decided he wanted her. He was ten years older than her, and he was her first lover. My father can be very charming, when it suits him. The way Mum tells it, all the girls she grew up with settled for a couple of Babychams and the back seat of a Ford Anglia. She held out, and got vintage champagne and a palazzo in Venice. A mostly ruined palazzo, but still a palazzo.'

Kaz finished her coffee, her mouth twisting. Damn! Devlin had done it again. Diverted her into an old story about her parents, and away from him. How did he do that? This time she was going to nail him. She leaned forward. 'You didn't –'

'*Signor*?' The bartender was standing beside the table. A girl, with a denim jacket slung over waitress' blacks, hovered behind him. 'This is Giuliana. She here to pick up her wages. I tell her about photograph. She wants to see. Yes?'

Devlin was already on his feet, sliding the picture out of his pocket. Giuliana stepped towards him, a sexy smile on her face. Her fingers rested against his, to steady the picture as she stared at it. Kaz held her breath.

The girl narrowed her eyes. Looked up flirtatiously into Devlin's face. '*Si*. I know him.' Long eyelashes fluttered. '*Signor* Elmore. Jeff. That's his name, *si?*'

Chapter Twelve

Kaz stood in the foyer of the hotel, watching Devlin crossing the square towards her. The long-legged lope was faster than it looked. She felt the flicker, low in her abdomen. Everything about the man spelled competence – and sex.

In response to the slight tilt of Devlin's head, which chimed with her own instinct, she'd melted into the darkness, leaving him alone to question the girl.

She had the glass door open by the time he reached it. He gave her a swift, hard kiss, that flickered her stomach some more. 'Thanks for that. You were so quick.'

'It was obvious that you were going to get more out of her if I wasn't there.'

'Including her phone number.' The smile was wry. He ran a hand through his hair. 'She knows Jeff all right. Way I read it, there's some jealousy going on, with one of the other waitresses, or she wouldn't have been so willing to talk.'

'Jeff's never been known for his exclusivity,' Kaz said dryly. 'Shall we go upstairs and you can tell me all of it?'

Kaz sat cross-legged on Devlin's bed, absently sipping the glass of wine he'd poured for her. Devlin was sprawled in the chair, nursing a glass.

'Jeff eats at the place she works lunchtime, on a regular basis. Big tipper. You've seen our girl. That wouldn't be the only thing to catch her interest. At a guess, they've walked out a few times together and Jeff is cooling, letting his eyes stray. So she was willing to take my money for information. He eats there usually at the weekend, sometimes Thursday also.'

'Tomorrow is Thursday.'

'And I guess we know where we'll be eating lunch.' He paused. 'I questioned her as closely as I could, Kaz, without making her suspicious. It didn't sound as if she'd ever seen Jeff with a child, or heard him talk about one.'

Devlin saw something in her face crumble. It hadn't been much, just a tiny glow of hope. She chewed her lip, head down. Then she looked up, eyes so brave he had to grit his teeth.

He'd beat Jeff Elmore bloody, when they found him.

'We didn't really expect it, did we?' She sighed. 'After running into Gwen like that, it must have made him cautious. He has to have someone looking after Jamie for him. He'll have a place outside the city. Fiesole maybe. Jamie will be there.'

'We'll find her.' Devlin reached over and took the almost-full glass out of her hand, hooking up a strand of hair. 'We can plan in the morning. Jeff has no idea that we know about Jamie. We can work with that. You need to sleep. You want to go back to your own room, or stay here?'

'My own room,' she said, after a second. 'I need some time to think. Thanks, Devlin.' She laid her hand over his. 'Thanks for everything.'

She lay face down on the bed, a pillow under her chin, putting her thoughts into order. She pushed Devlin, and sex, to the back of her mind. She had to focus on Jeff, how to draw him out, get him to admit –

The phone rang. She reached over.

'Mum? What is it? No, we were out.' Guilt flashed through her. She'd turned off her mobile when she went to Devlin's room, and never turned it back on. Her mother was crying. 'What's the matter? Tell me.'

Devlin finished his wine, looked at the glass Kaz hadn't drunk and left it on the side table. The maid hadn't been in. The bed was still rumpled from the afternoon. Wrecked actually. He straightened the covers, picked up a pillow from the floor. The faint scent of vanilla drifted up to him and his belly contracted. *Scent is the deepest trigger.*

He jumped when someone thumped hard on the door, and kept thumping.

'Kaz!' She almost fell in when he opened it. The quip about changing her mind died on his lips when he saw her face. 'What the hell is it?'

'Uncle Phil. Mum just rang. She tried earlier. He … he was killed this afternoon.' She looked up, her eyes wide and blank. 'Someone shot him.'

'Money.' A light breeze blew across the hotel's breakfast terrace, stirring the tablecloth. Kaz buttered a chunk of bread, hesitated, then put it into her mouth. Devlin watched her. Her face was still pale from shock, but she was functioning. He relaxed a little.

'Sounds like a plan.' He stirred his coffee. 'How?'

'Doesn't really matter. It's just a cover for me needing to find him, one he'll go for.' She shrugged. 'Something left over from the marriage that needs both our signatures, before I can realise the asset. A painting of Oliver's? He gave us one for a wedding present and another when Jamie was born. It would make sense if I wanted to get rid of them. Jeff won't be interested in all the lawyer stuff.'

'But he will want his cut.'

'Of course.' She met Devlin's eyes squarely. 'He doesn't know that I know about Jamie. He's bound to be wary but he won't know that's the real reason I'm here. But there is one thing –'

The way she paused, Devlin knew he wasn't going to like it.

'I think I should go alone. No – ' She put her hand up, to forestall his objections. 'I know Jeff. He's no threat, but if I have another man with me he'll jump to the obvious conclusion.' A flash of uncertain humour crossed her face. Devlin clenched his fist. 'I'm his *ex*-wife, but that doesn't mean he won't strut his stuff as the previous owner. And you'll respond, and all that testosterone will just get in the way.' She tapped the table for emphasis. 'Jeff has to be relaxed, unsuspecting, when we meet. Then we follow him, or get him somewhere quiet and persuade him to talk.' The grin was ferocious. 'I leave you to decide about that.'

Devlin leaned back, sorting options. Everything Kaz said made sense. He didn't *have* to like it.

'I think we follow,' he responded after a moment. 'Priority one is finding Jamie. If you can convince Jeff that he has nothing to worry about, he could lead you straight to her. And you're right. You will be better alone. If he realises I'm the one who found the crash site, it won't take much to work it out. But I won't be far off, and I'm going to get us some backup. A few guys I know.' He answered the question in her eyes. 'Are you sure you're going to be okay with this today, with Phil and everything?'

He'd checked the story on the Internet. It had been a clean, professional kill, over in seconds. Phil himself would barely have had time to react. Ice-cold nerve and complete confidence. The shooter had simply done the job and walked away, to disappear in the Park. No witnesses. Or none who were admitting anything.

Kaz was nodding. She'd finished her breakfast, pushed away her plate. 'It doesn't seem real, but being a policeman, it's always been there. The possibility of him getting hurt. Or killed. It's just so … He wasn't that far off retirement.' She stopped. Devlin saw the confusion and the glitter of tears. 'He was married twice, no kids. He didn't know much about children, but when we went back to England, he did his best to be a father to me.'

Devlin reached to take her hand. 'If you're not ready we don't have to do this today. We have the whole weekend.'

'I don't want to wait.' Her eyes were dark with intent. 'If Jeff is going to be at that restaurant, then I'm going to be there, too.'

Kaz sat at the counter, sipping *acqua minerale*, watching the traffic of customers in and out of the restaurant. There'd been no sign of Giuliana waiting tables. Kaz's tentative enquiry to the bar tender about her had been answered with an indifferent shrug. She chewed her lower lip. The clock over the bar showed it was quarter-to-three. The lunch trade was all but over and she was going to have to admit defeat in the next few moments.

There had been a few men eating alone. Once her heart had started to pump when she spotted the back of a dark head but when the man turned it wasn't Jeff. The disappointment had been like a punch in the face. She hadn't realised how much she was depending on this.

She shifted uneasily. Devlin had done a walk by about fifteen minutes ago and the men he'd recruited were somewhere around, though she didn't know who they were. Or where. They were doing all this on the say-so of a woman who had probably quarrelled with Jeff. Who knew what game she was playing? Or Jeff himself? Maybe he –

"*Scusi?*' Kaz looked down. A small boy had come up to the bar, from somewhere in the back. He had dark floppy hair, falling over one eye, and an envelope clutched in a small hand. 'You are Katarina Elmore.' He pronounced the words carefully, as if he'd been coached.

He looked up anxiously, breaking into the widest smile when Kaz responded. '*Si. Di dove sei?* Did someone tell you to look for me? How –'

'This is for you.' The boy thrust the envelope at her and turned quickly.

'Wait! *Ferma*!' Kaz slid off the stool, reaching out, but he evaded her. 'Please! Wait a moment. I need to know who gave you this ...'

The child dodged a waiter and two exiting diners, weaving around a high chair with a mewling baby, towards the door.

As Kaz started after him, the strap on her bag caught on the edge of the bar and she dropped the envelope.

By the time she'd retrieved it, the child was gone.

Chapter Thirteen

'Nothing.' Devlin opened the car door and slid behind the wheel. Kaz was sitting in the passenger seat, clutching the crumpled note. 'No one at the restaurant remembers seeing the kid before. He doesn't belong there, or in any of the streets around, as far as I can tell. And Giuliana does not work in this restaurant. You okay?'

'Mmm.' She'd been trembling when she darted out of the restaurant. She was calmer now. 'It's Jeff's writing.'

'You sure about that? It's not much to go on.' Devlin tweaked the paper out of her hand. 'Santissima Annunziata. Ten o'clock tomorrow. Come alone,' he read aloud. 'Not even a bloody signature!' If the note was from Elmore the arrogant prick still thought his ex-wife should recognise his handwriting, and come when he called. 'Melodramatic crap!' Frustration bubbled. The steering wheel was there, in his face. He thumped it. Kaz flinched. The impact juddered up his arm. His knuckles stung. *Great move, Devlin. Very adult, very productive.* He slumped down into the seat, disgusted. 'Why pull a stunt like this?'

'Because it's the kind of thing Jeff gets off on. We've been stirring things, showing his picture around, which pissed him off. This is him pissing back.'

Kaz's fingers, kneading his rigid shoulder, were small balm to his wounded ego. 'C'mon, Devlin. This is not a screw up. We've got what we wanted. We found Jeff.'

Kaz's eyes narrowed as she stared through the windscreen. They watched a fat black cat trying to decide whether to jump on the bonnet of the car. It squinted at Devlin. When he scowled it decided against, slinking off instead to a sunny door step. Kaz exhaled gustily. 'We've been played. Giuliana, last night. She was told what to do and say. Jeff wants to turn the tables. Now he's the one calling the shots.'

'You think?'

'Why else?'

Devlin buried a hand in his hair. 'I suppose it figures. You think he'll show, or is this just a windup?'

'I don't know.' Out of the corner of his eye, Devlin saw her mouth sag as he reached for the ignition. 'I'll find out tomorrow.'

'We,' Devlin corrected. 'You're not going into that church tomorrow alone.' He rammed the car into gear. 'I'm coming with you.'

'Jamie is my child,' Kaz's pronounced through gritted teeth. 'Which means I do exactly as it says in that note.' She stabbed a finger at Devlin. 'What happens if you come with me? You beat the truth out of Jeff, on the altar steps?'

'It's an idea.' Devlin was prowling the room, like something caged in a zoo.

'You don't think I'm not tempted?' Kaz sat down heavily on the bed. 'But I have to try talking to him. First,' she added as Devlin turned towards her. He was being unusually pigheaded. Arrogant. She should have left him and gone to her own room, not followed him in here, trying to convince him.

'Assuming the guy shows tomorrow, you think he's going to give you your daughter, just because you ask him?' Devlin bounced round as he reached a wall. Kaz shut down the splinter of her mind that wanted to admire the way he moved. She was getting nowhere, trying to argue. Time to go.

She stood. Looking round for her bag, she located it on the window ledge. She padded across.

'Kaz!'

'All right.' She held up a hand. 'No, I don't think he's going to hand Jamie back to me. It's just a matter of getting his confidence. *Then* maybe you come in. Maybe!' she cautioned, as Devlin growled. 'I'm still going with the story about needing his signature. No mention of Jamie at all.' She exhaled, exasperated, as she saw Devlin's face. 'What the hell is going to happen to me, in a church, in the centre of Florence?'

All she got in response was another growl. Looked like Devlin was turning tiger on her. Or cave man.

She shut her eyes. She wasn't changing her mind about going alone. She'd hired Devlin as an investigator, not as a bodyguard. His instinct to protect her, to take charge, was as ingrained as breathing. And as seductive as silk. To sink into it would be so easy. *And when Devlin is gone, where will you be? Still dependent, needy, hollow. Looking for a man to structure your life.*

She opened her eyes. Devlin was scowling, with something in his glance she couldn't read. Frustration was coming off him in waves.

'This whole thing – ' he began, as soon as he had her attention. 'It's just so much crap. Creeping about in churches –'

'Jeff is getting back at me. He's mad because we embarrassed him with the photo thing. Maybe we worried him a little, too. I hope so. That doesn't make him dangerous.' She reached for her handbag. 'Actually, I don't know why we're even having this conversation. We both know he probably won't be there.'

'So it really doesn't matter if I'm with you,' Devlin put in smoothly. 'Come on, Kaz. I'll be at the back of the church. Jeff won't even know I'm there.'

Kaz felt her chest constrict as Devlin's face softened. Nerveless fingers let go of the strap of her bag. He was reeling her in, pulling her close, cupping her cheek. His knuckle was treacherously warm on her skin, tracing her cheekbone with a feather touch that ran through her like hot liquid. His hips were close against hers, nudging her towards the bed. As his hand dropped to the vee of her sweater, her breasts began to tingle.

'Your ex thinks he's smart.' Devlin's voice was soft, close to her ear. 'He doesn't know who he's dealing with. I can –'

Deep in Kaz's brain, something connected.

'Whoa!' She jumped back, pushing Devlin's hand away from her. 'Is that what this is? Some macho thing, between you and him? Just because I went to bed with you!' She spun away, shoulders rigid, evading as he tried to pull her back.

'Kaz, just listen –'

'No, *you* listen.' She stood her ground. 'I'm going to that church tomorrow, *alone*. If you think you're going to seduce me into changing my mind –' her eyes flicked to his groin – 'you're going to have a long, *hard* wait.'

Grabbing her bag, she swooped on the door and slammed it behind her.

Devlin stood, staring blankly after her. He put his hands up to the back of his neck, stunned. The air in the room was still vibrating from the impact of door on frame. Slowly he dropped his hands, shaking his head.

'Christ.' *Well you handled that well.*

He flopped onto the bed, grimacing. Kaz was right on the money. He was tight, heavy and hard. And she'd just cursed him with staying that way. What started as a groan turned into a reluctant laugh. He gazed thoughtfully at the door, his mouth twisting. If he knew anything about women, and he was beginning to wonder, he was the one who was going to have to make the moves here. If he ever wanted to get laid again. And Kaz was one hell of –

He jerked his mind away from the thought. This whole thing was in danger of getting out of hand. If the woman wanted to see her ex alone, what did he care? That crack about macho bullshit stung. He'd never been possessive around a woman. He didn't really know why he'd come on so strong about the meeting in the church. It was just an … unease, griping in his gut. Something that didn't sit right. He didn't know what the hell it was, but he was pretty damn sure he wasn't going to rationalise it away. And Kaz wasn't about to change her mind, even if *he* was about to tell her about this … feeling. Which meant he had to do this thing some other way.

He sat up and reached for the phone.

In her own room, on her own bed, Kaz couldn't stop the tears. Tension, disappointment and pent-up grief for Phil all spilled out in a hot, angry wave that she couldn't control.

When it was over she scrubbed her eyes, blew her nose and stared at the ceiling. She felt drained but still rebellious. Somehow she had to get to that church tomorrow, without Devlin.

After an hour, she was still no nearer a plan to shake him off.

The knock on the door was so soft she barely heard it. The second one was louder. Irritation blossomed in her chest.

'If that's you, Devlin, you can just clear off.'

Next thing she knew, the door was opening. She'd stormed in and thrown herself on the bed, without locking it. She glanced round frantically, looking for a missile. One of her shoes was the closest thing. When the white flag appeared around the edge of the door, she had to stuff her fingers into her mouth to keep from laughing.

'Truce?' Devlin's head followed the flag.

'No!' But she put the shoe down. Devlin slid the rest of him into the room. 'A closed door is meant to be a signal,

Devlin. That people outside the room should stay outside,' she grumbled. 'What's that?'

He was setting a carrier bag down on the end of the bed.

'That is what is known as a compromise.'

Kaz prodded the parcel. 'It looks more like a lot of electrical stuff.' She prodded some more. 'Hey! Is this – what d'you call it? A wire?'

'Uh-huh. You wear *that* when you go in the church. I get to hear what goes down. From outside.' He lifted one of her hands, kissed the knuckles and gave her a grin that was pure evil. '*Now* can I seduce you?'

But it wasn't like that. It was soft and slow and bone-meltingly sweet. And when he finally slid inside her, they were closer than each other's heartbeat.

Chapter Fourteen

Kaz slipped into the church, closing the heavy door behind her.

She paused, to let her eyes adjust after the brightness of the square. As far as she could tell, the church was empty. The walls were heavily decorated, but the frescoes here, by lesser-known artists, didn't draw the crowds. Which was probably why Jeff had chosen it. She took a few cautious steps. Candles flickered. The funereal scent of dying flowers drifted towards her. Bridal bouquets, heaped in offering around an image of the Virgin.

A muffled clanging noise, from somewhere at the back of the church, made her start. She glided towards a niche in the wall, where a light was burning. Eyes down, she might be studying a tablet set low in the wall. Or praying.

'Can you hear me?' Even the whisper sounded loud.

'Every breath you take.' Devlin's voice was soft in her ear. 'It's kind of sexy.'

She knew what Devlin was doing, but it still made her smile. 'There's no one here.'

'It's not ten yet. We're picking you up fine, so no more talking, and don't fiddle with the earpiece. It's a dead giveaway.' With a guilty start, Kaz dropped her hand. Could anyone be watching her? From behind the statues? From somewhere above? Her head tipped as she considered the painted ceiling. There was nothing to be nervous about. If Jeff turned up, they'd talk. She had her script planned. She was here about money – the sale of a painting. The hardest part would be keeping a hold on her temper. She needed to get Jeff's confidence, arrange another meeting. If he didn't suspect anything, they could follow him when he left the church. Devlin wanted her to get Jeff outside, into the square, where they could be seen, but she wasn't so sure about that. What could happen, here in a church? Whereas outside – if Devlin thought he should take a hand …

She moved to stand at the entrance to a side chapel. She was perfectly safe. And if there *was* anything to alarm her, which there wouldn't be, Devlin and the two Americans were just a shout away, beyond the church door. Munroe and Rossi – big, taciturn, built in the same mould as Devlin. He'd introduced them simply as associates, with a security business here in Florence, but there was more to it than that. They'd worked together in the past, she was sure of it. It didn't matter. If Devlin trusted them, then so could …

She didn't hear him approach.

'Kaz.' She jumped. 'Don't look round.' His voice was hoarse, low-pitched. He moved to stand beside her and she risked a sidelong glance. His hands were resting on a low rail in front of them. The wedding ring was gone, but she recognised the gold signet. The wristwatch was new. And expensive.

On a spurt of impatience, she began to turn. 'Jeff, what the hell is all this? I'm only here to talk –'

'Don't.' It was almost a hiss, no more than a whisper. Anguish?

The hairs on the back of her neck rose. Something here wasn't right.

'Jeff, what –'

'You have to stop this, Kaz.' The words were rapid now, breathless. 'If you don't –' His voice hitched, rose, fell back to a frantic whisper. 'You have to stop coming after me. It can only be about Jamie. But I don't *have* her any more!'

'What?' Kaz spun round in shock.

And froze.

In all the years they'd been married she'd never seen fear on her husband's face.

'Jeff, please –' She reached out, grabbed his arm, saw the fear ratchet even higher. 'Jamie *is* still alive? Where?' Hands tightened into claws. 'What have you done with my daughter?'

'She ... she's safe.' Jeff's eyes were everywhere, scouring the recesses of the church. 'You have to stop, Kaz. Stop looking. Go home. Before we all die. Go home!'

With a violent jerk, he broke her hold.

Behind them the door of the church slammed open.

Kaz jumped and swung round. A chattering group of tourists poured towards her, led by a woman with a striped umbrella. She swerved sideways, to avoid being engulfed, pushing her way to the edge of the crowd. The space beyond the group was empty.

Jeff was gone.

Chapter Fifteen

When she erupted out of the church into the sunlit square, Devlin was running towards her.

'It's okay.' He caught her in a tight hug, against his chest. 'Munroe and Rossi are following. They picked him up as he left the church.' He dived into his pocket as his mobile phone chirped. 'Yeah. We're on our way.' He nodded to Kaz. 'He's heading out of the city. Let's get the car.'

Munroe walked towards the hire car, shaking his head. Devlin shoved open the door and got out.

'Sorry, man. That car of his has one turn of speed. He just disappeared.'

'That may not be entirely true.' Rossi snapped open a map and spread it on the bonnet of the car. Kaz slid out to join Devlin, as Rossi traced a finger over the unfolded chart. 'I know this area. I did a job out here a few years ago. Elmore must have turned off here. There are only three properties off that road. Shouldn't be too hard to find out which.'

It was, of course, the third and last. They could see Jeff's dark red Lotus from their vantage point in the car, on the hill overlooking the property. It was a tile-roofed, white farmhouse, with a cluster of outbuildings – what looked like a couple of rental cottages, in the process of refurbishment, stables and a barn. The blue of a pool showed beyond the house. Jeff's car faced the barn. Devlin studied the terrain with a pair of field glasses.

'No sign of anything moving.' He handed Kaz the glasses. 'Wonder why he didn't put the car inside?' The barn door stood open.

'Maybe he's planning to go out again?' Kaz speculated. 'He can't have realised we were following.' She lowered the glasses. Munroe and Rossi had driven on, beyond the house, checking for any more approaches – or exit routes.

His eyes still on the buildings, Devlin pushed the start button on the recorder that lay between them on the seat. The exchange in the church re-played, soft but clear. 'He was pretty keen for you to back off.'

'He was scared.' Kaz shivered. 'I've never seen Jeff like that. He doesn't scare.'

'How good is his acting?'

'Very. But not this time.'

'All that stuff about everybody is gonna die. Sounds like cheap theatrics to me.'

'You had to be there. He was trying to make it look as if we didn't know each other. As if someone else might be watching.' She slewed round in her seat. 'He knew I was looking for Jamie.'

'Or assumed it. Guilt has a habit of jumping to conclusions.' Devlin avoided her glance. 'Yes?' He flipped the buzzing mobile phone open, frowning. Kaz tensed. 'Rossi and Munroe are in position.' Devlin dropped the phone back in his pocket. 'I guess we can go down and pay your ex-husband a visit.'

There was nothing threatening about the house. It was just a building shuttered against the sun. No sign of Jeff. No sign of anyone. Kaz's chest was tight. What did she expect? That he'd come flying out, yelling at her to leave? Heart thumping, she surveyed the courtyard and the building.

The silence suddenly seemed odd, oppressive. She tried to imagine Jamie running around, splashing in the pool. Had her daughter been here? Was she still? Were she and Jeff hiding, somewhere in the house? Had he told her they were playing a game?

Behind her Devlin was turning the car, so that it was facing the road, but she hadn't been able to wait. Unexpectedly unwilling to approach the silent building alone, she craned to peer into the red Lotus. Would there be something – a child's book or toy? There was nothing but an empty mineral water bottle and a man's linen jacket, tossed over the seat. She prowled around the car to look on the opposite side, checking the barn through the open doors.

And saw. And screamed.

Devlin came up behind her at a run. He had her around the waist in a second, pulling her back. She hit out blindly, caught him on the chin and heard him curse. 'Let me go!' She squirmed to face him. 'For God's sake, we have to get him down. Get help –'

'Kaz.' Devlin shoved her head hard against his chest, holding her eyes away from the thing that was hanging inside the barn. 'It's too late for that. He's dead.'

'How can you know?' She was shaking, teeth rattling against each other. 'He might –' She looked up, saw the bleakness in Devlin's face and abruptly stopped struggling. 'How can you know?'

'Think about it. We've been here watching for at least half-an-hour. No one's been in or out of there.' He jerked his head. 'He was dead before we got here, baby. We go in there and all we're doing is contaminating a crime scene.'

'Oh, God.' Kaz put her hands to her mouth. 'After he saw me he came straight out here and did that. He killed himself.' Abruptly she twisted out of Devlin's grip, to retch into a patch of weeds.

Devlin waited until she was done, studying the scene in the barn from the safety of the doorway. Jeff's body hung from a beam, swaying slightly in a cross breeze. Even from a distance the distortion and discoloration of the face was visible, and the unnatural angle of the neck. A set of steps lay overturned under the dangling feet. The guy could have been dead before they hit the floor. Devlin turned away to hand Kaz a handkerchief as she straightened up.

'Thank you. I'm sorry …'

'Natural reaction.' Devlin shrugged, looking back at the house.

'We need to call the police.' Kaz put her hand to her head.

'Not yet.'

'What?'

'Once we call the cops, we get hustled straight out of here.' The phone was in his hand. 'Munroe? Get down here. We have a situation.' He folded the phone. 'Another ten, twenty minutes isn't going to matter. If there's any trace of Jamie here, we'll find it.'

'Anything?' Devlin came out of the dining room, into the hall, intercepting Munroe as he came down the stairs. Munroe was shaking his head.

'Most of the top floor is empty. Nothing that looks like a child's room.' He slid off the thin latex gloves, storing them in his pocket. 'We've been here long enough. You need to call this in.'

'Yeah.' Devlin stared back through the open door of the dining room and the French windows beyond. There was a battered-looking football resting against a pot on the terrace. Would a five-year-old girl play with something like that? 'You and Rossi head out. I'll take it from here.' Slipping off his own gloves, he handed them to Munroe and went to find the house phone.

Kaz was sitting on a bench outside one of the partly renovated cottages. He paused to give them a critical once over. Typical rural idyll stuff. Pretty. Elmore would have done well with them. He sat beside Kaz on the bench. If she'd been crying, she wasn't now.

'I called the cops.'

Kaz nodded, eyes distant. 'If she'd ever been here, we'd have found something.'

'I think so.'

She turned stiffly, focusing on him, eyes bleak. 'Where is she? What are we going to do now? Jeff was –' She broke off, swinging round.

Devlin was listening, but not to her. The distant sound of sirens was growing louder, more strident. She watched, open-mouthed, as three police cars bounced along the drive towards them. Devlin hoisted himself to his feet as the cars rolled to a stop, spitting a dozen yelling, gun-wielding police into the courtyard.

Chapter Sixteen

'Tell me, *Signora* Elmore, your ex-husband – he was a violent man? Jealous perhaps?'

'No!' Kaz put her hand to her temple, trying to ease the pounding in her head. Her Italian was too rusty for a police interrogation. Finding that she was having trouble keeping up, the policeman had switched to English. The events at the farmhouse were a dizzy blur. She and Devlin had been bundled into separate cars and driven away, as the police swarmed over the house. Now she was sitting in a windowless room, being asked the craziest questions.

'Look, I don't understand what you want.' She pulled herself up straighter in the chair. 'I told you already. Jeff didn't have a violent temper, he didn't drink to excess, he didn't do drugs. Not when I was married to him.' *He was a serial adulterer. That's all.* 'I don't know what this has to do with him killing himself.' Her voice cracked. 'When I met him this morning he was frightened, not angry.'

'Ah, yes. Your meeting in the church. Can you describe please the clothes your husband was wearing?'

Kaz closed her eyes and opened them again. 'Chinos, dark shirt and jacket – linen, loafers, I think.' The policeman was making notes.

'None of these clothes were marked or stained in any way?'

'No. There wasn't much light where we were standing, but I didn't see anything.' She gripped the edge of the table. 'Will you please tell me what all this is about?'

'Mrs Elmore, do not distress yourself. I will get you a cup of coffee and then I wish you to tell me again all that you have done here in Florence. This time it is for the record.

What you would call making a statement? You will do that?' He was already on his feet. Kaz found herself nodding blankly at a closing door.

Outside in the corridor a young officer, smoking a cigarette cupped guiltily inside his palm, was leaning against the wall. He looked up as his colleague joined him, raising his eyebrows. 'Well?'

'Their stories match. *Signora* Elmore came here looking for her daughter.'

'You think the child is still alive?'

'With what we saw this morning? No. Jeff Elmore was a head case.' The first man made a gesture of distaste and shoved himself away from the wall. 'Let's get this finished.'

Kaz sipped coffee she didn't want and stumbled again through her story, trying to read the police officer's expression. He was plump and balding, probably in his mid-40s. He'd given her his name and rank, but she couldn't remember it. When she'd stammered to a close, finally, he lifted a file and put a photograph in front of her. 'You recognise the woman in this picture?'

'Yes.' Kaz had no doubt who the laughing, dark-haired girl was. 'That's the waitress who told me about Jeff – Giuliana.'

'Giuliana Sforza.' The policeman nodded. 'And this?'

It looked like a school photograph. The child's hair was carefully combed, the shirt and sweater unnaturally neat.

'I think … I think it may be the little boy in the restaurant. The one who gave me the message.'

The policeman nodded again. His eyes were grim, but his mouth suggested satisfaction. 'Dominic Sforza – Giuliana's son,' he confirmed. 'And can you tell me, Mrs Elmore. Is this your husband's writing?'

The paper was in a plastic bag. Kaz smoothed it down.

'*I never meant things to end this way. I'm sorry for Dom and Giuliana and for my daughter. I didn't know what I was doing. I couldn't stop it. This is the only way I can repay.*'

Kaz nodded sharply. Her throat was too tight to speak.

'It was found near to your former husband's body.' The policeman pushed it back into the folder. 'Thank you, *Signora* Elmore, you have been most helpful. If you would now like to wait in my office –'

'No.' Kaz put her hand up to hold him, her mouth working. 'A moment, please.' She swallowed. 'I have to know what this is about. Giuliana and her little boy. Has something happened to them?'

She saw the indecision in the man's face, swiftly resolved. He shrugged. 'You will be able to read it in all the papers tomorrow.' His voice took on a formal inflection as his face hardened. 'Giuliana Sforza and her son were found in her apartment at ten-thirty this morning. They had both been stabbed to death.'

Chapter Seventeen

'Jeff killed his girlfriend and her little boy and then took his own life,' Kaz said hoarsely.

'That's the scenario the police are working with,' Devlin confirmed.

'Was that why he was scared this morning, when he saw me, because of what he'd done?' They were sitting outside a bar. An untouched glass of brandy stood on the table in front of her. Devlin nudged it forward. Kaz picked it up and drained it, almost choking, her eyes filling with tears. 'Nothing makes sense. Why would Jeff do any of this?'

'Giuliana knew too much,' Devlin suggested. 'That's what the cops think.'

'You understand Italian? – You listened in on their conversation.' For a second Kaz felt her face lighten into the ghost of a grin. Devlin nodded, not looking the slightest bit guilty. Then her features, and her control, crumbled. 'That suicide note ... The police think my daughter is dead. They aren't looking for Jamie, they're looking for her body.'

The shift in Devlin's eyes was tiny, quickly masked. It covered her skin with ice.

'Kaz –'

'You think that, too.'

'Kaz –' This time he leaned to take her hand, but she evaded him, curling her fingers into fists.

'I can't make it add up. That Jeff is a killer, that he would hurt Jamie? It *doesn't make sense.*' She heard the rising note in her voice and swallowed. 'He was never violent, even when we argued. Now I have to believe that he killed Jamie, then murdered his girlfriend and her son?'

Devlin grimaced. 'Whatever happened, Jeff regretted it to the point of taking his own life.'

Kaz sat, staring at the empty glass on the table. 'I don't understand any of it.' She lifted her head. 'But with Jeff gone, everything comes to an end. He was our link. There's nowhere else to look. I may never find out what happened to Jamie.' Abruptly her throat choked on a sob. 'I've lost her, all over again.' With a helpless gesture she stood up, almost overbalancing her chair. Devlin righted it, tried to pull her into his arms. When she resisted he dropped his hands. 'Where are you going?'

'Back to the hotel, to pack. Mum needs me – because of Phil.' A fresh wave of pain shuddered through her. She'd had half-a-dozen text messages from her mother, each sounding more urgent than the last. She needed to get back. Her crazy daydream, that when she left Florence Jamie would be coming with her, was over. Loss twisted deeper in her chest than tears. 'There's nothing to stay for now. My daughter is never coming home.'

Devlin stood by the window, looking down into the square. He'd booked two seats on a late evening flight, paid off Munroe and Rossi and left contact details at police headquarters. His holdall was packed, waiting on the bed. The hire car would be left at the airport. He'd see Kaz to her house and be back at Heathrow for a plane to Chicago before morning. Extraction complete. Case closed.

Except that this one would never quite be closed.

He watched a pair of pigeons on a nearby roof, the male strutting his macho stuff, neck feathers puffed to impress, the female turning a cold shoulder.

He wasn't kidding himself. The police thought Jamie Elmore was dead, and he couldn't argue with their logic. What he'd seen in Kaz's eyes, down in the square, was the end.

All he'd brought her was a whole heap of agony. He'd forced her to mourn her daughter, all over again. She was going to want to bury the memory of that, and of him, in the blackest hole she could find.

He was the one who'd brought all this shit down on Kaz, so if something was biting inside him, something that he could barely identify, and didn't have the first idea how to handle, it served him fucking well right.

Kaz was only dimly aware of Devlin as she went mechanically through the check-in procedure, the wait, the flight itself. The small part of her that wasn't in a fog of confusion and pain was very grateful for the way he was taking care of her, and the warmth and strength of his shoulder as the plane powered into the night. She wanted to tell him, but the words wouldn't come. She put her hand on his chest, fingers curled into his shirt.

As she faded into exhausted sleep, the last thing she remembered was Devlin's hand covering hers.

They were waiting just outside baggage reclaim. A man and a woman. Plain clothes and blank faces. Warrant cards.

'Mr Devlin? If you wouldn't mind coming this way, sir?'

'Sure as hell I mind!' Devlin let out a long breath. 'Not that it's going to make a damn bit of difference.' He looked from one to the other and then at Kaz standing, dazed, beside him. 'Any chance of telling me what this is about?'

He thought he could read the glance that went between them. This was pain in the ass, not panic button.

It was the man who spoke. The woman was watching Kaz, with something like concern in her eyes. 'We have a few questions. It concerns the murder of Inspector Philip Saint.'

Devlin knew his jaw had slackened. Of all the things it could be, he hadn't expected this.

Kaz's head came up 'Uncle Phil?' The bewildered look on her face spiked his gut. *You and me both, baby.*

He forced a hand through his hair. 'Does it have to be now?' Silence. 'I guess it does.' With a sigh he retrieved his bag from the luggage trolley and pushed the trolley towards the woman. 'I'll go with him.' He jerked his head. 'You see Mrs Elmore gets out of here. There should be a car with a driver waiting, in my name. Get her in the car and I'll answer anything you want.'

That look between them again. An infinitesimal nod. The woman took the trolley. Devlin hesitated, then reached down to kiss Kaz on the cheek. Her skin felt cold. He gave her a gentle push, towards the exit. Her eyes were huge and dark in a pale face. 'It's OK. Go on. Go find the car.'

For a moment she looked up at him, face unreadable. The female officer tapped her on the arm, pointing. Kaz turned to follow her.

Devlin stood and watched her walk away.

Chapter Eighteen

Kaz held the phone in a grip tight enough to crush it. 'Devlin's gone!'

'I thought you'd know that, darling.' Suzanne sounded distracted. 'He got a flight back to the States, right after the police finished questioning him. Never left the airport. I can't remember who told me – oh yes – the police liaison officer – did I tell you we had one of those? He really –'

'Do you know why the police wanted to question Devlin about Uncle Phil?' Kaz cut in.

'I think his name was on some papers on Phil's desk. He had been looking into him, hadn't he? And the police have to investigate every possible line of enquiry.' Suzanne caught herself up. 'I'm babbling, aren't I? I just don't seem to be able to concentrate. They want to put it on that programme on television – where they get the public to ring up with information,' she said abruptly. 'They have CCTV footage. They want to put pictures of a man murdering my brother, on national television.' Her voice rose and broke. 'I still can't believe Phil is dead. And that poor girl and her little boy, in Italy, and Jeff and Jamie. When did the world turn into a nightmare, Kaz? Oh!' Her voice changed, sharpened. 'Oh, no!'

'What's the matter?' Kaz demanded, alarmed.

'Something's burning. That bloody toaster is jammed again.' The ear-splitting whine of a smoke alarm came clearly over the line. 'Oh sod! I have to go, darling.' The phone went down with a crash.

Kaz sat on the stairs, arms wrapped around her waist, rocking. Devlin had left, without saying goodbye. Those last moments at the airport. Should she have known? She'd been in emotional meltdown, wiped out by shock and grief.

And guilt. Recollection dug into her brain, like glass shards. She'd threatened, so casually, to ring Jeff's neck ...

Gasping, she fought her way back from the memory of that ghastly, sickening fog that had enveloped her at the airport. To Devlin.

He'd kissed her cheek. His lips had been so warm on her skin. And then she'd walked away and left him alone. Had he walked out of her life, or had she walked out of his?

Sometime soon she was going to have to deal with this. And with Jamie.

The police thought Jamie was dead.

But Jeff had said she was safe?

A scared man and a killer?

Nothing safer than death. Nothing to hurt her now.

How do you tell a woman you killed her child?

I don't have her any more – because no one does?

Kaz set her jaw. However hollow and empty she felt, however high the brick wall that was facing her, she couldn't give up. Jeff was gone, but there had to be *something* more she could do. Whatever it took, she *was* going to find out what had really happened to her daughter. And bring her back home. At this particular moment, though, she had to concentrate on her mother.

Before the whole of Notting Hill went up in flames.

This time, the telephone at the top of the house was answered before it reached the second ring. 'For Christ's sake – I didn't order a bloodbath!'

The laughter at the other end of the line was low and mocking. 'You have the result you wanted. How I arrange it is my business. I was rather pleased with the effect. The woman and her son were an unexpected entertainment. An inspiration of the moment. I throw them in, no extra charge.'

'You've already collected your fee.'

'So I have.'

There was a pause.

'You're sure everything is secure?'

'Nothing leads back to you ... but there is one small, loose end.' The voice faded. Waiting.

The question came at last, low and wary. 'What is it?'

'The police are looking for the child's body.'

An indrawn breath. 'And?'

'I think it's time we gave it to them.'

'Ground control to Devlin. C'mon, dude, are you in there?'

'Uh!' Devlin focused back on the office and on his partner, lounging in the chair in front of him.

'Shit man – I've been briefing you for the last twenty minutes on the O'Hara job – a contract bigger than any we've handled so far. Which *I* did the deal on, while you were making your number with half the police forces in Europe – not that I'm bragging, you understand. And you haven't listened to a fucking word I've said.'

'O'Hara, big new film festival, back to the guy's roots, West Coast, stars, directors, producers and all that crap. Security and protection,' Devlin mumbled.

Bobby nodded grudgingly. 'So – you can look stupid and listen at the same time. Good trick.' He leaned back, dangerously, in his chair. 'If the thought of cosying up to Cameron and Catherine Zeta isn't bringing you out in a sweat, then you might try to show some interest in the money we'll be making,' Bobby suggested.

He took a good look at Devlin. 'This isn't working, is it?' He got up and walked round to prop himself against the end of his partner's desk. 'Half your head is still in Europe. Is it the job or the woman?' He saw the small movement in Devlin's eyes. '*Both?* Oh, Jeez!' He kicked Devlin's chair. 'Want to share?'

'Who made you my shrink?'

'No one. I'm dumb enough to volunteer. Which, considering you tried to shoot the last one, is pretty big of me. C'mon, Dev, spill it.' Bobby gestured impatiently. 'I got the basics. Kaz Elmore is hot and the job was a major fuck up. Do I need to beat the rest out of you?'

'Wanna try?' Devlin growled.

Bobby stared at him. 'If it will help.'

Devlin was the first to look away. Bobby waited.

'None of this has anything to do with Kaz Elmore.'

Denial.

Bobby straightened up, regarding his friend with a mixture of pity and sympathy. Well-hidden, because if Devlin spotted it, he was toast. The flicker was there again, in his partner's eyes. Devlin had either done Kaz Elmore and was desperate to do her again, or he hadn't, and was in the painful position of a man trying to kick his own ass. Bobby stifled a grin. He might offer that one out. There'd be people taking numbers. He'd really like to meet this Elmore babe. She had to be hot and more to get the Iceman this shook up. The prospect of Devlin thinking with his cock, like every other poor slob on the planet was … awesome.

Bobby took a deep breath and straightened his face, sobering up instantly. This was serious stuff. He'd be there, if Devlin wanted to talk about the lady, like when the order for snowmobiles came through from hell. Which meant he had to go with the screw up over the job. *That* they might be able to fix. And he had an angle on that himself.

'Okay – so suppose I go along with this obsession? What do we need to do?' With some amusement Bobby watched Devlin's eyes widen.

'We?'

'This thing is about two little girls, remember?' Bobby said quietly.

'I saw those women. Sally Ann's mother ...' He paused. He'd been thinking about that, wondering just how much pain and guilt there was, behind the hostility and the anger and the booze. He shrugged. 'Her grandmother is grieving. Knowing her granddaughter is dead won't make anything better, but right now we can't even give her that. We have to prove Jamie Elmore wasn't in that crash, before we can prove that Sally Ann *was*. Until we bring Jamie Elmore home, one way or another, no one gets closure.' He straightened up. 'So – again – what do we need to do?'

Devlin hesitated. 'Thanks.'

Bobby raised a finger. 'None of this hearts-and-flowers crap means I'm going soft. You're gonna haul your sorry ass back from whatever planet you're on and we work this and the O'Hara deal and all the other regular shit. You got that?'

'Just about,' Devlin drawled. 'And it's still thanks.'

'Yeah, well.' Bobby ducked his head. 'We've been buddies a long time. Too fucking long.' He shrugged himself off Devlin's desk. 'O'Hara is expecting to meet with us in the next couple of weeks. We need something to show him by then. I reckon we've still got space to do a little sniffing around.'

'You know we could dig up a whole heap of stuff, and it still might not tell us a Goddamn thing that's of any use.'

'Chance we have to take.' Bobby was philosophical. 'You're thinking about how Sally Ann came to hook up with Elmore's girlfriend?'

'And where she was in the missing time. And how Elmore got his daughter out of the country.' Devlin reached for the phone. He dialled, waited, then left a terse message. 'Munroe and Rossi,' he explained to Bobby's enquiring stare. 'I want to see what they can do from their end. The whole Elmore thing ... ' He shifted restlessly. 'It all fits together so damn well.'

'Too well?'

114

'It makes perfect sense, and no sense at all. Elmore killed his daughter, his new girlfriend and her kid, then tops himself in a fit of remorse. Nice neat story. But why snatch the kid, just to kill her?'

'An accident? He covers up and the girlfriend blackmails him?'

'Could be.' Devlin looked off to the side. 'Everyone is assuming that Jamie is dead. Again.'

'But if she's not –'

'– where the fuck is she?' Devlin finished softly. He fixed his eyes back on Bobby. Bobby took a jolt as he looked into them. Wide, troubled, defenceless. Not a look he'd ever thought to see on Devlin.

They'd first met when? Six years ago? Seven? The Carstairs job. He hadn't been impressed, being partnered with a Brit, but orders were orders – international co-operation and all that. And shit, what did you know, it had worked. 'They' had been delighted and crowing, curse their black, shrivelled souls. Six months later Devlin had saved his ass, when another international thing went spectacularly belly up. He'd returned the compliment a month after that. So, when things were getting stale and Devlin came looking for him with his proposition – new identities, new business, new life – he'd been ready to go. Now he was Bobby Hoag, with money in the bank, Hollywood babes on the horizon and a partner who looked like misery in a smart suit.

Devlin was still talking. 'This thing has been bothering me, right from the get-go. I've felt – I don't know what I've felt. Like there was something or someone out there.' He scraped his hand over the back of his neck. 'Now tell me I'm crazy.'

'You're crazy,' Bobby said, obediently. *Or so desperate to give Kaz Elmore back her little girl, you're clutching at fog.* 'Can you nail down anything particular that's been off?'

'I ... no ... ' Devlin stopped. 'Nothing.'

'Except?' Bobby prompted, wondering if he'd get it. Or would Devlin blow him off? When it came, it wasn't anything that he'd expected.

'Something in that barn. It put me in mind of Luce.'

Bobby swore ripely. 'Luce is dead.'

'Did you ever see a body?'

'Huh? Obsession *and* paranoia? You've got it bad, dude.' Bobby rose and crossed to the small fridge beside the window. He took out two beers and handed one over.

Devlin slugged from the bottle, eyes narrowed. 'It's the paranoia that keeps you alive.'

'Yeah, okay.' Bobby leaned a hip against the wall. 'You're thinking about that time in Austria. Murder made to look like suicide. Body found hanging – in a barn,' he finished slowly.

'Mmm.' Devlin nodded. 'That's the one. Though I don't recall you being there – not until the waking up in the hospital bit.'

'I wasn't, but your description was vivid and, as I recall, exceptionally profane.' Bobby shook his head. 'You're bent out of shape on this one, buddy. Apart from being dead, how the hell would Luce be connected to Jeff Elmore?'

Devlin shrugged. 'He can't be. That's why it's paranoia.'

Bobby took a thoughtful pull at his beer. 'Tell you what, if Luce isn't dead and he finds out that *you're* not ... Might be quite a party.'

'I'll get tickets printed.' Devlin's voice dropped. 'I don't think it would be a case of finding out I'm alive. If Luce is still out there, then he already knows.'

Chapter Nineteen

Devlin leaned into the car, took a gulp from the lukewarm bottle of water and dropped it back on the seat. He and Bobby had been on the road three days, working out of Atlanta, tracking Elmore's movements. At least, that was the theory. So far they had zip, and one small town was beginning to blur into another. And this was the last day. O'Hara and the rest of the crap were still on hold. Waiting.

Across the street a gleaming sign welcomed him to the Happy Days Motel. Was this the fourth Happy Days, or the fifth? He'd lost count. This one looked like it might live up to its name. Clean and well kept. His cell phone juddered against his thigh. He pulled it out and stabbed the button. 'Yeah?'

'You got anything?' Bobby was working the other side of town. In about an hour of motels, hotels and guesthouses, they were going to meet in the middle of Main Street.

'Nah. You?'

'Two maybes and the phone number of a laundry maid who thinks I'm cute.'

Devlin snorted. 'Anything with the maybes?'

'Not really. One of them was a hotel coffee shop. Waitress thought that Elmore had breakfast there a couple of times. Left a big tip. Couldn't be sure if there was anyone with him. Too long ago.'

'The tip sounds like Elmore.' Devlin sighed. 'Got to go. See ya.'

'I'm sorry, sir – the motel's records –'

'I don't want to see your records. All I need is a yes or no.' Devlin laid four photographs on the reception desk. 'Have you seen any of these people before?' Devlin was expecting the no. He wasn't listening to the mouth, he was watching the eyes.

The quick, blessed flash of recognition, told him everything.

'No. Sorry.' The clerk began to sort papers under the desk.

'Too bad. Thanks for looking.'

He found what he wanted outside unit twenty-four. A maid's cleaning cart. A small, olive-skinned boy was sitting on the floor beside it. Even better. Devlin hunkered down.

'Your mamma – she's inside, cleaning up?'

Cautious nod.

'You come to work with her, every day?'

Wariness. Another nod, less certain.

Devlin reached in his pocket for the photos. 'Did you see any of these people, when you were with your mamma? Did they stay here?'

He fed over the photographs, one by one. His heart speeded up when he got a nod for Elmore, and a nod for Gemma. He was palming the picture of Jamie, when there was a clatter behind him. 'Paolo, what are you – oh!'

'Sorry to startle you, ma'am.' Devlin was on his feet and turned in an instant towards her, smiling. 'Just asking your boy a few questions. No trouble.'

'What questions?' Her eyes, the mirror of her son's, were balanced between anger and alarm. 'I don't bring him to work before. This first time –'

'It's okay.' Devlin dammed the flow of justification with an open-handed gesture. An open hand with a twenty-dollar bill in it.

The bill disappeared. Devlin explained the photos and produced them. The maid shuffled through them, her face lighting up. 'This *Señor* and *Señora* Elmore.' She sighed as she looked at the photographs. 'Two beautiful little girls, one so dark the other so fair, like an angel. A nice family. They stay here five days.'

'Five days? Both kids? They were staying there as a family?' Bobby whistled. They were sitting in the local diner. Bobby was inhaling a burger and fries. Devlin nursed a cup of black coffee.

'According to the maid. End of September. Before they moved to the motel near the accident site, that the Sheriff checked out. She remembered them because her kid played with the two girls. Got upset when they left.'

'But that's –' Bobby shook his head, baffled. 'They must have known they were harbouring a runaway.'

'Had to,' Devlin agreed. 'Plus the timing is off.'

'Five days,' Bobby mused. 'Looks like I may have to be paying another visit to Luanne Cheska.'

Devlin nodded. 'Looks that way.' He grimaced. 'You know that bad feeling I've been getting?'

'Don't tell me.' Bobby rolled his eyes. 'It's just gotten a whole lot worse?'

Bobby stood at the entrance to the bar, letting his eyes get accustomed to the gloom. From the jukebox a country-and-western singer that he couldn't identify was wailing about her cheating man. A familiar bar-room haze, years of old smoke and stale booze, came to envelop him. He identified his quarry in the mirror over the bar. She looked up as he slid onto the stool beside her.

'Beer,' he ordered as the barman came over. 'And whatever the lady's drinking.'

'That would be club soda. Don't forget the slice of lime,' she added, as the barman looked towards her. The barman grinned, and gave her the finger. Luanne grinned, and gave it back.

She swivelled around in her seat. 'Do I know you?' She studied him. 'You were the guy that came asking questions about my daughter.' A small spasm flickered across her eyes when Bobby nodded. 'Never forget the cute ones, even when I'm drunk. I was pretty damn drunk that day, wasn't I? Go on,' she prompted, when Bobby hesitated. 'I can take it.'

'Yeah,' Bobby drawled. 'You were.'

'Eddie'd just walked out on me. That and Sally Ann.' Her hand tightened on her glass. 'I'm not drunk now. Threw away the bottle right after you left and haven't touched a drop since. Must have been your reforming influence.' She nodded thanks as the barman set a fresh drink in front of her. 'You got a name, cute guy?'

Bobby told her. She repeated it, rolling it round her mouth as Bobby studied her, with a small feeling of shock. The heavy make-up was gone. The platinum hair was fastened away from her face, spilling down her back in a long fall, and while the plain pink dress didn't exactly disguise the lush figure beneath, it didn't throw it in his face either. He felt an unexpected stirring in his belly. Without the stale paint and provocative clothes, Luanne Cheska was an attractive woman. More than attractive.

'You moved out of the trailer park.' He'd started there, before trying the bars.

'The trailer was Eddie's. Gone back to my own place, in town. Apartment the size of a dog kennel.' She sighed. 'It's clean and it's cheap. Got my job back, too. Waitress.' She indicated the dress. Looking closer, Bobby could see it was a uniform coverall. 'I can do that you know, Bobby Hoag. Clean up my act. I reckon my little girl is dead. Least I can do for her memory is get myself straightened out.' Her mouth puckered. 'A bit late, but what the hell.' She slanted him a sideways look. 'Men, they're my big problem. I'm a lousy picker, and I get restless. Sally Ann's father now, should have tried harder with him. He was one of the good guys. Not as cute as you.' She sipped her drink. 'But cute enough. He was a keeper, and I was too dumb to know it. Why am I telling you this?'

'I've got that kind of face?'

'Maybe.' She fiddled with her purse, lying on the bar. 'You got more questions, ain't you? About Sally Ann.'

Bobby took a chance. 'I know she didn't go missing when you said she did.'

'No.' Luanne's mouth turned down. 'It was before. Me and Eddie, we were, kinda out of it ... I don't rightly know when Sally Ann took off. Maybe we can piece it together.' She swivelled to look at him, full in the face. 'You're going to have to tell me why you want to know. No bullshit.'

Bobby considered, went with what his gut was telling him. *Only his gut?*

'That's cool. You want to go sit over there?' He indicated the booths, off to the side.

'Can't.' She'd drained the soda. 'Gotta go to work.' She hopped off the stool, grinning. 'You can come along with me, Bobby Hoag. Come to the diner and sit in the corner and drink coffee and eat Marylou's pecan pie. Best pecan pie in the State. I get off at ten-thirty.' She gave him a long, level stare, with a trace of the old provocation lying in the back of her eyes. 'After that you can keep me company. Keep me out of bars like this.' She put her hand on his thigh. 'Help me make it through the night, Bobby Hoag, and I'll tell you everything you want to know.'

Devlin was ploughing his way through bacon and waffles when his partner flopped into the seat opposite him. Something in Bobby's face made him bite down on the first wisecrack that entered his head. Bobby nodded at the hovering server, who filled his cup and offered the menu. 'I'll have what he's got,' Bobby ordered without looking at it.

'In your dreams, my son,' Devlin said smugly. He didn't get a rise. Bobby was staring into his coffee.

'The maid at the motel got it right. Luanne doesn't know exactly when Sally Ann disappeared, except that it wasn't when she told the cops. She says maybe two or maybe three days more, and before that the kid had been missing for long periods during the day. When she came back the last time, she took her stuff.'

'Sally Ann was already spending time with Elmore and his girlfriend, then she moved out for good.' Devlin was thinking aloud. 'Elmore played her, then reeled her in. You think they promised to take her to her grandmother?'

'It would work.'

Devlin scrubbed his hand over his face. 'Elmore was one cold-hearted son of a bitch.'

Bobby's breakfast arrived. Bobby poked at a piece of bacon. 'I had to tell her – Luanne – why we wanted to know about Sally Ann. I went with the story about Elmore taking his chance and snatching his daughter, after the wreck. Didn't tell her about all the other stuff. Told her I couldn't prove anything, but that was what we were trying to do. She ... she won't talk about it to anyone.'

Devlin hesitated, looking at Bobby's down-bent head. 'No problem.' He pulled his jacket off the back of his chair. 'I'll get the check and see you at the car in about half-an-hour.'

'Where you going?'

'Whatever gas station in town has a tow truck.'

'What exactly are we looking for?' Bobby surveyed the junkyard with disfavour. Wrecks of what had once been cars, and pieces of industrial machinery, were stacked all around. At least there was no dog.

'The car Gemma was driving.' Devlin was looking over the heaps of metal. 'According to the guy who towed it, after the wreck, this is where it ended up. We're going to find it, buy it and get it taken apart by the nearest forensics lab.'

The finding took two hours. Bobby watched as Devlin handed over a roll of notes for a rusty pile of metal.

'You think that heap is going to tell us anything, after all this time? Something that the Sheriff missed?'

'Sheriff didn't look. Didn't need to. Car was turned over by a drunk who was also high on drugs. Case opened. Case closed.'

'The car was fixed, or run off the road?'

Devlin nodded. 'You know that bad feeling? This is part of it, too.'

Chapter Twenty

It was raining in Chicago. Which was just fine, as it matched Devlin's mood. Everything had a grey edge to it these days, even when the sun shone. Especially when the sun shone.

He dumped a folder and three envelopes down on his partner's desk. Bobby grinned as he leafed through the file. Preliminary work for the O'Hara proposal. 'Looking good, man. I can hear those dollars stacking and see those sexy babes sashaying down that red carpet.'

'Don't start dusting off your tux. You're gonna be in a drain in the road, checking for deranged fans and paparazzi.'

Bobby grinned as he raised a finger, reaching for the envelopes. Devlin tapped the top one. 'Statements from Gemma Smith's doctor – don't ask – and her ex-flatmates. The girl was clean. A college friend overdosed. Died in front of her, after a party. She never took drugs, didn't even drink.'

'Always a first time.'

'Check out the rest.'

The report from the forensics lab, and the accident investigator, ran to five pages. Careful, detailed, thorough, and expensive. The pay dirt was on page three, the report on the airbags and the brakes, and page four, the scratches on the rear and side paintwork. Frowning, Bobby opened the last envelope, sliding out an e-mail that had the logo of an insurance company at the top. He read it and whistled.

'A million? What's that in dollars?' Bobby frowned, then gave up on the mental arithmetic. 'Not chump change,' he decided, stacking the envelopes. 'None of this is conclusive.'

'Separately no, but together? It doesn't have to stand up in a court of law.'

'Where the hell is this taking us?'

'An accident that was no accident. But did Jeff Elmore set it up?' *I don't have Jamie any more.* 'Or was it someone else?'

Devlin's feet slapped down on the pavement. One. After. The. Damn. Other. He heaved in air, speeding up. This time in the morning, there were plenty of other runners about. Joggers, too. Some ran in pairs, a lot had earpieces and music players. One ran with a dog with silver fur and sky-blue eyes loping at her heels. A human would need contacts to get eyes that colour. Physical activity. It was healthy, social, productive. For Devlin it was just running. He did it because he had to, because the speed and strength of the muscles in his legs might one day be what would keep him breathing.

He slogged along another road. He could be anywhere. It wasn't Japan because the faces were wrong. It wasn't Amsterdam or Venice, because there weren't any canals. It wasn't Alaska – no snow. Other than that, who knew?

How could he be home sick, when he didn't have a home? He turned right, looking for a hill to take down.

The shower was hot and wet and went on a long time. Dressing, Devlin's eyes kept returning to the chest where the envelopes he'd shown Bobby yesterday were piled. There were two new ones on the stack. Nausea growled in his belly. He and Bobby had put it together and now what was he going to do with it? Take it to her, in London? See her look at him with blank, dead eyes, because whatever he'd pieced together, it still wasn't going to give her her daughter back?

Or maybe he'd tell her how he woke at night, reaching for her, hard and aching. That if she'd let him –

With a sharp curse, he grabbed his jacket off the bed. It could wait a little longer. He still hadn't heard back from Munroe and Rossi. Opening a drawer and sweeping the envelopes into it, he headed out of the room.

The phone kept ringing. No answer. At last Devlin threw it back down on the rest. Still nothing from Munroe and Rossi, together or separately. The answer phone at their office had stopped picking up. He had to quell the prickly feeling between his shoulder blades. They were out of town, on a case, on vacation –

He dragged his attention away from the phone as Bobby ambled into the office.

'Got a suggested venue list from O'Hara. Preliminary, subject to our opinion on suitability.'

'Yeah?' Devlin held out his hand, glanced down, felt his eyes bulge. 'Community hall, art and craft centre,' he read, dangerously. 'You said O'Hara wanted to give something back to his roots, to the small towns on the West Coast. You didn't fucking think to tell me that he meant the west coast of fucking *Ireland*?'

Bobby's face was as innocent as an altar boy. 'I did mention it. I don't think you were listening.'

Normal. An ordinary day at work. Regular tasks. Routine. The familiar surroundings of the yard, the greenhouses, the up-market shed that served as an office. The twinge in her back as she leaned over the cold frames. Normal. Kaz heeled in the sweet pea seedling with brisk, firm strokes and moved on to the next. Trowel into the soil, trowel out of the soil, shake the next seedling out of its pot, untangle it from its fellows, pop it in the hole. She could do normal. The early morning sun was shining. A perfect May morning. She could hear the voice of a guide, showing a VIP party around the Chelsea Physic Garden, next door, before it opened to the public. An ordinary day. She could pretend that her uncle hadn't been murdered and that her ex-husband hadn't killed himself. She could pretend that her daughter wasn't missing, probably also dead. She could certainly pretend that she'd never met a man called Devlin, much less slept with him. She could pretend until her teeth fell out.

Letting out a deep breath, she leaned back on her heels to survey the hanging basket that she was filling. At least now there weren't any more tears. She was all cried out, for Phil, for Jeff, and for Jamie. She certainly wasn't crying for Devlin. He'd thought it was time to go, and that was fine by her. She didn't need him. Wanting wasn't the same as needing. That was what those few days had been about. Proving that she didn't have to have a commitment to have sex. Devlin had given her a gold standard for a lover, and for herself. His job was done.

'Tea?'

'Uh? Oh, thanks.' Kaz flopped back onto the path, accepting the mug, scattered with pink frogs, that her assistant Trisha was holding out to her. 'Thanks, Trish, you're a star.'

Trisha tested a convenient wheelbarrow for stability, before draping herself elegantly over it. The frogs on her mug were blue. 'How are you doing?' she asked softly.

'You know –' Kaz made a balancing gesture with her hand. 'Some days up, some days down. I've got an appointment tomorrow with an investigator who specialises in children who go missing abroad. I'm hoping he can suggest something.'

'It didn't work out then, with the American guy?'

'He was very helpful, but it wasn't a long-term thing. He had to go back to the States.' Kaz prodded an errant sweet pea into its proper place.

Trisha nodded, accepting. 'Keep hanging in there. We're all cheering for you. Oh.' Trisha looked up, pointing. 'I think you're wanted.' She giggled. 'Either that, or Tom is having a funny turn.' The site foreman was standing in the office window, making telephone gestures. 'I'll finish the baskets and put them on the van.' Trisha offered. 'Go and see what he wants.'

Kaz scrambled to her feet. Tom met her at the office door, his face creased with concern. 'It's the police on the phone. From Italy.'

Kaz stood still, her hand on the door knob. She had to do this, however hard it was. Her suitcase was packed and waiting in the hall downstairs. She'd checked everything in her handbag. Twice. Passport, currency, hastily printed flight schedule. The bag bumped gently against her side as she looked at her watch. Trisha would be here in less than twenty minutes to drive her to the airport. They'd check over the work schedule for the week on the way. *This* was all that was left to do. The Italian policeman had been very specific about what he needed. She'd switched off when he had talked of packaging and couriers. She couldn't just sit here, tamely, and *wait*.

She swung the door handle with a swift jerk, pushing the door open.

And rocked back in shock.

Jamie's room. She'd forgotten. The baby pastels and dainty patterns of memory were gone. A joyous celebration of light and colour came to meet her, as the door reverberated gently against the wall. A room befitting a young lady who was no longer a baby, but coming up to her fifth birthday. They'd chosen it together, the pale wood furniture, dark blue carpet – and the walls. Kaz took a hesitant step over the threshold. Sunlight glittered on the exotic birds and foliage Jamie had chosen over the competing charms of fairies and ponies and cartoon characters. Parrots and love-birds swooped and dived and peeped quizzically through leafy branches, heads cocked.

'Oh, baby, you never got to see it.'

A choking ball convulsed Kaz's throat. She stood for a moment, eyes closed, teeth clenched. She had to get on with it. There was no *time*.

The fat bristle hairbrush was on the dressing table. Kaz blinked, looking down at it. They'd bought a plastic travel set, a bright pink brush and comb, especially for the American trip. Jamie had been particularly pleased with it. Brush and comb were probably still in the hastily packed suitcase of her daughter's things that Suzanne had taken away and hidden, out of sight and tears, in the storeroom at the shop. Kaz snatched up this brush, hauling the plastic bag out of the pocket of her jeans and shaking it open, to drop it in. Her fingers trembled as she pushed the bundle deep into the recesses of her handbag.

She stood for a breath-shuddering moment, letting her emotions settle. The room enfolded her; safe, quiet, dust free. She'd suspected for a while that Suzanne crept in here regularly, with a duster. She'd not been able to face it. It had been finished just the day before ... the day before ...

She looked round now. It was a fresh, grown-up room, waiting for a little girl to come home. A happy surprise, to find it completed, after a holiday with her father.

Except ...

Abruptly Kaz's knees gave way. She sat down on the bed. The eyes of the birds looked knowing now, mocking. Eyes. Something else was watching her from the pillow. Someone else.

'Oh! Patchy.' Kaz scooped the skinny horse against her chest, holding him tight, feeling the familiar lumps and bumps of the long-nosed head and knobbly, floppy legs. Jamie's long-time companion and comforter.

Kaz tried to swallow and found she couldn't. Her daughter's face, solemn and resolute, swam before her eyes. A small hand, holding out the toy. 'I'm not taking Patchy to 'merica because he might get losted. He says he'll stay here, to look after you.'

'Oh, my darling.' Kaz rocked, gripping the piebald horse even tighter to her chest.

Sunshine and silence, but for the sound of her own ragged breathing. Then, from downstairs, the chime of the doorbell. With a convulsive indrawn breath, Kaz released her death grip on Patchy. The little head was tilted, looking up at her. The black-button eyes glittered.

The police wanted something that Jamie had handled. A hairbrush was a hairbrush, but Patchy had been *loved*. With a low-pitched groan, Kaz dropped the little horse into her capacious handbag, hefted it on her shoulder and headed for the door.

Trisha was standing on the step. Behind her, Suzanne was coming up the street. She waved as she crossed the road. 'I'm glad I caught you. The gate to your yard was closed, so I was going to drop these off.' She held up a file of papers. 'We need to choose ...' Her voice hitched. 'For Phil, for the memorial service.' She stopped as she took in her daughter's expression. 'Darling? What is it? What's happened?'

'The police rang, from Italy. They've found another property Jeff owned.' Kaz hesitated, looking at her mother's strained face, and knew she had to lie. 'They ... they're searching it.' She saw Trisha's eyes widen, then go blank as she understood. 'They want ...' Kaz's hand convulsed on the strap of her handbag. 'I gave them a sample, for DNA, before I left Italy.' It had been remarkably quick and simple, just a cotton bud, brushed on the inside of her mouth. And not something she'd ever imagined having to do. 'Now they want something of Jamie's, for a full match. In case they find ... any evidence. They asked me to send it, but I can't just wait here. I have to *go*.' She heard her voice rising, and clamped down on pain and panic. 'But you ... I didn't think. The arrangements for the memorial service. I should be with you.'

Suzanne shook her head emphatically. Her face was pale, but composed. 'There's no need. I can cope, darling. We know what happened to Phil, and nothing will bring him back. You *must* go. Are you off now? To the airport? I can drive you. The car's outside the yard.'

'No!' The word came out too loud. 'Trish has offered,' Kaz continued more quietly. If her mother accompanied her to the airport she couldn't be sure she'd be able to keep silent. Mercifully Suzanne had turned to Trisha, giving her a quick hug. 'Get her safely on the plane.' She turned back to Kaz. 'Go – but ring me when you land.'

It was raining in Dublin. Devlin shook water off his hair as he entered the hotel foyer. The rain clouds were following him around. Or his mood was generating them. He'd left Bobby in the dining room, eating his way through the breakfast buffet like food was going out of fashion. He'd been walking, pounding the streets. There wasn't anything better to do, until his partner was ready to go to work, checking out venues.

Bobby was standing next to the reception desk. The girl behind it had just handed him a folded paper.

'O'Hara wants to reschedule?' Devlin stared at the hotel message sheet in disbelief. 'What sort of fucking message is that?'

'It's code,' Bobby explained. 'It means O'Hara wants to reschedule.'

'Wiseass! The guy gets us here all the way across the fucking Atlantic –'

'Dev!' Bobby hustled his partner sideways, towards a corridor. It was empty. With a quick look both ways he opened the first door closest to the foyer and half-shoved Devlin, still protesting, into an empty conference room. He yanked his cell phone out of his pocket and held it out. 'Call her.'

'Call who?' Devlin ignored the phone, mooching over to the window to scowl into the rain-washed street.

'You know bloody well who.' Bobby followed him to the window, still with the phone in his hand. 'O'Hara has postponed the meeting. We have an extra day. London is what, an hour, two hours away? If you don't call her, then I will.'

'And tell her what?'

'That I may be forced to shoot you and dump the body in the nearest bog?' Bobby rolled his eyes. 'Just do it, will you?' He brandished the phone, dropping his hand when his partner didn't take it. 'Hell, Dev, we've put together all that stuff about what happened when her daughter disappeared. Don't you think she deserves to know about it?'

Devlin leaned against the wall, hands stuffed into his pockets. 'None of it will bring the kid back.'

'Does that matter?'

'Of course it matters.'

'Maybe it doesn't. Maybe she doesn't expect that from you. Maybe what matters is that you've done this for her. Think about it. Then do us both a favour and call her.' Bobby turned towards the door. 'If she doesn't hang up, then you'll know.'

'Know what?'

'That you're not fucking Superman, but the woman doesn't care.' Hand on the door, Bobby looked back. 'You have to tell her, Devlin. If she doesn't want to hear, that's a whole different story. Then I still may have to shoot you.' He made a gun with the fingers of his right hand, popped off a shot and left his friend staring at a closed door.

Devlin watched the door for a while. Nothing happened. No one came in. After a while he hitched his wallet and his cell from his pocket, extracted a business card, with fingers that shook very slightly, and began to dial.

Bobby lounged in a chair in the foyer of the hotel, long legs spread out in front of him, wary eyes on the corridor and the door to the empty conference room, wondering what sort of explosion he might have set in train. He'd backed a hunch, giving Devlin a shove in what he hoped was the right direction. *Hope* was the right word. If Devlin came out of the door looking for trouble then it was going to be touch and go on some of Bobby's favourite body parts.

The door opened. Slowly. Devlin's face looked curiously blank. *Oh shit.*

'She wasn't there.' He stood in front of Bobby's chair. 'I spoke to some guy, at her business. She's on her way to the airport. The Italian police located a vineyard that Elmore owned, away from the farmhouse. They found a grave.'

Chapter Twenty-One

'*Signora* Elmore is here. She is in the interview room downstairs.' The messenger delivered the news and shut the door behind him, leaving the occupants of the room alone, to consider the information.

The police Inspector sighed. 'She has wasted very little time in getting here. Ah, I was afraid she would do this, when I telephoned her in London. A woman, searching for her child …' He made a what-can-you-do gesture. 'I cannot say I was not warned. Our colleagues in Florence cautioned me, when they knew I would have to contact her. They anticipated this.'

'It would have been better if she had not come. You requested her to *send* the additional test material. She can achieve nothing here.'

The Inspector looked up at his junior officer, standing at the window, watching the street. He sighed again. The callousness of youth. One day he would understand.

'You have no children.'

'No.' The younger man turned from the window, frowning. 'She arrives here, unannounced, expecting information –'

'Not exactly unannounced.'

'A telephone call, from Pisa airport?' The junior officer indicated his disapproval, with an abrupt sweep of his hand. 'You will see her?'

'How can I not?' The Inspector looked down at the brief forensic report on his desk. 'But what am I to do with this? Until the … Ah!' He lifted the phone as it began to ring. The call was brief. 'The man from the forensic laboratory has arrived. Would you show him up? And then see that *Signora* Elmore has everything she needs. Tell her I will be with her soon.'

He waited, impassive, fingering the report, until his visitor was brought in and seated. He offered coffee and it was declined.

The Inspector surveyed his visitor and sighed. When had experts become so young? This one might perhaps begin shaving in a month or two. He was very nervous, fidgeting in his seat. Or was that the congenital inability to sit still that seemed to afflict the young these days? The report he'd presented had been careful and thorough, as far as it went. The Inspector felt another sigh rising, and stifled it.

'Your results.' He tapped the folder. 'I realise this is only your initial report, but it presents me with several difficulties.' He steepled his hands. 'I requested your presence, in the hope of resolving the most pressing of them. You will appreciate my dilemma. Downstairs, in another office, I have a young woman, waiting to be told if we have found the body of her daughter.'

The expert took off his glasses, polished them on the sleeve of his shirt and put them back on again. The Inspector knew a delaying tactic when he saw one. He waited for the younger man to gather his thoughts.

When he had, 'That report contains only my preliminary findings. I make that clear. The body was ... not in a good state. I would wish to do more tests before presenting you with my final statement. As you are also aware, the remains had been moved.'

'Buried at some other location, then reburied at the vineyard.' The Inspector nodded.

'Both those factors have complicated the situation. Also we cannot, at this point, determine the cause of death.' The younger man ducked his head. 'You already know that.'

The Inspector acknowledged, with a wave of his hand. 'But the findings of the DNA tests?' he persisted. 'You compared the sample from the body with that provided earlier this month, in Florence, by *Signora* Elmore?'

The young man wriggled as if the chair was uncomfortable. 'Yes, but that cannot be considered conclusive. I did not make a comparison with the father. There was a delay with the samples. I am *still* awaiting them,' he declared, aggrieved. 'But that does not matter. I will make further tests, with something from Mrs Elmore's daughter. That is the approved course. *Then* I can make a commitment.'

'But this report – ' The Inspector put his hands flat on the desk. 'The DNA matches.'

The expert sat up straight. 'I did not say that. I am not prepared to say that.'

'Then what would you be prepared to say?'

The scientist looked down at his hands, swallowed. 'There are more similarities between the DNA of *Signora* Elmore, and that of the child's body, than would be expected in two random samples.'

'There is a relationship between *Signora* Elmore and the child who was buried in the field.'

The scientist gave the Inspector a hunted look, before inclining his head. 'My findings would support that. My *preliminary* findings,' he emphasised. '*Signora* Elmore and the body share similar DNA.'

'Just as they would if they were mother and daughter,' the Inspector confirmed sadly. He stood, walking around the desk, to put his hand on the younger man's shoulder. 'Finish your tests as soon as you can, *per favore*. *Signora* Elmore will undoubtedly have brought the item you need. I will make sure it is at the desk downstairs, for you to take away with you.' He moved towards the door.

'What are you going to tell *Signora* Elmore?'

'I can only tell her what you have told me.'

'Do you have to tell her anything at all?'

The Inspector considered. 'I believe I do. She seems an intelligent woman. She will understand your position.'

'You know what she's going to think! That we have found the body of her child.'

'Of course. And I will explain that until you conduct your further tests, we cannot declare ourselves certain. But in the circumstances it is difficult to see what other conclusion can be drawn. What other possibility is there?'

Devlin leaned against the car he'd hired at the airport, watching the entrance to the police station. He'd been re-directed to the small hill town from police headquarters in Florence. An enquiry at the desk had confirmed that *Signora* Elmore had arrived. He hadn't been invited to wait.

He studied the building, inspecting the line of windows overlooking the street. Kaz was in there somewhere, learning God-knew-what about a small, abandoned grave. Devlin felt his stomach give an unaccustomed lurch. How the hell did a woman take that kind of news? Everything about Kaz Elmore turned him inside out and he was still coming back for more, but how did you ever make something like that right? All he could do was stand and wait. He'd positioned himself here, where she couldn't fail to see him when she came out. Giving her a choice. There was sweat running along his spine. If she walked straight past him –

He straightened up as a small figure appeared at the entrance to the building. God, he'd never realised how tiny she was. Fragile, delicate, but indomitable. Every muscle in his body tensed as she looked directly at him. For a second she stood, just looking. Then she crossed the road and walked straight into his arms.

Chapter Twenty-Two

He could feel her trembling, or maybe it was him?

'What ...' She coughed, tried again. 'What are you doing here?'

'I was in Dublin. I spoke to a guy in your office and got on the next plane. I guess it was the right thing?' He scanned her face. She was God-awful pale, with dark smudges under her eyes. And still beautiful. She gave a tiny nod. Something in his chest shifted.

'Can we get out of here?' She was looking at the car, then up at him. 'I'd like to ...' She stopped, swallowed. Wordlessly Devlin opened the car door, settled her in the seat, fastened the seatbelt around her, then loped around to the driver's side.

'Would you take me ... I'd like to go to the place where they found her.'

'It ...' Devlin all but gagged on the words. 'It is Jamie?'

Kaz knotted her hands in her lap. 'They can't say for certain. Not yet. They found the place just after we left, and they've done some forensic examinations ... enough to suspect ...' She stopped. 'They still have to do more tests. The Inspector was very kind. He explained it to me very carefully.' Hesitantly she repeated what the man had told her. 'I want to still have hope. I want to think that they're wrong, but how can it not be Jamie?'

It was very quiet. A pocket of land, with a few rows of vines, under a hot blue sky. Police markers still surrounded an area in one corner, where the ground had been extensively disturbed. Devlin leaned against a rock that marked the field boundary. High overhead a bird hovered, and a small lizard darted across the boulder and disappeared under it. Kaz went quietly up to the edge of the markers and stood for a long time. Then she came back to him.

'It's a good place. If she'd stayed buried here, it would have been okay.' She looked around. 'I had no idea Jeff owned this.' Her face worked. 'The farmhouse, and all this land? The police said he bought it outright.'

Devlin leaned back against the rough surface of the rock. There were a lot of things about Jeff Elmore that his ex-wife didn't suspect. Now was as good a time as any.

'Did you know that Jeff had Jamie insured?'

'What?' Kaz turned from her minute inspection of the ground, tilting her head. 'Well yes – travel insurance. I signed some papers. It was for medical expenses, lost baggage, that sort of stuff.'

'No,' Devlin corrected. 'Life insurance. Just over a year ago, Jeff insured Jamie's life – for a million.' He leaned forward, cursing, as Kaz swayed slightly. He gathered her hard against his chest. 'Sod it, I'm sorry. I shouldn't have thrown that at you, after everything else.'

'No.' She put a hand to his mouth, to cut him off, looking up intently into his eyes. 'There's more, isn't there?'

Devlin nodded. 'Me and Bobby Hoag – we've been digging. That's why I rang your office. Get in the car, and I'll tell you.'

They sat in the shade of a tree, with the doors open. There was no breeze. Foraging bees hummed. The lizard came back out, to bask on the rock.

'When I got back, I wanted ...' Devlin stopped, looking at his hands. How could he explain why he'd done what he'd done, when he didn't understand it himself? 'Bobby had already talked to a few people – the other girl's mother, her grandmother, someone from the sheriff's office, so he had a stake in it. We just carried on from there.'

139

He stared through the windscreen, reluctant to continue. He'd sat like this before, in out-of-the-way places, making reports in terse phrases, but never to a woman who had lost a child. He almost flinched as Kaz's hand found his forearm, fingers tentative against the tense muscles, prompting him to go on.

At last he turned. 'Bobby and I put this together. A lot of the stuff – I got it through contacts, people who have to stay anonymous, who'd deny flat out what they told me, or gave me, if they were asked. So – there are gaps, and not much of it can be proved. Not like a lawyer would need to prove it. It's ugly, and it may not be true.'

'But you think it is?'

'Oh, yes.'

'Then I want to hear it.'

Devlin shifted, cleared his throat. 'Okay, then. This is what we have. Jeff and his girlfriend picked up the other little girl, Sally Ann, way before the accident. She was with them and Jamie for five days at a motel. The day of the crash they moved to another place, fifty miles away. Jeff checked them in alone – two adults, one child. The Sheriff confirmed it when he investigated. It looked perfectly above board. Sally Ann had already dropped off the radar.'

'You mean ...' Kaz's voice wavered.

'Sally Ann was selected for the switch. She wasn't anything like Jamie, but that didn't matter. She was *there*. Running away from her mother. They probably promised to get her to her grandmother in Lynchburg. On the night of the accident, according to Jeff's account to the Sheriff, he and Gemma were breaking up. He was tired of her drinking and suspected she was taking drugs. Didn't want her around his daughter any more. He bought her the car, as a sweetener, and told her to go. There was a row and she took off. The Sheriff checked it out. A few people at the motel remembered a bit of banging and shouting around about the time, but no one saw anything. When Jeff found out Gemma had taken Jamie with her, as some sort of revenge, he chased after them. She'd been downing vodka and popping pills. He was frantic to catch them, but he chose the wrong direction.'

'That wasn't the version I got.' She pushed her hair away from her face. 'I didn't talk directly to the police. Thinking about it now, Jeff made sure that he kept me away from them. I wasn't a witness, so they didn't need to see me, and it never occurred to me to ask to see *them*. Jeff said he had no idea why Jamie was with Gemma in the car. That he'd left them at the motel, by the pool.' Her voice iced in horror. 'He knew all along that the girl in the car wasn't Jamie.' Her hand crawled down Devlin's arm, found his fingers and held on.

'Neither version was true. None of it was.' Devlin's voice was flat. 'Gemma Smith didn't drink and she didn't do drugs. Hated them, in fact. I don't know how she was persuaded to take the stuff. It was probably forced into her. If she'd been assaulted and terrified, she would have been desperate to get away, even though she wasn't fit to drive. She ran, and she took the other child with her. She was allowed to get away, and to take the old wreck of a car Jeff supposedly bought to sweeten her. That car ...' He stopped, shaking his head. 'It was an accident in waiting. The airbags were blown and the brakes were defective, and there's evidence it was deliberately run off the road. I don't think Jeff did go looking in the wrong direction. I remember a car passing, when I was ... when I was with Sally Ann. I'm betting that Jeff was meant to be the one who found the wreck. He must have been shitting bricks when I got there first.' Devlin gave a harsh bark of laughter, with no warmth in it. 'The whole thing was a setup, from start to finish. They picked up a suitable child, and kept her with them until they had everything in place, then they got Gemma Smith high, scared the living daylights out of her and shoved her off the road. It was a very carefully orchestrated plan. And I walked into the middle of it.'

'You said "they". Jeff ... he didn't ...' She couldn't go on.

'He didn't do it alone. He may not even have been there until it was time to find the wreck. It was a professional job. Hell, it fooled me.' He turned to look at Kaz. 'Jeff was part of it, he had to be. I guess he commissioned it.'

'For the insurance money?' Kaz frowned.

'It hangs together.'

'He got Jamie and all that money,' Kaz spoke slowly. He could hear her putting it together in her own head. 'It wasn't just that he saw an opportunity to identify the wrong girl and took it. The thing was planned – for over a year.'

Abruptly she doubled over, leaning out of the car to retch, dry heaving. Devlin dug a bottle of water from between the seats and handed it to her. When she gave it back, her eyes were dark not just with pain but with fury. 'He paid for his girlfriend and that little girl to die. No wonder he killed himself.'

'Yeah, well.' Devlin looked away. He wasn't ready to share what he felt on that, when it *was* no more than a feeling. A memory, and something cold at the back of his neck. It was impossible, yet it all fitted. And if anyone could organise that accident, and scare a women into driving to her death ...

He stared out, over the vineyard. 'You only have my take on this. This was the guy you married. Fathered your child.'

'Are you telling me I shouldn't trust you?'

'I don't know.' He swung round. 'I guess I'm checking that you do. Asking. I don't know,' he repeated. Something was catching in his chest, something important that had come out of nowhere. 'You know sod all about me, yet you believe me.'

Kaz closed her eyes, thinking back. When *had* she started to trust? Then it came. It hadn't been a matter of starting. She'd trusted him, ever since he'd sat at her feet in her own sitting room, after she'd realised he wasn't a journalist after a story. In what felt now like another life.

'If the body they found in that field is my daughter, and I don't see how it can *not* be, then that proves the key point of what you told me. My daughter didn't die in a car crash.'

'Christ.' She could see the tension in his jaw. 'I'd rather any way but that.'

'You didn't make it that way. Jeff did. And I would rather know than not.'

There was silence between them for a while. Devlin broke it. 'There were a couple of other things. After the accident, Jeff wasn't the one who took Jamie out of the country. When he left, he left alone.'

'He had professional help. You said so. I suppose if you can arrange a double murder, you can arrange for a small girl to disappear. Jeff simply handed her over to someone. A stranger.' Kaz drew in a deep breath. The silence lengthened as she stared bleakly at the dug-over area amongst the vines. After a while she roused herself. 'What do you think happened here? How did Jamie die?' she asked softly.

'It had to be an accident, or an illness.' He didn't voice what was in his mind. Had Jeff Elmore been afraid to seek medical help for his daughter, in case it gave him away? He went with the practical. 'I've been trying to get hold of Munroe and Rossi. I asked them to see what they could find out. I haven't heard from them. They've gone to ground.' Kaz turned, enquiry in her eyes. 'In our line of work, it happens.' He wasn't comfortable about it, but it could just be coincidence. He put out a hand, holding her fingers tightly. 'What do you want to do now?'

Kaz looked around, at the car where they sat, shaded

by the cypress trees, at the man, at the brilliant sunshine streaming over the peaceful vines. Was this almost her daughter's last resting place? 'Do you think we could get in the back, and you could just hold me for a while?'

Kaz stirred. It was dark. When they'd finally left the vineyard Devlin had found them a room in a small hotel close by. Her luggage was sitting in a room at the Florence hotel she'd hastily checked into, before getting a taxi to the police station in the hills outside the city. Devlin had bought her a toothbrush and other necessities, without being asked. He'd brought her a large glass of wine and coaxed her to eat more of her dinner that she'd thought she would, then left her to bathe and get herself to bed. She had been the one who persuaded him not to sleep on the sofa.

He hadn't expected to make love to her, and that touched something inside her.

She'd needed his comfort, his warmth beside her in the narrow bed.

The curtains were open. She could see the stars. She'd helped Jamie count them so often. There was nothing she could do for her daughter now. Pain curled in her chest. She reached for Devlin, nestling against him.

Eventually, she slept.

Chapter Twenty-Three

Bobby squinted at the bright pink hotel message slip. The words on it blurred at the edges and the colour stung his eyes. His head was buzzing a little. No, make that a lot.

Devlin had taken off for the airport and Italy yesterday, like there was a shark with its nose in his ass. Which was interesting in itself. Looked like his old buddy was really taking a fall for Katarina Elmore. Bobby shook his head from side to side, gingerly, pleased when the floor and ceiling stayed relatively where they were meant to be. When his brain was clearer he was going to have to think about that one. Right now it needed to focus on the words on the paper, which wasn't easy.

His mouth curved, without doing major damage. Cool! Semi-return of motor function. The full Irish breakfast he'd just consumed in the hotel restaurant was getting to work. A cigarette would top it off nicely. Pity he'd quit. Again.

It had been a good night, with the head he had on him this morning.

Alone and adrift in Dublin, what was there for a man to do but visit a pub or two, and sample the Guinness? It was what was expected of an American on the loose, after all. No one was going to say that Bobby Hoag was backward in upholding the honour of his homeland. He'd spent the day checking out potential red-carpet venues in the city, prior to meeting O'Hara, just as he and Devlin had planned. They'd be covering the west coast later, with O'Hara's people. Duty completed, he'd done the tourist thing, and sunk a few dollars into the local economy. As he recalled, more than a few, along with chatting up – he'd learned the phrase and liked it – a few, what were they called – colleens – along the way. The Irish girls were beautiful, sassy and friendly, just the way he liked them, but now he needed to concentrate. The words on the paper weren't that difficult. 'Please call Mr O'Hara. ASAP.' Followed by a number.

Bobby patted down three pockets, cursing softly, before he remembered. His cell had gone walkabout sometime last evening. Left on the bar of one of those pubs probably, after he'd programmed in the number of one of those beautiful girls. He'd retrace his steps today, but he doubted he'd get it back. Making a mental note to see about a replacement, he smiled at the girl behind the reception desk. 'Is there a phone down here I can use?'

The connection went through, smart and fast. The woman at the other end was soft-voiced and efficient.

'Thank you for calling, Mr Hoag. Mr O'Hara has asked me to make his apologies, but he's not going to be able to join you in Dublin, as planned. He's going to be tied up here in London until the end of the week. Would it be possible for you to meet him here, at his office, late this afternoon? Mr O'Hara would consider it a great favour.'

Bobby thought about it. Did he want to do a favour to an eccentric millionaire film fanatic, looking to return to his Irish roots? For three seconds Bobby wrapped his rapidly unfuzzing brain around favours, megabucks and hot babes, which left him nearly a second to wonder whether Devlin might be back in time to catch a meeting late in the day. 'What time this afternoon did Mr O'Hara have in mind?'

Chapter Twenty-Four

'At last.'

Kaz looked up from twisting her hair into a knot on the top of her head. She'd managed a few hours sleep, comforted in Devlin's arms. She could hold it together, if she didn't think too hard.

Devlin was scowling at his laptop. 'I don't fucking believe it. What is it with everybody? Munroe finally gets back – and now Bobby's dropped out of sight.' He turned the laptop so Kaz could see it. 'Munroe wants to start another fucking treasure hunt.'

'Piazzale Michelangelo.' Kaz read the e-mail. 'What's wrong with meeting him there?'

'He has an office,' Devlin grumbled. 'All this third statue from the right-hand corner crap –'

'Café.' Kaz pointed. 'He says he'll meet you at the open-air café at eleven. Maybe he has to be there for some other reason.'

'Yeah.' Devlin gave her a long, what-planet-have-you-landed-from stare. She stared back. Devlin was the first to laugh. 'Okay. Looks like that's where we're going this morning. Whatever Munroe has, it had better be good.'

'At least we'll get to look at the view.'

Devlin grimaced and flicked out his cell phone, trying Bobby's number, which went straight to voicemail. Again. He left a terse, crude message, which had Kaz raising her eyebrows. Shrugging, he grabbed her hand, hustling her towards the door. 'Breakfast. I *need* coffee and carbohydrate.'

On a hill, on the south side of the city, the church of San Miniato al Monte was airy and light, the walls glittering with mosaic. They'd made good time reaching Florence.

When Devlin suggested they look round the church, before meeting Munroe, Kaz was happy to agree. Now the sound of singing drifted across the cool space, intricate harmonies sending cat's paws shimmering down Kaz's back.

She and Devlin wandered towards the sound as it came to a triumphant, soaring close. Passers-by broke into spontaneous applause as the small choir of teenagers began collecting backpacks and jackets, heaped on the floor while they sang. Diverted, Kaz joined a group of tourists clustered around, asking questions.

'This is our fourth city in twelve days.' The girl, obviously American, was explaining. 'It's like, the trip of a lifetime. Our church put it together for us. We sing wherever we go, sort of like saying thank you.' One of the boys came up, draping an arm over the girl's shoulder. 'Europe really rocks. Everything here is like, so *old*.'

Charmed and amused, Kaz turned, to find Devlin was staring off into a corner of the church.

'What is it?' She put her hand on his arm.

'Something caught my eye. It was nothing. You ready to go and look at the view from the Piazzale?'

'Just like all the postcards.' Kaz shaded her eyes with her hands, picking out landmarks. Behind them, across the square, a long flight of steps and a winding path led down from the church they had just left. Below, on the other side of the Arno, the Duomo lay serene, embedded in the city's roofs. It shimmered in the heat, looking almost like a model of itself. The Piazzale was a plateau between, crowded with tourists. Cameras clicked and sightseers exclaimed.

Devlin stood a few paces behind Kaz. His eyes were on the Piazzale, not on the Cathedral and the maze of Florentine streets, basking in the sun. At least his own personal rain cloud had stopped following him around.

Amongst the stalls peddling cheap souvenirs there were a couple of booths with tables and chairs, selling drinks and ice cream. Before he'd figured out which might be the one, a man stepped out from behind one of the stalls. Devlin gawped at the baseball cap, the loudly patterned shirt and the low-slung camera.

Munroe?

Devlin followed the garish figure towards the dark shade beside a stall that was selling plastic replicas of Michelangelo statues and fifteen kinds of printed T-shirts.

He put a hand on Munroe's arm. And felt him shaking. In an instant every muscle tensed. His fingers jerked, moving automatically towards his shoulder, then dropped. The gun and holster hadn't been there for a while now. 'What?'

'You have to get out of here.' Munroe was leaning up, fingering the shirts, the rictus of a smile plastered over his face. Making like a tourist and covering Devlin's presence beside the stall. 'It's all gone bad. That stuff you wanted. We can't get it. You need to leave. Take the woman and go back to London.'

'What do you know?' Devlin eyes skittered around, body tense. 'Talk to me, damn it!'

'I can't say any more.' The whites of Munroe's eyes were showing. 'I'm too fucking scared. I've got to get out, Dev.' His voice hardened. Briefly Devlin saw the ghost of the old Munroe. 'I've done you a favour, coming here. Rossi has already gone and I'm following in the next few hours. This Elmore thing is a fucking mess. Stop digging.'

Munroe stepped around the back of the stall and out of sight.

Devlin stood completely still for a moment, before turning to locate Kaz, still looking at the view. He reached up quickly to thumb rapidly through the T-shirts hanging above him.

'Where did you get to?' Kaz greeted him with a smile, but Devlin could see the pain, deep in her eyes. His gut contracted. How did you ever do normal again, after you'd lost a child? He wanted to gather her up, right here, and pour everything he had into her, until he made it right. *As if.* All he could do was keep her safe.

He exhaled. 'Just looking around.' He held out the gaudy carrier bag.

'What is it?' She rifled the contents curiously, pulling out the T-shirt with the print of Michelangelo's *David* on the front, mouth curving. 'Thank you.' She tilted her head, provocative. 'Although I still think that his hands are too big – in comparison, I mean.'

'Comparisons are odious. I read that somewhere.' Devlin forced himself to relax and respond. 'I don't think Munroe is gonna show.' He scanned the crowd. 'You seen all you want here?'

'I don't know if I ever could.' She was laughing but the eyes were still dark, way too dark. Again it caught him in the gut. 'But yes, I'm done,' she agreed, with a sigh. 'You ready to leave?'

'How would you feel about another look at the church?' He kept it as casual as he could, pulling her into his side, reclaiming the bag. 'Something I want to check out.'

'Whatever you want.' She looked surprised, but not suspicious. 'You're sure we've waited long enough for Munroe?'

'Yeah. I don't expect to see anything of him now.' Devlin turned back in the direction of San Miniato, trying not to stiffen up, not to keep running his eyes around the crowd. 'Munroe wants me, he knows how to get in touch.'

The choir had been persuaded to sing again. Devlin made sure that Kaz was focused on the music, safe in the group of tourists making up the impromptu audience. He drifted up a shadowy aisle to slide into the vacant seat beside Rossi.

'Thanks for waiting.' Like Rossi, Devlin kept his eyes facing front.

'No problem.' Rossi was sitting forward, arms on his knees. 'Better you saw Munroe first. He was down in the square?'

'Mmm. He said you'd left.'

'Not yet.' Rossi continued to gaze ahead. 'I think our partnership is officially at an end. He's gone over to the dark side.'

'Is there a dark side?'

'Oh, yes.' Rossi's voice was very soft.

Devlin inhaled. 'Dark side or not, Munroe was scared.'

'With good reason.'

Devlin risked a side glance, meeting Rossi's eyes. Rossi grimaced. Devlin could see a light film of sweat on the other man's face. Automatically his shoulder muscles tensed.

Rossi twitched the bag, identical to the one containing the T-shirt that Devlin had bought in the square, from between his feet.

'Everything we found is in here. Don't open it in front of Kaz. There are pictures.' He passed over the carrier. Devlin dropped the bag with the T-shirt inside it, frowning.

'You're going to be okay?'

Rossi nodded. 'There's a job in Johannesburg. Probably take me six months. Plane leaves this afternoon.' He stood up. 'You look in there.' He indicated the bag. 'You'll piece it together. There's stuff that doesn't mean crap to me. I think it'll make sense to you.'

'It's bigger than Elmore.'

'Much bigger.'

Devlin stared across the church at a statue of the Madonna. Mother, holding her child. 'Thanks, Rossi. Looks like I shouldn't have got you into this, so I owe you. Take care.'

'You, too.' Rossi stood for a second. 'You're going to have to fix this, Dev.' The grin was crooked. 'You do, then I guess we can call it quits.' The smile faded and the eyes went bleak. 'If you don't, then none of us is safe.'

Chapter Twenty-Five

Devlin walked around from the back of the car. Kaz raised an eyebrow. 'Trunk wasn't fastened properly.' He opened the door, and dumped the carrier bag with the T-shirt on the back seat, before getting in. Kaz was fiddling with her seatbelt. 'I think I should take you home. Back to London.' He leaned an arm on the steering wheel. Kaz had stopped moving. He waited.

'Yes.' The sigh came up from somewhere very deep inside. 'There's nothing more we can do here, is there?' She turned towards him. Her lower lip was caught in her teeth. She was holding it together. The sight tore at him. And there was nothing he could do about it. Except, maybe now there was something. Depending on what he found in the bag he'd just put in the boot.

'The police in Florence wanted you to sign some papers, right?' She nodded. 'So, we go and do that now?' Another nod. Her eyes were swimming. 'You want to go back out there, to the vineyard?'

'No.' It was barely a whisper. 'She's not there any more.' He saw the shudder that ran through her, as she hauled her emotions back under control. 'Let's just go and get the formalities over.'

The alarm was loud and insistent. Kaz touched Devlin's arm. 'Is that ours?'

'Looks like it.' Devlin was striding towards the vibrating car. They'd parked as close as they could to the police station – but the only available space had been several streets away.

'Oh!' Kaz's hand went to her mouth as she saw the cubed glass from the shattered window glittering on the floor.

Devlin was shaking his head as he silenced the alarm. She walked towards him. *How much more? What next?*

He'd opened the door and was carefully pushing out the remains of the glass. She touched his arm as a man approached them. Devlin straightened up. 'Did you see what happened?'

'Not much. I heard glass breaking, and then the alarm.' The man gestured to the small sandwich kiosk at the corner of the street. 'I was cleaning up. Someone ran past, but I didn't see his face.' He raised his hands in an apologetic gesture. 'Is anything missing?'

'Just a couple of bags from the back seat – souvenirs,' Devlin confirmed, shrugging. 'Thanks.'

Kaz leaned forward to peer in. The T-shirt bag was gone and a small parcel of postcards she'd bought. She shook her head, dazed. 'Should we go back to the police station?'

Devlin was looking around, his eyes hard and sharp. She saw the shift of concentration as he came back to her. 'It wasn't anything of value. You want to spend another hour filling in forms?'

'No.' She shivered. 'Let's just go.'

Devlin leaned down on the boot to close it, eyes scouring the small shady courtyard, behind Kaz's hotel, where the car was parked. The plastic carrier was crumpled into a corner of the boot. The envelope it had contained was thrust into the front of his jacket.

He gave the broken side window of the car a long, assessing look. Thieves took their opportunities where they could. This could simply be bad luck, but he didn't like the feeling it was giving him.

He glanced up. Kaz was upstairs, washing her hair. He thought he could see a shadow as she moved around the room, but it was probably imagination. He leaned his back against the wall, conscious of the weight of the envelope against his chest. Pretty soon he was going to have to go into the hotel and find somewhere private to look at the contents, but just now –

He looked up at the window again. Kaz was up there. He didn't quite understand the curious lift in his chest as he stared at the window. Somewhere between pain and ... what? He knew pain. Mental and physical. If he could take hers into himself, spare her even a few seconds of it, he'd do it. Without hesitation. The knowledge twisted his mouth into something that wasn't a smile. *You're quite safe, buddy. No one's found a way to do that yet.*

All he could do was what he did. Keep her safe. That was his job. He didn't have a shred of doubt that what was in this fucking envelope, that was right now burning a place in his chest, was going to lift the game to a whole new level. He rubbed his hand across his mouth. Better go and find out – and pray that he had enough in him to deal with it.

He shoved away from the wall and went inside.

It was a small office. Probably belonged to the housekeeper, from the lists and rotas pinned to the wall.

Devlin wedged a chair under the door handle, testing the fit, before sitting down and taking out the envelope. He weighed it in his palms. Heavy. Rossi had done a good job. He fingered the seal, reluctant. For a second he let his hand drift over to the cell phone in his pocket, wondering if he could raise Bobby or if the guy was still AWOL. *Oh, for fuck's sake, Devlin. Let's just get this done!*

He slit the seal, letting the contents fall out onto the desk. Paperwork. Phone and credit card accounts, bank statements, even copies of property deeds. Elmore's life, in paper. Devlin scanned them, whistling softly before pushing them back into the envelope. They would take time to study.

Which left – another envelope.

The muscles of his back tensed. He ducked his head and undid the flap.

He left the photocopied report alone, fanning the photographs onto the desk in front of him.

It took a full second for his eyes to make sense of the shapes and colours. Then the bile rose in his throat, thick and acrid. He didn't need the printed dates and locations to tell him this was a crime scene.

He closed his eyes, then forced them open again. The thing in the photographs had once been a woman. A young attractive woman; Giuliana, Jeff Elmore's girlfriend. Now she was meat, barely human. The slashed and peeled flesh had him swallowing hard. And that was nothing to what had been done to the child. She would have watched her boy die, before her own long, slow agony.

Cursing in a flat monotone, Devlin crammed the pictures back into the envelope, away from sight, only to tip them out again a moment later. Rossi was right, Kaz should never see these. The police had spared her the grim details. She mustn't get them from him.

Quickly he assembled what he needed. The ashtray was on the windowsill, the matchbooks, bearing the logo of the hotel, stacked on the shelf. He tore the photographs in half, then in half again, before putting them to the flame, watching the grotesque images curl and burn.

When all that was left was a pile of soft, clean ash, he scattered it out of the open window.

He gathered up the envelopes and dragged the chair from the door, half-formed promises of revenge and atonement beating in his skull.

Jeff Elmore had been scared.

Munroe had been scared.

Now Devlin knew why.

Chapter Twenty-Six

Bobby scanned the building, frowning. He was at the right address. Just across and down a way from the multi-storey car park where he'd left the car. He'd found that easily, following the PA's instructions. Lowest floor, spaces specially reserved for O'Hara's company. That was impressive enough, but this place, where the meeting was scheduled, looked disappointingly ordinary. Not what he'd imagined for his get-together with O'Hara. A nondescript office block, in some town that he'd never heard of, on the edge of Heathrow. The man had seemed more like the hotel-in-Mayfair type. Or maybe that was just wishful thinking. *Come on, what did you expect – 5 stars, and the guy swinging in with Scarlett on one arm and Keira on the other?*

The PA had been quite clear. It was probably like a tax thing, having a place out of town. This meeting was with the money, accountants and stuff. For that you needed an office. This was business, big time.

Bobby yanked at his unaccustomed tie. He'd had to buy the damn thing and it was just about choking him. Now he remembered why he always shoved Devlin, kicking and screaming, into the meetings that needed the suited-and-booted stuff. The dude did that buttoned-down look so much better.

Most clients didn't give a shit about the Hoag laid-back style of doing business, which no way involved a suit and a tie. If they were that bothered about what the hired help looked like, they could go hire someplace else. But occasionally, with some, you did need that little bit more. He'd figured O'Hara for one of them, which was why Devlin should have been here.

For this his partner was going to pay, and pay good.

There was a brand-new cell nestling in Bobby's pocket – they called them mobiles over here – and if he'd been able to remember Devlin's frigging number, he'd have rung him, to tell him about the debt he was running up.

Bobby cursed softly. He didn't even have that satisfaction. Shit – you lost a phone and you lost, like half your frigging life – phone book, speed dial. Of course, he should have *known* Dev's number. Getting lazy. Sloppy. A wake-up call to sharpen up. In the old days he'd never have relied on a mess of plastic and micro-chips to do his thinking for him. As it was, it was going to take hours to reprogramme all that crap, not to mention the numbers of all those babes that he'd never get again. Some lowlife kid was probably going down the list right now – and he was standing on the sidewalk waffling inside his own head.

Truth was, although he'd set up the deal, just like he'd set up a hundred others, he'd kind of relied on Devlin being around to help him close it. Mr Cool, he just *looked* the business. Impressed the hell out of the suit-and-boot clients, all that silent menace stuff.

Well, tough shit. Devlin is in Italy, chasing after his woman – which in itself is a pretty weird concept – and this deal is gonna be done, and Bobby Hoag is going to do it. So get your butt in there.

Bobby straightened his shoulders and gave the tie another yank. Showtime. Pretty soon he was going to have a whole new list of babes in that brand-new phone – Hollywood babes!

Devlin was back in the courtyard. The envelope was safe in the car, buried deep in his overnight bag. His gut was settling, but he didn't want to go in just yet. He scraped one hand through his hair and then the other, making it stand on end. He had to forget what he'd seen, what he knew, before he could face Kaz. He had to get things straight in his own mind, before he could think of telling her. And if he told her, would she even want ...?

He flattened himself against the wall as a door at the back of the hotel opened and a maid emptied a bucket of water into an outside drain.

Devlin leaned into the cool stucco, concentrating on the pattern that was emerging in his mind. It seemed too incredible to believe. What he was groping towards chilled his blood, but he just couldn't see what else –

He thumped his palm against the wall. He needed to run this by someone. To find out if it still sounded just as crazy when you said it out loud. He'd got used to kicking things around with Bobby.

The thought had him reaching for his phone.

It went straight to voicemail.

Swearing under his breath, Devlin gathered his thoughts. 'I don't know where the hell you are Hoag, but it had better be a good one. Call me as soon as you can. As soon as you get this.' He hesitated. 'Rossi came through with some stuff.' He glanced round, eyes sharp. 'Looks like Luce isn't as dead as everyone thought he was. And he hasn't lost any of his skill with a knife.'

Bobby stalked into the murk of the multi-storey car park, where he'd left the car. His shoulders were hunched, his stomach seething between fury and panic. He couldn't fucking believe it! He'd come to the wrong fucking place! Cold sweat dripped down his spine. He wanted to hit something. He'd made a stupid, *stupid* mistake. Right now O'Hara was sitting waiting someplace else, ready to close the deal with Bobby Hoag ... And Bobby Hoag was stuck in some fucking parking lot, at the back end of nowhere.

He stared around, trying to locate his car. Maybe it wasn't too late to fix this. He dragged the piece of paper with the address out of his pocket. If he could just figure out …

He stared at the paper, squinting in the dimness of the parking lot. The overhead lights were out and the lowest floor, this one, seemed to have been dug into the back of a hill. He didn't remember it being this dark when he drove in. But then he'd been buoyed up and buzzing, ready to get to the meeting. He turned the paper until he could make out the words. The address wasn't wrong. He'd checked it twice, got the girl to spell it out for him. And the place existed, as he'd written down. He'd just been there. Except O'Hara could never have had an office there, because the address that he'd copied and checked was the local police station.

Fury of a different kind powered through him as realisation dawned, making him see red. He hadn't fucked up. He'd been *set* up. The whole thing was an elaborate scam. He'd fallen, like a prize asshole. Let himself be sucked right in. Hollywood megabucks and movies stars! Christ, was Devlin going to laugh, or what?

He stopped. Why would someone –

The slight sound of a footstep behind him made him turn, so the first blow missed connecting with the back of his head. Instead the padded cosh cracked down on his shoulder, breaking bone, sending him to his knees.

The second blow tumbled him into the dark.

Chapter Twenty-Seven

Her hair clean and dried, Kaz sat down on the bed, wondering where Devlin was. She shifted uneasily. Could he have taken off again? There was nothing at all of him here. The few articles scattered around the room were hers. Devlin had turned up yesterday and they'd spent the night in the place he'd found near the vineyard. He'd never even been in this room

She gathered her knees up under her chin, rocking slowly, gradually relaxing. She didn't have to worry about it. Her mouth curved slightly. She'd forced herself not to be reliant, not to expect *anything*. And then, when she needed him, there was Devlin.

He'd just been there. Waiting outside the police station, as if it was the most natural thing in the world. Even when he'd left her before, and gone back to the States, he'd been putting all that information together. About Jeff.

She shivered. She wasn't going to think about that now. Or analyse what it meant that Devlin had come for her. She would simply be grateful that he had. It didn't have to mean anything at all.

When she'd recognised him outside the Questura and realised she didn't have to go out alone to a grave site in the corner of a quiet field ...

Her lower lip quivered. She controlled it ruthlessly. She couldn't look back, and she wasn't ready to look forward. All she could do, for the present, was *be*. Minute by minute. She stared into space, watching dust motes dance in a column of sunshine, slanting in from the window.

Devlin's knock made her start. She slid off the bed and went to the door. He looked pale, eyes smoky. The line between his brows was more deeply etched. She put out her hand to draw him in. Pushing the door closed, she raised her arms to his neck, resting her head against his chest. They stood like that for a while. Then Devlin stroked his hands down her back.

'We have a couple of hours yet, before we have to get to the airport. Do you want ...' His voice faded. She could feel him holding himself together. Puzzled, she ran her hand over his chest, probing the tension of muscles held rigidly under control.

'I want whatever you want,' she said cautiously.

'Right. Good.' The way his breath exhaled made his chest rumble under her ear. She snuggled in, inhaling him, comforted, content to stay, until something happened. They could both just *be*, for a while.

Devlin dipped his head, nuzzling his face into her hair. She was warm and real and she had nothing to do with pictures of tortured flesh. He shifted to hold her more tightly. He'd been out of it too long. Once he'd been able to wade through that sort of crap without being touched. But this ...

Mothers, and children. Lost children.

He thought of his own mother, then stopped. No need to go *there*.

'What is it?' Kaz must have sensed a change in him. She tipped back her chin to look up into his face. He just shook his head, dumbly. She shifted her hands until they were splayed at his hip bones. Abruptly the tension dropped out of his shoulders. He studied her neck, and the scoop of rosy skin revealed by her slim-fitting cotton top. There was a sweet spot, just there, at the curve ... he could taste it already, on his tongue. He bent his head ...

Kaz let her head drop back, enjoying the kiss. The feel of

this man's mouth was something she was never going to tire of. He'd relaxed, muscles smoothing out under her fingers, holding her, just poised, against him. His lips whispered up over the length of her neck, to find her mouth, probing gently until her whole body was humming with it. Her whole body. Shivers. All over.

When he picked her up and deposited her on the bed it groaned and so did she. The creak, when he knelt beside her, made his eyes widen. 'Christ, is this thing going to hold?'

'I don't care.' She was laughing, pulling him closer. He could feel her smile on her mouth and it went through him like a drug. His lips moved on, her jaw, her chin, the tiny soft cleft of dimple. She wound her arms around his neck, still smiling, welcoming him into her warmth.

The bed hadn't collapsed. Miracles still happened. Kaz was lying sideways across it, Devlin sprawled half on top of her. His eyes were shut, but he was grinning. Kaz felt a proprietary glow. She'd put that grin there. With a groan he flopped onto his back, eyes still shut.

Kaz leaned over to look at him. With guilty indulgence she examined his body, drinking the perfection as well as the flaws. There were a few. Most of the skin on view was mouth-wateringly firm, smooth and slightly tanned. *Everywhere. All over. Hmm.*

There were silver, puckered lines of old scars, visible above the elbow and just under the rib cage, and another high on the thigh. Kaz winced. That had to have caused a few moments of panic. She shook her head. She wasn't going to think about how the marks came there, of the blows and the pain. Devlin was here, warm, breathing. Reality was out there, on the perimeter, stalking, but she wasn't letting it in here. She traced the curve of his hip. Warm, sexy. A man's hipbone as an erogenous zone? Who knew?

'You keep doing that and we're not going to make that plane.' His eyes were *still* shut. His voice sounded hoarse. Obediently she removed her hand. With a groan Devlin found it and moved it back again. Not quite in the same place.

What she could see of the room was spinning. And dark. In the late afternoon? It took a second to realise that her hair was all over her face. Pulling in the deepest breath, she raised herself on one elbow, scooping curls out of her eyes.

'Damn, but you're good at this!'

Devlin's eyes were closed and he was flat on his back again. He raised a hand in acknowledgement. 'Ditto, sweetheart.'

'Have you ever –' She stopped, shocked at what she had been about to say. How could her mind even go there?

'Have I ever –?' Devlin prompted. He'd found a pillow from somewhere and propped it at his back. The rest of them were on the floor.

'It's nothing.' She knew her face was flaming. 'Doesn't matter. Stupid.'

Her hand fluttered. Devlin caught it and kissed the knuckles. 'Have I ever done this as part of my job?' he supplied softly.

Kaz shook her head, appalled at the way he'd read her mind. 'I have no right to ask that sort of question. I shouldn't even have thought it.'

'Why not?'

'Because … ' She was floundering. Devlin had turned her hand to kiss the palm.

'You can ask, Kaz. I might not always tell you, but you can ask. We do this.' He glanced around the tumbled bed. 'I reckon that gives you the right to want to know things.' He hesitated. He was still holding her hand. 'Yes. I have had sex as part of the job. Not often. I wasn't pretty enough for the honey-trap stuff. Thank God.' He shrugged. 'And not recently.' His mouth quirked. 'These days any of that stuff is down to Bobby. He adores the ladies and they adore him right back, so there's no harm done.' He leaned against the headboard, exhaled. 'I can't believe that I'm sitting here, naked, talking about Bobby Hoag's sex life.'

Kaz smiled. 'You're fond of Bobby, aren't you?'

'Don't know if fond is the word.' He grimaced. 'I've got used to having the stupid asshole hanging around.'

'Will I meet him?'

'Maybe.' Devlin thought about it. 'Yeah. Why not?' He shrugged off the bed and began to gather up crumpled garments. 'You want first shower?'

'We could share.' She could see that the hopeful look in her eyes almost convinced him, before he decided that someone had to be the tough guy around here. 'Uh – not if you want to be on that plane. Go on. Shoo –' He handed her a bundle of clothes, as she scooted off the bed.

'Kaz.' She paused in the doorway to the bathroom. His eyes lingered on her silhouette, then up to her face. 'You want to know anything, you ask.'

Kaz turned on the shower and stepped under it, soaping herself absently as her mind wandered. Her body was still vibrating. She raised her arms above her head, luxuriating in the warmth of the water.

Devlin was an incredible lover. Whoever amongst his bosses had decided that sex wasn't his metier – well, it certainly wasn't a woman. Hell, the man oozed sex appeal from every pore.

She paused to let the thought develop. No one could be that stupid. Devlin hadn't been called on to play the seducer by his bosses, because he simply wasn't good at it. She knew it as clearly as if she'd been told. He wouldn't play those sort of games at someone else's bidding. She stifled a smile.

Devlin knew plenty about seduction, but for him it would be something personal and private. There was a guardedness about him. An inner core that was the real man, something she suspected that had its own morality, its own sense of decency. That core was his and his alone. Devlin didn't share it, didn't share himself. *And now he's let you reach in and touch some of that part of him, just brush your fingers over the edge. And told you that you can have more.*

She shivered and turned up the thermostat on the shower.

Devlin sat on the end of the bed, his jeans and shirt over his knees, wondering what he'd done. He'd just given Kaz something out of his past. There were maybe three, four people who might remember, who went that far back with him, but he hadn't seen any of them in years. It had only been a tiny shard he'd given her, but it was still his past. He'd offered it up, unadorned. And she'd accepted it. Strangest of all, he didn't care that he'd done it. He'd wanted to. He welcomed her curiosity. He just hadn't expected … that.

With most women, and there hadn't been that many, it was the scars. She'd seen them, too. Even with his eyes closed, the heat of her exploration had prickled his skin. It had made him feel vaguely ashamed, as if he ought to cover himself. But she hadn't asked about them, and she hadn't run.

She'd touched him. Not the scars, *him*. And she had asked, just a small question, and he had told her. And now he wanted to tell her it all. The whole sad, sorry mess that had been his life. Just pour it into her lap. He wasn't going to. But he wanted to. Looking for what? Absolution? Understanding?

A small sound from the bathroom made him turn that way. Kaz hadn't shut the door properly. He could see her, standing under the spray. Sated and satisfied to the last atom of his being, he could just watch her and enjoy the sight.

Water ran down her body as she turned and twisted. A body he'd caressed, kissed. She was lovely. Not perfect. She wasn't a girl and she'd borne a child. She was a woman. She was *the* woman. Devlin felt every muscle in his body melt into stillness

He was in love with Katarina Elmore.

Chapter Twenty-Eight

Bobby woke slowly.

Cold, darkness, pain, thirst. The last bothered him the most. He was in bad shape. The most economical of movements revealed that he was handcuffed to some sort of pipe work. His shoulder and his upper arm throbbed when he was still, screamed when he moved. Or maybe that was him. Clamping his teeth, he got himself up into a sitting position. Then he just sat like that for a long time, while the sweat cooled and the pain eased back from excruciating.

Christ, he wasn't used to this. He'd been in worse places, with worse injuries, but he was just so unprepared. He had to focus. This was a kidnap. O'Hara had been a scam. Someone had set him up. He took a second to curse himself. Babes and mega bucks. Greed and stupidity. Reeled in the suckers every time. Then he pushed all that away. Unproductive and a waste of precious energy.

He had to figure this out. He knew how. He couldn't do much with who. Unless he was meant to die here of dehydration, he'd find out soon enough. Which would probably give him why. He spared a moment for that. Forewarned was forearmed. As armed as you could be, sitting on your ass in the dark, with your legs cold and your shoulder on fire.

Anyone he and Devlin had pissed off lately? He leaned his head back, gingerly, to rest against the wall. No one. The guy from Wisconsin hadn't much liked the accidental CCTV pictures of his golf partner teaching his wife the meaning of swing, but he wasn't going to be doing this. Which meant it was something from the past. *Shit.*

Fear flickered in his body and he squelched it. He'd got out of worse than this, and Dev was still out there. Thank

Christ he was in Italy, or they'd both have been here, chained to a fucking pipe. Sooner or later Dev would come looking. *Sooner, please God.*

Bobby opened his eyes. He hadn't realised they were shut. Maybe he'd drifted a little. The only question he could do any work on was *where*. Where the hell was he? He couldn't see much, but there was light of a sort, just ahead of him. A long, narrow strip. Coming under a door. So, the escape route was that way. Hah! Behind him, and under his buttocks, the wall and floor were icy. He could feel the cold seeping into the damaged shoulder, doing it no good at all. *No point in going there.*

He explored with his good hand, stretching the fingers as far as he could. Smooth, cold and shiny – tiles. There was a familiar acrid smell, but it was faint, just teasing his nostrils. Urine. The uncomfortable fullness of his bladder told him that he hadn't wet himself, so the smell was part of the regular ambiance.

Put together with the pipes he was cuffed to, it gave him a bathroom. No – washroom, he decided. He could vaguely make out stalls beyond the door and sinks opposite. At a guess, he was tethered to the wall next to the urinals. The place was clammy but dry. No sound of any water. Disused? A washroom in the centre of a disused building? Old office block? The darkness made sense. This place would always have been lit artificially. Great. He was in an unused office block, somewhere in London. Did he know anyone who owned one, rented one? He dredged his memory, but there was nothing.

He listened, concentrating. Was there any sound that wasn't him breathing? Anything that would tell him something? There was a distant, periodic rumbling, that he could feel rather than hear, but it made no sense. Other than that, zilch.

He held his breath and shifted his position slightly, easing the cramp that was threatening his right leg. He had to keep the uninjured bits of himself in working order. When whoever it was came back, if they moved him, then he would have his chance. He needed to be ready. He sifted the evidence, looking for patterns.

Whoever had done this wasn't too worried about damage but didn't want him dead, or he'd never have made it this far. Comforting thought. He was useful alive. That was a bargaining chip. He needed all he could –

Noise. He stiffened, wincing as pain shot down his arm and across his back. Fighting nausea, he held himself still. Footsteps. Outside.

The door swung open and bounced off the wall. He couldn't make out the figure silhouetted against the light that stabbed into his eyes.

'Hello, Bobby. It is Bobby, now, isn't it? Nice to see you. After so long.' The soft drawl, with its distinctive lisp, curled into Bobby's ears. Pain and nausea flared together. With miserable desperation he fought to control the muscles of his bladder. It was a very small victory.

Was his voice going to work? He cleared his throat. 'Hello, Luce.'

Chapter Twenty-Nine

Kaz folded her sunglasses and tucked them into the pocket of her jacket. An assortment of bags was lurching unevenly around the carousel. None of them was hers. Devlin's carry-on was between his feet. His sunglasses were still in place, so she couldn't see his eyes. He'd seemed – distracted – on the plane. Withdrawn. And being here in the airport was making her itch.

She might as well ask the bloody question. 'Are you going to be disappearing any time soon?'

'Eh?' Devlin swivelled towards her. What she could see of his face had a blank why-would-I-do-that? look. Impatient, she tipped his glasses out of the way. 'Last time we did this, you walked away and never came back.'

It took her a few seconds to decode his expression. Surprise. Followed by something. Uncertainty? Devlin?

He gave her a twitch of the shoulders that wasn't quite a shrug. 'I didn't think …' She saw him swallow. 'Because of me, you'd lost Jamie all over again. I didn't think that you'd ever want to see me again. Getting the hell out seemed to be the best thing – I guess I called it wrong.'

The soft uncoiling of relief surprised her. She hadn't realised she'd been holding herself tight in anticipation. She splayed her hand on Devlin's chest. Warm, firm, strong. *And therefore dangerous. Oh, what the hell.*

'I never blamed you.'

'I guess I thought you should.' He put his hand up to cover hers. 'You were hurting. I didn't want to make that worse.' The puzzled look in his eyes almost made her smile. 'I didn't know how to help, so maybe it was easier to go,' he acknowledged softly. She could see it was a new thought.

'If you need to leave any time, you just have to tell me.'

She watched him blink. 'Okay.'

They stood for a moment. Something undecipherable hovered. Devlin's mouth moved. Was he going to –?

His eyes shifted. He pointed past her, to the rumbling carousel. 'That's your bag.'

It was almost dark. Devlin looked up at the neat, well-kept house. The window boxes had been changed. The flowers now were smaller, pink and white, just coming out. With trailing stuff. Ivy. He knew that much.

'You're not coming in.' Her voice was matter-of-fact.

'Er. No.' The pressure in his gut had started to gnaw again during the flight – for once nothing to do with the asshole who might be flying the plane. Now it was building higher. He needed to get somewhere alone and quiet, to look at the papers that Rossi had given him, that were just about setting fire to the bag at his feet. The patterns that were forming … He had to get it straight in his head, to make calls, and he couldn't, wouldn't, do that from Kaz's house. He wasn't going to bring all that into her home.

And he needed to think. About … that thing he'd just discovered. Him and … her.

'I'll get a hotel.'

There were circles under her eyes, but she was smiling. 'You trying to protect my reputation, Devlin?'

He summoned up an answering smile. 'Something like that.'

She didn't push it, just turned her cheek into his chest, head under his chin, hugging. Which made him want to stay. This woman had all the weapons, even when she didn't know she was using them. No bloody prisoners. Christ, he really had to deal with this, or the thumping of his heart was going to give him away.

She raised her head, smiled, and turned his knees to water. 'It probably won't hurt either of us to get some sleep. I do have a business to run.' Her mouth twisted. 'My team is absolutely the best, but they've had to manage without me much too often these last few weeks.' She flexed her shoulders, as if shaking off unwelcome memories.

He frowned. 'You going to call your mom, get her to come over?'

Kaz shook her head. 'I knew we'd be late. I told her I'd ring her in the morning.' She tilted her head. 'Will I see you tomorrow?'

'Yes.' He dropped his lips to her forehead, then let her go. 'You will.'

Kaz dumped her bag in the hall and wandered through the empty house, leafing through the post and checking on the health of her pot plants. Finally coming to rest in the kitchen, she brewed a mug of cherry-and-cinnamon tea and stood drinking it, eyes on the colourful drawings on the door of the fridge. Someday, soon, it would be time to take them down and store them away, but she wasn't ready to do it yet.

She turned to stare at her reflection in the glass of the window, sipping tea. Jamie was gone. For the second time. Her daughter would never run through the house laughing, chased by her grandmother in the guise of a wolf. Never kick her shoes across the room in a fit of temper. Never paint any more pictures to join the bright daubs that hung behind her.

Kaz turned, touching the paintings with her fingers. Not daubs, there was real talent there. She swallowed down the tears that threatened. There was a time, however great the pain, when somehow you had to move on. Everything she'd had with Jeff was gone, as if it had never been. Her marriage and her daughter were just memories now. No more possibilities. But she still had years of her life left to live. Years that still might have something good in them. Tonight – she was bone tired, too tired to think, but the thoughts kept coming anyway.

Was she ready to change?

She'd had the strength to let Devlin go, to do whatever it was he needed to do tonight. If he came back …

She sat down at the kitchen table. She wanted Devlin in her life. Especially in her bed. Even knowing that he'd been things, done things … things she didn't want to hear about. Or maybe she did? Was it better to know? He'd said she could ask. If she didn't ask would there be imaginings or would she be able to pretend none of it existed? What they *had* was powerful sexual attraction. Powerful sex. To hell with being a nice girl, *that* mattered.

Devlin was possibly the most complicated human being she'd ever come across – except maybe her father. *No, that's wrong. Oliver likes to think he's complex, but he's only writing his own hype and believing it.* Now where had that one come from? Kaz tilted her head. *Dangerous ground here, kiddo, thinking about your father and your lover in the same sentence.* She smiled. One thing Devlin *wasn't* was a father figure. There was so much more to him than he gave out. She sensed that he was struggling with that himself. He cared about that child – Sally Ann. And he'd kept looking for stuff about Jamie, even after he'd left. *So what was that about?*

Kaz drifted a finger down the mug. She trusted Devlin. The thought made her hesitate, but she faced up to it. She did trust him, but could she *accept* him? She'd have to take Devlin as he was, baggage and all, and accept that he would come and go in her life. That he might not always be there. *Is that what you want?*

She had to be able to trust herself, too. To take whatever Devlin was offering, and not expect anything more.

Kaz yawned. It was too late, and she was exhausted, which was probably why all this was oozing up now. She wasn't going to resolve anything, sitting here.

She crossed to the sink, rinsed her cup and left it on the draining board. At the door, with her hand on the light switch, she turned, for one last look at the pictures on the fridge. She would take them down. Soon. But now –

Heart cracking, she raised her hand to blow a kiss. 'Night-night, sweetheart.'

Devlin stared down at the bank statement. The columns of figures blurred and danced. He wasn't taking in any of it. Promises. *Shit.*

They were starting to come much too easily when he was around Kaz. To her. To himself. He stared morosely at the cheap print hung over the bed, a mess of lines and circles. They called *that* art. He blotted it out by shutting his eyes.

He shouldn't have left. Maybe she was in danger. Maybe he should go back.

He all but clambered off the bed. *Hold it! You want to go because you want to be with her, you jerk. No pressure, just like breathing.*

The room had suddenly got very hot. He yanked impatiently at his collar. That little epiphany in another hotel room, a few hours ago – *shit.*

What he was thinking had to be wrong. The smell of her, the touch of her, the feel of her – the woman was a great lay. The best. Absolutely. Why couldn't his body just leave it at that? Why did there have to be all this extra, in his head and his *heart?* He didn't know what the fuck love *was* for Christ's sake, so how could he tell if this was the real deal? How could it be ... oh Christ ... how could he be *thinking* a word like love?

It had to be just some overstretched hormone thing. Oh

yeah, hormones that made him want to rip down the moon, and every last star, and hang them around her neck. Or get some magic, voodoo or something, that would give her her kid back. *Christ, some hormones.* Oh yeah, and while they were at it maybe they'd rip his own tongue out too, before he burdened her with all this.

The woman had enough going on, without him dumping this on her. *'So, hey babe, I'm the guy with no past – I'm not offering anything – except a CV that's full of all the natural talents you could ever hope to avoid in your worst nightmares, but I'd be proud if you'd take my name – it's not mine, by the way – I stopped using my real name a long time back.'*

Name. Marriage. Fuck, fuck, fuck. He gritted his teeth. The old values that his grandmother had hammered into him really were crawling out of the woodwork now. Love, fidelity, marriage. He scrambled off the bed, as if the coverlet was on fire.

He needed alcohol.

Three of the whisky miniatures from the mini bar lay in the glass, like so much poison. He put it down after one sip. His gut was squirming and there was an evil little voice in the back of his head telling him how much he *wanted* to feel like this. That the churning, aching, unsatisfied *need*, that had nothing to do with lust, was something he *wanted* to be happening to him. Like how bloody twisted was that? Could you really *enjoy* tormenting yourself like this? Well yeah, you could. Like poking a half-healed wound, knowing it was going to hurt, but not being able to help yourself.

He looked frantically round the room. If he still had his gun, he could put it to his head and just pull the trigger and that would be that.

No.

Abruptly the freewheeling stopped. *Never that.*

Life was too damned precious, too easily thrown away. Sobered, he looked again at the whisky. He took a mouthful, then another, then set it to rest on the night stand. He would keep all this to himself. He would do for Kaz whatever needed doing, using whatever of his miserable talents that were required. God help him. To the extent of his worthless life, if it came to that.

With the precision of long practice, he took the bundle of emotions he had let ride him, rolled them up and stuffed them into the back of his brain. With ruthless control, he forced himself to look at the heap of papers dumped on the pillow. Those from the package Rossi had given him and a few of his own, new stuff that he'd shoved in the bottom of his bag when he'd left Chicago for Dublin. About half-a-century ago. He hauled in a breath. Dublin. In the morning he had to track Bobby down and fix that. Right now ...

Starting the familiar rhythm, the professional machine took over as he sorted and sifted the papers into piles across the bed.

Bank statements, phone accounts. If Elmore had come into serious money, where had it come from? Was all of it from an insurance payment? Was any of it? There were phone calls, three in particular, that caught Devlin's interest. One was to a number that Devlin recognised. One, when he checked with the service provider, was to a defunct cell phone. And then there was the last one, on the morning that Jeff had died.

Devlin looked down at the neat bundles. So many deaths. A young woman and a child on an empty road, a mother and her son in an apartment in Florence, Jeff Elmore. And Jamie Elmore? Devlin's hand hovered over the first pile of paper, one of the ones he'd added. It was mainly press cuttings. The death of Detective Inspector Philip Saint. Shot dead, in broad daylight, in a central London park. There was nothing to connect the death of Kaz's uncle to the rest – except that one phone call.

Listening to his gut, Devlin pushed that pile in with the rest. A traffic accident, an execution, a suicide, a double murder. Death on two continents, strung together by fear, and lubricated by money. Big money. If he was right, then this thing was bigger, deeper and darker than he'd ever imagined, with roots that maybe went back years. Maybe almost a lifetime.

Devlin yawned suddenly, and stretched. It was twenty-to-two. He scraped his hands over his chin, finding stubble. He could shave, shower, sleep, but the papers pulled him. There were two people lurking here, amongst the debris on the bed. Two shadows. The executive – shooter, executioner, murderer – and behind him – The reason for all this. The Paymaster.

Devlin stacked the papers. Mothers and children. But what about fathers …

He got up from the bed, picking up the phone. Only one of the calls he made woke someone.

He stared at the slim black cell, in the palm of his hand. The whole thing was coming, sickeningly, together. Did he really need to make the fourth and last call? His finger was poised over the keypad when the phone began to ring.

Chapter Thirty

Bobby's head swam. He could taste something bitter in his mouth and his face was wet. Sweat, or blood. There was a lot of blood. Too much. His clothes were gone. So was most of the skin on his thighs. He'd known that when he'd still been able to focus.

There had been a moment, when Luce came to move him from the washroom, out onto the open floor of the office. His hands had been free as Luce pulled him to his feet. He'd faked grogginess and got a punch in. Two. Felt the surge of joy when Luce's head snapped back, and he heard it crack against the tile. He'd been through the washroom door, down the short corridor and half-way across the empty space – disused office, just as he'd thought – getting away from the brightness of a string of naked electric bulbs, that Luce must have rigged, looped along the wall and across the ceiling, fast as he could. But not fast enough. On the very edge of the pool of light, with the blessed dimness beyond, the thrown knife had caught him, just beneath the knee, and brought him down. The pain had been hotter than hell, the ache in his heart, worse.

Now he couldn't feel much of anything, in amongst the rest.

He was cold. Teeth chattering. The chair under his buttocks felt like ice. His hands were fastened somewhere at the back. Didn't much matter now. Not much feeling in them. There was one thing, though. One thing he wanted to know. Been buzzing round his brain for quite a while. Might as well ask.

'Hey, Luce.' He raised his head.

The dark figure, standing to the side of him, moved into

his sightlines. The darkness was foggy but that was probably something to do with his eyelids. Lots of tiny cuts there. He'd figured out what the rumbling noise was. Trains. They were somewhere near a railroad. Hadn't been any going by for a while now, though. Just the muffled quiet of an empty building. He sat straight. He'd been about to ask something. Still had his tongue. So far.

'Luce.' Breathing hurt, but he wanted to know. Just how much of a sucker had he been? *Money and babes – what was a guy to do?*

Luce was in front of him now, fiddling with that damn bloody knife. Concentrate. Ask. 'O'Hara. None of that was for real right? You set that up?'

A low laugh. The bastard really did sound as if it was funny.

'No, Bobby. O'Hara is for real. A genuine eccentric, with money to burn. I intercepted his message rescheduling. In a few hours time – ' Luce looked at his watch. Fucking Rolex. – 'he's going to be sitting in that fancy hotel in Dublin, wondering where you are.'

'Shit.' Did he want to laugh or cry? *That close. They'd come that close to the money. And the babes.*

'You should have been more careful, Bobby. The little blonde *barista*, from the coffee shop? The one you chat with every day? You really shouldn't have boasted to her about O'Hara. Not when the lady has a younger brother who wants to play professional basketball. A badly broken leg – that can really ruin a promising career.' A low, satisfied chuckle. 'You came to Europe and straight to me. So much easier to be working on home ground. I might have left you out of this, if Devlin hadn't disappeared to Italy. But then I thought, why not? I can use this. And you were as bad as the others. You turned on me. You all turned on me.' The voice rose slightly, and was controlled. 'Collateral damage,

Bobby, you're just collateral damage. And a means to an end. A much-desired end.'

Luce was looking at him. Assessing, like looking at a piece of meat. Of course.

'Time, I think.'

Alarm stabbed through Bobby. He tried to pull himself up, get his shoulders back against the seat. One shoulder. The other was … broken.

'No sweat.' The bastard was laughing again. 'You're going to ring Devlin.'

Triumph warmed Bobby's depleted veins. 'Can't. Dunno Devlin's number.'

'I do.' Luce held up a cell phone, close enough for Bobby to see. 'He's been trying to get you, left a number of messages.'

'That's my fucking phone!'

'Picked up off the bar in Dublin, by the sexy brunette in the red dress.'

'Red dress?' Bobby tried to think. So much was a blur. 'Samantha?' He could hear the slur in the word. *Shit.*

'That's the one. Surprising what a woman will do, for a few hundred euros. I had her too, in the alley behind the bar. She wasn't expecting that.' He was fingering the knife, relaxed, close. Bobby tried testing his heels. If he could get in one good hit. He flexed the muscle in his leg, to try to get it to move.

If he could drag the chair –

No feeling in his feet.

Luce was still talking. 'She wasn't quite as good a fuck as the woman in Florence – she was willing to do *anything.*' Bobby could see Luce's eyes gleaming. Sicko. Major sicko. Always had been. Even before he was supposed to be dead. 'Stupid little whore thought I was going to let the child go.' With a brisk movement he sheathed the knife. 'Enough romantic reminiscence. Business.' He thumbed the phone.

'Devlin? Or should I say Michael? Oh, come now, you *know* who this is. You left me a message. No, let's be correct, you left a message *about* me. No, he can't come to the phone, not just this second. Yes, well like they say, these things can get exaggerated. A meeting. I have our friend here. Quite a party. I believe he can talk to you now.' Luce thrust the phone in Bobby's face.

'Stay away, Dev.' Bobby put all the energy he had into bawling the words. 'I'm gone. Get the hell away – ' The phone was pulled back.

'No. Didn't think you would. Alive, yes, but not in good shape.' Soft laughter. 'This is what I want you to do.'

Chapter Thirty-One

Devlin peered through the window of the cab. There had been rain when he set out, but it had blown over. At this time of the night/morning the A4 was quiet. Not empty, but quiet. Lorries mostly.

He felt his hands tightening on the edge of the seat and deliberately loosened them. Ice calm was the only way he was going to get through this. Forget Bobby and the way he had sounded, and that it was probably already too late. That bastard Luce knew him too well. Knew that he'd have to come, no matter what.

The turn off for Hayes was approaching fast. He hadn't been this way for years. Memory and apprehension curled in his gut, quickly stifled. He would have felt better with a weapon, but there was no point in wishing for one. He'd figure something out.

No question but he was going to take Luce down and this time he was going to see a fucking body. See Luce's blood. He might be seeing his own, too. *Bad thought.*

Regret gave him a moment's pang. If he didn't get through this, and the odds were probably not good, Kaz was going to assume he'd run out on her again. He thought about a phone call and discarded the idea. Maybe this was best anyway. What did he have to offer her –?

Christ. He pulled himself up short. Where was he heading? If he didn't make it through this, then no one was going to make sense of the paper trail that was spread out on the bed in a West End hotel. So he had to make it through. And get a name. From Luce.

He leaned forward, scouring the dim maze of suburban streets, looking for the landmarks Luce had given him.

It was a small office block, alongside the railway line. Derelict. Devlin had the cab circle around, paying off the cabbie outside the deserted station. There were steps on the opposite side of the road that led down to the street he wanted.

The narrow terraced houses opposite were quiet, curtains drawn, no signs of life. A thin ginger cat weaved around an empty milk bottle, mewling forlornly. *You and me both, buddy.*

He looked at his watch. Fifty-five minutes since the phone call. Luce would be expecting him any time soon. He didn't have long to reconnoitre.

The entrance Luce had specified was at the end of the block. There was a tarmacked yard, around the front and side of the building, set behind a brick wall. Devlin prowled the perimeter, not caring for the open front gates. No need to announce himself too soon, crossing that exposed space to the main door. There was a gap in the brick work on the side, closest to the rail line. Demolition of the wall had already started in this corner. He climbed through and approached the front of the building from the side.

The outer door was propped open, as Luce had said it would be. Devlin studied it from the shelter of a rickety metal shed. Could be booby-trapped, but he didn't think so. Too risky – too easily tripped by kids, a dosser looking for a place to sleep, even a patrolling cop, if such a thing still existed around here. Besides which, a bomb would be over too quickly to please Luce, and that was what this was about. Devlin frowned. Maybe there were sensors or motion detectors, but why, when Luce knew he was coming? Only one way to find out.

He left the cover provided by the shed, crossing to the entrance and easing into the small foyer. The stench of damp and urine came to greet him. Luce had hotwired the power somehow, so that the lift, in the corridor beyond, was working. Devlin looked at it, and at the stairs beside it.

'I don't think so.' There was something else he'd noticed, outside the building. Impossible to know how far Luce was reading him. Surprise was doubtful, so which one would Luce expect?

After a moment's consideration, Devlin ripped a panel from what was left of the reception desk. Pressing a few buttons he jammed it into the lift doors. It wouldn't last long. Already the opening and closing of the mechanism had concertinaed it to half its size, but that was not the point. Luce wouldn't know for sure. Devlin took off for the front door, and the other side of the block, as the wood splintered.

The metal escape ladder was on the next building, but Devlin had seen the narrow connecting walk between the two and the punched-out window slot beside it. Luce had invited him to the top floor. The walk-way was a floor lower than he needed to be, but if he was lucky there would be internal corner stairs and no gun waiting in the darkness.

He was.

He came out, after a scramble over an unforgiving wall, to reach the next building, a tense, muscle-wrenching climb, and a short stumble up a dark stairwell, in the corner of the top floor, well away from the main stairs and central lifts. Once he was through the sagging fire door, at the top of the stairs, he could see his battleground. The open-plan space, stretching in front of him, was mostly empty. There was enough light from the street to make out a few abandoned pieces of furniture and some battered screens, that had once divided the area into small compartments. Devlin scooted round a coil of disconnected cable.

Tiles had fallen from the suspended ceiling. He stepped on one, and it crumbled, powdery, under his foot. Gaping holes exposed metal struts and the ducts and pipes of the service void above. Air was blowing into the building, through cracked windows. It was getting light outside, the soft grey of predawn. Towards the centre of the floor, near the lifts, electric bulbs cast a harsh light.

It was the smell that warned him, bitter and metallic.

What was left of Bobby was suspended, head down, from one of the ceiling struts. Devlin didn't need to look at the slashed throat. The dark pool, spreading across the ragged carpet, was enough. *That* had once been his partner and best friend. Nausea and cold, hard fury welled behind gritted teeth. He turned sharply away from the body.

'Luce, you bastard.' The words echoed. 'You wanted me here. You got me. So come on out and let's finish this.'

The part of his brain that was still functioning the way he'd been trained was screaming at him to get down, take cover, spread-eagle, anything. If Luce's chosen ending was a bullet between the eyes, he was already a dead man. But that wasn't Luce. This was the two gunslingers, facing off at the end of the movie, the man-on-man crap that would prove, finally, who was *the* man.

'Michael.' The soft voice had Devlin letting out a pent-up breath. *In front of him, not behind him.* Luce moved slowly into view. 'Didn't fancy the elevator, or the main stair?' Luce's voice was even, conversational. 'Can't say I blame you. Nice trick with the wood in the doors. Tried and tested and simple – but still effective.'

Devlin was scanning Luce feverishly. Hands relaxed and in plain sight, no visible weapons. But when were Luce's weapons ever visible? Wrist holsters for the knives, and maybe one at the back, too. Bulkier body, new lines on the face, a slight stoop to the wide shoulders? Older, softer, flabbier, slower?

'It's been a long time.' Devlin had to clear his throat. 'You didn't have to do that –' he jerked his head backwards – 'to get my attention.'

'No.' Luce was walking forward. Devlin held his ground, wary. 'But I knew how much it would upset you. And there were scores to settle, not like those between you and me, but enough.' He shrugged. 'All done now. But I'm disappointed.' The full mouth pouted. 'You were not as surprised to hear from me as I expected. Has someone been talking?'

'Nah. I kind of deduced that you were still around. Elmore – the woman and her son in Florence. Had your stamp on them. Phillip Saint and the crash outside Atlanta? Yours, too?'

'Of course,' Luce acknowledged, hands spread, with obvious delight. 'So sharp,' he approved. 'I have to say that what was meant to be a small, private commission escalated spectacularly when you came on the scene. When I recognised you there, at the crash site. Well – be still, my beating heart.' He put his hand to his chest. *As if the bastard* had *a heart.*

'After you ran the car off the road, you waited on the ridge opposite, to watch.' *Of course.* 'In case the crash didn't do a complete job.'

Luce inclined his head. 'Observe with field glasses. Standard procedure. Too far away to be noticed, but also too far away to intervene when you appeared. You were much too fast in calling the authorities. If it hadn't been *you*, I would have been *so* annoyed.' He was smiling. 'But please, indulge my curiosity. Why did you come out of the dark for this? And why wait so long before stirring everything up? It created *so* many loose ends that had to be … attended to.'

'The crash was simply wrong time, wrong place.' Devlin felt an icy shaft shivering through his guts. All that death, down to him? *No, Luce, playing mind games.* 'When I next came to London I contacted the mother. And found out the children had been switched.'

'Ah!' Luce let out a sigh. 'The lovely Katarina and the operation of chance.' He shook his head, marvelling. 'Of all the people, in all the world –'

'Can it, Luce,' Devlin cut in, hoarser than he would have liked. 'If you've been alive all these years, why didn't you come after me before this? You could have found me, if you'd wanted, staged an accident. No one would have known.'

'But then you wouldn't have known either, Michael. That is *so* important. I've always dreamed of us having this encounter, but I'd almost given up hope. The Service protects its own, you know that. I hate to admit it, but I couldn't find you. I was – incapacitated – for quite a while after our last meeting.' The eyes flickered. 'And wishing to remain *dead* rather limits one's ability to hunt someone down. So much risk of showing one's hand and becoming the hunted. When I saw you at the crash site, I knew the gods were smiling. You were finally mine. Even then it took a while to trace you to Chicago. And of course there was the *preparation*. I have somewhere all set up. A secluded little venue, well away from prying eyes. We're going to have such good times together, Michael, before I let you go. I thought I was going to have to lure you home on some pretext, but then you came to me.'

Luce's voice changed abruptly, rasped. 'You came to *me*, Michael. Remember that. As you die.' Luce hammered the words out, taking one pace forward, then another. Devlin held on, didn't step back. Any moment now – he could see light in Luce's eyes, pupils that were usually flat sparked with venom.

'I want you to feel it, every second, just like *he* did.' The light in the eyes now was flaring, otherworldly. He might have been talking about Bobby, but Devlin knew he wasn't.

'That was a fucking stupid … *accident*. No one imagined –'

'No!' The voice shuddered. 'It was you. Just as if you'd used the hammer yourself. But now you'll *know*.'

Devlin threw himself to the side as the knife whistled through the air. He rolled and was on his feet as Luce slid the other from the sheath at his wrist. Devlin kicked the blade out of Luce's hold and moved in.

It was close, brutal and dirty. Another knife clattered away, pushed aside inches from Devlin's face. They jabbed and punched and kicked. Devlin's body was soaked in sweat. Head ringing from a sideswipe that he dodged a second too late, Devlin staggered before catching his foot behind Luce's knee and yanking hard. Luce pulled him with him as he fell, and kept pulling.

Devlin controlled panic. His assessment had been right. Luce was much slower, but he had the weight. If he got it across Devlin's body – Devlin squirmed into an ungainly move that flung him clear, splattering him on the deck, at the expense of most of the breath in his lungs. His ear was bleeding. Luce was already scrambling to his feet. Devlin was almost too winded to roll aside as Luce's boot stomped into the space where his abdomen had been, two seconds before. He rolled again, and again and then again, gaining precious space. Luce had stopped advancing, standing still to watch, his chest heaving. Devlin shuddered as the pale eyes raked his prone form, deciding where to strike first. His hand scrabbled, of its own volition, searching frantically around on the floor. Something to hit out with. Something to throw. *Any bloody thing.*

Luce was walking forward. Devlin nearly sobbed in relief as his fingers connected with a thick cable, snaking across the floor. Desperation powered his arm as Luce set his foot on the loose end. He jerked the cable, hard. Luce went down with a thud that rocked the floor.

Devlin was on his knees and then his feet, circling. Luce

wasn't moving. There was a portion of a broken desk under his head. Had he –

With a roar, Luce came up off the carpet and straight at him. Devlin jumped back, catching his foot and falling, arms flailing. He hit the ground again as Luce advanced, a piece of the desk held out like a spear. Devlin grabbed it, feeling splinters bite into his palm, and ripped it away. But Luce was too close to avoid. He grabbed, lifting Devlin bodily, to slam him down.

Kicking out at Luce's groin, and turning in the air, Devlin miraculously got his feet under him, only to stagger as he landed. He sprawled, all his weight on his left wrist, and felt the ominous crack as the bone impacted against the floor. Pain shot up his arm. On his knees as Luce loomed over him, he grasped his useless left hand in his right and powered both up into Luce's face, clamping his teeth down over the hot needles stabbing his forearm.

He was upright and backing off, panting, as Luce swayed, blood dripping over his mouth from a smashed nose. Devlin heard something between a groan and a whimper. He wasn't sure who it was coming from. He was flagging, his left hand hanging powerless.

They'd edged, slowly, towards the windows. Behind the mangled glass the sun was rising. Bobby's body swung eerily in the breeze from a partially shattered pane. Devlin feinted to one side, just missing the slick pool of blood that would have taken his foot from under him.

He had to end this. His strength was failing and his hand was useless. Which left low, animal cunning.

He backed away, nursing his arm. Luce's head was up again, his gaze hard and focused. Devlin powered in, fingers of his right hand stiff, going for the eyes, only to be flung back. He let himself relax, collapsing slowly against the bank of windows. Cracked glass juddered. His head flopped to one side. Luce was coming for him, hands outstretched, horrible triumph on the ravaged face.

At the very last second, just as Luce reached him, Devlin bent his knees up to his chest and pitched himself sideways, with all the strength of his screaming calf muscles. Luce hit the damaged window, headfirst.

For a silent second it seemed as if nothing had happened. Then the glass shattered into fragments and Luce hurtled through it, screaming.

Devlin flopped over onto his hip to watch, stomach like ice. Luce's body rocketed forward, in a hail of splintered glass, then described a wide, lazy arc, out over the rail line and right into the path of the approaching goods engine.

The sound of protesting metal and screaming brakes drifted skywards, curiously divorced from the scene playing out below, as the train ground ponderously to a halt.

Devlin sat up slowly. His whole body was shaking. It took three attempts, with unsteady fingers, to get the phone out of his pocket, two to tap out the number he'd never expected to use again. He hadn't forgotten it. And it hadn't been changed.

The call was answered on the second ring. Devlin spoke the required words. There was a pause, and another voice came on the line, controlled and unruffled, the questions brief and incisive. Devlin breathed deep, riding on that clarity and letting it focus him, stirring responses that he hadn't called on in years.

Eyes averted from Bobby's body, he made his report in terse sentences. Heard the almost imperceptible silence at the other end, when he came to the part about the train. There was another pause, a couple of clicks, and a new voice.

'If there's chaos and mayhem at this time of the morning I might have known it would be you, Michael.'

'Sorry.' He rubbed his ear. His hand came away with blood on it.

'Damage?'

He flexed his hand, wincing. 'Some.'

'You can still move?'

'Oh, yeah.'

'Then, as our American friends would say, haul your butt out of the building and into the street. Move away. Then wait. We'll be along.'

The line went dead.

Devlin folded the phone and stuck it back into his pocket. Painfully he pulled himself to his feet, took a step towards Bobby, then shrugging, changed his mind.

He turned and walked slowly back to the stairs.

Following orders.

Chapter Thirty-Two

There was a small group of onlookers, hovering beside the outer barrier. Early morning passers-by, a couple of joggers. The police had been briefed to expect her. The metal barrier was moved aside. Kaz drove in, as she'd been told, and stopped the car. A police vehicle was parked crosswise, ahead of her, blocking most of the road. She could see another, in an identical position, further along the street. Car-top lights winked and there was an occasional garbled burst of chatter from a radio, but otherwise the scene had a strange, hushed quality about it. A uniformed officer standing beyond the stationary car beckoned her forward. She edged gingerly past its bonnet, two wheels on the pavement, a blank brick wall too close for comfort on her other side.

She stopped again, then nosed the car into a space, opposite a set of gates, as directed by the policeman. There were other vehicles within the barrier, and a few more scattered in an empty parking area, behind a wall. Through the sagging gates she could see a couple of cars and two large vans, one black, one blue. The centre of attention seemed to be a derelict building. As she watched, a group of men emerged, pushing a black-wrapped bundle on a trolley. Kaz was dimly aware of some sort of muffled mechanical noise coming intermittently from the direction of the railway line. She couldn't hear any trains.

She got out of the car, hunching her shoulders at the early morning chill. The policeman guarding the gate stepped forward, but before he could intercept her another man had slipped past him and was walking towards her. Something in his build, and the way he moved, reminded her of Devlin.

'Mrs Elmore?' He stopped about a foot away from her.

Kaz registered a round, unremarkable face, with ice-shard eyes. This time the shudder had nothing to do with the cold.

'I had a phone call.' She winced over the recollection. Phone jolting her out of sleep. Handset, clock, fumbling. Scooping her hair from off her face. Hands trembling. *Nothing good at 5:57 a.m.*

It was a stranger, clipped, precise, who knew her name. Then *his* voice, husky strained, subdued.

'I'm here to collect Mr Devlin,' she said carefully.

'Mr ... Devlin. Ah ... yes.' He looked as if he hadn't heard the name before. 'If you'd like to follow me.' There was some nudging and pushing going on amongst the gawpers around the barrier. A couple of mobile phones were raised, to take pictures, before a burly policeman stepped in to block the view.

'Thank you for coming, Mrs Elmore.' Her escort spoke over his shoulder. 'As I believe he explained, Mr ... Devlin has been slightly hurt. In the circumstances it was felt advisable to contact you to pick him up.'

Kaz chewed down the questions that were seething under her tongue. The guarded way Devlin had spoken, when they'd handed him the phone, had alerted her. She'd wondered, for a giddy second, if she was being invited to *bail* him out. But he had just asked her to come for him. No explanations, and she'd known not to ask. The first voice had told her where, and how to get there.

Whoever this guy ahead was, and he had high-end spook written all over him, he certainly wouldn't be bothering to answer questions. It was fine to turn her out of bed, when it was barely morning, and expect her to drive immediately to an unfamiliar part of London, but God help anyone who told her why.

At least she knew Devlin was alive. The body bag hadn't been him. They weren't handing her a corpse to dispose of. She stepped cautiously through the broken gates. Something nasty had happened in this derelict office block, and Devlin had somehow got right in the middle of it. Which meant *she* was right in the middle of it. She put her hand to her temple, massaging it. Devlin had left her last night – about ten hours ago – to get a hotel room. Now he was here, on the outskirts of London, after some sort of *incident*. It was her job to get him out. Then she could kill him.

Her escort took her to the blue van parked inside the perimeter wall and produced a pile of forms from somewhere. Incredulous and impatient Kaz signed where he indicated, shoving the copy he offered her into her bag. He frowned, started to say something, then closed his mouth abruptly when a woman glided out from behind the van. She was short, even dumpy, with a long thin face and curly grey hair. Eyes like razors. The effect on Kaz's escort was electric. She watched, fascinated, as his whole languid body tightened and straightened. It was a salute, in all but the hand gesture. This, then, was the boss. She was smiling. Nice teeth. All the better to eat you with? The smile, surprisingly, reached her eyes. Kaz wasn't reassured.

'Mrs Elmore?' The woman put her hand briefly on Kaz's elbow to urge her forward. All these people had her name. None of them had offered her theirs.

Devlin was slumped, half in, half out, of the back seat of a dark grey car, parked out of view at the side of the building. Kaz's heart spiked. He was pale, there was a smear of blood on his face and more on the front of his shirt. He was nursing one arm in the crook of the other.

Kaz took a very deep breath. She felt it all the way down to the scruffy trainers she'd stuffed her feet into, in the daze of early morning. If she'd known that she was going to meet a woman dressed in an Armani jacket, that looked as if she only wore it to walk her dog, she'd have taken more care in her choices. *But then again, perhaps not.*

Devlin was squinting up at her. Possibly he looked a little apprehensive. *Good.* The woman had melted away again.

'Is much of that blood yours?' she asked, after a while.

'Not much.' He shifted and grimaced. 'At least I don't think that it is.'

Kaz nodded. 'Is this the point where I ask what the other guy looks like?'

Devlin swallowed. 'The other guy's over there.' He jerked his head towards the railway line. 'Under a train.'

'Ah.' Now it was beginning to come together. 'And you –?'

'Put him there? Yeah.' He was studying his hands. 'We fought. If I ... it could have been me.'

Kaz felt dizzy. She and Devlin, here in the early morning, discussing violent death. As if it were a stock order from the nursery.

Devlin was staring at the side of the building. 'There's a lot of stuff I need to tell you, Kaz, explain.'

'Like your whole life, maybe?'

He chewed his lip. 'Something like that, but not here.'

She nodded again. Scratched her nose. 'When you said last night that you'd see me today, I didn't expect it to be this early.'

'Uh, neither did I.'

'Yes. Well.' She moved her weight from one foot to the other. Looked at the trainers. Wondered whether Armani woman was watching, from somewhere behind them. *Probably.* 'I think I'm supposed to take you home now.'

'A&E, first. This –' he indicated his left wrist – 'is broken.'

'Oh.' She rocked back a little on her heels. 'Did you know, last night, when you left? That this was going to happen?'

'No. He called me. He had Bobby.' Devlin shuddered, looking away again. 'Bobby is dead, too.'

Kaz thought about the black bag on the trolley. Her fingers twisted. She wanted to touch Devlin. And then again, not. 'Shall we go now?'

There was unmistakable relief in Devlin's eyes as he shrugged himself carefully out of the car and on to his feet. There was other damage, besides the wrist. She could see that. And more. Mental, not physical. But now wasn't the time. *Will it ever be?*

Ignoring the tell-tale flutter her stomach gave, she led the way to the car.

She had to help him with the seatbelt. With elaborate concentration she turned the car. The on-lookers had drifted away, or been dispersed. The last thing she saw, in the rear-view mirror, was the woman and the man, standing together in the shadow of the wall, watching them leave. A car, large but discreet, pulled up beside them, doors opening.

Chapter Thirty-Three

It was full daylight, and the traffic was thicker than when she'd driven down, heart in her mouth.

'The nearest hospital is Hillingdon.' Devlin roused himself as they approached a junction.

'Fine.' She glanced up at the road sign. 'If that's what you want.'

'It will do.'

Kaz changed gear and got in lane. Devlin had gone back to his intense contemplation of whatever he could see out of the side window. A quick glance showed her an averted profile. Even then, she could see the mouth was pinched.

'How are you going to explain it? When we get to the hospital?' she asked abruptly. She wanted to hear this.

'What? Oh, whatever.' He gestured with the good hand. 'Something. Maybe I fell over the cat.'

'Mmm.' She pretended to consider. There was a white van behind her, too close, and another in front. She was a white-van sandwich. She could feel the dangerous edge of hysteria. 'That doesn't really account for all the blood on your shirt,' she suggested.

'Nosebleed.' He was still looking out of the window. 'It was. Just wasn't my nose.'

She digested this. 'You think the doctor is going to buy that?' His face was bruised, but only along the jaw and cheekbone.

'Some knackered kid, in their dad's white coat, at the end of a long night shift? You think he, or she, will care?'

'Well – your experience of this kind of thing is greater than mine.' She assumed he nodded. Her eyes were on the rear-view mirror. He'd turned towards her now. She felt him shift.

'Afraid they'll think you belted me?'

'Don't tempt me!' Without warning, fright and relief segued effortlessly into fury. Now she'd started, she had a list. 'Just who the hell *are* you, Devlin?' She seared a glance across at him, saw the shock in his eyes. *Goodie, goodie.*

'I'm hauled out of bed in the middle of the night ...' She gestured away his protest that it had been early morning. Wisely he shut his mouth. 'Someone I've never spoken to before *insists* that I have to come all the way *out here* to collect you. When I get here there are *police*. And a scary man and a *really* scary woman, even scarier than you. And I have to *sign* for you, like a bloody parcel!'

'Um.' She could almost hear him thinking about which bit to go for first. 'I don't think what you signed was a delivery note, Kaz.'

They had reached a set of traffic lights. On red. Kaz delved one-handed into her bag. A glance at the heading on the sheet of paper was enough.

'*I just bloody well signed the Official Secrets Act!*'

'Er, yeah.'

'Is that all you've got to say?' Her voice was shaking. Luckily her hands weren't. How the hell had she missed *that* the first time around? *Because you were crazy to get to Devlin, terrified of what you would find – and determined that no one else was going to know it.*

Devlin was still keeping quiet. 'Hah! You think I don't know,' she accused. 'You're hoping I'll yell myself to a standstill, aren't you?' She let in the clutch with a jerk as the lights changed, splaying her fingers on the steering wheel in a repudiating gesture. 'Okay. I'm done.'

They drove on, without speaking. Kaz turned on the radio and pretended to listen to it. An ambulance skated past them. They were nearing the hospital.

'I'm scary, huh?' Devlin asked conversationally. 'Even when you've got me naked?'

Kaz clenched her teeth. She was *not* going to give in to the sudden burst of laughter that was forcing its way up her throat. Oh hell, yes she was.

'Maybe not so scary naked.' *And maybe I'm a liar. It's just a different kind of scary.*

She swung into the hospital's car park and stopped, slewed across two spaces. 'Why the hell am I laughing?'

It was coming up now in waves, making her body judder. Laughter that wasn't laughter, but half-way to tears.

Devlin snapped his seatbelt off, and hers. Wincing, teeth gritted, he gathered her clumsily into his good arm. He couldn't tell whether the shaking was tears or mirth. Or maybe it was coming from him? 'I'm sorry, sweetheart.'

He brushed back her hair, stroked it, soothed and took his own comfort. Christ, he *was* shaking. He was getting way too old for this aftermath shit. That's why he was supposed to be retired. *Pity no one told the bad guy.*

Right now he had a woman half-way between sobbing and hiccups in his arms. A woman, God help him, who mattered. He ignored the ice in his gut, concentrated on the warmth in his arms. So sweet, the fit. And he had to make this good.

He shifted her upright, looking into her tearstained face. She was snuffling, but the tears had stopped. 'All that stuff was supposed to be behind me, Kaz, I swear. I ... I have a new life, new name, everything.' He looked up, over her shoulder. Some things were better without eye contact. 'I've done a lot of bad things. They were meant to be for good reasons, but hell ... I don't know. That's why I stopped. But things sometimes come crawling back out of the past. Luce was one of them.'

She sat up, rubbing her nose with the back of her hand. He'd have offered her the sleeve of his shirt, except that it was kind of messy.

'But you didn't know – that this might happen?'

He remembered in time not to shrug – too many bruises. 'Luce was supposed to be dead.'

'Oh … And now he is.'

'Oh, yes.'

She rocked a little against his arm. 'How?'

'It was a fair fight, as far as these things go. I don't know if that matters.' Yes it did. He could see it in her eyes and feel it in his gut. 'I was down, the wrist was already gone. He ran at me and went through the window. I set it up that way. He'd already killed Bobby.'

'And he would have killed you.'

'Yeah.'

'Then that doesn't make it right, but it does make it … something. I don't know.' She shoved a weary hand through her hair. 'Come on, I think we'd better get that wrist seen to.'

Kaz straightened the car and stuck the payment ticket on the windscreen, then they headed for the entrance to A&E. Thankfully the place wasn't crowded. Devlin handed the receptionist a chit of paper. Her eyes widened and she made a call. After that the formalities were whistled though, without question, in record time.

Kaz raised an eyebrow as they took their seats in the waiting area.

'Sometimes it pays to know someone.'

'Obviously.'

The triage nurse gave the bloodstained shirt a narrow look, but didn't ask questions. Kaz wasn't sure the doctor even noticed. The nurse in the plaster room was sharper, but accepted the story of a fall.

The car park was full when they came out. Kaz led the way to her vehicle and they got in. Devlin's face looked grey. There was stubble on his chin and white lines beside his mouth. They'd given him painkillers, but Kaz knew they weren't enough. He needed to rest. But first. 'Look. If you need – ' She held out her arms.

'Yeah, well.' He hesitated, then leaned over, and into her shoulder. She settled her chin on the top of his head and just held on. Despite everything, he felt strong and solid and so right in her arms. *Oh hell.*

After a while, Devlin sat up. Kaz started the car and the radio spluttered to life.

'– at the junction with the M25. And on public transport, there are currently no trains running in or out of Paddington station, following an earlier incident in the Hayes area. Passengers are advised –' Devlin punched the channel changer. Rachmaninov floated into the car.

Kaz knew her eyes had saucered. 'That was you.'

'I guess.' Devlin shut his eyes. 'First time I've ever brought part of London to a halt. I think.'

'My place, or your hotel?' They were about to come off the A4.

'Hotel.' He needed to get out of these stinking clothes – and preferably burn them – and into a shower.

'Oh, bugger' he groaned, lifting the cast. 'How the hell am I going to shower and keep this dry?'

Kaz grinned. 'You come to my place. I have everything you need.'

'Cling film?' Devlin narrowed his eyes as Kaz herded him into the bathroom.

'You wrap the cast, and put it into a plastic bag. You still need to take care, to keep it out of the water, but it helps.'

'And you know this how?'

'Mum fell in the snow last winter and broke her arm,' Kaz explained. She was already working on the buttons of Devlin's shirt. He twitched away from her, fumbling, one-handed. 'Devlin, you're practically out on your feet. Let me help.' She fixed him with a killer stare. 'I have *seen* you naked.'

She watched reluctance struggle with exhaustion and pain on his face, before he dropped his hand and let her get on with peeling off the shirt and jeans. She drew in her breath sharply as she saw the bruises blooming on his lower back and thighs. There was blood matted in his hair, behind his ear, and the palm of his right hand was grazed and swollen, when she turned it over.

'Wood splinters,' he explained, when she held his hand up. He leaned against the wall.

'They would have dealt with this in A&E.' She inspected the swelling, frowning.

Devlin shook his head. 'Didn't want to hang around. Don't like hospitals.' He squinted at his hand. 'Antiseptic should do it.'

Kaz treated him to a sceptical look, but his eyes were on the jeans he'd just kicked off.

'Do me a favour? Do you have a bonfire, garden incinerator or something?'

'Yes?' She was rolling up the stained clothing.

'Burn those in it.'

Kaz looked down and registered the state of the bundle, shuddering slightly.

'Yeah.' Devlin eased himself off the wall. 'You gonna wash me, too?'

'Don't push your luck – go on.' She tapped his back, feeling the tingle of awareness, touching his skin. *Come on, the man's bloody and exhausted. Let him alone.*

She looked up and found him grinning lopsidedly. 'What if I drop the soap?'

'If you do, you pick it up yourself.' She grabbed the clothes and turned away, as Devlin stepped into the shower stall.

She left the door to the bathroom open though, just in case.

She got him dry – he jibbed at having his hair blow-dried, until she pointed out the disadvantages of a wet pillow – and into her bed. Whatever the hospital had given him was making him drowsy. He docilely gave up his good hand for her to tease the splinters out of the palm, and was asleep before she'd finished. Kaz straightened the covers and brushed his hair off his face.

He was naked under her duvet, which might raise some interesting possibilities for later. Keeping him nude in her bed for a while, now there was a thought.

She had the name of his hotel, and the key card for his room, retrieved from the pocket of his jeans, so she could go and check him out and get his stuff. She didn't have to tell him about it, though.

The key card slid smoothly into the slot. Devlin had put out the *Do Not Disturb* sign before leaving. Kaz left it there. The curtains were closed and the room was gloomy. She pulled them back and went straight to the wardrobe, dragging out Devlin's half-full case and scooping up the jackets and shirts which were all he'd hung up. She carried them over to the bed, to fold them. And realised the geometric shapes covering it weren't part of the duvet design but piles of papers neatly spread out all over it.

She dumped the clothes in a chair and stood uncertainly for a moment. Did she want to look at this? Should she? Was this why Devlin had left last night? Something he didn't want her to see?

She stepped forward, shifting the piles gingerly, with one finger. Most of them she didn't understand. Copies of bills and lists of figures. Except the cuttings. She slid them apart, heart beating a little faster. They were all about Philip's death. Headlines screamed. *Daylight Cop Killer, Death in the Park*. And the bold, single-word slash *Assassination*.

Something cold clawed at her chest. What had Phil's death to do with Devlin? Was this stuff – oh, God – was she looking at *trophies*?

She sat down heavily on the bed. Devlin was a self-confessed killer. What did she really know about him? Sex. They had sex. Brilliant sex. Even this morning, after everything and the state they were both in, she'd wanted his body. But she still didn't *know* him.

'Oh, don't be such a bloody fool. He was with you when Phil was killed.' *But today another man died*. 'He's never lied to you about what he is.'

He'd called her this morning. When he'd needed help he'd called *her*. And she'd been scared. Scared that something really bad had happened to him.

Because if it had …

She smoothed out the topmost cutting. Phil stared up at her. It was an official photograph. He'd been collecting an award for gallantry. Tears welled.

She looked around the room, focusing on a truly awful abstract painting that hung over the bed, to hold down a wave of grief. After a while the blobs and squiggles worked. She sniffed and stood up

Devlin would explain it all to her. She had complete confidence of that. Complete confidence in *him*.

She collected the papers carefully and put them into an envelope that was lying beside them on the pillow. It only took a moment to repack his clothes and fasten his laptop to the carrier on the case. When she left, she tossed the *Do Not Disturb* sign into the room behind her. In the foyer she dropped the key card into the box marked express checkout. The hotel would take the credit card charge automatically.

Now Devlin had nowhere to run. She had a hostage. She'd make him talk.

After she fed him breakfast.

Chapter Thirty-Four

Devlin fell out of the nightmare into blind panic. His body was slick with sweat. Naked body. *Jesus.* Where the fuck was he? Who the fuck had him? Why the fuck couldn't he lift his left arm?

It took ten seconds before he remembered.

He lay on his back, waiting for his heart to slow down. He was in Kaz's bed. Her scent was on the sheets. He inhaled gratefully. The weight on his wrist was a couple of pounds of plaster and bandage. Courtesy of Luce. He winced. In his dream Luce hadn't gone through the window alone. At the last minute he'd hauled on Devlin's leg and then they'd both been falling. And Bobby. He'd been there, too. Flayed, bloody flesh, shredding and splattering blood, as he fell through the air.

Devlin put his hand over his eyes. He needed coffee. He needed to pee.

He swung his legs over the side of the bed, reaching for his trousers, and stopped. No trousers. If Kaz had done as he asked, his clothes were probably at the bottom of the garden right now, smouldering.

He padded, stark naked, to the top of the stairs. The house was very quiet, like Kaz had gone out somewhere. He called her name. No answer. There was probably a note somewhere downstairs. He thought about going down. Nah! He still needed to pee.

The reflection in the bathroom mirror wasn't encouraging. Basically, he looked like shit. The bruises down the side of his face weren't too bad, but the rest of him more than made up for it. There was a tender spot behind his ear. When he investigated, he found a swelling the size of an egg.

He craned over his shoulder to see the bruises on his back. He guessed, from the stiffness, that his butt wasn't in much better condition. In the absence of coffee he skimmed his teeth with Kaz's brush and took a glass of water back to bed. He drank it and lay down again, to stare at the ceiling and contemplate being totally and utterly at the mercy of Katarina Elmore.

Kaz looked down at Devlin, stretched out in her bed. The arm with the cast was splayed awkwardly beside him. A wicked smile twisted at the corner of her mouth. All the stuff for breakfast was laid out on the counter down in the kitchen, but first ...

The second time Devlin woke, something was tickling his face. He brushed Kaz's hair out of his mouth, without opening his eyes. She was laughing, close to his ear. The familiar Kaz scent of green fields and vanilla swirled in his head. He could feel her warmth.

He did a mental status check. The broken wrist was supported on a pillow and there was another propped under his back, easing the pressure on the bruises.

'I know you're in there, Devlin,' she purred in his ear. 'Your breathing changes when you're awake. You've been awake now for a minute-and-a-half.'

Cautiously he opened his eyes. She was leaning over him, smiling.

His heart jolted hard against his ribs. He stretched his good hand to the back of her neck, pulling her gently towards him. The soft, lingering kiss was as necessary as oxygen.

Making love while in a plaster cast was awkward, but nothing was impossible if you took it slowly. Long, slow and languorous, and infinitely sweet. With laughter, and passion and a deep, poignant, unspoken undertow of regret and relief. The joy of being alive, spiked with the deep-dredged pulse of sorrow.

In the aftermath she lay with her head on his chest. He stroked her hair away from her face.

He'd almost said it, at the end, when she came apart in his arms. *I love you.*

The words still whispered in his head. He couldn't, shouldn't say them. But there was something else he could give her. Something just as dangerous, in a different way.

'Stuart Adams.'

'What?' She raised her head sleepily. He waited a beat. Her eyes widened, blank for a second, then she understood. 'Your name.'

'The one I grew up with. The real man.'

She was shaking her head, half-propped on her elbow to look down into his eyes. Hers were so clear and so dark. Transparent, pure, untouched. And what was he? What did he have to offer that wasn't stained with blood? The ache in his chest was threatening to choke him.

'*This* is the real man.' She spread her fingers against his chest. 'It doesn't matter what name you go by. It's *you*, Devlin. Body and soul.'

He pulled her down then, fiercely, to lie against his heart, because he needed so badly to hold her, and so that she wouldn't see the sheen of tears in his eyes.

The afternoon sun filtered softly into the room as they both slept.

'Food.' Kaz kissed Devlin's nose and wriggled away from him, to sit on the edge of the bed. 'Breakfast?' She patted his good arm.

'Breakfast in the nude.' He opened one eye. 'At 4:30 p.m.'

'You can eat it how you like, but you do have clothes.'

She rose and grabbed her dressing gown from the hook on the back of the door, and slithered into it. 'I collected your stuff. Your bag is on the landing.'

Devlin sat up, carefully, frowning. 'You went to the hotel?'

'I've seen the paperwork. That's in the bag, too.' She sat down again, on the edge of the bed, to be level with his face. The blue of his eyes was chilled with pain. 'I'm hoping you will explain it to me,' she said softly. She heard his breath hiss out, in relief.

'I wasn't keeping it from you. I just needed to sort it out in my own mind first.' He still looked troubled. She bent and kissed him, quick and hard. 'Eat first. Then we'll talk.'

Chapter Thirty-Five

Devlin grimaced then grinned, as Kaz put his plate in front of him, with the bacon and sausage neatly cut into small pieces. Having only one hand didn't hamper him in putting away the food in record time. Kaz re-filled his mug of coffee and pushed it towards him.

'Before we get to that –' she jerked her head towards the envelope sitting on the counter – 'I'd like to know what happened last night. And why.' She touched the handle of her own mug, decided against picking it up. 'All those security types. You're still one of them?'

'Hell, no!' The speed and the shock of Devlin's response unclenched a small part of the tension that had racked up at the back of her neck. 'At least –' Her chin came up as Devlin hesitated. 'Officially I retired three years ago. They set me up with a new life, and a new identity. A fresh start, but I guess you really never leave. I was in a hole and I called them. They came.' He reached over the table to touch Kaz's hand. 'I never intended to use that number again, but when it came down to it …' He shifted one shoulder, wincing. 'They still own a piece of me. Always will. That cuts two ways – what went down last night.' His grin was crooked. 'Something like that is capable of being a major embarrassment if it's not handled right.'

'Mmm.' Kaz nodded. 'Which might explain this.' She pulled a copy of the *Evening Standard* out of her bag. 'Cop Killer Suicide?' She read the headline blasted across the front page, before passing the paper over the table.

Devlin was scanning the article. His mouth had gone hard. 'Suicide? Ties the ends up nice and neat. For which I guess I should be grateful.'

'It doesn't actually *say* that this man Luce murdered Phil –' Kaz began hesitantly.

'He did.'

Devlin dropped the *Standard* and looked up, straight into her eyes. *They* weren't hard. They looked … naked. The same way they'd looked upstairs for those few seconds, when she'd told him she'd seen the papers he'd collected. Desolate, and alone. Kaz shivered. This was real. She sat still and let him speak first.

He sighed. 'Luce was the professional fixer who was hired for all this. The car crash … everything. I need to tell you it all.'

'Please.' She wetted her lip. She had to ask. 'Was … was it something that we did that got Phil killed?'

'No.' Devlin squeezed Kaz's hand and let go. 'At least, in a way maybe I did, starting all this. I honestly don't know.' She saw the doubt in his face. Something rocked a little, deep down. Devlin vulnerable? He was letting her see it all. She fiddled with a strand of her hair. He was still speaking. 'I'll tell you what I know, and what I suspect, but first I need to tell you about Luce. The guy I *finally* watched die at 4.30 this morning.' He rubbed his fingers over the knuckles of his left hand, just visible over the cast. The skin was split and scuffed. 'Luce and I were in the same line of business.' Kaz watched Devlin as he took in a deep breath, then let it out. 'I worked for … well, you saw them, this morning. Luce was mostly freelance. Liked to move around.' Devlin's eyes were dark, turned inwards. 'There were rumours, even then, about how he got his results. Bottom line was, he got them. It doesn't pay to ask too much. Well –' He paused. 'We were never going to be buddies but we did okay together, when we had to. Then Luce started bringing this kid along with him to the party. The boy was about seventeen or eighteen – nephew, brother, cousin. I never got to the bottom of who

212

he was. Might even have been Luce's son – his protégée, anyhow. Some people said they were lovers, but I don't think so.' Devlin shifted restlessly. 'There was a job – it should have been routine – we needed someone to work on the inside. Luce suggested the boy. There was no reason not. It was *meant* to be routine, but somehow the job went bad. I don't know whether they made the boy, found out who he was, or whether the kid panicked and blew it. Perhaps he tried to sell us out. Who knows?' Devlin looked away, staring through the window to the garden. 'They dumped him in a disused office block, out beyond Canary Wharf. He was still alive when Luce and I found him, but he was in bad shape. And they were expecting us. Maybe that was the object of it all along, us, not him. Maybe the job never *was* routine.' He swallowed. 'The place was rigged. Not a bomb, incendiaries. They planned on taking us all out, in a nice, tidy fire. I got Luce away, but the boy ... he was dead before the fire took hold. Luce ... he went crazy, swore that the kid was still alive and accused me of leaving him because he'd fucked up – that he was an embarrassment. I'd saved *him* because he was more useful to my paymasters, and abandoned the boy.' Devlin stopped, eyes blank. Kaz pushed his mug towards him.

'Thanks.' Devlin gulped coffee. 'Luce and I ... ' He looked for a while at the mug, then lifted his head. 'My bosses kept us apart, which was fine by me.' He lifted his hand to make a gesture, registered the weight of the cast, and put it down again. Kaz stayed where she was, waiting until he spoke again. 'The stories about how Luce got results got worse – the things he'd begun to enjoy, with women especially. And the word went out. He wanted *me*. My people had stopped hiring him, and made sure I was well out of his way, but Luce wasn't a fool and he was patient. He set up a scam.' Devlin put down his mug carefully, so that it made no noise on the table. 'Something he said today. About making preparations and us having a good time together before ... before he killed me. I think that his plan then was to fake two deaths, his own and mine. That way I was his – for as long as he wanted. Didn't work.' Devlin's voice was clipped. 'He put me in the hospital, but he didn't get me. Three people died. Officially, Luce was one of them. So was I. I suppose it should have tipped me off when they didn't find Luce's body.' He looked up. 'I'd been thinking for a while about quitting. Had a plan, for the security business. I knew Bobby was getting restless, too. Didn't take much persuading to get him to come in with me. It seemed like the right time. We moved off the radar. New lives, new names.' His grin had an edge to it. Not quite on the mark. 'Hell – it worked for three years.'

'Until I asked you to help me.' Nausea made her stomach lurch.

'It was a billion to one shot that Luce was involved in this and that he and I had history. Not your fault. He saw me, at the crash site, before I even knew you existed. He'd been looking for me ever since.' His eyes looked very clear on hers, cool and steady. 'None of this was your fault. Luce was hired. Someone *bought* all those deaths.'

She couldn't let it go. 'And Bobby?'

'Ah.' He leaned back in the chair, head down, the thumb and forefinger of the good hand pressed above his eyes. Kaz gritted her teeth. What did she have to give him that could repair that hurt?

The silence lengthened, barbed.

Devlin straightened, dropped his hand. The stricken look on Kaz's face caught him in the gut.

'If Bobby is down to anyone, he's down to me,' he said softly. 'Luce took him to get me.' *And if he'd known how things are, it would have been you.* The chill hammering through him wasn't like anything he'd ever felt before. Desolation.

'I'm the one who has to live with that,' he went on. 'But Bobby was a pro. He should have been paying attention. He made a slip, had to have. When it comes down to it, all of us are responsible for our own lives and our own safety. Our own mistakes. Whatever Bobby did, or didn't do, he paid.' *But way too much.*

'You really believe that?' There was hope, laced with suspicion in her eyes. This woman was scary the way she could read him. *And isn't that why you're in this mess?* She was looking at him. He hauled himself back to her question. 'I try to believe it. Mostly it works.' He gave her the truth. 'You have to have something, or you go nuts.'

'I suppose you do.' She was turning over an idea. When it came, it wasn't what he expected. 'Is there anyone else out there likely to be coming after you?'

'What? No.' He stopped, thought. 'No. A couple I've pissed off maybe, but no one who'd want to see me bleed.' *The ones who might, those that are left, never knew who I was.*

He watched her curiously. There was still something going on in her mind, but she wasn't sharing. When she got up and took the envelope from the counter something inside him closed down, cold. She upended it on the table. Papers spilled. She sat down and gathered them into a pile. Her fingers were jerky. Then she was looking at him again.

'What is all this, Devlin? What does it have to do with Jamie?'

Chapter Thirty-Six

Devlin hunched down on the cold feeling, pushed his thoughts away from the messy, touchy-feely emotional stuff. Debrief. Marshal evidence and present the conclusions. *Oh, shit.*

No way out of this now. She'd seen. She'd kissed him, loved him, taken him into her body – was that going to be the last time? Was there still some way out? *Never mind about saving your sorry ass. Doesn't she have the right to know? No one here to tell her but you. So get your thumb out of your butt and do it.*

He shifted the papers. Start with what was written. And then ... He didn't want to think about *'and then'*.

He pulled out the two key pieces. The bank statement and the phone account. The one she could see for herself, the other he'd have to interpret for her.

'This –' he tapped the bank account – 'is what Jeff had in his checking account when he died.' He watched her eyes go round with shock. 'The farm, the vineyard and the car were also all his, all paid for. Cash.'

'But that –' Her voice faded.

'Money from your wildest dreams.'

'No.' She was shaking her head, disbelief carving lines in her face. 'Jeff never had that kind of money. Where *could* he get it?'

Don't go there. Not yet. Get to the phone bill. That's the way in. He pulled the bill to the top.

'See these three calls?'

'Yes?' Her face was shuttered, not hostile, but ...

He hesitated. *Get the hell on with it.* 'This one –' He pointed. 'Last in the series to a-pay-as-you-go cell – virtually untraceable – except that the phone turned up in the Arno, the day after Jeff died. Caught up in debris under one of the bridges.' He smoothed the paper. 'Rossi located the police report.'

Kaz took a breath. 'You think Luce had that phone?'

'It's a pretty standard MO.'

'For someone in your line of work?'

He grimaced. 'Yeah.'

'So, Jeff may have been calling Luce.' Devlin could almost hear her brain leaping to connect as she studied the printout. Clusters of calls of short duration, one after the other. 'Calling and getting voicemail?' she guessed. 'He was desperate.' Her voice was low, talking almost to herself. 'Trying to placate Luce, or to call him off from whatever he was doing?' Her voice hitched. Devlin watched intently. She was pale, but her chin was up and steady.

'Looks that way.' He watched her swallow and put it aside.

'What about the others?'

'This –' Devlin indicated. There was no good way to say it. 'It's a private line. To Scotland Yard.' He waited, and saw realisation flair in her eyes.

'Oh, God – That's why Phil was killed.'

'It's a connection.' Devlin reached over with his good hand to take hers, felt her relax instantly into his hold. 'Maybe Phil found out something and tried to contact Jeff. Maybe Jeff was looking for help. We'll probably never know exactly what the truth was. But there *was* a link.'

Kaz shut her eyes, drawing in a long breath. 'If Jeff was desperate – he might have thought Uncle Phil would help. Phil was quite old-fashioned. He'd have done what he could, even though Jeff and I were divorced. He didn't deserve to die for it.'

Devlin lifted her hand and brought it to his lips. Her fingers were cold. And there was more to come. And the last was the worst. He kept hold of her hand, jerking his head towards the papers that lay between them.

'The third call – ' he swallowed – 'was to the château in France.'

'The château. Oh. No.' Kaz surged to her feet, eyes suddenly livid in a white face. 'You think my father? No, oh no!' She shook her head, violently. 'That's just sick, preposterous –'

'Kaz!' Devlin was up and round the table as she began to pace. He caught her and led her gently back to the chair, pushing her into it and standing over her. 'Think about it. Who would want Jamie and who had the money to buy all this?' He waved to the pile of papers.

'But why? No, it can't be.' Her eyes were dark with disbelief.

'It's all circumstantial.' He couldn't lie and he couldn't prove a line of it, but he hadn't been out of the game so long that he did not know a pattern when it stood up and bit his ass. This one gagged in his throat like rank meat. 'But it's all there.' He gestured to the papers.

Horror and disbelief were battling in those pitch-dark eyes. He savaged his lip. Get this *done*.

'The other little girl – Sally Ann, she was with Jeff and Gemma and Jamie for a couple of days before she died – staying at a motel, like a family. The maid remembered them. Sally Ann was a run-away and she suited their purpose. The whole thing was rigged – the crash, Sally Ann and Gemma dying. Jeff had professional help. Luce's help. Luce rigged it. It was one of the guy's specialities. Accidents.'

It had always prickled on the back of his neck. Ever since he'd stopped beside that quiet road, as the sun set and a child died. That tiny feeling that something was *off*. That what he was seeing had been *put* there. He'd thought it was just that bloody sixth sense that had pulled him off the road in the first place, and made him an intruder in what he wasn't supposed to find – and got him into this … morass.

He looked up and froze. It was a toss up which was paler, Kaz's face or the white T-shirt she was wearing. *Spit it out, and be done.*

'Jeff didn't do what he did for any insurance money.' His vocal chords were gritty. He sounded as tired and as old as dirt. 'I'm not even sure that there *was* insurance money. That was a cover. Jeff was *paid*. With this.' He tapped the financial statement, with its column of unbelievable figures. 'And then, once he was in – maybe he was blackmailed, probably threatened.'

'And then we found him. Put more pressure on.' Kaz's voice wasn't much above a whisper.

'I can't say that it didn't happen that way.' Devlin sat down slowly. His bruises were aching like a bitch, and there was still more of this to do. He pointed a finger. 'No blame, Kaz. This was a guy who connived in the death of his lover and a child, for money.'

'That's what he couldn't face. Why he killed himself –'

Devlin shook his head. 'Jeff didn't kill himself.'

'What?' Kaz's eyes flared open. 'But – I saw his body. The police, they said he'd stabbed the waitress, and her little boy –' She put her hands to her mouth.

Devlin wanted to reach out to her, but her eyes were too dark, too huge. He had to get past this first.

'Jeff didn't murder them. That was the first scenario, but it didn't stand up. There were other DNA traces on the scene. The police know there was another man, but they haven't released that information. I've seen the report and the pictures. That crime scene had Luce's hallmarks all over it.' He clamped his jaw tight for a second. 'Jeff didn't kill Giuliana and her son, and he didn't kill himself – it was murder made to look like suicide. Luce killed them all.'

He watched as her eyes widened even further. She had to be reeling under the weight. 'Did *we* make that necessary? Asking questions? Stirring things up?'

Luce said so. But when did they make him the fountain of truth? He was goading you, wanting you to feel like this. Go with what your head is telling you, not with the guilt. She doesn't need to share that burden.

He shook his head. 'We stirred things up, but the stuff was there to stir. Jeff was a liability, long before we showed up. While he was alive, there was always a possibility that he'd tell someone about what he'd done. Or demand more money. If I had to take a guess, I'd say it was always planned that way. He was going to die, whatever happened. Luce tidied house. He'd done it before, in almost exactly the same way. A hanging in a barn. When I saw Jeff, I remembered. That's what first started me wondering ... the way Jeff died.' He gave a tight laugh. 'What do they say – thinking the unthinkable? I asked Munroe and Rossi to dig. Things began to add up, but in the wrong way. It turned up your father, Kaz.' Now he put out his hand to clasp hers. She didn't pull away, but her fingers just lay, limp, in his hold. There was a deep, dark, cold spike, down into his rib cage. 'I'm sorry.'

'No.' Her eyes focused. She shook her head gently. Her fingers curled to close over his. Balm trickled over the pain in his chest. 'It ...' She stopped. 'You really are *sure*, about Luce?'

Devlin looked away. If he'd been faster, slicker, *better* maybe Luce would still be around to talk. Except that he never would have.

But he did tell you. He told you who died, but he never told you who paid. Fool.

Memory of a lisping voice, triumphing in the half-light of early morning, threaded through his mind. 'I'm as sure as I can be. He confirmed it, this morning, when he thought he was going to kill me. I can't *prove* it – but it's what he does

220

– did. Arrange accidents. There was never any one better.'
He leaned away, detached himself reluctantly from Kaz's
hold. 'The whole thing was a setup – Jamie was the prize.
Someone was prepared to expend money and blood to get
her. This kind of thing – any kind of crime. You have to
ask – who benefits? We've been looking at this the wrong
way round. Jeff didn't need to go through all this to get
his daughter. He could have challenged you in the Courts
if he'd wanted more access. More access wasn't enough. It
had to be *everything*. If Jamie had simply been snatched, if
Jeff had disappeared with her, would you ever have rested
until you found them?' He didn't need Kaz's vehement head
shake to confirm it. 'You had to believe it. That Jamie was
never coming home. This ...' He put his good hand down on
the pile of papers lying on the table. 'It took planning and
money. A whole heap of it. Jeff – I don't believe he was up
for planning something like this. But he couldn't resist the
money. Your father has the cash to fund this, the connections
to find Luce. There's some shady stuff in the art world. It
would take a while to find someone with Luce's talents, but
if you have patience *and* money, everything is out there, to
be bought. It all comes back to that. Who had money to buy
this? It's the only thing that fits. And Jeff tried to ring your
father, just before he died.'

'But ...' Kaz stopped. Devlin waited. Her eyes were
turned inwards, to her thoughts. Terrible things that he'd
put there. 'This is difficult to say about my own father, but
Oliver really has no time for children. Trust me on that.'

Something that was the vestige of a smile twisted the edge
of her mouth. Devlin felt the shudder run through him, the
urge to kiss her, to blank out the anguish with something
more powerful – except who said that it was more powerful?
He looked away. *What the hell are you thinking of?*

'Oliver has only ever remembered intermittently that

I exist,' Kaz said slowly. 'He never really wanted me. Not *me* –' Devlin heard old pain in the drawn breath. 'Why would he want –?'

He saw the payoff hit her, like the force of a blow. The answer to her own question.

'Because Jamie had talent. I don't.' Her voice had hollowed out. 'No.' She scrabbled in the air, as if trying to clear cobwebs from around her face. 'It can't be – children get snatched, people take them, evil people –'

'Kaz.' Devlin rose and turned her, gently, towards him. 'Jamie wasn't snatched off the street, enticed into a waiting car. There was an elaborate plan to make it look like she was dead. The only person who could have set that up was Jeff. Everything points to him having expert help, and being paid to do it. Whoever paid him didn't want just any child, they wanted *your* child. Insane as it seems, who else is there?'

Kaz's head was down. He watched the long shudder ran through her. 'If it's true …' She raised her chin slowly. Her eyes had gone from bleak to fire. 'He had all those people *killed* to cover up the fact that he'd taken my daughter – because he thought she could *paint*. He wanted me to give her to him – ' Recollection spiked her voice with wonder. 'I brushed him off. I thought he was joking. I told him that maybe, when she was older, she could spend some of her school holidays with him. If she wanted.' She made a choking sound. 'He was angry, but that wasn't anything new. That's just Oliver. Oh, God … he took my little girl, just to feed his ego, and something happened and she died. She died in a strange place, away from me, away from everything she knew. She wasn't even with her father.'

Devlin gritted his teeth. Kaz's face had set and hardened into something beyond pain. Her hand shot out, trapping his good arm. 'Devlin, if that bastard took my daughter, we have to prove it. And then we have to make him pay.'

Chapter Thirty-Seven

Kaz stared down at the grey water. The delicate struts of London's prettiest bridge soared above her, but she didn't see them. She'd got here almost at a run, drawn by – what – the power of the water, the memory of her child? She'd had to get out of the house, to deal with the adrenalin rush of emotion that was threatening to burst right out of her skin. But now she was here – her limbs seemed leaden. All she could do was lean on the parapet and stare.

A young man jogged by, then stopped, pulling earphones out of his ears. 'Hey, I say, are you all right?'

Kaz looked up at him blankly, then focused abruptly on the concern, overlaid by a heavy dose of alarm, in his face.

'Yes.' She dredged up a smile, wondering what it looked like. *No, I'm not planning to jump off Albert Bridge. I'm just coming to terms with the idea that my father, a man I respected, even if he was difficult to love, is a kidnapper. Who hired a contract killer to cover it up. Oh, and I have another killer in my bed. An ex-killer, but maybe not too ex –.*

The escalating panic in her Good Samaritan's face brought her back to her surroundings. His eyes were skittering all over the place, searching for help. He'd flipped, in a second, from fear for her safety to fear for his own. She made a gigantic effort at a smile that wasn't just the baring of teeth. 'Thanks, but I really am okay. Just trying to straighten something out in my head.'

'Oh. Oh, well, if you're sure –' His relief was almost comical.

Kaz watched him jogging towards the end of the bridge. The sun was going down and a cold, brisk wind had sprung up off the river. Gulls were diving on something embedded in a dirty tide mark of sand, at the lip of the water. She closed her eyes against a wave of desolation. Oliver. Her father. Could she really believe that he would do this? Had genius turned to madness? Had she signed her own daughter's death warrant when she'd laughed in her father's face?

Her throat closed, over a bitter ache. She'd enjoyed it. Just for a second. She'd finally had something that Oliver wanted, so she'd enjoyed that brief, mean flash of power. Retaliation for years of trying too hard and being ignored, of never being good enough to hold her father's attention. Small and petty and childish. If she'd known then what he would do –?

She put out her hand, to feel the cold metal of the bridge. How could she have known? How could anyone? Even now she couldn't be sure, but it made horrific, horrible sense. She trusted Devlin. That small shock, that wasn't really a shock, went through her once more. The man was a killer, which made him just the man she needed. She could figure out what a killer was doing in her *bed* later. Sometime. *Or you could just forget it. Take what the man is now, not what he was.*

She turned away from the water. This wasn't just about her. Suzanne ... would her mother believe it? She'd loved the man, lived with him ... Kaz exhaled. No need to go there yet. Before she had fled out here, she'd asked Devlin for proof. Whatever they could get. She'd left him reaching for the phone. By now he might have something to tell her.

Devlin stretched out on the couch, staring at the ceiling, the cast resting uncomfortably on his chest. The arm was awkward, but not painful. The rest of his body was doing overtime to make up. He had a bruise the size of Africa blooming, in a hundred shades of purple, on his hip, and the tenderness of his back and buttocks suggested that they were pretty much in the same state. He could get up and go in search of painkillers, or he could lie here and wait for Kaz to come back and hope she'd kiss it all better. She could just about kiss him every place she chose. *Please.*

She might have decided to add a few bruises of her own. He'd asked her to believe incredible things about the man who'd fathered her. A man half the world venerated. She needed something more than gut instinct and patterns, if it could be found. He didn't blame her. She'd asked for proof, then she'd lit out, at the speed of light, in what he hoped was just adrenalin rush.

He dragged his mind back to the phone calls he'd just made. He'd done what he could. Now it was just a matter of waiting. Devlin shut his eyes. To sleep would be good. Classic avoidance tactic. Except it wasn't working. His mind circled back to the dawn, to a derelict building next to a rail line. He scuffed his hand against his cheek. The kill had been virtually an accident, the desperate, gut instinct of an animal to survive. And there wasn't a creature on the planet that would mourn for Luce. Hell – they'd be lining up and taking numbers to dance behind his coffin. But a kill was a kill. And it was the last.

Devlin pushed his tongue up against his teeth, feeling the flicker of pain. He was reaching for unfamiliar emotions, exploring areas in his head he hadn't visited in – Christ knew. Maybe never. It was like a minefield in there and he had a blindfold instead of a map. There was sweat on his face. Kaz knew he'd killed a man and she'd accepted it. More than that, she'd taken him – Hell! His body was getting hard just remembering where it had been ...

He'd told her things he'd never told a woman and the really crazy thing was, he didn't care. But could he ask her –

The phone rang. He almost fell off the couch as he reached for it. Behind him a door slammed. Unexpected relief flooded his body when Kaz called his name. She appeared briefly in the doorway and waved a hand when she saw he was occupied. He wrenched his mind back to the telephone call.

When she came back, she brought more food. Sandwiches and a hunk of fruit cake and an enormous chrome teapot.

'Afternoon tea?' He consulted his watch. 'At nearly nine o'clock.'

Kaz had dumped the tray and was nudging his legs out of the way, so that she could sit. Her face was pale, but there was something in the set of it that told Devlin she'd come to some sort of resolution. He shifted his knees as he dragged himself into a sitting position. Kaz dropped a couple of painkillers into his hand. There was a glass of water on the tray. She wasn't planning on slow torture then – except that the warmth of her bottom against his legs was making him twitchy. This had to be some sort of emotional release from nearly getting killed. Or it could just be old-fashioned, down-and-dirty lust.

He accepted a sandwich when she offered it.

Looking up at him, eyes wide against fragile skin, she looked almost the same age as her daughter – the child she'd now lost twice. A pain Devlin had never experienced before sliced into his chest, taking him unawares and unprotected. He could feel sweat forming again. He took a bite of sandwich and chewed. Kaz was still looking at him. 'You're not feverish, are you?' she asked abruptly.

'Eth? – no, or maybe, a little.' Maybe that was it. Physical weakness. He was *definitely* getting too old for this shit. *Or maybe it's all this stuff waking up and moving about inside your head that's making you feel like …*

Just making you feel?

She finished her scrutiny of him and picked up a plate. 'What have you found out?'

226

He cleared his throat. 'If anyone knows what Oliver's doing now, they're not talking. Not yet. I wouldn't really have expected it. Maybe in a few hours ...' he said cautiously.

She didn't wince, or yell. Wherever she'd been, she'd made some decisions. He could feel it. Purpose was sparking off her in deep intense waves.

'I do have something –' He took another sandwich. 'I got to thinking –' He'd sifted every scrap of information she'd ever given him about Jamie and come up with a fragment that might just grow. 'That reporter you told me about, the one who was so interested in Jamie's drawings?'

'Ye ... es.' She couldn't see where he was going with this and it showed. Her eyes narrowed as she dredged up recollections. 'His name was Hugh, Hughes, something like that. I found him with two of Jamie's drawings in his hands. If I hadn't come into the kitchen when I did, I'm sure he would have taken them.' She was frowning, digging cherries out of a slice of cake. Devlin tried not to watch her popping them into her mouth. *That mouth.* 'You think he knew something? That he'd been told something?'

'Could be.' Devlin tried to force his eyes back to the sandwich plate. They didn't want to go. He gave up the struggle. He might as well suffer the cake thing, along with all the rest. 'Best way of finding out is to ask him.'

Kaz's eyebrows went up in a gratifying way. 'You found him? When do we go?' She was half on her feet.

'Not tonight.' Devlin grinned. 'His name is Giles Pugh. He used to be a stringer for some of the nationals in London.'

'But now?'

'Art editor for something called the *Western Daily Tribune*, based in Cardiff. If we want Mr Pugh, we have to go west ...'

Kaz's eyes were shining, with a disturbingly predatory gleam. 'Oh, yes,' she said softly. 'We want him.'

227

Chapter Thirty-Eight

Devlin hunched over the computer. Above him he could hear the soft sounds of Kaz moving between bedroom and bathroom. He'd resisted the urge to join her. The woman needed some space. The phone was quiet. No one was ringing in to tell him anything. If he wanted information he'd have to go out there and get it.

He tapped Olivier Kessel into the search engine and waited. The Wikipedia entry ran to six pages. The search engine cranked up ten pages and counting. Devlin got up to fetch a bottle of water from the refrigerator, and settled in for the long haul.

After two hours searching, his eyes had begun to cross. What he was looking at was Kessel soup. Academic treatise, magazine articles, museum listings, blogs from critics and enthusiasts. The recent stuff was mostly puff pieces and speculation. 'Kessel Heads in Bold New Direction' 'Now I'm 64 – Olivier Kessel to Embrace New Primitivism?' 'Kessel to Re-define Naive Art?' Hints and teasers from 'sources', stirring the pot about the next big thing, stacking up the next ten million. Nothing concrete.

Devlin leaned back, risking upsetting the chair he was sprawled in, staring at the screen. Kessel wasn't just an artist, he was a showman. A media hound who didn't seem to have given a direct interview in eighteen months. Devlin frowned. None of this stuff was going to take him anywhere. He tapped his fingers on the table. What had he expected, an internet confession?

The man had planned the project down to the last inch. Like preparing a canvas for paint. Except he hadn't counted on the wild card. Devlin grinned ferally at the screen. *Him.* Wrong road, wrong place, wrong time.

Kessel must have nearly got a rupture from holding his breath. Nothing had happened for six months. Was the whole lot fucked, or not? Devlin picked up a pen and rolled it along the surface of the table. For six months after the accident there had been zip. Kessel had probably begun to breathe again. And then – hell in a hand basket. No wonder he'd sent Luce in. And then, after all, to lose the child. When did she die? Was Luce protection or merely damage control? Devlin slid away from that one.

Idly he scrolled back the pages to Oliver's bad boy years. Kessel in impossibly tight pony-skin flares and flowered shirts, making faces at the camera with his mates, falling out of doorways, drunk or stoned, snapped backstage at rock concerts, in fracas at high-price hotels and galleries, with his arm around a succession of doe-eyed, mini-skirted beauties, with endless legs and long, heavy curtains of hair. And with Suzanne. The most stunning of all, blonde and fragile and adoring, with a child in her arms.

Devlin sat up straight. Kaz was looking directly at the camera, curious and unafraid. The dark hair was a wild circle around her head. Someone had plaited coloured ribbons into the front and tucked a flower behind her ear.

Devlin turned off the screen and eased out of the chair. The adult Kaz was upstairs and even more beautiful. He lifted a flower out of a vase as he passed. If she was still awake, maybe he'd get lucky. It never hurt to be prepared.

Chapter Thirty-Nine

There was a sharp wind blowing. It carried the scent of the sea. Overhead, squalling gulls hovered, waiting for the platform to clear before they swooped on a discarded sandwich wrapper. Kaz looked at her watch. The train journey to Cardiff had taken a little over two hours. Services out of Paddington had returned to normal. If Devlin had been thinking about what had happened on the rail line the day before, he hadn't mentioned it.

Kaz surveyed him critically through lowered lashes. It had taken a while to get him dressed, not helped by the fact that he hadn't wanted to accept her assistance. It was a lot easier getting his clothes off him than getting them on.

In the end she'd left him to struggle, waited fifteen minutes and gone back into the bedroom. He'd been sitting at the end of the bed with an unbuttoned shirt, an untied tie and a neatly folded pair of socks, still beside him on the bed. She was very proud of the way she *hadn't* burst out laughing at the expression on his face.

Now he was smart and sinister in a dark suit. As well he might be, considering the designer label she'd spotted on the inside pocket and the bruises which had come out all along his jaw, in full multicolour glory. If you had a journalist to intimidate, it was a good look.

'What?' He was staring at her suspiciously.

'Nothing.' She looked away, sucking in her cheeks to control the grin. 'Any idea where we're going?'

'Just across there.' Devlin indicated the building that loomed next to the station.

'What if Mr Pugh isn't there?'

'We wait.'

'Would it be about an exhibition?' The receptionist looked uncertainly at Devlin. 'You can leave an invitation – or if it's a book for review –' She nodded towards a small pile of volumes on the shelf behind her. 'Mr Pugh hasn't collected them yet this week. I'm sure when he gets in –'

'No.' Devlin took a card out of his pocket. Kaz watched as he weighted it with the cast and jotted something on the back. He handed the card to the girl. 'If you could see that he gets this?'

'Um ... yeah.' The girl took the card, as if she was afraid it would sprout teeth.

'Can you write with both hands?' Kaz asked, as Devlin piloted her towards the pub that was almost opposite the entrance to the building. There were unoccupied tables on the pavement outside. 'Only if it had been the other wrist you broke –'

'Write, shoot, and punch out a guy's lights, I do with either hand, otherwise I specialise.' He gave her an evil leer, pulled out a chair and handed her a menu. 'You want breakfast? They serve all day.'

They gave their order and two unexpectedly good cappuccinos had arrived before Kaz gave in. 'All right. What did you put on the card? And why are we sitting here?'

'Something that should bring Mr Pugh to us.' He looked at his watch. 'He should be here to meet us in about – one minute?'

'Not two?'

'No.' Devlin pointed a finger at a man standing on the opposite pavement, waiting to cross the road. 'There he is.' He grinned as Kaz raised her eyebrows. 'The receptionist was doing her job, fobbing us off. He wasn't out of the office. I figured five minutes to give him a message, two to come down in the lift –'

Kaz squinted; the man looked familiar. 'How you know things is creepy,' she accused. 'How did you guess he was in the building and that he'd come?'

'I *knew* he was in the building, because I can read a list of names upside down.' Devlin's grin got wider. 'The receptionist had a signing sheet – Pugh was marked in but not out. It wasn't much of a long shot that Oliver's name on the card would bring him.'

'Huh!' Kaz knew she was covering nerves by teasing Devlin. There was a coiled tension in him, too. 'Simple, when you know how.'

'Giving away secrets here.' Devlin reached over and took her hand, brief, warm, just right.

She exhaled. 'You didn't explain what you expect me to do, when he gets here.'

The lights had changed. Pugh was approaching.

'All you need to do is look enigmatic. Inscrutable, too, if you like.' Kaz kicked him under the table, but he moved his leg too fast. This anticipation of her moves was getting disturbing. Particularly the way she was enjoying it. She resorted to making a face at him. Devlin just gave her the wolf grin.

Giles Pugh had almost reached the table. He was hovering three feet away. Kaz remembered the thin dark features and wary eyes.

'Are you Devlin?' Pugh covered the final feet.

Devlin simply nodded, hooked out a chair with his foot and gestured for Pugh to sit. Kaz considered the move. A little over the top, but it had impressed the hell out of Pugh. There was an interesting mix of eagerness in his eyes and sweat on his upper lip. Kaz didn't see a signal, but the waitress appeared immediately with another coffee. Pugh's glance was flicking between her and Devlin.

'I ... You're Katarina Elmore.' Good memory, no fool.

He rose and held out his hand. Kaz shook it. Pugh subsided back into his chair. Kaz sucked in a grin. He'd made no move to offer Devlin his hand.

There was a pause. Pugh sampled his coffee, then sat back in his seat.

'You have something to sell? Information?' His eyes were still darting from her face to Devlin's, and back again. The move didn't quite fit the relaxed body language. The man was confused, but trying not to show it. Excitement warred with caution.

Devlin was shaking his head. He leaned forward. Pugh's eyes swivelled back and Kaz heard the in-drawn breath as he took in the full strength of the bruises.

'Look, what the hell is this?' Alarm flared. The man was half-out of his seat. 'I have work waiting. If you've got something for me, then get to the point.'

'Relax, Mr Pugh. Drink your coffee. We haven't come to sell you anything. Not yet.'

Pugh's jaw worked, as he decided whether to go or stay. 'What do you want?'

Devlin looked out towards the end of the street. 'In October last year you visited Mrs Elmore at her home. Mrs Elmore was at the time in a distressed state, following the loss of her only child. After interviewing her you attempted to remove a number of drawings –'

'Hey! Forget this, whatever it is.' Pugh made a repudiating gesture, scraping back his chair. 'I'm out of here –'

Devlin uncoiled from his seat. Pugh balked. 'What do you *want*?'

'The name of the person who sent you to Mrs Elmore and the reason you tried to take those pictures.'

Surprise splattered over Pugh's face. He leaned one hand on the back of his chair. The waitress had come to the door of the pub, frowning in their direction. Devlin inclined his head towards Pugh's chair as he returned to his own. Pugh subsided with a grunt. The waitress retreated.

'You want me to give up a source.' Pugh took a swig of coffee. 'Just like that?'

'Exactly like that.'

'I …' Pugh stopped. 'What's in it for me? There's a story, has to be.'

'There could be.'

'I don't see – 'Pugh stopped again, clearly trying to work out an angle and coming up with nothing.

Kaz shifted her chair slightly. The gunslinger circling was entertaining to watch, but it was time to move on. Delving into the outsize handbag that was sitting beside her chair, she pulled out a small package and passed it across the table to Pugh. 'This is yours. If you tell us what we want to know.'

Devlin made a small, jerky movement, then went still. Kaz kept her head turned away from him. Pugh was staring at the parcel with his mouth slightly open. His Adam's apple bobbed.

'Go ahead, open it,' Kaz encouraged.

His fingers were trembling as he unfolded the wrappings. Kaz could hear him breathing. He knew what it was, from the way it was wrapped.

'This … it's …'

Reverently he ran the tip of his thumb along the very edge of the heavy piece of card. It was the simplest of sketches, ten black slashes on a faintly lined background. A bird, soaring with joy and power. One edge of the paper mounted on the card was ragged, as if it had been torn from a child's exercise book.

'An original Olivier Kessel.' Pugh breathed the words, his Welsh accent broader with emotion. His eyes came up, almost round with disbelief. 'You're prepared to give me *this*, just for a name?'

'It's yours. You can take it away with you now. If you give me your address I'll send you the document for provenance.'

His eyes were back on the picture, unable to stay away. Kaz almost heard the wrench as he pulled his gaze from it and focused on her. 'Why would you give this away? Just *give* it. You want that information very badly.'

'I do.' Kaz didn't see any point in denial. 'I also want your silence. You tell us what we want to know, then forget we were here. And you get the documents to prove that you own *that*.' She nodded towards the sketch.

Pugh's eyes sparked. 'And if I don't, I get a visit from the cops investigating a theft?' Suddenly he was grinning.

Kaz grinned back. 'Could be.'

Pugh looked for a while at the picture. Kaz let him. She could feel his hunger for possession fighting with journalistic instinct to hold on to a source. It was what she had counted on. She was maybe seventy per cent sure which would win.

Beside her Devlin was lying back in his chair, unmoving. She wasn't going to risk a look at his face. What she sensed coming off him was amusement. *You hope.*

Pugh had folded his hands in his lap. Kaz guessed it was to stop himself pawing at the picture.

The waitress broke the mood. Approaching silently, she pounced to clear the table. 'You want anything else then?'

Pugh snatched the sketch away from the risk of disfiguring spills as dirty cups slopped. His hand came out to stop the woman as she prodded the discarded wrappings from the picture, about to crumple them onto the tray. 'Three more coffees, please.'

They waited in silence until the order arrived. Pugh was nursing the flying bird on his knee. Holding it by fingertips only, ready to snatch it from harm. He still didn't seem able to take his eyes off it.

At last when the coffee was served, and the waitress had

left, he raised them. Kaz pushed the wrappings towards him. Reluctantly he fitted the sketch back into its coverings. The deep sigh came up from a very long way down.

'I'll answer your questions. And I'll keep my mouth shut.' Pugh heaped sugar into his latte. 'But I want an exclusive on the story. Come on.' He gestured with his spoon as Kaz finally glanced over at Devlin, and found his face blank. For now, this was her show. 'Don't tell me there isn't any story,' Pugh persisted. 'I want the first chance of telling it.'

Kaz turned her head towards Devlin. He shrugged. She could almost hear his thoughts. *What did you expect? The man is a journalist. It's what he wants, balanced against what you want.*

'All right.' She swallowed. 'When you came to interview me about my daughter, who sent you?'

Pugh had bent down. The sketch was safely stowed now in a briefcase at his feet. When he straightened up, his face reflected surprise. 'That really *is* it? That's all you want to know?' Now he was grinning. He spread his hands. 'The answer to that one is easy. No one. No one *sent* me.'

Chapter Forty

Devlin resisted the urge to feed Pugh his fat smile. He was getting better at restraint, but it still made his toes twitch. A fast glance at Kaz showed him a pale, disappointed face. She hadn't heard it, the slight nuance in Pugh's speech. *Why should she? She's a civilian. Smart, determined and sneaky, but still a civilian. Thank God.*

Pugh was preening himself, smug. The guy would be lousy at the poker table. Kaz didn't know that she hadn't struck out; that she'd just asked the wrong question. And Pugh was using it to muddy the water. And prove what a clever bastard he was.

'No one *sent* you.' Devlin stared straight at Pugh, echoing his inflection and playing it back amplified. 'But something *prompted* that visit. Who gave you the idea?' He stretched one leg forward, to block Pugh's way out. Should the man be thinking of leaving. He nudged the case on the floor with his foot too, a reminder that the guy had already been paid for what he was giving up. 'Mrs Elmore has been very generous with you. In exchange, I think you should give her a proper answer,' Devlin suggested mildly.

Pugh was looking a lot less happy. And a lot confused. Abruptly his face crumpled into surrender. The pull of the sketch was too much. Plus underneath he was probably a decent guy. Most of the time. He was puzzled, that was clear. Warning bells were sounding softly in Devlin's head. Pugh didn't really understand why they were asking, because he thought they should already know. No wonder he was confused.

Devlin glanced over at Kaz. The bones of her face seemed to be standing out, but he suspected he was the only one who would see it. A hand clenched hard round his heart. She had her eyes on Pugh.

'Look, if this is some family argument, I don't want to get into the middle of it – I never used the story.' Pugh was wriggling in his chair, flashing glances back and forth between them again. 'I'm not involved. You must know ...' He sighed. 'I don't know what you *want*.' It was close to a whine. 'You want me to admit that it was Kessel himself who gave me the idea? Is that it?'

He was looking at Kaz, clearly unable to read her face, and floundering as a result. Devlin wasn't surprised. He couldn't read it either, though he had a sickening idea of the turmoil that might be going on in her head. He'd felt the tiny jerk of her leg, when Pugh spoke Kessel's name. Here it was. Her father, about to be dismantled in front of her, by a man who didn't understand what he was saying. It was what they'd come for, but that wouldn't make it any easier to hear.

Kaz's expression was working on Pugh. Getting no reaction, he was floundering on. 'Look, I interviewed Kessel eighteen months ago. Before he dropped out of sight. He was in town to discuss a retrospective. He told me about his plans then, but it was strictly off the record. When I saw that his granddaughter had been killed, well it still seemed like a story. Tragedy, human interest. Of course I wanted some of the little girl's paintings, but I shouldn't have tried to take them like that.'

The man's ears were going pink, Devlin noticed with interest.

'It was crass.' Pugh jerked his shoulders. 'In the event, my editor wouldn't run it. Not when I couldn't get hold of Kessel, to comment. I'm sorry if I caused distress,' he finished, with a small, stiff gesture, that was almost a bow, in Kaz's direction.

Kaz started to speak, then stopped. Devlin let his arm brush hers. They needed more. *She* needed more. He had to play Pugh to get it.

'Kessel told *you* his plans.' The inflection of disbelief was just enough.

Pugh, ego close to the surface, fell straight in.

'If you don't believe that Kessel shared his hopes and dreams with me –'

'To hell with this!' Kaz's sudden outburst had both men looking at her. 'Just tell me what my father *said* to you.'

Pugh visibly gulped. Devlin almost felt sorry for him. 'He told me about your daughter, how she was going to be his successor – about the training programme.'

Devlin looked at Kaz and felt the hand squeezing tighter in his chest. She looked as if someone had dripped acid into her heart. After all the fencing, here it was. Pieces falling into place. Her eyes hadn't left Pugh's face. 'My father told you about his programme for developing my daughter's talent,' she said distinctly.

'Yes.' Pugh nodded, for emphasis. 'I don't think he meant to, but he couldn't keep it in. He was just so amazed and delighted. About all he was going to achieve. When the little girl died like that, he must have been devastated.' Pugh had his hands on the table, suddenly eager. 'Is that why he's still avoiding the press? Or is he really working on something new? Look, if you can get me an interview –'

Kaz was getting to her feet. Her eyes looked blind. 'I think we're done here.'

Devlin rose, to help her with her chair. It would have fallen, if he hadn't caught it.

'Hold it.' Belatedly the journalist in Pugh surfaced. Pennies had begun to drop. 'You didn't know any of this, did you? This was all a con?'

Kaz swung round on him. Devlin heard the chill in her

heart spilling into her voice. 'A con that just got you a very impressive addition to your art collection, Mr Pugh.' She put her hand on his shoulder and Devlin saw him stiffen. 'If you want to hold on to it, you'll forget we were here.'

She started to move away, then turned back. 'One more question. You said my father dropped out of sight. What did you mean?'

Pugh gaped at her. 'Just that. He disappeared, not long after he gave me that interview. No one I've talked to knows where he is.'

Chapter Forty-One

'Kaz?' Devlin was watching her face. Her eyes were shut and her head was back against the seat. Mercifully the train carriage wasn't crowded.

'I didn't expect it to come out like that.' She opened her eyes. Two dark pools of hurt. 'It was all we thought. What you thought, but I ... proof, in a bundle, just like that.'

'It wouldn't stand up in a court of law.'

'I'm not thinking of a court of law.' Kaz's mouth twisted. 'My father told that journalist about Jamie and what he had planned for her. Then I refused to let him have her, but he didn't give up. He dropped out of sight and he just kept on planning.' Her voice wobbled. 'Pugh came looking for a story about a dead child prodigy that day and it was my father who gave it to him.'

The pain in her face and her voice was shredding things in Devlin's gut.

'We don't have to go on with this. We can leave it, right now. Nothing is going to bring Jamie back.' Kaz's mouth was a line of anguish. Devlin felt like howling. Emotions, families, trying to love someone, the dark side of the moon. He was a live grenade, rolling from one horror to another. The more he did, the worse it got. 'I should never have begun this.'

'No!' Kaz sat forward, eyes blazing suddenly. 'This is *right*. I need to know. And I want to hear it from my father's own lips. We look for him.' She glared at him, as if he'd refused her.

'Okay!' He held up his hands in surrender. 'Whatever you want.'

A very shaky half-smile flickered, and was gone. It felt like the first shot of morphine after hours of pain.

'Thank you.'

'Whatever you want,' he repeated. 'Just tell me.'

Kaz dipped her head. 'My mother will have to know.'

Devlin grimaced. 'You're sure?'

'I ... yes.' Kaz fell silent.

Devlin watched her face, hoping maybe she'd sleep, but the eyes were too bright.

'What are you thinking?' she asked eventually.

'That Pugh is a lucky guy. And not just because he's walked away from this with a priceless Kessel sketch.'

'Not exactly priceless,' Kaz corrected. 'But worth quite a bit. I have a stack of exercise books. Oliver did them for me, when I was a kid. I was supposed to copy them.' She flinched. 'I've had one or two of them mounted. They've come in handy.'

'Why did you bring it with you today?'

'Instinct? We knew he might have information. From what I remembered of him, it seemed the sketch might be what would shake it free. It worked.' She gave him a wry look. 'Sorry if I stole your thunder.' Devlin made a doesn't-matter gesture. What mattered more was the shade of warmth creeping back into her face. There was a tiny, beautiful frown between her eyebrows. 'What did you mean, that Pugh was lucky?'

'He's still breathing.' He watched her eyes go big, eyelids fluttering. Those long lashes got him, every time.

'Should we have warned him?'

'Maybe.' He wasn't going to lie, but he wasn't that troubled over Pugh. 'I don't think he's much at risk now. If he'd been seen as a threat he would already be dead. Luce is gone and it's only us that can put any kind of story together that would incriminate your father. Oliver either forgot that he told him, or banked on the connection being too slim to worry about.'

'Didn't bargain on you, did he?'

'Few people do,' Devlin agreed dryly. 'It's your call, Kaz. We *can* let this go.'

'No.' Her voice was very soft. 'And it isn't vengeance. At least, I don't think so. Well, maybe a little.' She gave him another hesitant smile, holding up her finger and thumb to indicate a small amount. 'It's ... retribution? Oliver did all this and he still lost Jamie. I want to see his face. See that knowledge. How must it have felt? I want to *see* it.'

'Looks like first we have to find him.'

'You can do that.' Her utter confidence stole his breath, and chilled his gut. Dark side of the moon.

'Suzanne will help. That's why we have to tell her everything.'

Kaz washed her hands in the tiny bowl, swaying with the movement of the train. She looked at herself critically in the mirror over the sink, then got out her blusher and glided a healthy dab over her cheeks. Better.

She stood for a moment, staring. Her father had never been big in her life – as a great man, yes, but not in the way a *father* should be. Now she didn't even have that. But now she didn't have to struggle either, to try to reach him. To *earn* his love. The relief was small, crowded with pain, but it would grow.

He'd wanted Jamie, but her mother had simply been a cipher, easily blanked off the canvas. No more than a vessel for the Kessel gift. Did that hurt more than the missed birthday parties and the inappropriate gifts of her childhood?

She shook out her hair, and stared herself down in the mirror. None of it mattered now. She would live with the hurt and learn to cope; that was what living was all about.

But first she would look in her father's face and tell him that she *knew*. Knew what he had done. Then she would walk away, for the last time.

Closure.

And the beginning of the rest of her life?

Chapter Forty-Two

It wasn't just the need for Suzanne's help, Devlin realised, as he listened to Kaz laying out the evidence for her mother. It was something else there, too. A kind of hunger. For confirmation? *The man who fathered me is this much of a monster?*

At some time during the train journey he'd picked up a sense of peace in Kaz, and been grateful for it. But a whole lifetime's mind set wasn't going to change that fast. Kaz still had a way to go.

Suzanne stayed quiet through Kaz's careful explanation. So quiet that Devlin wasn't sure that she was taking any of it in. When her daughter ended, with that morning's visit to Pugh, there was a complete, pithy silence. Outside in the street a car stopped. Doors slammed, people called their goodbyes. Devlin could almost feel Kaz holding her breath.

'Oh, darling.' Suzanne spoke at last. 'I'm so sorry.' She stood, opening her arms, and Kaz went into them.

Devlin looked away, an unfamiliar weight in his chest. His arm, and all the other bruises, were aching. He'd been hit a lot harder than this, but his body didn't cope so well any more. Not just his body. His bloody soul, too. Assuming he had one. Couldn't take the punishment.

He rose, looking around Suzanne's compact, cosy sitting room. There were books and papers, ornaments and pictures. Home, family, all that stuff. Over the mantle three small frames hung in a row. An exquisite series of studies of a child's hand. Olivier Kessel's work. And his daughter the model? The sight griped Devlin's stomach. He was never going to be able to look at a Kessel canvas again without seeing blood.

A movement behind him made him turn.

'This man, Luce, he murdered my brother?' Suzanne's grey eyes quizzed him. Her face was much thinner. She looked fine-boned and bleak, like a woman staring at a field of ice. She was waiting for his answer. He swallowed.

'Yes, he did.'

She considered for a moment. 'Then I believe I owe you a debt.' She raised her hand to stop him speaking. He hadn't been about to. Didn't know what he could say. He'd never had a woman thanking him for ... doing what he did. The whole world was coming apart at the fucking seams and his chest was tighter than ever. Suzanne inclined her head, like a queen accepting some sort of unspoken acknowledgement. Some of the pressure in his chest eased. She moved her gaze over to her daughter. 'You want to know whether Oliver is capable of this?' She cut to the heart of it. Unerringly. He watched Kaz's mouth tremble as she nodded.

Suzanne's face didn't alter. 'I'm afraid the answer is yes. Perfectly capable. There were incidents ... ' She stroked Kaz's hair 'I did my best to keep them from you, darling. Your father ...' She shook her head, swallowing. 'What do you need from me?'

Devlin moved over and hooked Kaz into his good arm. Sooner he got rid of the cast, the happier he was going to be. But a lot of other stuff would be happening before then. Suzanne was looking at him, with what he hoped was approval, as he backed her daughter over to the couch, to sit beside him.

'We need to know where we might find him.'

'At the château. If he's not there, then I don't know where. The last time I spoke to him was August last year. He was here in London, at his lawyer's office.' Suzanne's mouth curved. There wasn't a lot of humour in it. 'He was a tad annoyed with me, because I'd sold a small oil. It still irritates

him when I dispose of his work without telling him first.'
She looked speculatively at the pictures over the mantle.
'Maybe I'll just burn the lot. When you find him, you can
give him the ashes.'

'Mum!' Kaz stirred against Devlin shoulder.

'It would be fitting. All Oliver has ever respected is his
work. Respect is the wrong word,' Suzanne corrected
herself. 'The work is his obsession. Everything else –' She
made an abrupt, expressive gesture.

Devlin was calculating. 'If he was here last August, then
he hadn't dropped out of sight totally. Would you be able to
get anything from the lawyer?'

'Doubt it, but I will try. Kaz, darling.' Suzanne reached
out and touched her daughter's hand. Devlin looked down
at her strained face, and felt his bones constrict. He should
have known, but he hadn't got the hang of this emotional
stuff yet. Kaz's whole world view was shifting. She was
composed on the outside, but underneath? What did he know?

All he was thinking of was how to find her father.

*But then that's what you do. She wants that, and you
want to give it to her. You hunt, you bring back the kill, you
lay it at her feet. Job done. Just like men have been doing
for centuries. But there's other stuff. Stuff you have to learn.
Shit.*

He eased round, adjusting his hold. Kaz's attention was
on her mother. She was the one with the information. His
job here was physical comfort. Relief flickered through
him. That he could do. Kaz's arm was across his lap, hand
clenched over the cast. From the look of her grip, if his wrist
hadn't already been broken she was having a damn good try
at it. Anything of his she wanted to squeeze, it was fine by
him. *We live to serve.*

He shook himself away from inappropriate thoughts and
back to what was going on in the room. Kaz's muscles were

taut, to the point of quivering. He ran his hand up her spine, rubbed. Felt the tension give a little.

'You … when I was growing up, after you'd left him … you never stopped him from seeing me, when he wanted to.' The tension spasmed again. 'You didn't come between us. We were father and daughter, as much as Oliver was capable of that. I accepted what he was prepared to give. He was … is … a great man.' There was the tiniest shade of accusation in her voice, but mostly she sounded … lost. 'I think you need to tell me. Why did you leave him? It wasn't about the Russian countess, was it?'

'No.' Suzanne sighed the word. 'She came later. After I'd left. I used her as an excuse. I didn't want to tell you the real reason.' Suzanne shifted her position in the high-backed chair.

Another woman protecting Oliver Kessel's sodding reputation, Devlin thought, as he watched.

'I'd been getting bored and restless for a while, unhappy with the way Oliver lived. The château – most of the time it was like a zoo.' Suzanne smiled again, reminiscently. 'I had what I suppose you'd call an epiphany. Standing at the foot of your father's bed.'

Chapter Forty-Three

'He was in it at the time, along with a gallery owner from Paris. And her husband. When he invited me to join them, I suppose you might say scales fell from my eyes.' Suzanne gave a shaky laugh. 'For one thing they looked so stupid, sprawled all over that enormous four-poster. You remember it? It was supposed to have belonged to Eleanor of Aquitaine or someone. Oliver loved that kind of stuff. Anyhow, he and Pierre or Marcel or whoever he was – they were both stoned and giggling like a pair of schoolgirls. The woman was crawling about, looking for something to cover herself with. I remember, she had the most enormous boobs. They were flopping up and down, while she tried to grab one of the sheets. I suddenly had one of those *what the hell are you doing here* moments. I was the mother of a twelve-year-old girl. It was time to grow up. Take some responsibility. Oliver was never going to change … And what he was …

'I'd packed our stuff and we were out of there in an hour. Oliver laughed when he saw the cases, and called me an uptight, narrow-minded bourgeoisie. He always expected me to go back to him.' Suzanne's eyes narrowed. 'He was right on one thing. I was sufficiently bourgeois to have stored away all the paintings and sketches he'd given me, over the years. Two of them were enough to keep us going until the tenants left this house and I got the business started. We lived at the Ritz for three months. Do you remember, darling?' she queried Kaz.

Devlin felt Kaz nod. Suzanne's face had become dreamy with reminiscence. 'You know how Oliver grumbles when I sell anything, but he's never asked for any of it back. That was the one thing that stopped me from telling you what your father was really like. There was enough guilt in him to leave me the means to keep us both.'

And enough love or passion left, both ways, to keep that tie alive, Devlin saw, with a sudden flash of instinctive knowledge. A pile of canvases kept them together. While Suzanne still had the work, she still had Oliver, but when she sold a piece, a small part of that connection crumbled away. And maybe neither of them realised it. It all came back to the work.

Suzanne rubbed her eyes. 'I should have left him a long time before I did. There were incidents ... Flares of temper that went deeper than artistic tantrums. One of the girls – there were always girls – had a dog. It used to bark incessantly. It drove us all nuts, not just Oliver. Someone from the village found it, in a ditch, with its head bashed in. It could have been run over, but it wasn't a very busy road. There were fights, sometimes fires.' She put her hand to the back of her neck. 'Once everyone but Oliver had the most awful bout of food poisoning, that was never properly explained. He was punishing us for something. I'm not sure what. And I think ...' She was looking way into the past now, eyes a very deep grey. Devlin knew that look – a woman facing something she'd never faced, looking back at something horrible.

Kaz's hand slid up Devlin's arm. He kept her close, wanting the scent of her.

'I think that when Jed drank that bleach, or whatever it was ...' Suzanne paused. 'I've never been sure that it was an accident.' Her voice broke. 'How could I tell you these things? Oliver acknowledged you, when he didn't need to. He did his best to be a father. I really didn't think he'd ever hurt *you*.'

'He didn't.' Kaz's voice was very soft. 'Until I had something that he wanted and I wouldn't give it to him.'

Abruptly Devlin felt the tension leach out of Kaz. She moulded into his side. 'We have to go to the château.'

'It's a place to start,' Devlin agreed.

'Darling, do you really think ...'

'Yes, Mum. I do need to see him. If I can. And Devlin will take care of me.'

He felt the shock go through her body at the same time as the finger prodded into his heart. Confidence. She trusted him to take care of her. Mouth had got there before her brain. And he wasn't giving her the chance to back out.

'I'll look after your daughter.' He hauled himself to his feet, bringing Kaz with him, and held out his hand, cast and all. Suzanne rose and took it. Now it was a done deal. A mother/daughter/lover triangle. Kaz couldn't go back on her admission, because now he'd promised her mother. Worked for him

They stood for a moment. Devlin looked from one drawn, beautiful face to the other, drinking them in.

Two women, protecting the reputation of a murdering bastard who didn't deserve it. And now the whole thing was unravelling. This was on his shoulders now, and he wasn't about to put it down.

Chapter Forty-Four

Kaz stood at the long window, staring down. The tops of the trees were moving in a hot, dry wind. They were bigger. Seventeen years bigger. She could barely see the ruined tower that was all that was left of the original building on the site.

Oliver had never changed the locks. Suzanne's ornate key, to the even more ornate front door, had turned easily. She almost hadn't brought it, but Suzanne had pressed it on her. 'Just in case.'

It had been clear, even as they approached the building, that it was uninhabited. A walk through silent spaces had confirmed it.

She turned abruptly. The room behind her was empty, bare walls, bare floorboards. Darker patches showed on the walls and floor, where paintings and rugs had been removed. She shivered, remembering cold. In the winter the place had been icy. There had never been much furniture, but what there had been was gone. Even Eleanor of Aquitaine's monstrous bed. Wherever Oliver was, he wasn't here.

Kaz ran her finger along the wall. The wallpaper, faded blue with a strange silver sheen, was coming away, showing patches of plaster underneath. This suite of rooms faced north. They felt damp, even in the summer heat. Tall and echoing. She'd expected that to be a trick of childhood memory, making them seem bigger than they were. The height swallowed everything, warmth and sound. She'd lived here for three years of her childhood, in this place of half-furnished rooms and endless corridors.

She stood still and shut her eyes. Scent came first. Patchouli and joss and other things she'd been too young to recognise, and under it a heady, pervasive smell of linseed oil. From

Oliver's studio, at the top of the building. She teetered on the edge of memory. There had always been that sense of things happening in other rooms, snatches of loud music and conversation, laughter behind closed doors.

You never belonged here.

She'd been a child in an adult world. She'd probably seen and heard things that she shouldn't have, though she didn't remember now. And over and behind it all was Oliver. The man who could make lines and splashes of colour sing, who could catch a bird on paper with a few quick strokes, who'd tried to teach her.

He'd offered her all he could. His art, the closest thing he had to love.

Failure tasted bitter in her mouth. She could still remember those breathless evenings, when her father had sat with her on the terrace, drawing endlessly in those cheap exercise books, trying to will her to see what he could see. She'd treasured those times. The scent of cigarettes and oil, which always clung to him, and the quick movements of paint-stained hands. But it had always been about the drawing, the siren call of the paint, when what she'd really wanted was to walk with him in the garden and the woods. To look at butterflies and lizards and the colour of the old roses, climbing over half-ruined walls.

Her father had always been there and always been just out of reach.

'Kaz?'

She turned. Devlin was standing in the doorway. Light from the corridor silhouetted him. Big, solid and awkward in the plaster cast. *There.*

She didn't have to ask him to take care of her when she needed it. He just did it. Why hadn't she known that?

Her blunder the other night, in her mother's sitting room, that she'd covered up by completely ignoring, had been the truth. Devlin would take care of her. It wasn't a matter of her being clinging, or needy. It was Devlin. He was taking care of her now, concern in his face. It was the easiest thing in the world to step into his arms.

'What?' He pulled her into his chest, holding her in place as he stroked her hair. She was trembling. She hadn't noticed. And her legs would barely hold her, but it didn't matter.

'I thought he loved me, because I loved him. Or tried to.' Her voice sounded thin, swallowed by the room. 'I wanted him to be proud of me, to notice me. I never understood.'

Devlin's face, above her, seemed to be distorted, misty at the edges. Her eyes were swimming with tears. 'He didn't see *me* at all. It wasn't just that I wasn't good enough. He had nothing to *give* that a small girl could use. We barely breathed the same air. It was all about the painting. The groupies and the parties and the busted hotel rooms, those were only trappings. He couldn't love me, because he didn't have room. If I couldn't share what obsessed him, there wasn't any space for anything else. It ate him, from the inside. Everything he did, he did because of his art.'

She took a small, hitching breath. 'All the capacity to love that he had, he gave to my mother, and that wasn't much. But she was part of the painting. His muse. He has no morals, no scruples, no conscience. He never has had them. He isn't like other people. Genius walks past all the rules. Why did I never see it?'

Realisation lifted her voice. Now she could say it out loud. 'I don't have to try any more. I'm never going to get his attention, but it doesn't matter. What *I* am has nothing to do with him.'

Pain was bubbling up and out, freeing her, making her feel light-headed. 'And because he doesn't care about anyone else, that bastard stole my daughter.' It came out as a wail.

Then the dam broke. She gave up trying to contain the tears and burrowed into Devlin's chest, sobbing.

Chapter Forty-Five

He didn't really know how he should handle this, but the hair stroking thing seemed to be working, so he went with that. Kaz was making the front of his shirt wet. He'd never in his life had a woman cry in his arms, until Katarina Elmore. This made twice now. His mind shied away from an early morning in a hospital car park. That had been ...

This time it felt ... incredibly good. Not that Kaz was crying, but that she was letting him hold her while she did it. A tiny, hope-shaped spark, had lit, very gingerly, in his chest. It was in unfamiliar territory and it knew it. If Kaz ...

Shit. Not the time, not the place. Not the man?

'Better now?' When she got to the hiccupping and rubbing her nose stage he eased back, brushing hair out of her face.

'Mmm. Sorry.' She was scrubbing the damp patch on his shirt. Now *that* was starting another response entirely. Huh!

He covered her hand. Would it be too much to bring it to his lips? He decided regretfully that it was. Guaranteed to bring the shutters down. He studied her face. No shutters. She wasn't blocking him out. Her nose was a bit red and there was a trace of pink across her cheekbones, but that was all. Devlin had a sudden desire to kiss her until she was pink all over, and then get her naked, just to make sure. It sounded like a plan. *Later.*

'There's nothing here.' His voice was raspier than he expected. Not enough blood to the vocal cords. She was shaking her head slowly. 'Doesn't look like it. There's just one more place.' She stepped away from him, to lead the way.

The staircase was behind a door. From the outside it looked like the entrance to another room or a closet. Narrow, dark-varnished treads rose steeply.

'Oliver's studio,' he queried.

'Closest he could get to the sky, and away from the rest of the house.'

Kaz went first. Devlin tried not to be distracted by the rear view as she climbed. The space stretched the entire expanse of one side of the building. Huge skylights let in a steady northern light. The floor was scarred and stained with paint splotches. The smell of linseed still hung heavy in the air. One wall was defaced by a wide blue stain. Whatever had made the mark it had hit the bricks hard.

'That's it.' Devlin detected a tiny tremor in Kaz's voice. 'Very few people ever came up here, but it was still the heart of the house. If there's nothing *here*, then Oliver is gone.' She was turning slowly, surveying the walls as if they might have a message.

'We can ask in the village. Moving furniture would have taken a while and more than one truck. Someone might have seen something.'

'Mmm.' She turned to look at him. 'The locals hated it when Oliver bought this place.' She turned away again, back to the room.

'You okay?'

'Yes.' She sounded surprised. 'He used to let me sit up here with him, while he worked. Over there.' She nodded towards the corner. 'There was a dais and I'd make myself a nest with the old draperies. I used to organise jars of pigment and acrylics into groups of colour. I didn't remember. He hated people to be up here when he was working but I could come and go as I pleased.' She took a long look round. Devlin waited. 'Some of my best memories of this place are up here.' There was wonder in her voice. 'Nothing here now. Shall we go down?'

Kaz closed the door at the bottom of the stairs and leaned against it. She stood for moment, then held out her hand.

Devlin threaded his fingers through hers and they made their way down through the quiet building.

'There must be an agent or someone, taking care of the place, and keeping control of the garden.' Kaz looked round thoughtfully. The floor and stairs showed signs of recent sweeping. 'If we find out who, they might know something.'

They'd reached the ground floor and the main hall. Devlin stooped to lift the handset of a phone, pushed into a corner. He listened, then put it back. 'Still connected. When Jeff rang, someone answered. But not the person he needed.'

'They must have told him the place was empty.' Kaz gave a small shiver. She swivelled slowly, considering. 'We looked at the kitchen. We can't get into the wine cellar, where Oliver kept his paintings, because of the steel door. I doubt if there's anything left there, anyway.' Her gaze came back to Devlin. 'There's nothing much else to see, unless you want to look at the grounds. I used to ride my bike along there.' She nodded to a wide corridor, stepping forward. 'Through the hall and out on to the terrace – there's a door – oh!'

Devlin moved fast, to push her behind him. The door was open and a man stood in the frame, with a naked blade in his hand.

Chapter Forty-Six

The scythe was old, and stained with rust. The hand that held it was twisted and spotted. And shaking visibly.

'*Arrêtez!*' He might be old and scared, but it wasn't stopping him advancing down the corridor, brandishing his weapon of choice. '*Qui êtes vous? Ne bougez pas.*'

Kaz wasn't listening to the commands to stay still. She stepped forward eagerly, right into the man's path. 'Maurice! You're still here.'

'Mademoiselle Katarina?' The scythe clanged as it dropped to the floor. Devlin moved forward smartly to pick it up and store it on a convenient window ledge. He leaned against a wall and watched as Kaz was petted and stroked and marvelled at. Her wild curls were remembered and her beauty exclaimed at, until she was blushing. Devlin loved that look.

'*Votre mari?*' The old man was looking him over now, bright-eyed, like a cock on his dunghill.

Kaz's cheekbones had gone even deeper pink. '*Non. Un ami.*' She introduced Devlin. Handshakes were exchanged. 'Maurice was the first person to teach me about plants. I used to follow him all over the garden.'

Devlin waited again while Maurice exclaimed over the success of his protégé. 'I read about you, in the magazines, and now, on the internet. Jean finds things for me. But you are not here to talk about the plants and flowers,' Maurice suggested at last.

Kaz shook her head. 'We're looking for my father.'

If Maurice thought that this was strange he didn't show it. He spread his hands. It was a totally Gallic gesture. 'Alas. Gone.'

'Do you know where?'

The old man shook his head. 'The lorries, they came at night. Three, not local men.' Devlin sensed that he might have spit but was too respectful of his surroundings. 'In the morning. Poof, all gone.' His head bobbed up and down 'Who knows where?' he demanded dramatically.

'Oh.' Disappointment flattened Kaz's voice. The old man took her arm. 'You come with me.' The eyes were still bright and birdlike and lit with amusement. 'You talk to Jean.'

'Jean?' Devlin quizzed out of the corner of his mouth as they headed for the hire car.

'Maurice's son. I think this might be the local version of *I don't know, but I know a man who does.*'

Maurice was hoisting himself into an immaculate grey 4×4. They followed him down the narrow road to the village, and parked in the main square.

Jean, the scrawny urchin who had run wild with Kaz in the château's grounds, was now the well-padded owner of a smart roadside bistro. He was standing at the open door, dressed in a white apron, surveying the street. Maurice ushered Kaz out of the car, a hand on her arm, to present her proudly to his son, before leading the way into the restaurant, with its welcoming miasma of garlic and fresh herbs.

The pâté, cheese and new-baked bread were excellent. The information was even better. Jean poured wine, wiping his hand on his apron. Kaz picked the black olives out of a bowl on the table and sipped from a small glass.

'The trucks took the furniture into storage last September.' Satisfied that his guests' needs were attended to, Jean pulled out a chair and sat with them. It was late afternoon and the restaurant was empty. 'Monsieur Le Brun has a cousin who works at the storage depot. It wasn't a secret.' Jean grinned. 'But the furniture wasn't all that was moved. There was another truck, a few nights later. I saw it go through the village as I was locking up. Smaller. Specialist hauliers.' He looked at Kaz, waiting expectantly.

'Moving the paintings and Oliver's studio.'

He nodded. 'And not into storage. The driver and his mate had breakfast here before they left. One of them made a call on a mobile, confirming their instructions. He went outside, but the kitchen window was open.' Jean's grin got wider. 'The paintings went over the border. To Italy. To Lake Garda.'

Chapter Forty-Seven

Kaz sat in the tiny church, across the square from the bistro, breathing in the fragrance of incense and old stone and silence. She'd lit a candle on the stand next to the altar. She watched the flame, burning steadily. She'd prayed. She wasn't quite sure who to, or what for. Strength? Justice? Peace?

The deep core of grief inside her was never going to go away, but it might change.

She wrapped her arms around her chest, pulling her cardigan closer.

Something had happened at the château. More of the pieces she'd been missing in her relationship with her father had fallen into place, mysteriously moving her yet another step towards freedom. Her heart felt ... open?

She *would* confront Oliver. She needed that, deep down, somewhere too deep to analyse. It was the last piece in the picture. Once that was done, she could walk away. But what would she be walking to? Devlin?

Did what they have amount to a relationship? What did he want? What did she want?

She sighed, letting her shoulders drop. The candle flame flickered higher, fed by a fugitive draught. There were already layers in her relationship with Devlin that she'd never had with any other man. Trust. Care. Shivery sounding words.

Is this what real love looks like?

The whisper seemed to come out of the air.

She got to her feet and headed for the door.

The bistro let rooms. When she got back two new mobile phones lay on the bed, alongside a pair of train tickets dated for the following day.

'We drop the hire car back to Avignon station, pick up another at the other end, in Desenzano, if we need it.' Devlin stuck his head out of the bathroom as she came in. He was managing to shave one-handed. Kaz raised her eyebrows. 'Taking a lady to dinner,' he explained.

'Hmm.' Kaz looked at the phones.

'Old habits. We're going into the field. We need clean equipment.'

'Are we? Going into the field?' She dumped her bag and kicked off her shoes. 'I suppose we are. Do ... do you have a weapon?'

Devlin's eyes slid away. 'Not yet.' His head came up. 'You know, as far as I'm concerned, if you wanted me to put a bullet in your father's head, it would be justified, with the things he's done. And I could do it.' He paused for a beat. 'That's not how you want it. I respect that you don't want any more violence, but it doesn't mean that other people will. We have to take care. We go into this as hostile terrain, so we prepare accordingly. It feels better to me that way. Humour me.' He gave her a level look. 'And if you change your mind, about the bullet in the head, let me know.'

He ducked back into the tiny shower room. Kaz looked thoughtfully after him, then took one of the phones over to the deep window seat. She rang Suzanne, giving her an update and the new number.

Call ended, she was standing by the window, looking out at the street, when Devlin emerged. 'What do we do now?'

'Whatever you want.'

'I think I'd like ... just to walk? Spend some time ... out of time.' She turned around and offered him her hand.

They explored the grounds of the château and climbed the ruins. Kaz showed Devlin the places where she and Jean had hidden, the rose garden that had first sparked her interest in flowers and the overgrown maze on the edge of the trees.

'What?' Kaz tilted her head.

Devlin was lounging on a dilapidated seat, at the furthest end of the château's garden. Kaz had settled on a large, flat-topped boulder, her knees drawn up under her chin. The roofs of the village were just visible below, tucked into the valley.

'I'm imagining you here, as a child, all skinned knees and pigtails.'

'Pervert,' she suggested amicably

'Nah – I've never gone for the schoolgirl thing. But you must have been cute.'

'I suppose I was.' She looked around, considering. 'We weren't here that long, just three years, but I had a good childhood here, as far as it went. Small villages are very conservative. They totally disapproved of everything to do with Oliver, and life at the château, but they accepted me. I rather think they conspired to protect me, in a funny sort of way, to give me something normal. I went to school, and played with all the other children, and rode my bike and ate ice cream. All the usual kids' stuff. I was more interested in helping Maurice in his greenhouse than what went on up here. I'd lived with that lifestyle for years. It was just Oliver, messing about as usual, and a bit boring. The paintings he produced here were amazing, but I was used to that.' She grinned. 'Planting out geraniums and picking beans and tomatoes was a novelty, after Venice, and far more fun.' She turned slightly, and took a deep breath. 'What about you? Your childhood?'

She waited for the eyes to hood, and close down. He'd turned his head and was looking off, at the view. 'Yeah. I had one.'

'I kind of thought you might have.'

Devlin sighed. She was watching him. He could see, out of

the edge of his vision. Not exactly expectant, but hopeful. He concentrated on the view. What had gone on in his childhood *really* didn't interest him. It hadn't interested his mother much, either. He sighed again. Kaz wouldn't pry, if he kept silent, but then she might *imagine*. And remembering wasn't painful – it was just … just … He didn't really know what it was. Just that he didn't much care to go digging about there. He'd buried his memories, as required, when he entered the Service, without too much regret. They rarely surfaced now, and if they did, he could soon shove them under again. *Oh, what the hell*. Kaz had shared, so could he.

He leaned forward, arranging his good arm and the cast on his knees. 'What do you want? It was a dark and stormy night? All that stuff?'

'Was it? A dark and stormy night?'

'Might have been. It was a hot summer, I know that much. Ma wasn't too happy, being pregnant in temperatures in the 90s.' Kaz leaned forward. He could hear his voice going flat. 'She wasn't too happy being pregnant at all.' He looked up. 'She was two months short of her seventeenth birthday when I was born.'

'Oh.' The soft exhalation of breath said it all. Compassion, pity, understanding. Words he'd never had much time for.

'I'm pretty sure she would have got rid of me – and I don't know that I'd blame her – but she was too far along when she realised what was happening. By the time my grandmother found out, it was way too late. Ma was 16, and stuck with a baby, when she should have been worrying about her O-levels and going to Bay City Rollers' concerts.'

'Your father?'

He shook his head. 'If Ma knew, she wouldn't say. My gran blamed the mechanic from the local garage. Swore that I was the image of him. Apparently he did a runner just after I was born, so she was probably right. My gran brought me up.

She thought she was done with all that, and then to be landed with a kid from the wrong side of the blanket.' He gave Kaz a smile that he knew was lopsided. 'There you go – we're both of us bastards – only I work harder to live up to it.' Kaz's soft exclamation of protest straightened the smile a little. 'Gran fed me and clothed me and taught me right from wrong, but I always knew –' He stopped. It *didn't* hurt. It was just how it was. 'I was a mistake. Something to make the best of. That's it. Childhood. It was a long time ago.' He wiped his hand across his knee.

The look on her face told him he wasn't getting away that easy. Her eyes were very dark. They always got that way when she was ... involved. She looked like that at night. In his arms. He shifted his position. There were bees and butterflies amongst the bushes that sprawled around the seat, and now and then a pleasant, pungent smell. Lavender? Something green and spiky. He leaned over and picked a leaf, as a diversion.

'What about school?'

He hesitated. A flippant *What about it?* wasn't going to be good enough.

'I liked school. Sports and reading science books and –' He stopped again. *Petrie*, he hadn't thought of him in years.

'And?' Kaz prompted.

'There was an old guy, living up the street. Old guy – I thought he was about 100, but he was probably only in his 60s. You know how kids are. Mr Petrie. He was a friend of my grandfather.' Granddad – a pale wraith, slumped in the corner, fading slowly out of life in the grip of emphysema. 'They used to play chess. Then my grandfather died and Petrie taught me to play. He'd been in the War and he had stories.' Devlin frowned. 'Looking back, I think he'd probably been in military intelligence, but the stories were boys' own stuff – desert battles and beach-head landings.'

Had it begun with Petrie? Had he been the first talent scout, all those years ago? 'Between him and my grandmother, they pushed me into going to university.' He grinned as he saw her eyes widened. 'Didn't think I had brains, did you?'

'I just ... never pictured you as academic. What did you study?'

'Physics and Electronics. In the last year I got a work placement – a government research laboratory approached my tutor, I think ...' Had that been the last stage in the selection process? 'Graduation day –'

Graduation day. The loneliest day of his life. Petrie and his gran were gone, dead within a few months of each other, in his final year, and his mother run off, God-knew-where, with a car dealer from Peckham. All his friends in excited family groups. The girl of the moment, what was her name – Ellie, or Emma? She had her family around her, too. They'd made him welcome, but somehow it had pointed up how alone he was. He'd been easy meat for the stranger in a sharp suit who'd approached him, almost as he staggered off the platform, with a diploma in his hand and no one to show it to. 'A man offered me a job.' He sat back abruptly, jerking the cast.

'*The* job,' Kaz said softly. 'MI5? MI6?' She raised her eyebrows at his expression. 'I have signed the Official Secrets Act.'

'And so you have.' He exhaled. 'I never worked for MI5 or MI6. My ... employers ... were a lot deeper and a lot darker. The unit that no one acknowledges exists.' Until they want something particularly dirty done. *Send for the magicians. They make things disappear.* 'You've seen, Kaz. You know a little, or I wouldn't even be telling you this, but you can never reveal it, to anyone.'

He heard the short, sharp hitch in her breath. 'Would ... would they harm you?'

His chest tightened. First thought for him, not herself. 'They would not be happy.' He laughed. 'Making them happy is not one of my ambitions these days. But they don't like to be talked about,' he warned softly. 'I accepted their job offer, got the training and eventually was let loose on the world.' Re-made, in their chosen image. 'When you sign on – your whole past ceases, as of that moment. To all intents and purposes, Stuart Adams no longer exists. I became someone else, so deep undercover that there's no connection now between me and that university student.' Except in his own mind. He kept the thread, the finest of gossamer strands. He'd never been back, but he knew now where his mother was, and with whom. She had a new life and he wasn't going to trouble it. 'Then, when I left the Service, I changed again. New life, new name.' Compartments, each one watertight. No links, except for the flesh and blood that strung them all together. Him. Whoever *he* was? 'There you are.' He spread his good hand on his knee. 'That's me.'

'Devlin.'

'Devlin,' he agreed. 'That's who I am now.'

The man I'm in love with? Kaz clenched her hand against the rough fabric of her jeans, shaking down her hair to hide her expression. She'd listened to his words, flat and matter-of-fact, but she'd watched his face too. Seen the pain and the loneliness of the unwanted child, and of the man, valued only for what he could be made *into*. He didn't know, she was sure of it. He'd buried that so deep too, along with the child Stuart. He didn't know how much he'd lost. Lost children. Damaged.

She hugged her knees. You and me both. Two peas in a bloody pod. And now he was Devlin, and she was pretty sure that she was in love with him. But could *he* learn about love? Would he even want to?

'You okay?'

'Oh. Yes.' She raised her head. A breeze was blowing up. She slid off the rock and held out her hand. 'Thank you for telling me.' She looked up into his face. 'I will respect your confidence.' It was formal, but it seemed the right thing to do.

The ghost of a smile dispelled his worried look. 'I know you will.' He put a finger under her chin, to tilt her face further up. 'Don't worry, Kaz. It was a long time ago. It doesn't hurt.'

She nodded and took his arm, a coat of anguish lying over her heart. Hurt, and he doesn't even know it.

Devlin watched Kaz across the tiny dinner table, tucked into a corner of the bistro. It was a popular place, pleasantly full and humming with conversation and the scent of good food. She was wearing a deep purple dress, with shiny narrow straps, and a bizarre-looking necklace, which might have been lifted from the neck of a tribal statue. A purple stone winked like an eye when she moved. She was feeding him *frites*, dipped in garlic mayonnaise, from a bowl in front of her.

You would *kill for this woman.* He clenched his fingers on the stem of his wine glass. He assessed her carefully, checking. She'd been very quiet on the way down from the château, but she looked fine now. He didn't want her thinking that there had been anything wrong with his childhood. It wasn't anything special, the mix of tedium and powerlessness that you had to endure, until you got old enough to do something about it. His training for the job, now that had been pretty brutal – weaponry, tactics, combat, languages, so that you could disappear, wherever you were. He'd valued that. Even now, he still did it. He'd picked up Bobby's speech patterns – a spasm across his chest when he remembered Bobby – and

267

now, being around Kaz was bringing up the English in his speech, he was sure of it.

Satisfied that she wasn't brooding about his non-existent unhappy childhood, he relaxed into his surroundings, listening to the snatches of conversation around them. Someone had a new baby; someone else was leaving for Paris on business in the morning and was hoping to get lucky tonight. The couple in the corner were arguing amicably over the colour to paint the bathroom. It was ordinary, normal family stuff. He didn't have a clue about any of it. The char-grilled lamb cutlets on his plate; now that was a completely different matter. He stopped analysing and started to eat.

The quiet dinner in the bistro developed into a party, once word got around that Mademoiselle Katarina had returned. Curious villagers thronged in, swelling Jean's coffers as another bottle circulated. Kaz was breathless and a trifle tipsy when they finally made it upstairs. The clock on the town hall was chiming twelve. She collapsed backwards onto the covers.

'The witching hour.' For some reason that seemed to be very funny.

Devlin was switching on table lamps and drawing blinds. Soft pools of gold lit up the sheen of antique furniture, and traced designs in shadow over the faded, time-washed rugs that covered the floor. Kaz stretched, and felt warmth floating over her skin.

Devlin sat beside her on the bed, looking down at her. She couldn't focus on his face properly.

'You're sober,' she accused. She'd seen that the bottle of excellent local wine, bottles, she corrected herself, had passed by him more often than they'd stopped. 'I'm not,' she confided happily.

Devlin was smiling in a very promising way. Kaz wriggled closer.

'I can see that.' The amusement in his voice sparked her indignation. She started to wriggle away again, but he caught her, rolling her on the bed and trapping her, slightly awkwardly, between both arms.

'Look. No hands,' she giggled.

'I have a hand.' He proved it by planting it on her waist, to hold her in place. 'And I have this.' His mouth slid over hers and her brain did a long slow glide that had nothing to do with any wine. 'You taste of blackberries and plums.'

He'd finished with her mouth and was nibbling his way along her jaw. 'And you smell of vanilla and fresh green grass.' He was nuzzling the pulse point behind her ear now, making her heart jump.

She lost the thread for a moment as his mouth travelled down the length of her throat.

'Shower gel,' she gasped, as his mouth hit the slope of her breast and began to move down. 'I … I suppose you don't need to know that.'

'No.' He'd found something impossibly delicious to do with his tongue, that involved licking her skin and then blowing gently on it.

'You have a fabulous mouth.' Kaz writhed as he found a sensitive spot. 'Don't stop.'

'No intention. No intention at all.'

Chapter Forty-Eight

The sun was already heating the air over the police station to shimmering point.

The Inspector paused on his way in, to survey his domain. Clean windows and paintwork, no litter, the public notices up-to-date and straight in the glass cabinet. Exactly as he liked to see it. A swell of proprietary pride puffed his chest. He acknowledged it, grinning. And why not? A mild obsessive-compulsive with a liking for order. So?

He fumbled the pristine white handkerchief out of his pocket to wipe a bead of sweat from his forehead. The temperature was already in the high twenties, at this hour of the morning. What it would be like later in the day, down in the centre of Florence …

He folded and replaced the handkerchief and strode up the steps, pausing in the doorway, with a frown. Early as he was, someone else had been earlier. There was a man loitering in the vestibule, clutching a large briefcase.

The forensic scientist who had been working on the DNA in that distressing case of the British child – *Signora* Elmore's daughter.

His presence here –

The Inspector stepped forward, with a quick glance at the officer at the desk. He was engrossed in completing a pile of forms.

The forensic scientist's face lightened when he saw him. Some of the tension lifted from the thin shoulders.

'Inspector? I …' His voice tailed off and he shuffled his feet.

The Inspector crossed the hall to him. 'You have something? Something new,' he said softly.

A nod.

'Come to my office.'

Once behind a firmly closed door, the technician recovered some of his composure. He delved into the briefcase that he'd been clutching against a slightly concave chest and held up a folder.

'The full results of the tests.' Clearly he wasn't going to say any more.

The Inspector smothered a sigh, took the folder and sat behind his desk, gesturing the young man to a seat. 'I'm not going to like this, am I?'

The scientist's eyes widened. 'Inspector?'

'Never mind.' The Inspector opened the folder and looked at the neatly tabulated results and lines of formulae. There were graphs, too. The crucial conclusion was, of course, right at the bottom of the page. The Inspector forgot himself so far as to swear. 'You're sure of this?'

'Certain.' The young man nodded. 'It changes things, doesn't it?' There was an air of suppressed excitement about him, now that he'd delivered his burden.

The Inspector nodded curtly, already reaching for the phone. 'We need to speak to *Signora* Elmore, as a matter of urgency.'

Chapter Forty-Nine

Kaz watched the early morning ferries criss-crossing the lake, shielding her eyes as the sun hit the water. She looked up as Devlin dropped a handful of paper onto the table and his body into the chair beside her. Her mouth had gone a little dry. She couldn't help it. The way he moved got to her, every time.

'Properties that have changed hands, lakeside, in the last two years, which should more than cover the time that Oliver would have been house-hunting.' He was examining the papers. 'Not so many, when you add up all the requirements.'

'Big, secluded, accommodation capable of being converted into a studio and a place to store several million pounds' worth of art in progress,' Kaz recited the list.

'You're sure about it not being a rental?'

'Oliver likes to own things.' Where had that knowledge come from? A new clarity when it came to her father?

'There's really only one.' Devlin pushed over the paper. 'Special feature – temperature-controlled wine cellar, which might be modified to store paintings?'

'Sounds exactly what we're looking for.'

'It's the other side of the lake, at Bardolino.'

Kaz's heart was beating faster than it should. 'Shall we go and look?'

They took the ferry. The boat puttered gently from pier to pier, letting off passengers and taking them on. Mostly holidaymakers and tourists, a few locals with business in another part of the lake and time to spare.

Devlin offered her a pair of field glasses as they neared

Bardolino. She'd stopped wondering where he got these things. If she'd wanted an elephant or a balloon ride or a toffee apple no doubt he'd have conjured it up. A package had been waiting for them at their hotel last night. Hand-delivered. Kaz didn't ask what else it had contained. She had a pretty good idea. The thought of Devlin with a lethal weapon didn't bother her. She put the glasses to her eyes and focused where he pointed. Her breath came out in a startled hiss. 'That's it.'

She handed Devlin the glasses, waited while he raised them.

'It might be a carbon copy of the château. The size, the tower, the outbuildings.'

'Did you see the skylights in the roof?'

Devlin let the glasses drop. 'Oliver's studio.'

They were back at the hotel, waiting for the hire car.

'We don't have to go there ourselves. I can send someone.' Devlin was pacing the room, which was enough to get Kaz's attention. Devlin didn't often pace. 'Let me send someone. To reconnoitre.'

'We may as well do it ourselves; if we have the wrong place we apologise and leave. If not ...' She savaged the inside of her lip. Her heart was drumming uncomfortably in her chest, but she had to do this.

Then she could love Oliver and hate him *and walk away from him.*

She crossed over to stand in front of Devlin. 'No one is forcing me to do this. He's my father.'

'He's dangerous.'

That's what I thought about you when I first saw you. That, and hot sex on legs. Still do.

She saw the bafflement in Devlin eyes when she smiled. *No, I'm not going to explain.*

'Oliver hires people to be dangerous on his behalf.' She edged her mind around the fights and the tantrums that were dim memories from her childhood. 'He's 66 years old.'

'That's not old.'

Their eyes locked. She kept hers on Devlin's face. Saw the precise second that he gave in ... and loved him for it.

Hey – wait one damn minute here.

Can't now. No time.

'What?' He was staring at her.

'Nothing.' She tried to sound calm. It must have worked, because he stopped glaring at her. Now she wanted to reassure him. 'I go to the house. I call my father every foul name I can think of. I walk out. Nothing simpler.'

'Yeah? And what's he doing all this time?' Devlin demanded, frustration clearly spiking.

'Sitting in a chair with his mouth open, wondering where I learned words like that?' She had to be flippant; she was too close to the edge. She dug her nails into the palms of her hands. Her heart was trying to climb into her throat.

Forget Devlin, focus on Oliver.

She'd tried to imagine the scene when she confronted her father, but she hadn't been able to do it. She wanted grief, she wanted guilt. 'He won't hurt me.' She had to hang on to that.

'Nothing I can do is gonna talk you out of it, short of knocking you out and tying you up,' Devlin was grumbling for form's sake. She knew there was concern under the growl. It warmed and hurt, in about equal measure.

She laid her hand on his arm. 'I *will* be all right.'

She could see he wasn't convinced, but he knew when to stop wasting breath. She watched as he stalked over to the dressing table to pick up her phone and punch buttons. He held it out to her. 'I'm coming with you. I'll stay outside,' he forestalled her protest. 'You leave this switched on.

You need me, if anything seems off, in any way, you hit three on the speed dial.'

She managed a crooked smile. 'And you come running to the rescue?'

'You'd better believe it.' He hauled her into his arms for a short, hard kiss. She could almost taste his frustration. 'Let's get this over.'

She had expected heavy-duty gates, but these were for ornament rather than security. They swung open under Devlin's hand. He slid the thin probe he'd intended for the padlock back into his pocket and waved Kaz through.

'Well, at least that takes care of explaining to strangers how we came to break into their house.' Devlin slid back into the car and peered through the windscreen. 'This way for Bluebeard's Castle.'

The car crunched along a narrow drive, edged with bushes and shrubs. Kaz tried not to be diverted by the sights on either side. She'd remembered a write-up of the villa in *The Garden* magazine. It had belonged to an English plantsman before the First World War. 'Which will give me a reason for being here, if they do turn out to be strangers.' Devlin only grunted in response, but she felt some of the tension leach out of him. '*Do* you have a gun?'

'What do you think?'

Kaz cast a sideways look at him. 'Don't shoot the first thing that comes running out. It might be me.'

The car crawled forward.

'Stop!'

Alarmed, Kaz trod on the brake. Devlin winced as the car jerked.

'Did you see something?' She was craning to look round.

'No. This is where I get out.' He gestured ahead. The

foliage cover was thinning in front of them. 'Better if you go on alone.'

He took a quick, professional look round. Checking for cameras in the shrubbery? 'Leave the car somewhere conspicuous up front and don't take the keys.' He pulled her close. The kiss this time was long and deep. When he let go, she tried to control the trembling.

'We can still turn round and go back.' He gestured to the passing place alongside. When she shook her head he cursed softly. 'Go on then.' He had the car door open and his feet on the ground. 'Go. Do what you have to do. And if you need me, *use the phone*.'

He'd faded into the bushes before she had the car moving again.

The drive ended in a wide sweep of dusty, compacted ground. Kaz turned the car to face back the way she had come, before getting out.

The house was big and imposing, approached by a terrace with two sets of steps, flanked by statues. Sea gods and monsters, as far as she could tell. There was a jumble of outbuildings, garages and what looked like a dovecote. And behind that the tower they'd seen from the lake. A plantation of citrus and olive trees stretched away to the side of the house.

Kaz reached for the car keys then, remembering, left them where they were. She got out slowly and leaned against the car. She'd come to the right place. A woman had come out onto the terrace, with a watering can in her hand. Kaz walked forward.

'Hello, Valentina. Is my father around?'

Chapter Fifty

Devlin had found a vantage point, just on the edge of the foliage cover. It would have relieved his nerves to stay with Kaz and wait in the car for her. But if her father was holed up here, Kaz arriving alone was one thing, arriving with *him* in the passenger seat was something else entirely.

This was hardly a covert op, but old habits were harder to kill than rats.

'Good girl,' he approved softly as Kaz turned the car. She was getting out. Leaning against the car. The slim woman in black, who had just come out of the house, put down her watering can and was descending the steps. Devlin watched her hesitate, then reach out to embrace Kaz and lead her inside.

Valentina? Oliver's latest mistress and mother of Kaz's half-sister? Who else could it be?

Showtime.

Kaz fought to keep her mind on her surroundings, not on her pounding heart. The proportions and construction materials of the villa were beautiful. She saw glimpses of mellow stone and marble, with pale wood and gilding. The understated furnishings, in soft shades of ivory and sand, let the paintings and sculptures sing.

Kaz caught her breath, swallowing a sudden rush of tears, as they passed a portrait of her mother, holding a mirror. She concentrated instead on the woman ahead of her. Her mother's replacement.

Even as the thought came, Kaz dismissed it. Valentina hadn't arrived on the scene until long after Suzanne had packed her bags. Kaz studied the young woman who was walking slightly ahead of her. They were almost the same age. It was Valentina's taste that had arranged these rooms and hung these pictures. She'd made a home for Oliver and her small daughter. The scatter of toys under tables and a familiar children's book, abandoned face down on a chair, brought a lump to Kaz's throat. She focused again on Valentina.

The woman didn't look well. The chic linen top and narrow-legged jeans hung on her, as if she had lost weight, and her movements were jerky and nervous. Kaz remembered meeting a blooming young girl, shy but exultant at her conquest of a great man. They'd dined at The Ivy and Oliver had scarcely been able to keep his eyes, or his hands, off her.

Was living with Oliver taking its toll?

They'd reached a small drawing room, giving onto a second terrace which overlooked the lake.

Valentina gestured to a chair. 'Sit, please.' She gave Kaz a hesitant smile. 'I will tell Oliver that you are here. Help yourself to a drink.'

Left alone, Kaz poured a small glass from a pitcher of orange juice and drifted out of the terrace doors and over to the balustrade. Clear water lapped on a small pebble beach below, stirred by passing boats and the wake of the ferries. Nothing else moved in the gardens on either side of the building.

Devlin was somewhere out there. Kaz fingered the phone in her pocket. In most households a visiting daughter would not have been kept waiting in an ante-room while her father was asked if he wanted to see her. In most households a daughter didn't arrive with the intention of accusing her father of murder. Kaz's shoulders sagged a little. Even now, she didn't have to do this.

Minutes passed. Kaz finished her juice and looked at her watch. Her father would know by now that she was here.

A boat skimmed close to the shore. The wash made choppy waves on the tiny beach. Oliver was taking his time, deciding if he would see her. Would he really refuse?

There was a sound behind her. She spun round. Valentina was coming back. The woman was smiling. Somehow it made her face look even more haggard. 'Oliver is in his studio. Would you like to come up?'

It was shady in the lee of the garage block, but Devlin could feel sweat on his back. He was standing downwind of an enormous urn of pink lilies. The heavy scent caught in his throat. The urge to reconnoitre was another hard habit to break. Restless, once the two women had disappeared from view, he'd penetrated further into the outbuildings, towards the back of the villa. More than half his mind was with Kaz in the house. Not a good move, but he just couldn't help it. He took out his phone, to make sure it was still on, then stuck it back in the pocket of his jeans. Should he go back and wait near the car? Or take a longer look around?

Curiosity won. Once Oliver knew that Kaz was here, the surprise card had been played. Secrecy didn't really matter. Even so, he moved cautiously out of the shade.

Ahead of him was a small, squat tower, built of yellowing brick. It looked as if it was older than the villa. An exterior staircase led up to a door at the top. Devlin walked round it, and found two heavy doors, big enough to take a cart, on the other side. Some sort of storage tower?

The doors at ground level didn't look as if they'd been opened in years, but there were new windows under the roof and they were all open. Intrigued, Devlin went back to the steps and began to climb.

The door at the top had been fastened on the outside by the simple expedient of stuffing a metal rod through the handle. Devlin took it out and shoved it in his pocket.

The door swung inwards silently. The familiar smell of oil paint came to meet him. A quick burst of panic flared, before reason reasserted itself. Unlikely that anyone would be locking Oliver Kessel into his own studio. So what was going on here?

Inside the door was a small hallway and another set of steps. The walls and the treads were freshly plastered and painted white. A high, narrow window gave a glittering view over the lake.

Devlin waited for a moment, listening. There was a small scraping noise from above, then a silence that sounded like someone holding their breath. Devlin hesitated, then propped open the door behind him with a doorstop shaped like a shell, that he found in the hallway. He turned back to the inner stair.

'Katarina. Such a surprise. How lovely to see you.'

Oliver was leaning elegantly, hands propped behind him, on a high stool in the centre of the room. Relaxed, casual, the great man at leisure in his studio, in front of his easel. Kaz halted a few feet away from him. She couldn't make herself go any further. Valentina had opened the door and ushered her through, then left them.

She was alone with her father.

Every muscle in her body tensed. She felt as if she were standing on the tips of her toes, even though she knew her feet were flat on the floor. She hadn't planned what she was going to say, just trusted to the moment. Now she was here, there was only one thing she could say. Only one question capable of being asked. She had to get the words out, before they choked her. This man …

'You must know why I'm here.' Her voice came out in a harsh croak. 'I want to know how my daughter died.'

'Katarina!'

His face was a masterpiece of control – no expression, except maybe a hint of concerned bewilderment, but she got what she was looking for in his eyes – a tiny flicker of fear. Relief flooded through her, followed by searing pain.

It's all true.

'My dear.' He was leaning forward. 'What do you mean? What's happened to you? You know how Jamie died –'

'I know what you wanted me to believe, what you set up for me to believe. Jamie didn't die in a car crash. She died here, after you abducted her.' She took a step closer and then another. 'How did my little girl die?'

He reared back as she approached, swaying slightly, eyes widening. 'Katarina, you clearly don't know what you're saying. This is wild talk. You need help –'

'I know everything. About Jeff and Phil and the child you had killed in Jamie's place – Sally Ann Cheska. Did you even know her name?'

'Stop!' Oliver put a hand out, only to draw it back. 'This is outrageous. You're talking nonsense!'

Kaz stared, hearing the outrage and denials, but searching instead, in his expression, for evidence. And finding it.

He was playing injured surprise to perfection, but something in his posture had changed. The facade was falling in; cracking with every accusation she threw at him. A savage joy leapt horribly in her chest, as she took another pace closer.

From the pocket of her dress, her mobile phone began to warble.

The staircase came out on the edge of a circular room. There was no ceiling, just the roof of the tower, lined in wood. Light spilled in through a series of shallow windows. All of them were open, admitting the faint breeze that came off the lake to cool the air. The room appeared to be empty.

Devlin took all this in, during one assessing glance. It was the furniture in the room that took his attention. At first he couldn't make sense of what he was seeing. It looked like an artist's studio that had been miniaturised. A tiny easel, low tables holding paint and equipment. Then he got it. Not miniature, child-size. He moved slowly into the room, hands at his sides, shoulders relaxed, every sense at the stretch. When he came to the middle of the room he stopped and listened.

It was the smallest of movements, but he traced the source immediately. There was a heap of cushions piled against the curve of the wall. He made straight for them, before swinging round, at the last moment, in a ninety-degree turn.

There was a squeal and clatter.

Crouched at the end of the equipment table, dark eyes wide with alarm, her mother's eyes, was Jamie Elmore.

Chapter Fifty-One

The child was dead, twice over. It didn't make sense, but his eyes weren't lying. It was Kaz's daughter cowering in front of him.

'Oh, shit.' Devlin could hear Kaz's voice, whispering in his ear. 'What do you know about five-year-old girls?'

The little girl's eyes had travelled up his whole height and back down again. Now they were getting wider. Any second and she was going to scream. Shoving down panic, Devlin put his finger to his lips.

The scream got swallowed, but not forgotten. The small head tilted, in a heartbreaking echo of her mother. Pulling in a shaky breath, Devlin marshalled his scattered wits.

He could do this. It was female. Pint-size but still female. Although the usual passwords, Manolo Blahnik, diamond earrings, weekend in Paris, weren't going to work here. He'd just have to go with charm.

He hunkered down, careful to keep his distance, and tried out a smile. He got a wary, watery grimace in response.

'You're Jamie, aren't you? Hi. I'm Devlin.'

Ah! He'd established some credentials by knowing her name. The tension in the small shoulders slackened a fraction. 'I'm a friend of your mom's, your mummy,' he corrected quickly. 'She and your grandma, Suzanne, they asked me to help them find you.'

'My mummy is here?' Heartbreaking hope lit the little face. Devlin gritted his teeth. The child was stretched so thin, even an unpromising stranger looked like salvation.

'Yes,' he said carefully. 'You want to go look for her? She's just gone to talk to your granddad.'

Bad move. The child's lower lip trembled. 'I'm not C'ara. And I don't want to paint any more pictures.'

Devlin rode out the fierce stab of anger, schooling his face and body. If the kid caught even a glimmer his credibility would be fried. She'd think it was aimed at her. When he could trust himself. 'You don't have to paint, if you don't want to.'

She'd shut her eyes and screwed them up tight. Maybe it was meant to make her invisible. One of them blinked open, cautious. 'You promise? You'll tell Grandpa?'

'I'll tell him. Cross my heart.' Devlin did it, solemnly.

Oliver Kessel was 66 years old, and a genius, and the father of the woman he loved. He might still lose a few teeth when Devlin found him.

Jamie had both eyes open now, looking speculatively up at him. He held out his hand, palm up.

'What say we go find your mummy's car? You can sit in the back seat. I'll go get your mom and it'll be a big surprise.'

Jamie thought about it. 'If I *hide* in the car, then no one will know I'm there. Not Grandpa, or Valentina, or Guido or anyone, except Mummy, when she comes. And you,' she added after second. 'But that's cool.'

Devlin felt as if someone had pinned a medal on his chest. He turned a choke into a cough when the child fixed a beady stare on him, the exact same way her mother did.

You're losing it, Devlin.

Hah! He'd been losing it ever since he met Kaz Elmore.

Jamie was waiting for his opinion. 'That sounds good.' He hustled to provide some input. 'There's a rug. You could hide under the rug.'

She was getting to her feet. 'We'll go now,' she decided.

Devlin looked towards the staircase. Narrow and steep. Not a good place to meet someone else coming up. The faster they got out of here, the better. 'You think it would be okay if I carried you down to the car?'

She thought, head on one side. 'I won't be too heavy? Mummy says I'm heavy.'

'You won't be for me. I'm a big kind of guy.'

'Yes.' Jamie's eyes widened again, clearly remembering her initial inspection of him. 'But you have a bad arm.' She pointed to the cast.

'I do, but it only goes up a little way.' He showed her. She touched the cast and then his arm. 'Okay.'

Negotiation completed, she stood still and waited to be picked up. Devlin scooped her into the crook of his arm, next to his shoulder. She smelt of paint and something sweet. Now they were at eye level. She was taking an inventory of his face. He remembered the bruises, but they didn't seem to be what was on her mind.

'You come from America?'

'That's where I live,' he agreed.

'That's nice. I want to go to Disneyland,' she confided. 'Have you ever been there?'

'No.' Was this going to jeopardise his street cred? Apparently not.

'Maybe you could come with Mummy and me,' she suggested.

'I'd like that.'

'Good,' she confirmed, with the air of settling a bargain. Then in the same tone she dropped the bomb. 'Are you in love with my mummy?'

Devlin's heart stuttered. Jesus! To the point. Forensic. Just like her mother.

He swallowed, floundering. She was frowning, right into his eyes. *Oh, what the hell.*

'Yes.' It felt good to say it, even to a five-year-old. 'I am, but I haven't told her yet.' He paused. 'That's our secret. Okay with you?'

'You'll take care of her?'

'When she'll let me.'

Jamie weighed the answer. 'That's all right then.' With a blinding smile, she pointed to the stairs. 'Let's go and find her.'

'Hadn't you better answer that?'

All Kaz could feel was rage. With a shaking hand she reached for the phone, to flip it off. The mood was broken. She'd had Oliver on the run. Now he was laughing at her.

The second before she pushed the switch, to stop the phone's demanding crow, realisation hit her. Sweat coated her palms.

Devlin.

New phone. Who else could it be? Devlin must need her.

She snatched the slim cell to her ear, almost sending it skittering across the floor in her slick-palmed haste.

'Kaz? Is that you?'

'Oh, God, not now, Mum.'

'Your father is there.' Suzanne understood at once, but her voice was sharp. 'Don't cut me off. You need to hear this. The Italian police just rang. They have the detailed forensic results from that poor child in the field. The DNA was close, but it *wasn't* a match. And the body had definitely been moved to the vineyard. The child didn't die there, and it wasn't Jamie.'

In a small part of her mind Kaz felt the phone drop out of her hand and heard it hit the floor. Emotions were fighting each other in her chest and her brain. Joy, amazement and a bone-crunching, teeth-wrenching anger, that launched her straight at Oliver's throat.

Chair and man went flying. 'You bastard! Who else did you kill?'

When the easel crashed, Kaz pulled up short, shuddering for breath, staring down at her father. He was lying at her feet, trying to find a handhold on the closest bench and drag himself upright. Without thought or ceremony, she grabbed him by the collar and hauled him up, propping him against the bench.

'My daughter is *here*. You killed *another* child. Oh, God.' Her hand went to her mouth. 'Chiara, my sister. You killed Valentina's daughter and put her in that field.'

Oliver had his hand to his head. Blood was oozing from a small cut beside his eye. He dabbed ineffectually at it, hand trembling. He looked dazed. Gaping at her. Poise and resistance gone. 'It should have worked. Luce said the DNA would be close enough, everyone would assume –'

'They did, at first, but the police weren't satisfied. My God, I don't believe I'm having this conversation.' Kaz spun round, paced away and paced back. Oliver hung on to the bench, pale-faced. Somewhere a door slammed. 'You did this, just to hold on to my daughter. You took her from me, just so that you could teach her to paint. You're insane.'

'No,' Oliver barked the word, voice suddenly strong. Kaz jerked her head. 'Not insane. Desperate. Look at me, Katarina. Really look.' He reached out and took a handful of her sleeve, forcing her to turn towards him.

Kaz looked up into his face. Seeing the profile that was more familiar from photographs than in the flesh. Oliver looked as he always did. Older, maybe more tired. The face was thinner and curiously blank, the eyes a little sunken … with something hovering in their depths.

With a cold bolt of fear, Kaz finally understood.

'What is it? Cancer?' she breathed

'I wish.' Oliver gave a harsh laugh. 'Parkinson's Disease. A perfect, ironic gift from the fates, don't you think? An artist who can't hold a brush steady?' He held his hand out. 'Look. It's not bad, not yet. You can barely see it. I can still control a pencil. But it won't last.'

'Oh, God.' Kaz raked her hand through her hair. 'Look – there are drugs, advances all the time – you can afford the best that money can buy. People live for years –'

'Live! Live! I don't just want to *live*! I want to *create*. I am *Olivier Kessel*. I'm not just *people*.' Oliver's voice was a vehement, escalating hiss. 'Drugs? That's what the doctors said. With their hearty, back-slapping stupidity. *There, there old man*,' he mimicked. '*Soon get you sorted out – a bit less daubing on the canvas, but we all have to retire some day.* Idiots! What do I want with their drugs? Miserable placebos, for credulous fools! The whole world laughing at me. *Me!*'

He took a step forward. Kaz held her ground and looked into the stare of madness.

'I have to show them. The work has to go on. Before it's too late.' He shut his eyes, swaying where he stood for a second. When he opened them, some of the fire had dissipated. Instead there was a sly, secretive look. 'And after me, a successor. The Kessel name will go on. That's why I need Jamie.'

'You killed all those people to get her.' Kaz heard her voice sounding gritty, like a stranger's. 'Even your own daughter.'

'Yes, I killed her.' Oliver's head came up. 'After the crash. As soon as I knew Jamie was mine. I was desperate.' Now the voice was toneless, energy ebbing. 'You have no idea what it's like, to have all these images in your head, fighting to get out, knowing that a lifetime isn't going to be long enough. And then to find you won't even have that. That you're going to be trapped in a useless, rotting body, with the pictures screaming to escape.' His tone roughened. 'I killed her, and I put your daughter in her place. I'd do it again tomorrow. She's perfect, Katarina.' His eyes began to glow again, manic. 'So much talent. She will be greater even than I am. I know it.' He splayed his hand to his chest. 'The other one.' He shrugged. 'I had hopes, when she was born.

But she was useless. She wasn't even quiet, like you were. Noisy, destructive ...' He looked puzzled. 'I didn't think that Valentina would take it so hard. I bought her a pearl necklace.'

'A necklace?' Kaz felt bile rise in her throat. 'That was supposed to replace her daughter? Buy her off?'

'Not buy her off.' Oliver seemed genuinely confused. 'She didn't know. I told her the child died in her sleep. She believed me. She always believes me. I told her what the authorities would do to her daughter's body if we handed it over. That they'd mutilate it, in their arrogance, in the name of their stupid science. We buried her under the olive trees. Valentina thinks she's still there. She goes out every day to sit with her. I explained it all to her. Her daughter was dead, but now she had Jamie, to take her place. Jamie would *be* Chiara. My daughter. My *new* daughter. Your child.' He stared at Kaz. 'My power, my talent, living on. We could still do that. You could stay here. We could do this ...'

Kaz wondered if she was going to be sick. Oliver was rambling now. Talking not to her but to himself. She was listening to the voice of a madman.

Sweat was trickling down her face and across her ribs. The air in the room was stuffy. Suddenly Kaz couldn't breathe. There was a roaring in her ears.

It took a second for her to realise that the noise wasn't in her head. She wasn't fainting. All she was feeling was real. *Oh, no.*

She put her hand out, to jerk Oliver back to planet earth. 'Dad, I think we have to –'

'Katarina.' His face cleared and focused. 'You have to leave Jamie with me,' he said earnestly. 'I need to teach her. She's mine now. I have to keep her!'

'Dad –' Kaz dragged at his arm. 'We have to get out of here. I think something's on fire.'

She could smell it now, and see it, wisps of smoke threading across the floor. Oh, God. An artist's studio. Solvents and oils, paint-stained rags. A small explosion sent a rush of heat across her back. She swung away from Oliver, eyes darting frantically. The door behind them, open onto a small antechamber, the way she had come in, was already blocked. Smoke was writhing around the frame. She could see something beyond. A bucket or a paint tin, dancing with flames. And beyond that a pile of smouldering canvasses.

'Another way out?' She yanked at Oliver's arm, shaking him. He had begun to cough. 'Which way?'

'There.'

Kaz's heart spiked in relief as she saw the second door, untouched by any flame. 'Come on.'

Herding Oliver, dragging him when he stumbled, she scrambled to safety.

They were a foot away when the door ricocheted open, bouncing against the wall. Behind them the fire roared, fed with a new supply of air.

Valentina was standing in the doorway, with a shotgun in her hands.

Chapter Fifty-Two

The woman's face was a mask of pain. Kaz recoiled instinctively. Heat battered on her shoulder blades. 'Valentina, you have to let us out. The fire –' Kaz gestured behind her. *If the fire spread to the draperies, pinned to the walls and ceiling of the studio. If the flames flashed over …*

'You can go.' Valentina glanced at her briefly. All her attention was fixed on Oliver. 'You *must* go. Save your daughter. Your *child.*' She let out a howl that was more animal than human. Tears were coursing down her cheeks. 'You killed her, my bella Chiara, my light, my angel.' She was crooning, but the gun was steady, pointing straight at Oliver's chest.

'Stop this!'

Kaz turned, startled, feeling the heat now on the skin of her face.

Oliver had hauled himself to his full height, jaw set, eyes fixed 'Let us pass, woman.'

All he got was a shake of the head. 'You will burn. First here, then in hell.' Valentina sounded quite confident about it. 'With me. My angel, she will be in heaven.'

Kaz bit her lip as she saw the fight go out of Oliver. His spine sagged and the light in his eyes faded. His face was bathed in sweat.

'Go, Katarina.' His voice was urgent, though he was coughing again. Kaz felt her chest tightening. 'The tower. Save Jamie.'

Valentina took a sideways step, opening the doorway to let her pass. The gun was still pointing at Oliver. Kaz took a small shallow breath. She could try to take the woman down, but they both might get damaged in the process.

Or the gun might go off. Or both. Then the fire would get them. They would all die.

Oliver was on one side of her, Valentina on the other. A mad man and a woman crazed by grief, locked in a battle over a dead child. She could stay and try to part them or she could go and find her daughter and get help. With a half-strangled prayer for some sort of forgiveness, she stepped past Valentina. The woman didn't look at her. Oliver's face showed her nothing but relief. 'Find Jamie.' She saw him mouth the words. The flames were flaring behind him, hot and ragged.

She turned and ran.

Chapter Fifty-Three

Kaz fell twice on the way down. She arrived, sobbing for breath, at the main door, with grazed knees and elbows. She hauled the door open and fell out onto the terrace. Oh, God, more steps. She grabbed an urn, swaying drunkenly, gasping down air.

The terrace and garden were deserted. On this side of the building there was no sign of the fire. Just a roaring, that might have been in her ears, and the faint smell of smoke. She might have been alone on a stage set. The car was standing on the sweep of the drive, where she had left it.

And Devlin was straightening up, away from the back door. Relief almost pitched her over on her face. She slithered forward and hurtled down the steps.

'Kaz!' Devlin caught her as she fell off the last two, into his arms. 'What the heck – ' She gestured, panting too much to speak.

Above them there was an abrupt explosion. Flame and smoke billowed out of the windows under the eaves. She felt Devlin's muscles tense, already primed for the stairs.

'Valentina has Oliver up there. He killed her daughter. Jamie is alive.' She cast wildly round. 'We have to find her.' She was clinging to Devlin, fighting for breath.

The rear door of the car creaked open, propelled by a small hand. 'Mummy?'

'Oh, God, baby!' Kaz stumbled forward. 'You found her.' Kaz had one hand on Devlin and the other outstretched to her daughter. Tears began to spill.

Devlin kissed her hard and swift on the lips, and shoved the car keys into her hand. 'Get out quick, fast as you can. It's not safe here.' He looked up at the pluming smoke.

'Get help. I'm going up.' He was already half-way to the terrace.

'Valentina has a shotgun,' Kaz yelled after him.

He made a sign to show that he'd heard, before plunging through the main door to the villa.

Kaz turned towards the car. Jamie had tumbled out, and wound herself around her mother's legs. Kaz gathered her up into her arms, covering her face with kisses. 'We have to go, sweetheart.' She hurried her back into the car and ran round to the driver's side. She could hear the sound of sirens. Someone had seen the smoke. She started the engine and rammed the car into gear.

The sirens were getting closer. If she left now, she would meet them head on in the narrow space near the gate. There was a grassed area on the other side of the drive, half-sheltered by young trees; safe from flame and falling masonry. Kaz pulled into it and stopped the engine. Swinging round she leaned over the seat to her daughter. 'Granddad's house is on fire, sweetheart. There will be lots of people and fire engines. We just have to sit quietly here while they put the fire out.' She slid out of the car and into the back seat to cuddle her daughter.

'Where are the fire engines? Can I look at them?' Jamie bounced on the seat, ready to scramble up to the back window.

Kaz bit her lip. 'I don't think they're here yet, sweetie, but listen, you can hear them.' The sirens sounded even nearer now. She twisted round. The little she could see of the front of the house was unscathed. There was no sign of Devlin. She tried to relax the tension in her body, but Jamie had already picked it up. Her small, beloved face screwed up into a frown. 'Where's Mr Devlin? Is he fighting the fire?'

'He's doing what he can, yes.'

Jamie eyed her carefully. 'I think you should go and help Mr Devlin,' she pronounced solemnly.

'No, sweetie.' Kaz hugged her close. 'Mr Devlin can take care of himself.'

Jamie was shaking her head. Her jaw jutted mutinously. 'I want you to go and find Mr Devlin. I *like* Mr Devlin.'

Kaz looked down helplessly at her daughter. Another Elmore female under the Devlin spell. She tried again, 'Wouldn't you rather I stayed here –'

Jamie's headshake got even fiercer. 'You go and help Mr Devlin.'

'Oh, darling.' Kaz didn't know whether she was laughing or crying. She held her daughter close, dropping a kiss on the dark head, then let go. 'Just for a minute then.'

She was half-way out of the car when she remembered. She dived into her bag, rummaging in the depths.

'Patchy!' Jamie let out a crow of delight when she saw the splayed-legged, piebald horse. Kaz hugged them both. 'You look after Patchy and he'll look after you.' She kissed her daughter again. 'I'll be quick as I can. You stay in the car now.'

'Yes, Mummy.' Jamie curled up, cuddling the toy horse, already whispering her adventures into his ear. Kaz carried the image of her smile as she quickly crossed the drive.

In the moments that she'd been with Jamie, everything had got a whole lot worse. Flames were licking all around the top of the building. Muffled explosions flared over the roar of the blaze. She stuffed her hands in her mouth as a plume of fire flashed suddenly out of one of the windows. Glass cracked and pattered on the stones of the terrace. Thank God she'd moved the car. She cast a glance over her shoulder. It, and its precious cargo, stood serenely, guarded by the trees.

When she looked back, Devlin, smoke-stained and coughing, was shouldering open the main door. He had Valentina in his arms. Kaz leaped forward to help him carry her down the steps and across the drive, to lay her on the grass behind the car.

'Is it smoke inhalation?' Kaz bent over the unconscious woman.

'Some.' Devlin dropped onto the grass, head between his knees, breath rasping. 'She wasn't planning on leaving. I had to persuade her.'

'Oh.' Kaz could see the small round bruise coming up on Valentina's jaw. 'Oliver?'

'He wouldn't come, either.' Even in the midst of chaos the disgust in Devlin's tone almost sent a quiver of laughter through her. 'He was trying to pull canvases away from the flames.'

Devlin's breathing had settled. He looked up at the car, shielded by the trees. 'You didn't get far.'

'I was afraid of meeting the fire brigade coming up.'

Devlin nodded. 'Jamie OK?'

Kaz followed his glance. No sign of a small face at the window. 'Yes.' *Thank heaven for Patchy.*

Devlin was heaving himself to his feet. 'I have to go back. Christ!'

A fire engine was making its way up the last section of the drive, but that wasn't what had Devlin's attention. He was looking up.

Above them Oliver was inching his way along a ledge, beside the villa's turret. He had a picture under his arm and the shotgun in his hand.

Kaz was dimly aware of men tumbling from the vehicle, of orders being shouted and equipment marshalled. Her eyes were riveted to the tableau above her. Oliver had reached the widest part of the ledge. He stopped.

Kaz bit down on her lip and ground her nails into her palm as he swayed dangerously. She felt a touch on her leg and looked down in panic. Surely Jamie –

Valentina was struggling to get up. Kaz dragged her to her feet, but didn't let go. The woman's face was ashen, eyes drenched with fear and pain. They clung together, mesmerised by what was playing out above them.

Oliver had the picture clutched to his chest. The gun waved wildly for a moment, threatening to overbalance him.

'The illness ... his hand trembles,' Valentina breathed in Kaz's ear. The woman's body was rigid in her arms.

Oliver had the gun under control. Kaz felt the churning in her stomach ease. He was going to throw it and the painting down.

Behind them ladders were being broken out. Men in breathing gear were already on the terrace.

Kaz saw it at the same second as Valentina, felt her own and Valentina's indrawn breath. Oliver was tucking the shotgun under his chin. Valentina's hands went up over her eyes. Kaz couldn't move.

With a curse Devlin spun Kaz round, holding her against his chest, as Oliver pulled the trigger.

Chapter Fifty-Four

Kaz wondered if she'd talked to every policeman and fire investigator in Italy.

It felt like it.

The police from Tuscany, investigating Chiara's death, had arrived shortly after the fire engines. Kaz thanked them, with a few tears. Valentina was led away sobbing, in the care of a nurse. Back at the hotel a doctor put salve on her knees and elbows and checked Jamie over, pronouncing them both fit. Various policemen and officials took statements. Devlin disappeared for a while, and came back with a new plaster cast and dressings on his singed hands. Food appeared, and was eaten. Sometime in the evening Suzanne swept in, with a full set of luggage, trailing an old flame in her wake.

'Who else was I going to call, darling?' She winked at Kaz and hugged Jamie fiercely. 'He has a private plane.'

Jamie sat in her mother's lap through it all, until Devlin gently disentangled the sleeping child, to carry her to bed.

Devlin had watched as Kaz fussed, settling her daughter. He'd been uncertain whether the presence of even one near-stranger was appropriate, but Jamie seemed to have accepted him without comment. Briefly he recollected the feel of the child's head, resting against his chest as he carried her down the tower steps, and the small hand, confidingly in his, as she scrambled into the car. He swallowed down what felt like a golf ball lodged in his throat.

They'd eaten room-service pasta together.

Like a family?

Kaz had sat for a while beside her sleeping daughter and Devlin had taken a chair and joined her by the bed. He'd never sat at a child's bedside before. It was one of the most peaceful hours of his entire life.

Now it was midnight. Kaz leaned her weight back into Devlin's arms as they stood near the window, watching the new moon. The police had moved Kaz and Jamie to a small suite of their own. Suzanne was down the hall. With or without the old flame. They hadn't asked.

Jamie was fast asleep, barely visible in the wide bed. One of Suzanne's cases had contained every soft toy she'd been able to find in the house in Chelsea, but Patchy still had pride of place on the pillow.

Kaz shivered and Devlin held her a little tighter.

'What the hell happened today? Why did he do it? Because I was taking Jamie?' she asked softly.

Devlin moved restlessly against her body, then forced himself to be still. 'He did it because he'd schemed and cheated and killed, not once, but over and over – he was obsessed, Kaz. This has nothing to do with you.'

'You think?'

'I *know*.' He kissed the top of her head. 'You didn't give up and you have your daughter back and she'll grow up with a proper childhood and she'll paint if she wants to. Or not.' Kaz looked up over her shoulder, clearly puzzled at his vehemence. 'What was the alternative?' he asked softly. 'Oliver gets away with a trail of killing? He knew it was all over, Kaz. He was a sick man, whose scheme had fallen apart. What else was there for him?' Devlin shifted his grip, wrapping his arm around Kaz's waist. 'I think he'd made up his mind what he was going to do, before I got up to the studio. He wasn't trying to save the paintings, he was hunting for one. The one he was holding when he fell. It was a portrait of your mother, Kaz, with you in her arms, when you were a baby. Perhaps he'd finally realised what he was and what he'd done and decided to end it – on his own terms.'

'I …' Kaz sighed. 'I still can't believe …'

'He killed his own daughter, Kaz. That was always Oliver's plan – to substitute the gifted child for the unwanted one. In time, Jamie would have become Chiara.' Maybe. A small, defiant face drifted across his memory.

'That poor woman – she was kind to Jamie.' Kaz looked towards the bed. 'Jamie said she cried a lot.'

'She overheard what he said to you, about her daughter. She set the fire. The investigators were quite clear that it was started deliberately.'

'Destroying Oliver, and all his work?'

'Those she could get at. There was a time lock on the cellar.'

'If he'd explained to me, about his illness –'

'*Don't* go there.' Devlin turned her round, to face him. 'Would you really have handed Jamie over to him, because that's what he would have demanded?'

'The whole thing …' Kaz shook her head. 'How much could he have taught her, in the time he had left?'

'I don't know if it was just about teaching her.' Devlin had been thinking about it. 'There's been speculation lately about a new Kessel style, a new kind of naivety. I think he may have intended to pass Jamie's work off as his own.'

Kaz buried her face in Devlin's chest. He stroked her hair.

'When Oliver found out he was ill, he planned it all,' he said, into the soft curls. 'Jamie's death was staged, so she could be taken from you. Chiara was killed and her death was hidden, so Jamie could be put in her place. Then everyone else who might uncover or reveal anything was systematically eliminated. Oliver and Luce even used Chiara's body. They moved it, to throw everyone off the scent. It could have worked.'

'The only people he didn't get were you and me.'

'Mmm.' Devlin had his own theory on that. That Oliver Kessel had maybe valued his elder daughter more than she realised.

'I still can't believe he's gone.' Kaz straightened up. 'There's going be a hell of a lot of sorting out to do. And the press …' Her voice quivered to a stop.

'At the moment, the police are going with tragic accident. Once Valentina is fit to question, there may be charges. It depends on her mental state. You don't have to think about it yet. And when you do … You could give Giles Pugh his exclusive.'

'So I could.'

Kaz slid from his arms, crossing the room to the bed to bend close and kiss her daughter's cheek, unable to keep from touching her for too long. 'He gave her back to me.' She looked up at Devlin. 'Those were the last words he said. *Find Jamie.*'

She sat beside her daughter on the bed, curling her legs under her. Devlin stood, looking on. The small form was sprawled across the toy-strewn bed. Her hair had fallen over her face, like her mother's did, and she was sucking her thumb. Maybe later there would be shrinks and therapists, but right now Jamie Elmore looked like she was doing fine. Resilient, like her mother.

Kaz looked up, apparently aware of his stillness. 'I think I'll sit here with her, for a while.'

'Fine.' Devlin moved over, kissing her briefly on the lips. 'Don't sit up too long.'

'Not too long,' she agreed, eyes already back on her daughter's face.

There wasn't much to pack. He had it all in a bag in less than ten minutes.

He'd done what he set out to do. Kaz had her child back. They were a family again. He didn't do families. *Never learned how.*

All that was left for him to do was leave.

He stood for a while, looking at the door. The way out was that way. He'd promised the kid ... He'd promised the kid to take care of her mom. Best way to do that was let them both get on with their lives. *Without him.*

He stared at the door some more. Jamie Elmore was going home, with her mother, who loved her. He shut his eyes, just for a second, thinking of a child, dwarfed by a huge bed, and the woman who sat beside her, watching. And the most peaceful hour of his life.

When he was done, he went down the corridor to knock on Suzanne's door. She took a moment to answer. When she saw him, and the bag at his feet, she let the door swing wide and stepped back. There was no sign of the old flame he noted, in the part of his brain that wasn't solidifying into a dark grey lump of misery. And that was nothing compared to the pain in his chest.

'You're leaving.' Suzanne's voice was flat.

'What else can I do? Kaz has her daughter back. She has everything she needs. That doesn't include me.'

'Have you asked her that?'

'No. And I don't intend to. I'm not a settling-down kind of guy.' He tried a smile. He could see from Suzanne's face that she wasn't impressed.

'You love her, don't you?'

Devlin shook his head, tongue between his teeth.

'Oh, yes. I know,' Suzanne accused. 'Torture wouldn't get it out of you.' She sighed. 'Has it occurred to you that Kaz wouldn't care who you are, or what you've been?'

'I care.'

Suzanne gave him a long look. 'Yes, you do.' She raised her hand. 'Go then. If you think it's right.'

'It has to be.' He picked up the bag and headed for the door. 'Tell her goodbye for me.'

Chapter Fifty-Five

London, two weeks later

'I don't understand how a man can just melt into thin air.' Kaz pushed aside her preliminary doodles for a new commission. The sparkling water feature was coming out more like a gloomy duck pond.

'It's what he does.' Susanne was standing by the table, leafing through a magazine . She tapped a picture of a model wearing what appeared to be a bright-blue space suit. 'Do you really think we'll be wearing *that* this winter?'

'I don't know and I don't care.' Kaz took the magazine out of her mother's hands. 'Listen to me, when I'm whining at you.'

Suzanne sat down on the sofa and folded her arms. 'He didn't want to intrude on you and Jamie. That's why he left.'

'Intrude!' Kaz poked a cushion. 'It feels like running away to me. He wasn't prepared to take on a woman with a child. Which is fine, because I didn't ask him to.'

'But did you *want* him to?' Kaz contemplated throwing the cushion at her mother, but picked at the fringe instead. 'What did you think was going to happen?' Suzanne quizzed softly, when her daughter didn't answer. 'That Devlin was going to stick around? Audition as husband material?' Suzanne made a face. 'Kaz, that is not the man he is, and you know it. I doubt if Devlin has ever had a fully functioning relationship with a woman – head, heart … and the other thing,' she improvised quickly, when she saw her daughter's expression. 'Which doesn't mean he can't, but he doesn't know that. He doesn't believe that a woman would take him on, regardless of his past. And you are so pathologically afraid of being dependent on someone, *you* won't admit when you've latched onto a good thing. Neither of you is prepared to commit. To open up to each other and take a chance.'

'And that's your take on it, is it?' Kaz glared at her mother.

'It is. For what it's worth.' Susanne sighed. 'No charge for the psychoanalysis.' She took her daughter's hand. 'Kaz, forget common sense and pride for a moment. What's your *heart* telling you?'

'Nothing.' Kaz was studying the arm of the chair as if it was about to do something amazing. 'Devlin and I had a fling. It was never meant to be more than that. I'm just mad at him, because he didn't bother to say goodbye.'

'Oh, darling, it might have been meant to be a fling. But they don't always turn out the way you expect. Believe me, I know.'

Kaz took her hand out of Suzanne's and got to her feet. 'I need to do something about Jamie's tea. Are you staying?'

Suzanne shook her head. 'I have a dinner date.'

Kaz raised her eyebrows. Since Italy, the old flame had been burning pretty bright in her mother's social calendar.

'A least one of us knows a good thing when she sees it,' Suzanne said crisply.

Kaz made a growling noise and headed for the kitchen.

The letter came the next day. When Kaz saw the American postmark her heart did a painful war dance against her ribs.

When she opened it, the wave of disappointment had her reaching for the wall for support.

'Mummy?' Jamie wandered downstairs, dragging Patchy behind her by one leg. Kaz straightened up, to rearrange her face and ruffle her daughter's hair.

'Hello, pet. Want some breakfast?'

'I've had a letter.' Kaz hunched the phone between chin and shoulder, pouring cereal into bowls. Her eyes flickered to the folders and rolled designs stacked on the counter, ready for work. The envelope lay beside them 'Here you go.' She pushed one of the cereal bowls towards Jamie. 'I'm just talking to Grandma,' she explained as Jamie looked up enquiringly. Curiosity satisfied, Jamie dug in her spoon and left her mother to it.

'It's from Mrs Kettle. She's coming to London.' Kaz whisked herself and the phone out of the back door and out of her daughter's earshot. 'Sally Ann Cheska's grandmother. She wants to see where her granddaughter's ashes were scattered.'

Laura Kettle arrived in London in the third week of June and Kaz arranged to take her to the Albert Bridge. It was a lovely bright sunny day.

'I understand why you chose this place.' Mrs Kettle leaned over the parapet, looking down at the water. 'The bridge is pretty, and the river and the boats. So much to see. Everything to appeal to a little girl.'

'I ... I don't know what to say,' Kaz admitted. 'I thought Sally Ann ... I thought it was my daughter.'

'You don't have to worry.' Mrs Kettle turned away from the river. 'Mr Devlin explained everything to me.'

'Devlin! You've seen him? Recently?'

'Why, yes.' Mrs Kettle sounded surprised. 'Just before I wrote you. He came to visit with me. I can't say it wasn't painful, what he had to tell me, but it was best to know.'

'He was holding your granddaughter, when she died.'

'He didn't say, but I kind of thought that he was. It's a comfort to know she wasn't alone. I guess it was a comfort to you, too.'

'Yes. God, this is so weird.'

'Doesn't have to be.' Mrs Kettle put out her arms. After a second, Kaz returned her hug. 'You have a lovely daughter.'

Jamie was waving to them from the Battersea side of the bridge, towing Suzanne towards them.

'Thank you.' Kaz turned. 'I'm sorry for your loss,' she said formally. 'And for my father's part in it.'

Mrs Kettle shook her head. 'Not your fault, honey. The Lord takes, but He gives too. My Luanne, my daughter ... she's pregnant. This babe ... well she swears it's going to be different and I believe her.' Mrs Kettle cast a tentative glance at Kaz. 'It's Bobby Hoag's baby.'

'Bobby ... Devlin's partner?'

Mrs Kettle nodded. 'Seems like he and my Luanne hooked up for a night or two. Mr Devlin told me a bit about how Bobby died. We're not gonna tell Luanne. We agreed, Mr Devlin and me, that it would just be an accident. A road crash in Ireland, on those twisty roads they have there.'

'It sounds ... a good idea.' Kaz bent down as Jamie pelted along the bridge and threw herself at her mother's knees. 'Hey, you!'

'Come and feed the ducks.' Jamie had captured her mother's hand, and stretched the other out to Mrs Kettle. 'We kept some bread.'

They strolled on, to the park. Kaz sat on a bench with Mrs Kettle, watching Jamie and Suzanne throwing pellets of bread to a flurry of ducks.

'Er ... did Devlin say anything about what he was planning to do? Now he's lost his partner?' Kaz asked, after a moment.

'Can't say as he did, though I got the feeling he would be moving on.'

Kaz's heart accelerated uncomfortably.

Jamie danced back to them, and scrambled into her mother's lap.

'Have you been to Disneyland?' she asked Mrs Kettle politely.

'Can't say as I have.'

Jamie beamed at her. 'You can come with me and my mummy and Mr Devlin.' Kaz's knees jerked. Jamie looked up indignantly.

'Sorry, precious, cramp,' Kaz excused herself. 'I don't think that we'll be going to Disneyland any time soon, pet, and certainly not with Mr Devlin.'

'He said he'd like to come,' Jamie refuted, calmly. 'Mr Devlin is in love with my mummy,' she confided to Mrs Kettle, before clapping both hands over her mouth.

Her dismay would have been comic if Kaz's heart hadn't been thumping almost too hard to breathe

'I wasn't supposed to tell. It was supposed to be a secret.' Jamie's fingers twisted on the lapel of her mother's jacket. 'But it's all right, Mummy, because he's going to take care of you, when you let him.'

Chapter Fifty-Six

'What are you doing?'

'What does it look like I'm doing?' Kaz waved a shoe at her mother, before tossing it into the open suitcase. 'I'm going on a manhunt. I can't *believe* that sneaky bastard told my daughter he loved me, and somehow forgot to mention it to me!'

'Jamie probably tortured it out of him.' Suzanne ambled over to look in the case, removing a delicate lace top that was in danger of being snagged by the heels of the shoes. She looked up sideways at Kaz. 'Was it so important? That he should tell you he loved you, before you told him?'

Kaz sat down with a plump on the bed. 'Yes. I didn't know it though, until Jamie said it. I was just so mad. At him, at myself. I spent years trying to live up to Oliver's expectations, and when Jeff came along I threw myself into his arms. I know I did,' she confirmed, when she saw her mother's expression. 'I just *so* didn't want to do it all over again.'

Suzanne sat beside her on the bed. 'But the sneaky bastard got under your defences anyway.'

Kaz looked at her, saucer-eyed for a moment, then burst out laughing. 'He did. And how!' She put her hand up, to brush her eyes. 'I trust him, Mum. It happened, almost from the beginning, but I tried to ignore it. I never expected to say that about a man and especially about a man like him. I don't care what he's done, or what he's been. We're both going to have to deal with baggage. Apart from a tendency to run out on me, he's the most dependable guy I've ever met. If I have to go after him, to convince him of that, then that's what I'll do.' She chewed her lip. 'Will you take care of

Jamie for me? I shouldn't be leaving her so soon, but I have to. I might already be too late. Mrs Kettle told me he was getting ready to move on.'

'In that case the sooner you go, the better.' Suzanne nudged her elbow. 'Leave this, I'll do it. Jamie is still awake. Go and read her a story.'

'Thanks, Mum.' Kaz brushed her lips over her mother's cheek.

'Oh. You might need this.' Suzanne took the card from her pocket. 'Mrs Kettle gave it to me.' She grinned. 'I asked her for it. It's Devlin's address in Chicago. His home, not his office.'

Kaz brushed her daughter's hair away from her face. 'I think you need a haircut, kid.'

Jamie didn't look impressed. She tilted her head and squinted one eye. 'Grandma could take me, when you go to 'merica,' she suggested hopefully. Kaz smiled. The upmarket salon that enjoyed Suzanne's patronage treated young customers like visiting royalty.

'You'll have to ask her.' Kaz sat beside her daughter on the bed, and cuddled her close. 'It's OK, is it? For me to go? You'll be OK with Grandma?'

''course I will.' Jamie was already sorting through the storybooks Kaz had dumped on the bed, picking out her favourite. 'You're going to find Mr Devlin.'

'I'm going to *look* for him.' Kaz took a deep breath, a shiver of cold over her heart. 'He might have gone away.'

'But if he hasn't, you'll find him.' Jamie nodded. 'Patchy and me will look after Grandma,' she informed her mother kindly. 'You don't have to worry about us. You find Mr Devlin, and bring him home.'

Kaz stared out over the wing of the plane, willing it to fly faster. Was she going to be too late? Would Devlin have already disappeared into another life? If they had something, if he really did love her, *could* he walk away? *Of course he can, if he thinks he's doing the right thing. And if he's scared.*

She pondered the thought. Devlin knew even less than she did about holding a family together, and he was carrying so much guilt. A short, fierce burst of anger at Scary Woman and all her works made Kaz grit her teeth. Who had the right to do *that* to a young man, to take away everything he was ...

She watched a cloud drift past. She knew the answer to that one. No one had the right, but because it *was* done, hundreds of thousands of ordinary, normal lives were able to go on, every day. Ordinary men and women, like her, who had no idea what blackness might be out there, and who wouldn't want to know. They just went on living, and men like Devlin took it all into their souls and carried the burden alone.

The man on the seat beside her gave a loud snore. Startled, Kaz jumped, and then giggled. So much for deep, dark thoughts. If she could find Devlin, they would have their own try at being normal. See if they could make this home and family thing work. If she could find him ...

There was nothing she could do, sitting on a plane. She might as well follow her companion's example. She cradled her head in her hand, and settled down to doze.

It was the final box. Devlin stared down into it. He'd left Bobby's office until last and the bottom drawer of the desk, the personal stuff, until the very end. Half a pack of cigarettes, a handful of matchbooks, a well-worn baseball cap, three neckties, a couple of paperback books, a Spanish dictionary. The debris of a life. He hefted the shallow cardboard carton onto the cleared desk, and looked around.

He'd been holding it in all morning, regret and a simmering anger that dripped through his frame like acid. At least that pain was hot – not cold, like the other. Waste. The life of a friend, at the hands of a madman, and now there was another kid growing up without a father, down in Tennessee. Bloody circles – they never stopped. He folded the lid of the box closed and leaned against the desk.

The place was still, with only muffled sounds from the street outside marring the quiet. Most of the furniture was gone already, phones disconnected, the sign on the glass door rubbed clean. If he closed his eyes, he could see Bobby, standing in the doorway, grinning, and smell the smoke from his illicit cigarette, but that was all in his mind. There were no ghosts here, only memories.

It was all finished here. He could be on the road tonight, if he wanted. His life in Chicago was ended. And he was doing what he always did. All he knew. All he'd been taught. Move on and start over. *When it's not broken you don't fix it. But if it's broken beyond repair?* Less than three months, three sodding months, and his whole life had come apart at the seams. If he'd never met Kaz Elmore … If he'd never learned to love her … Then he wouldn't have the searing pain in the centre of his chest. He could manage the days, but the nights –

He leaned back and scrubbed a hand over his face. She hadn't come looking for him. He'd … *hoped* was the wrong word, but he'd kind of *wondered*. She hadn't come, and that was fine, because that really was how it should be. She was tending her child, and her business, and forgetting that any of this had ever happened. One day there'd be another man, a good man, able to give her the things she needed. The ache in his chest, because it wasn't him … He'd just have to get used to it. The need to punch his hand into the wall at the thought of another man in her bed – that was going to take a while to die.

Devlin took one last look from the window. He had a plan, of sorts. He was going to travel. See all the places he'd never seen. Sit on beaches and mountain tops and beside rivers and try not to think of *her*. Eventually the hurt would fade a little. He'd done this before, so he could do it again. And this time it was worth it. The pain might be eating him, from the inside out, but he'd been right to leave her. He was feral. He didn't belong in anyone's home.

But you might have tried.

Maybe he *would* try? He couldn't be a father to Bobby Hoag's baby, or even an uncle, but maybe he could be a friend to Bobby's son. Oh, Christ, maybe it would be a daughter, with her mother's blonde hair and her daddy's eyes.

Children. That's where all this had started. Two children, one with long blonde hair and the other with dark, and an ocean between them. Two young girls, and a need for justice. And now the grief he would always carry, until death finally took him. Love. The silent killer.

He shrugged away from the window, with one last look around. He wouldn't find her here. He wouldn't find her anywhere, not now.

He picked up the box and headed to the door, and the rest of his life.

Kaz unpacked the contents of the suitcase and laid it out on the bed, grinning. Her mother's idea of an outfit for a manhunt included the sleekly fitted lace top, a slimline skirt and killer heels. She slithered into the clothes, twisting her hair up high and anchoring it with a jewelled clip. Her hands were trembling as she fastened the matching necklace. A slick of lip gloss and she was done. She picked up her bag and headed for the door.

She paid the cab at the end of the street, looking around

curiously. She'd expected the address on the card to be an apartment in the city, but this was a neighbourhood of wide lawns and white-painted porches. She recognised Devlin's house immediately. It was the one with the For Sale sign outside.

There was a hire van parked by the kerb. Kaz caught her breath as Devlin emerged from the house, carrying a box. The bruises were healed and the plaster cast had been replaced by a brace on his left arm. The well-worn jeans, faded almost white, clung low on his hips. The writing on his sweatshirt was even more faded. His hair was brushing his collar.

Kaz took a shaky step and then another. 'If you ever run out on me again, Devlin, I'm going to hunt you down and shoot you.'

His head jerked round. She couldn't read his face. It looked completely blank. He set the box down carefully. 'Is that a promise?'

'Of course it is, you bloody idiot.' She cleared the last few steps in a leap, landing in his arms. She heard his breath woof out as she thudded into his chest, then her own breathing stopped entirely as his mouth came down on hers in a crushing kiss.

Her head was swimming and her knees were weak when they came up for air. She had to cling to him, to stay upright. She wasn't going to let that stop her. She thumped him, with the heel of her hand.

'I love you. I came all the way across an ocean to say that.' She thumped him again. 'I know you love me, you bastard, so say it.'

'Hey! Ouch!' He grabbed her hands, fending her off. 'The kid squealed.'

'Of course she did, she's only five, but it took a month.' Kaz wriggled in his arms, loving the feel of him against her body. 'You told my daughter you loved me, before you told me. What's she got that I don't?'

'Dimples?' He had her anchored now, solid against his hips and chest. She relaxed against him. Just sank in. The kiss this time was long and soft and languorous. He rested his forehead against hers.

'I love you.'

'At last.'

'I never said that to anyone before. Never knew what it meant. I do now. But I'm still not sure I should be saying it to you.'

Kaz flinched. 'You must know, I *have* said it. Which is why it's taken me a while to even think about saying it again.' She put her hands flat on his chest. 'I can't wipe out history. I had a marriage, I have a daughter. I come as part of a package, Devlin.'

'I know that.' He pushed her gently away from him. 'And that's why I can't ask … I can't expect … I don't know if I can do that. I don't know how to make a family.'

She held her breath. 'Is this about Jamie, or about your past?'

'God.' He swore. 'It's not about Jamie, it's about *me*. The stuff I've done, I shouldn't be around a child.'

'I wouldn't have my child, if it wasn't for you. And before you start on that tack, this isn't gratitude.' She waved a finger. 'The stuff you've done. Are you still doing it?'

'Well no, but –'

Kaz didn't allow for any buts. 'I've asked you this before. Is there anyone else, like Luce, likely to come after you in the future?'

He blinked. 'No.'

'In that case, done is done.' She looked up at him, clear-eyed. 'I know what I feel for you, Stuart Adams. I've never felt like this before. I trust you. I want you to take care of me.' Something shivered up her spine. 'I trust you with my life, with my heart, with my daughter. When I came around the corner and saw how close I got to losing you –' she gestured over her shoulder to the rental van – 'I knew exactly how much.' She waved her hand. 'Now I'm done. The rest is up to you. I, Katarina Elmore, *need* you. You want it in writing, you have it. You want to throw it all away, go ahead.'

The corner of his mouth was turning up. The smile, when it bloomed, took her breath away. 'You drive a hard bargain, woman.' He scooped her up and put paid to any remaining trace of air that might have been hanging around in her lungs.

'I want the whole thing.' He finally put her down. 'If we're going to do this thing, then I want marriage. I want to be a father to Jamie, if she'll have me.'

Kaz knew she was going to cry. The water just squeezed out of her eyes. Devlin wiped it away with his thumbs.

'She'll have you.'

'I figure I owe her.' He lifted his head. 'She's the reason you came, right?' Kaz nodded. He was frowning. 'Barbie dolls – little girls like Barbie dolls, right? Or what about a pony? Would she like a pony?'

'Probably.' Kaz was laughing now. 'I think a honeymoon in Disneyland will do, for the moment.'

'Honeymoon.' Devlin pulled her up off her feet again. 'Is that a yes?'

'It's definitely a yes.' She held him off from kissing her again, eyes sober. 'You were about to disappear. If you need … if Jamie and I need to make a new life with you, somewhere else, then that's okay.'

'I …' He stopped, thought. 'We should talk about that – but no, we don't have to go underground. I *will* have a new life. A wife and a family. Who'd have thought?' The wonder in his face tugged at her heart. 'Family.' He looked like he was tasting the word.

'I want six kids, you know,' she said casually. 'Jamie would love a little brother or a sister.'

This time he gulped. 'Uh – straight away?'

He was stepping up to the plate, even though his face had gone white.

She hid her delight, smothering the grin that wanted to burst out.

'We can negotiate. Let's see how you do with the family stuff first.' She narrowed her eyes. 'There are a few other questions and conditions.'

'Of course.' He'd straightened up, shoulders back.

'For a start, do I have to have the scary woman you used to work for, to give you away?'

Devlin shook his head. A grin was starting to form. 'Only if you want to.'

'Good.' She ticked off on her fingers. His eyes were gleaming now. 'Will this agreement involve a lot of crazy hot sex? Because if not, the deal is off.'

He sucked his teeth. 'I think I can manage that.'

'Good.' She nodded. 'Then this one is the clincher. I want everyone to know I belong to you. I want a rock. The hugest, most obscene diamond ring you can find.'

'No problem.' Devlin pulled her tight into his arms. 'It just so happens that I have these shares, in a diamond mine – '

About the Author

Evonne Wareham

Evonne was born in South Wales and spent her childhood there. After university she migrated to London, where she worked in local government, scribbled novels in her spare time and went to the theatre a lot. Now she's back in Wales, writing and studying history and living by the sea. Her membership of the Romantic Novelists' Association lets her enjoy the company of other authors and gives her an excuse to sneak back to London from time to time for essential stuff, like attending parties. She still loves the theatre, likes staying in hotels and enjoys walking on the beach, where she daydreams about her characters. She hopes that all those things come through in her books – drama, glamorous locations, engaging heroines and dangerous heroes.

This is Evonne's debut novel. Her second novel, *Out of Sight, Out of Mind*, will be published in 2013.

For more information visit www.evonnewareham.com and Evonne's blog at www.evonneonwednesday.blogspot.com

More from Choc Lit

If you enjoyed Evonne's story, you'll enjoy the rest of our selection. Here's a sample:

Starting Over
Sue Moorcroft

New home, new friends, new love. Can starting over be that simple?

Tess Riddell reckons her beloved Freelander is more reliable than any man – especially her ex-fiancé, Olly Gray. She's moving on from her old life and into the perfect cottage in the country.

Miles Rattenbury's passions? Old cars and new women! Romance? He's into fun rather than commitment. When Tess crashes the Freelander into his breakdown truck, they find that they're nearly neighbours – yet worlds apart. Despite her overprotective parents and a suddenly attentive Olly, she discovers the joys of village life and even forms an unlikely friendship with Miles. Then, just as their relationship develops into something deeper, an old flame comes looking for him ...

Is their love strong enough to overcome the past? Or will it take more than either of them is prepared to give?

Visit www.choc-lit.com for more details including the first two chapters and reviews, or simply scan barcode using your mobile phone QR reader.

Love & Freedom

Sue Moorcroft

*Winner of the Festival of Romance
Best Romantic Read Award 2011*

New start, new love.

That's what Honor Sontag
needs after her life falls apart,
leaving her reputation in
tatters and her head all over
the place. So she flees her
native America and heads for
Brighton, England.

Honor's hoping for a much-deserved break and the chance
to find the mother who abandoned her as a baby. What she
gets is an entanglement with a mysterious male whose family
seems to have a finger in every pot in town.

Martyn Mayfair has sworn off women with strings attached,
but is irresistibly drawn to Honor, the American who keeps
popping up in his life. All he wants is an uncomplicated
relationship built on honesty, but Honor's past threatens to
undermine everything. Then secrets about her mother start
to spill out …

Honor has to make an agonising choice. Will she live
up to her dutiful name and please others? Or will she
choose freedom?

Visit www.choc-lit.com for more details
including the first two chapters and
reviews, or simply scan barcode using
your mobile phone QR reader.

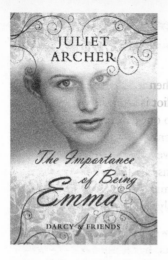

The Importance of Being Emma

Juliet Archer

Winner of The Big Red Reads Fiction Award 2011

A modern retelling of Jane Austen's *Emma*.

Mark Knightley – handsome, clever, rich – is used to women falling at his feet. Except Emma Woodhouse, who's like part of the family – and the furniture.

When their relationship changes dramatically, is it an ending or a new beginning?

Emma's grown into a stunningly attractive young woman, full of ideas for modernising her family business. Then Mark gets involved and the sparks begin to fly. It's just like the old days, except that now he's seeing her through totally new eyes.

While Mark struggles to keep his feelings in check, Emma remains immune to the Knightley charm. She's never forgotten that embarrassing moment when he discovered her teenage crush on him. He's still pouring scorn on all her projects, especially her beautifully orchestrated campaign to find Mr Right for her ditzy PA. And finally, when the mysterious Flynn Churchill – the man of her dreams – turns up, how could she have eyes for anyone else? …

Visit www.choc-lit.com for more details including the first two chapters and reviews, or simply scan barcode using your mobile phone QR reader.

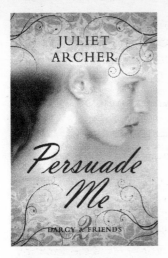

Persuade Me
Juliet Archer

When it comes to love, Anna Elliot is stuck in the past. No one can compare to Rick Wentworth, the man she gave up ten years ago at the insistence of her disapproving family. What if she's missed her only chance for real happiness?

Since Anna broke his heart, Rick has moved on – or so he thinks. Out in Australia, he's worked hard to build a successful career – and a solid wall around his feelings.

The words 'forgive and forget' aren't in Rick's vocabulary. The word 'regret' is definitely in Anna's. So, when they meet again on his book tour of England, it's an opportunity for closure.

But memories intrude – the pure sensuality of what they once shared, the pain of parting … And she has to deal with another man from her past, while his celebrity status makes him the focus of unwanted attention.

With Anna's image-obsessed family still ready to interfere and Rick poised to return to Australia, can she persuade him to risk his heart again?

This contemporary re-telling of Jane Austen's last completed novel is the second book in Juliet Archer's Darcy & Friends *series, offering fresh insights into the hearts and minds of Austen's irresistible heroes.*

Visit www.choc-lit.com for more details including the first two chapters and reviews, or simply scan barcode using your mobile phone QR reader.

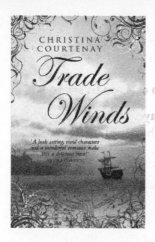

Trade Winds
Christina Courtenay

*Short-listed for the Romantic Novelists'
Association's Pure Passion Award for
Best Historical Fiction 2011*

Marriage of convenience – or a love for life?

It's 1732 in Gothenburg, Sweden, and strong-willed Jess van Sandt knows only too well that it's a man's world. She believes she's being swindled out of her inheritance by her stepfather – and she's determined to stop it.

When help appears in the unlikely form of handsome Scotsman Killian Kinross, himself disinherited by his grandfather, Jess finds herself both intrigued and infuriated by him. In an attempt to recover her fortune, she proposes a marriage of convenience. Then Killian is offered the chance of a lifetime with the Swedish East India Company's Expedition and he's determined that nothing will stand in his way, not even his new bride.

He sets sail on a daring voyage to the Far East, believing he's put his feelings and past behind him. But the journey doesn't quite work out as he expects …

Visit www.choc-lit.com for more details including the first two chapters and reviews, or simply scan barcode using your mobile phone QR reader.

Highland Storms
Christina Courtenay

Who can you trust?

Betrayed by his brother and his childhood love, Brice Kinross needs a fresh start. So he welcomes the opportunity to leave Sweden for the Scottish Highlands to take over the family estate.

But there's trouble afoot at Rosyth in 1754 and Brice finds himself unwelcome. The estate's in ruin and money is disappearing. He discovers an ally in Marsaili Buchanan, the beautiful redheaded housekeeper, but can he trust her?

Marsaili is determined to build a good life. She works hard at being a housekeeper and harder still at avoiding men who want to take advantage of her. But she's irresistibly drawn to the new clan chief, even though he's made it plain he doesn't want to be shackled to anyone.

And the young laird has more than romance on his mind. His investigations are stirring up an enemy. Someone who will stop at nothing to get what he wants – including Marsaili – even if that means destroying Brice's life forever …

Sequel to Trade Winds

Visit www.choc-lit.com for more details including the first two chapters and reviews, or simply scan barcode using your mobile phone QR reader.

The Scarlet Kimono

Christina Courtenay

Winner of The Big Red Reads
Historical Fiction Award 2011

Abducted by a Samurai warlord in 17th-century Japan – what happens when fear turns to love?

England, 1611, and young Hannah Marston envies her brother's adventurous life. But when she stows away on his merchant ship, her powers of endurance are stretched to their limit. Then they reach Japan and all her suffering seems worthwhile – until she is abducted by Taro Kumashiro's warriors.

In the far north of the country, warlord Kumashiro is waiting to see the girl who he has been warned about by a seer. When at last they meet, it's a clash of cultures and wills, but they're also fighting an instant attraction to each other.

With her brother desperate to find her and the jealous Lady Reiko equally desperate to kill her, Hannah faces the greatest adventure of her life. And Kumashiro has to choose between love and honour …

Visit www.choc-lit.com for more details including the first two chapters and reviews, or simply scan barcode using your mobile phone QR reader.

The Silver Locket
Margaret James

Winner of CataNetwork Reviewers' Choice Award for Single Titles 2010

If life is cheap, how much is love worth?

It's 1914 and young Rose Courtenay has a decision to make. Please her wealthy parents by marrying the man of their choice – or play her part in the war effort?

The chance to escape proves irresistible and Rose becomes a nurse. Working in France, she meets Lieutenant Alex Denham, a dark figure from her past. He's the last man in the world she'd get involved with – especially now he's married.

But in wartime nothing is as it seems. Alex's marriage is a sham and Rose is the only woman he's ever wanted. As he recovers from his wounds, he sets out to win her trust. His gift of a silver locket is a far cry from the luxuries she's left behind.

What value will she put on his love?

First novel in the trilogy

Visit www.choc-lit.com for more details including the first two chapters and reviews, or simply scan barcode using your mobile phone QR reader.

The Golden Chain
Margaret James

Can first love last forever?

1931 is the year that changes everything for Daisy Denham. Her family has not long swapped life in India for Dorset, England when she uncovers an old secret.

At the same time, she meets Ewan Fraser – a handsome dreamer who wants nothing more than to entertain the world and for Daisy to play his leading lady.

Ewan offers love and a chance to escape with a touring theatre company. As they grow closer, he gives her a golden chain and Daisy gives him a promise – that she will always keep him in her heart.

But life on tour is not as they'd hoped. Ewan is tempted away by his career and Daisy is dazzled by the older, charismatic figure of Jesse Trent. She breaks Ewan's heart and sets off for a life in London with Jesse.

Only time will tell whether some promises are easier to make than keep …

Second novel in the trilogy

Visit www.choc-lit.com for more details including the first two chapters and reviews, or simply scan barcode using your mobile phone QR reader.

Turning the Tide
Christine Stovell

All's fair in love and war? Depends on who's making the rules.

Harry Watling has spent the past five years keeping her father's boat yard afloat, despite its dying clientele. Now all she wants to do is enjoy the peace and quiet of her sleepy backwater.

So when property developer Matthew Corrigan wants to turn the boat yard into an upmarket housing complex for his exotic new restaurant, it's like declaring war.

And the odds seem to be stacked in Matthew's favour. He's got the colourful locals on board, his hard-to-please girlfriend is warming to the idea and he has the means to force Harry's hand. Meanwhile, Harry has to fight not just his plans but also her feelings for the man himself.

Then a family secret from the past creates heartbreak for Harry, and neither of them is prepared for what happens next ...

Visit www.choc-lit.com for more details including the first two chapters and reviews, or simply scan barcode using your mobile phone QR reader.

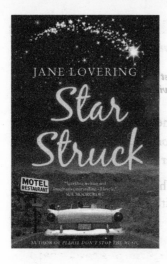

Star Struck
Jane Lovering

Our memories define us – don't they?

And Skye Threppel lost most of hers in a car crash that stole the lives of her best friend and fiancé. It's left scars, inside and out, which have destroyed her career and her confidence.

Skye hopes a trip to the wide dusty landscapes of Nevada – and a TV convention offering the chance to meet the actor she idolises – will help her heal. But she bumps into mysterious sci-fi writer Jack Whitaker first. He's a handsome contradiction – cool and intense, with a wild past.

Jack has enough problems already. He isn't looking for a woman with self-esteem issues and a crush on one of his leading actors. Yet he's drawn to Skye.

An instant rapport soon becomes intense attraction, but Jack fears they can't have a future if Skye ever finds out about his past …

Will their memories tear them apart, or can they build new ones together?

The UnTied Kingdom

Kate Johnson

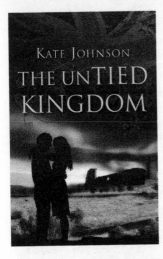

Best Book Award from Long & Short Reviews

The portal to an alternate world was the start of all her troubles – or was it?

When Eve Carpenter lands with a splash in the Thames, it's not the London or England she's used to. No one has a telephone or knows what a computer is. England's a third-world country and Princess Di is still alive. But worst of all, everyone thinks Eve's a spy.

Including Major Harker who has his own problems. His sworn enemy is looking for a promotion. The General wants him to undertake some ridiculous mission to capture a computer, which Harker vaguely envisions running wild somewhere in Yorkshire. Turns out the best person to help him is Eve.

She claims to be a popstar. Harker doesn't know what a popstar is, although he suspects it's a fancy foreign word for 'spy'. Eve knows all about computers, and electricity. Eve is dangerous. There's every possibility she's mad.

And Harker is falling in love with her.

Visit www.choc-lit.com for more details including the first two chapters and reviews, or simply scan barcode using your mobile phone QR reader.

Introducing Choc Lit

We're an independent publisher creating
a delicious selection of fiction.
Where heroes are like chocolate – irresistible!
Quality stories with a romance at the heart.

Choc Lit novels are selected by genuine readers like yourself.
We only publish stories our Choc Lit Tasting Panel want to
see in print. Our reviews and awards speak for themselves.

Come and support our authors and join them in our
Author's Corner, read their interviews and see their latest
events, reviews and gossip.

Visit: www.choc-lit.com for more details.

Available in paperback and as ebooks from most stores.

We'd also love to hear how you enjoyed *Never Coming
Home*. Just visit www.choc-lit.com and give your feedback.
Describe Devlin in terms of chocolate and you could win a
Choc Lit novel in our Flavour of the Month competition.

Follow us on twitter: www.twitter.com/
ChocLituk, or simply scan barcode using
your mobile phone QR reader.